Praise for Sarah Maine

'Maine adroitly weaves together the
three strands of her novel'
Sunday Times

'An echo of Daphne du Maurier'
Independent

'A beautifully crafted novel'
Publishers Weekly

'Maine writes beautifully about the wilderness'
The Times

'Maine's gift of setting the mood shines'
RT Reviews

'The historic mystery will keep readers guessing
right up until the end'
Booklist

'I predict great things for Sarah Maine'
The Book Bag

'A tremendous accomplishment.
So assured, so well-judged, and with
such an involving story to tell'
Ronald Frame

Sarah Maine is the author of *The House Between Tides* and *Beyond the Wild River*. She was born in England but grew up partly in Canada before returning to the United Kingdom, where she now lives.

Also by Sarah Maine

The House Between Tides
Beyond the Wild River

WOMEN
OF THE
DUNES

SARAH MAINE

HODDER

First published in Great Britain in 2018 by Hodder & Stoughton
An Hachette UK company

This paperback edition published in 2019

6

A CIP catalogue record for this title is available from the British Library

Paperback ISBN 9781473639737

Printed and bound in Great Britain by Clays Ltd, Elcograf S.p.A.

Hodder & Stoughton policy is to use papers that are natural, renewable
and recyclable products and made from wood grown in sustainable forests.
The logging and manufacturing processes are expected to conform to the
environmental regulations of the country of origin.

Hodder & Stoughton Ltd
Carmelite House
50 Victoria Embankment
London EC4Y 0DZ

www.hodder.co.uk

For Alasdair and Guy

Prologue

As the sun rose over a pale sea, Odrhan emerged from his dwelling at the end of the headland. Eyes closed, he stretched, reaching his fingertips to the sky, and felt the chill of dawn on his cheek. He offered up a prayer, and a gull's cry was blown back on the north wind as the sun set the water asparkle.

He stood there, a solitary figure, savouring the sharp stillness of early morning, and took long breaths, filling his lungs and belly with the salt-laden air, glorying for a moment in his own youthful vigour. The sea was well in. Waves lapped on the sweep of the twin beaches either side of the spit of land which formed a natural causeway, binding his rocky refuge to the shore.

Soon the tide would turn.

He prayed again, and a mist rose like breath from the ocean, changing form and softly gathering. He lifted his head and allowed his eyes to follow a pair of dark shags flying low over the sea's surface, casting fleeting shadows. The birds turned seaward, towards the distant stacks, and his gaze pursued them, then stalled.

A shape was emerging from the mist. It vanished, then reappeared, gaining substance and form. A sail!

A ship.

He studied it, eyes narrowed. Should he retreat inland? Something held him back – It was just a single ship, after all, and a small one at that. Time enough to wait, and watch.

He marked its progress as he went about his chores, and as it drew

1

closer he saw it was a high-prowed vessel with a square tan sail. A mile or so offshore it altered course to follow the coast, moving south towards the headland. And still he stayed . . . By midmorning prayers it was close enough for him to discern three or four figures on board. One of them pointed in his direction and then another rose and stood at the gunwale looking towards him.

A woman.

They stared across the water at each other. There was yet time to head inland, but he stayed, curious now, and then seemingly the woman spoke and the vessel altered course, coming in fast on the surf.

It beached moments later on the sand of the northern bay.

The time to leave had passed and Odrhan felt a strange presentiment as he watched the woman, unhurried, lift her skirts and climb out of the ship into the ebbing flow of the surf.

And she stood there on the strand line, and waited for him to come to her.

Chapter 1

When Libby Snow finally arrived, darkness was already falling. She decided to park the car anyway and walk out onto the narrow spit of land. The tide was well in and the only sound was that of the waves as they crept, hissing over the sand to the line of seaweed which marked the tide's turning point. Not an engine, not a voice, not a gull's cry. And out at sea the moon floated above the horizon, pouring silver across the dark swells and lighting the spume at the shore's edge.

It had taken a long time to reach this place. Eight hours of driving –

Or a lifetime, depending on how you looked at it.

The sun had set some time ago and the vibrant colours were fading in the western sky, draining away over a watery horizon; tomorrow she must make a point of being here earlier to watch it go down. March days were short, but by June, when she returned with her students, sunset would be late and lingering as long summer evenings merged with the early dawn. And once the planned dig started, there would be less time to savour such moments.

A breeze roughened the water and she pulled her jacket close, then shut her eyes and filled her lungs, absorbing the rank smell of high-tide seaweed and salty turf. Ullaness – a place of legend. She could almost hear Ulla's name whispering through the marram grasses.

There was an awesome beauty to the place, and she looked up, seeing gulls blown landward by the wind wheeling above her, their wingtips catching the moonlight against a darkening sky. Others circled out to sea, beyond the grey shapes of distant stacks, heading for the horizon over which lay the next landfall, two thousand miles away.

She had checked once in an atlas and been disappointed to find that if you followed the line of latitude eastwards from her grandmother's home on Newfoundland's broken coast, it went well south of Ullaness, south of Scotland in fact, to pass through the English Channel. And if you drew a line due west across the ocean from Ullaness, it fell north of that tiny Maritime harbour where she had spent her childhood summers, and went way up, above the tip of the Labrador coast, and entered the icy Hudson Strait. At the time this had seemed wrong! It should be possible to draw a line across the Atlantic, over the arc of the globe, and link the headland at Ullaness directly with Gosse Harbour, as her grandmother's stories had done.

But then again, she thought, nothing in her grandmother's stories made a straight connection either.

She could hardly believe she was here. The place was etched so deeply into her psyche it was almost part of her being. Familiar and yet quite unknown. She watched as a string of seabirds flying low above the ocean rose to become silhouettes against clouds now edge-lit by moonlight. What a sight! Timeless and unchanging. It must have looked the same to the nomadic people who once came here to gather shellfish, and to those who followed them and then settled, and built houses. Tides and time had sculpted the shoreline, but this view must be unaltered, and Libby felt the centuries shrink around her.

Ulla herself must once have stood here, a thousand years ago.

And Ellen too – her grandmother's grandmother, whose stories of Ulla had been woven into Libby's childhood – and she wondered again at the darker threads in the weave. Generations might divide them, but standing here now she felt herself bound by the connection to both these women, held by a sense of otherworldliness in the strange stillness of the place.

The archaeological work planned for the summer might throw light on Ulla's legend, but Libby had her own reasons for being here, her own questions to ask.

In a few hours, dawn would filter through her grandmother's bedroom window on the far side of the Atlantic, and the old lady would stir in her bed, emerging from under her gaily coloured quilts. As a child, in the summer holidays, Libby loved to go with her at daybreak, hand in hand, down to the fishing stages to watch the Gosse Harbour boats set off laden with crab and lobster pots, the chill morning air laced with salt and diesel. And when the boats had gone she would sit on the wooden landing, leaning her head against the mooring post, her short legs dangling, and think of the stories the old woman had told her. Of Ulla, and of Ellen who had come from Scotland, bringing the stories with her. And in her childish mind the two women had become hopelessly entangled, existing in a place she could only imagine, two thousand miles away across the ocean in Scotland.

And Libby had felt certain that Ulla must have been as good as she was beautiful: a lovely Norsewoman, blown in on a ship by the north wind, her dying lover beside her, fleeing her husband's wrath. In her picture book of legends there was an illustration of the fabled Isolde, and Libby had imagined Ulla to be like her, tall and slender and very beautiful, while Odrhan, the legendary monk, would have been as handsome as the knightly Tristan. The legend of Ulla had, for Libby, been as compelling as that of those star-crossed lovers, all the more so because it was personal, as Ellen's stories had connected her to this place, Ullaness, where the legend had been born.

It was only later that her grandmother had explained about Ellen's final years, when all was neither beautiful nor good.

Libby rose, reminding herself that she was also here to do a job, and made an effort to bring her mind back to the present. She swept a more professional eye over the landscape and tried to get a grip on how it all hung together. The ruined structure at her feet was Odrahn's cell, so they said, and, beyond the curving line of the southerly beach, she could see the roofless nave of St Oran's Church, where Ellen had once worshipped. Ferns had taken root in the crumbling masonry and birds nested in niches left by fallen stones. And there, beside the church, was the abandoned manse where Ellen had worked, its broken roof slates caught in the gutters. Planks had been nailed across the door. Beyond church and manse she could see the remains of cottages, disappearing into a tangle of brambles and nettles, and wondered for a moment where Ellen might have lived. The abandoned dwellings could tell her nothing, settling back into the landscape and returning to the natural world, mute witnesses to the fact that if there had ever been a larger community here, it was long gone.

Only Sturrock House, the landowner's residence, remained inhabited.

Her gaze followed the curve of the northern beach where, somewhere amongst the sand dunes, there was the mound that they would excavate this summer. From here it looked like just another dune, but she'd found it earlier and had stood staring down at the curved row of stones that the winter storms had exposed. It was now obviously a man-made feature, but was it a burial, and if so could it really be a physical part of the legend? Almost too much to hope for.

There had been a frisson of excitement amongst her colleagues when the news had reached them of what had been reported following a particularly wild storm, and parallels had quickly been drawn with similar stone settings which had turned out to be graves, significant graves, boat-shaped Viking-age graves – and there had been general agreement that the site should be excavated before the evidence was lost. Despite her own attachment to it, the legend of Ullaness had never been in the same league as that of Tristan and Isolde, but it did, after all, refer explicitly to the burial of a Viking warrior.

Professor Declan Lockhart, an early medievalist at the midlands university where Libby had a short-term contract, had been assigned to the project and an advertisement had gone out for an assistant to help him run it. For Libby, the job was custom-made, and she had applied. She'd not mentioned her personal connection at the interview, nor had she mentioned her grandmother's stories when she was offered the post. They had, after all, no bearing on the ancient site.

She moved off, back along the causeway. Tomorrow she would inspect the mound in daylight, putting the personal aspects aside, and start to think seriously about the summer. *A unique opportunity to match archaeological investigation with the surviving oral tradition and ancient legend,* their grant application had stated.

And, for Libby, a career-making opportunity which must go well.

That thought collided, as it had done all week, with the acute worry about the parcel which had arrived last Saturday from Gosse Harbour. She had opened it to find it contained an old sketchbook which she remembered from childhood, and she had thumbed through it, seeing the drawings she'd been told were Ellen's, and smiled at her own scribblings added on wet summer days. A fragment of the legend had been written on the back page, but as she turned to it an object, wrapped in a slip of paper, had slid out from between the pages and onto her lap. *This was Ellen's,* her grandmother had written on the paper. A trinket, she'd thought, as she carefully unwrapped it, and then stared down at the object in astonishment.

It was a cross about four inches across with four splayed arms, each decorated with a simple circular design while in the centre a larger incised circle framed a deep red stone, and the object seemed to glow against her skin. Gold? Carefully she turned it over, seeing how one of the arms had been folded over to make a loop through which a thong could be threaded so that the cross became a pendant. A simple design, but skilled craftsmanship, and her heart had started to pound as she recognised it for the real thing. An ancient artefact redolent of the early days of Christianity and the emergent northern church. It could only be gold, thin, hand-beaten gold, and the stone was almost certainly a garnet, a stone once much prized. Gold and garnet. The sort of thing that would be owned by an early bishop or other high-ranking churchman, or a devout layman – eighth century in date, if she was right.

So how had Ellen come by it? It was worth thousands.

She looked anxiously across towards Sturrock House. Over the years items had gone missing from there, it was said, valuable antiquities –

And she found herself wondering what else might have found its way to Gosse Harbour. The letter which arrived with the parcel had simply said: *Ellen used to wear it, my dear, so I thought you'd like to have it.* Libby had written straight back asking what else her grandmother could tell her about it, where it had come from, were there other items . . . ? But she had, as yet, had no reply. It was letters, stamps, and patience with Nan, not e-mail.

She looked again at the house. The cross had almost certainly come from there, but in what circumstances, and how on earth was she to broach the subject? And with whom? The house was set back within a garden bordered by a stone perimeter wall, masked by a line of shrubs and trees, and all she could see of it in the growing darkness was the roof, a silhouette of little turrets and chimneys. A right old mishmash of architectural styles and now the home of the seventh baronet, Sturrock of Ullaness.

It had started life as a late medieval tower house, she had read, and developed from there, with successive extensions and alterations reaching a crescendo in the nineteenth century embellishments of the third baronet. He had, by all accounts, embraced the Romantic movement with well-funded gusto and positioned himself in something of a dream world, rooted in the works of Walter Scott.

The family was at home, she noted, seeing thin grey smoke spiralling above the rooftops. Perhaps, in the summer, there would be an opportunity to have a look inside, but on this visit, for all sorts of reasons – not least the arrival of the little cross – Libby intended to stay well below the radar.

———

Declan had had all the dealings with the Sturrock estate, and had found them unhelpful and remote; it had taken forever to agree on terms for the excavation. The estate had refused to contribute a penny towards the project, and numerous conditions had been stipulated and legal contracts insisted upon. Uphill work, Declan had said.

Libby had thought right from the start that it would have been better to come up here and deal with matters face-to-face, but Declan was a busy man, and he did not delegate, especially to a newly appointed assistant. Nor did he take advice. The baronet himself was impossible to contact, he said, so why go up to talk to an intermediary? It had taken time, therefore, and a lot of backwards and forwards of e-mails and letters to get all the paperwork in place and all appropriate bodies satisfied. In the end they had

had to settle for a much less ambitious project than Declan had first envisaged, and had only secured permission to excavate the mound itself and do a building survey of the roofless church. All correspondence had to be directed to the estate's owner, Sir Hector Sturrock, but all negotiations were undertaken with his intractable land agent, who, Declan had told her, was uncooperative. Sir Hector himself remained unavailable.

She'd been in Declan's office when he had phoned and tried one last time to persuade the agent to let them excavate the enigmatic ruins at the end of the headland and dig a few small test pits in the bay area. It would enhance their understanding of the ancient landscape, he explained down the phone, rolling his eyes at Libby. Ullaness was a unique and complex site, '. . . and the chance to tie the oral tradition to the physical remains is exceptional, so if—'

'Haven't we been through this before?' The call was on speaker, so she heard the interruption.

'We touched on it —'

'And the estate agreed the extent of the work.'

Declan stuck up two fingers and continued in a tone which, in Libby's view, was guaranteed to fail. 'I know that, but what I'm suggesting is little more than a survey —'

'You'll have enough to do, surely,' the cool voice replied.

Declan handled refusal no better than he handled rejection, as she'd learned to her cost, and he let it show. 'I thought you'd welcome the opportunity,' he said. 'After all, the Ullaness chalice must have come from *somewhere* on the estate, and a survey might suggest where.'

The chalice! Libby gaped at him, and the cool voice on the phone became arctic.

'Really.'

The conversation ended swiftly after that and Declan put the phone down, avoiding Libby's eyes. 'He's a stubborn sod,' he said. 'And there's no getting past him. Everything's signed *Sturrock* but I bet it's that guy making the decisions.' He spun his pen on the desk and stared sullenly out of the window. 'Don't they realise they're sitting on one of the most promising sites on the west coast?'

Not mentioning the chalice and taking a more conciliatory tone might have produced better results, she'd thought, but said nothing; with Declan it simply wasn't worth it.

'It's the sense of entitlement that gets me,' Declan had continued. 'Just because some forebear chose the winning side and got the whole damn estate as payback . . .'

All this was before the parcel had arrived, but it was the furore around the theft of the Ullaness chalice which now fuelled her anxiety; she was torn between wanting to tell Declan about the cross and needing to know more before she did.

It was about a year ago that thieves had broken into Sturrock House and taken the chalice, and the burglary had made the national newspapers. A short article had been published describing what was known about it, which was, in fact, very little, given that the circumstances of its original discovery were vague. All that was known was that it had been found somewhere on the estate in the late nineteenth century.

And the cross, if she was right, belonged to the same period. And was valuable.

The family had been absent at the time of the theft, which had obviously been a professional and targeted job, triggering grumblings in the broadsheets about national treasures being held, inadequately protected, by private individuals. It had never been fully studied, but the few images that existed had led scholars to believe that it was originally Irish, probably eighth century in date, a beautiful vessel of silver and gilt encrusted with semiprecious stones, and well worth stealing. An insurance scam had been suspected until it became clear that the missing item had not been insured, and the art and museum world had groaned again at the hopeless ineptitude of the seventh baronet.

So Declan's reference to it had been bound to provoke, and she had said so.

'I meant it to,' he replied, with the mulish set to his jaw she was learning to recognise. 'Shows them no one's forgotten and that maybe they should cooperate more.'

'But if they're still smarting after all that publicity –'

'Yeah, well. The papers did rather go to town on it, I suppose,' he said, 'and speculating about more treasure being out there. I heard a rumour that the estate's gamekeeper fired at some metal-detectorists soon after.' She must have looked appalled, thinking of the students, and he had turned the subject. 'Only a rumour, of course.'

No wonder the landowner was keeping his head down.

So against this background, the cross was a problem and it was overshadowing her excitement in being here.

She'd planned a visit as soon as she'd come to England for university, but it had seemed less pressing then and her new life had taken over. And almost at once she'd become involved with Simon, an economics postgraduate. Involved, looking back on it, to the exclusion of all else. Simon was London-based. Very focussed. Ambitious. And when he'd announced at Christmas that he had the opportunity to go to New York for a year, Libby's growing concerns with that relentless focus had crystallised. Trailing in his wake was not at all what she wanted from life. She had felt vindicated by his expression of astonishment when she'd tried to explain her decision, and so she had stayed on, completing her studies, and let him go. They'd parted friends, more or less, and she had felt a sort of relief when she saw him off at the airport. She'd chart her own course now, and had no regrets.

And then the job with Declan had come up, and she was here! A further vindication of her decision.

She started picking her way back towards the shore. The place had had no real part in her life, of course, and yet it still provided her with the sense of connection she had felt in childhood. Did everyone feel that need? To be able to point to somewhere and say that they had ties there? Since her parents' divorce, many years ago, she had been passed between her mother in New Zealand and, less frequently, her father, who was constantly on the move. English boarding school had been endured because her summers had been spent, gloriously, in her grandmother's house in Gosse Harbour. Her father had occasionally touched down there to take her fishing, teaching her to sail and to drive a boat, but it was her grandmother who had been her fixed point, constant, serene, and unchanging, and Gosse Harbour became the closest thing to home.

So perhaps it was not so strange, she thought, watching the smoke from Sturrock House blow towards the old cottages, that she felt a connection with this place, even one that was generations old and built on the flimsy foundation of an ancient tale.

She scanned the bay one last time, noting where the estate had said they could camp behind the old manse for the prescribed two weeks in June. Declan would be in overall charge, but she was responsible for the day-to-day smooth running, and she wasn't sure just how hands-on he would be. He'd said from the start that he'd not be caught dead in a tent but would stay at the local pub, the Oran Bridge, which did bed and breakfast.

But somehow, between them, they would direct the students who would excavate the enigmatic mound, record their discoveries, catalogue any finds, and then go, leaving absolutely no trace of their stay there. This had all been spelled out in detailed, uncompromising print – *Any and all finds remain estate property. Nothing whatsoever is to be removed without explicit agreement.*

And that thought brought her back again to the little cross. She'd left it, still in the package with the sketchbook, in a drawer in her flat, but it couldn't stay there forever. If it had been Ellen's, as her grandmother's letter said, then it surely must have come from Ullaness. And if Libby was right, it was of the same period as the chalice and was hardly something Ellen, who had been in service, would have owned. So how had she come by it?

She knew that there was a darker side to Ellen's story – but had Ellen also been a thief?

Chapter 2

Libby had told no one that she was coming up here this weekend, not even Declan, and the journey had taken longer than she'd imagined. Driving away from the shore she was conscious of weariness, and she moved to straighten her shoulders. Eight hours it had taken her to get here, seven of them at the wheel. That was alright, though, she liked driving, it gave her time to think, but she was ready for bed. She'd stopped only once on her way north to the border, and then got lost in road works approaching Glasgow before being slowed to a frustrating crawl by a caravan on the Loch Lomond road. The pasty she'd eaten while waiting for the little ferry to cross back over a great sea loch now felt like a long time ago. A few cars and a delivery van had disembarked as she sat there, and then she and three other vehicles had been waved on board. Once across the loch, she'd still had an hour to travel, following the ever-narrowing roads towards the coast until she reached the tiny community of Oran Bridge.

She'd passed through it on her way to Ullaness, and it amounted to little more than a clutch of cottages, a shop and the Oran Bridge Hotel where she would stay tonight. She retraced her route now and pulled up outside where a soft light fanned out a welcome onto the road.

Food, and then bed. She took her bag off the back seat, locked the car, and went inside. The hum of conversation broke off as she entered, but resumed a moment later while the landlord fetched

15

the room key. The clientele was mostly middle-aged or old men, except for three young boys who were doggedly tucking into plates of sausage and mash over by the fire, and the sight reminded her again that she was hungry. 'Can I still order food?' she asked, and the landlord nodded her towards a menu. She ordered, then went up to her room to dump her bag.

Returning a moment later, she bought a drink and headed for a free table near the fire, conscious of eyes following her, a woman alone, a stranger, but the scrutiny felt curious rather than hostile. She threaded her way through the tables to a long wooden pew which looked as if it had once served Sabbath duties, and sat down next to the boys. The grey-bearded man beside them nodded at her. 'Shift along there, lads,' he said, 'make space for the lady,' and she smiled her thanks. He was a big man and had a good face, she thought, weather-worn with laughter lines etched deep beside his eyes. Their grandfather, perhaps? He was nursing a pint, dividing his attention between the boys and a companion on his right, and his eyes rested on her for a moment.

The boys looked like brothers, ranging from about seven to eleven years old, she guessed, and they studied her in that open way that children have. Their focus switched abruptly, however, as her plate of fish and chips arrived. 'Wish I'd had that,' the smallest of them muttered, earning himself a jab in the ribs. 'I *said* I wanted chips.'

'They do look good,' she agreed, and the boy blushed and turned away to chase the last of the peas around his plate.

The outside door opened a moment later and a man entered. The boy beside her leapt to his feet, chips forgotten. 'Dad! I caught a cod!' he called across the room. The man lifted a hand in acknowledgement and went over to the bar. 'A *cod*, Dad! The only one, all day, the others just got mackerel.' The newcomer ordered a drink and stayed chatting a moment to the landlord. 'Did you hear me?' the boy demanded, clearly affronted, and a low laugh went around the room. Someone said something to the man at the bar and he gave a wry smile.

'I did, Charlie, I did,' he said, and came towards them, pocketing his change. 'You'd no call to feed them, Angus. Alice's left us a pie.'

'But we were starving,' said the middle-sized boy, and the old man chuckled.

'And that would never do.'

'A *cod*, Dad!' the boy called Charlie insisted, tugging at his father's sleeve, and the man ruffled his hair and smiled down at him.

'Well done! And what about you two?'

'Five mackerel and a crab,' said the eldest. 'But we threw the crab back.'

The man nodded and took a long drink, then set his glass down and moved his neck and shoulders as if to ease their stiffness.

'How was the event?' the older man asked.

'Not bad. Not brilliant, but not bad,' he replied, dragging a chair over and sitting down. He was dark in colouring, like the boys, and he too had an outdoor sort of face. He was leaner than the older man, his face more angular, more drawn. Late thirties, Libby reckoned. 'Alice was pleased, at any rate. Seems anything that's smoked will sell these days, as long as it says *wild* on it somewhere and has a saltire on the packaging. Made some useful contacts too.' He glanced briefly in Libby's direction, then away, and gave his attention to the boys: 'So tell me about this cod, then. And the rest.'

Libby half listened as the anglers' triumphs were described in detail and ate her fish and chips. Once she looked up and saw that the man was considering her. Not many visitors came here, she thought again, or perhaps not at this time of year.

The food was good, hot and well-cooked, and slowly the warmth of the room crept into her muscles, reminding her that it had been a long day. Having eaten her fill she put down her knife and fork. Time for bed. She turned aside to gather her bag and scarf and stood, but unwittingly the newcomer rose at the same time, and they jostled for a moment in the restricted space.

The man sat. 'You first,' he said, and watched her as she eased herself past the table; then he stood up again and addressed his sons. 'Say your thank-yous, you two. And what do I owe you for the food, Angus?'

'Away wi' you, sir.'

A good-natured dispute ensued as she crossed the room and she turned to see a note being anchored under Angus's glass. Then the man bid the company good night and ushered just two of the boys through the door, leaving the third, the eldest, with the older man.

———

The pub's bedroom was papered in a faded chintz and rather cozy, she decided as she unpacked the little she had brought and then climbed into bed, pulling up the flannelette sheet and wool blankets. When had she last slept under blankets? Probably not since her last visit to her grandmother a year ago. And who else came here, she wondered, other than walkers or passers-by? Oran Bridge was well off the beaten track.

But this summer they would have Declan to stay, and she looked again at the pink chintz, and smiled.

They had begun recruiting students for the summer's excavation a couple of weeks ago, once permission to excavate, and funding, had been assured. Declan was to give a lecture setting out the importance of the site to whet appetites and get volunteers to sign up. Competition for student labour might be fierce, as alternative fieldwork options in Sicily and Jordan were on offer. Scotland, and midges, could be a hard sell.

She'd almost been late for the lecture and the lights were dimmed as she slipped through the door and found a seat, and watched Declan stroll across the front of the lecture hall with his hands in his pockets. Black jeans, a white open-necked shirt, and the inevitable black leather jacket; his trademark image. His career had gone well and he knew it, the youngest professor in the department, the cool one.

'So!' he began, pivoting on his heel to face his audience. 'Ulla-ness.' He played out the syllables one by one. 'Ul-la-ness. Ulla's headland. The enigma of the west. How many of you have heard of it?'

One or two hands went up, followed by others who hoped not to have to confirm their claim. Libby smiled. Chancers – but it was a good turnout. About thirty or thirty-five students, more than she'd expected, and far more than they could take if all chose to apply. Declan usually attracted a good audience though, and, inevitably, the front row was entirely female.

'Some of you, eh? And the rest are here to find out – if you manage to stay awake, that is. Heavy night, Danny boy?' A titter went through the hall and his victim grinned as he shuffled up-right in his seat. 'Don't worry. I'll be brief.' He touched the remote and an image flashed onto the screen of a breathtakingly white sand beach fringed by dunes which followed a perfect curve out to the rocky headland where she had stood this evening. 'Ullaness has a history which encompasses four or five thousand years, with everything from prehistoric shell middens to a grand estate house, not to mention' – he paused for effect – 'The Mound.' A pale turquoise sea lapped over the sands on the screen, but this eve-ning it had been steely grey, flecked with white. Declan's pointer hovered over a low, irregular mound set in the dunes behind the beach. 'And there it is, peppered with rabbit holes, eroding away with every storm, but apparently, and miraculously, undisturbed.'

If it *was* undisturbed, it would indeed be miraculous, especially given the recent talk of treasure, she thought as she pulled the blankets up under her chin, relishing the softness of their satin edging. But the mound had only been recognised as a man-made feature after last winter when a high tide had leapt over the protecting dunes and uncovered the setting of round white stones she had stared down at this evening.

'There're also the remains of what is thought to be an early Christian cell or oratory out on the headland,' Declan had continued, 'associated traditionally, though spuriously, with Saint Oran, to whom the church is dedicated and for whom the nearby village is named. Oran was an Irish saint who apparently spent his life dashing along the Celtic fringes sticking his moniker on every island, headland, or skerry.' Another unctuous titter ran through the students. 'And then there's the church itself. An early monastery, perhaps? Who knows, but there's some fine sculpture associated with it, and fragments of a tenth-century high cross now in Edinburgh.' She'd not had time to explore the church this evening, but tomorrow she would.

'The estate passed into the hands of the Sturrock family,' he had continued, 'following the 1745 Jacobite rebellion. They'd chosen the boring, but winning, side, so a baronetcy was created and the incumbent family got the push. A couple of generations later the third baronet got swept up with the Romantic movement and went mad on his home-grown legend, did an architectural makeover and wrote some ghastly poetry. We'll never know how much of the original legend he preserved and how much he made up, but he put Ullaness on the map, so to speak. And feudalism is still alive and well up there, my friends, believe me.' The remark had been unnecessary, as well as unprofessional, and

Declan had avoided her eye. 'Until recently they've resisted any suggestion that work be done in the area. But now, with erosion threatening to destroy what had previously been thought to be a dune, they've rather belatedly started to pay attention to what they have. And I'm happy to tell you today that not only have I got permission to dig there this summer, but I've secured the funds to do so.' He had paused for an appreciative splatter of applause while Libby thought wryly of the hours that she had spent poring over grant application forms, ticking boxes and jumping through hoops, and then the nail-biting delay in getting his signature on them before the deadline passed. Such was life.

'Some of you will remember,' he continued, 'the furore over the theft of the Ullaness chalice about a year back? Other artefacts were allegedly found, but they too have disappeared over the years.' This was before the parcel had arrived. 'The loss of the chalice is tragic, as it was one of the finest examples of Irish art discovered in Scotland, and all we've got to go on is a handful of black-and-white photographs and some old drawings. But perhaps its loss triggered a latent sense of responsibility in the estate – yes, Paula?'

'Where was it found?' the student asked.

'Somewhere on the estate, but no one knows precisely where. It came to light in the nineteenth century after the third baronet had pumped life into the old legend of Ulla.' He paused. 'For those of you who don't know, the legend describes the antics of a beautiful pagan Norsewoman called Ulla and Oran or Odrhan, a masochistic monk, one of those fanatical types who hung out on draughty headlands and islands.' His audience laughed. 'A ruin on the headland is traditionally associated with him but it's never been investigated, although I have plans, my friends, I have plans . . . Anyway the legend first surfaced in the seventeenth century although earlier fragments are known, and then it was almost certainly garbled by the third baronet, who milked it for all it was worth. Great cachet, you know, having your own legend to draw on. Walter Scott was said to have visited Sturrock House to discuss its place in Scotland's literary heritage. It's got all the right ingredients, though, I'll give it that – vengeful Vikings, pillaged loot, a hot temptress and an anguished celibate. Oh yes, and a complicated paternity issue. Sex, murder – and a reckoning. There's probably a kernel of truth in all of it, but folklore has a way of twisting things, so we'll put the antics of Ulla-the-fair-maiden and Odrhan-the-naughty-monk aside for the duration of the project and stick with the concept of *research*. Time to consider connections later. What we have to work with is a mound, an early church, a ruin on a headland – and a very careless baronet. Next question –'

Chapter 3

They had a wounded man on board, the woman told him. 'Do you have skills, holy man?' she asked, and he nodded, so the men fashioned a stretcher from two oars and brought him to Odrhan's cell.

The woman then issued further commands, sending the men back down to the ship while Odrhan knelt beside the injured man and began uncovering a deep wound.

'Can you save him?' the woman asked.

He looked up at her. 'With God's help, perhaps.'

Down on the beach the men were unloading baskets from the ship.

'But your god is not his god,' she said, and he saw that her eyes were a pale aqua, the colour of the ocean.

He made no response. Then: 'Your husband?' he asked.

She shook her head. 'It was my husband who did this.' Odrhan frowned as he removed the bloody bindings. 'We were fleeing from him but he stopped us at the shore, and they fought.' Odrhan bent to sniff at the wound. It was clean. 'They are brothers, Erik and Harald,' she added.

Odrhan looked up at her again. 'And you leave one for the other, lady?'

She returned the look evenly. 'I do not ask for your approval.'

'Only for my help.'

The men were clambering up the rocks, grunting under the weight of baskets which they set down beside the cell before returning for more.

23

The woman spoke again, quickly. 'Erik beat me, saying I was barren. But the lack was in him, not me. We dared no longer stay.'

Odrhan's frown deepened as he considered her. These were heathen folk and she stood there, defiant in her adultery, a tall and slender figure, asking him to save her lover. 'Lady – he began.

The men set the second load of baskets beside the first and the woman gestured towards them. 'If you can save Harald then I will give you gold enough to build a church here –'

'You think God's help can be bought?' And anger grew in him that she should be so lovely, and yet so full of sin.

'Then what must I do?' she asked.

'Pray to God,' he said, 'and repent.'

Chapter 4

'Sex, murder – and a reckoning.'

Declan might dismiss the legend in a single ill-formed phrase, but her grandmother had told it differently:

> *Odrhan stood beside his cell, and gazed out o'er the sea.*
> *A sail, a sail, his eye espied, and fell he to his knee.*
> *Save me, Lord, from the Northman's sword,*
> *Spare me from his wrath!*

'No, Nanna, not the poem. Tell me it like a story!' ten-year-old Libby had protested.

'Don't you like the poem, then?' Her grandmother had smiled.

'I like some of it,' she had replied, with youthful diplomacy. 'Especially the bits about Ulla.'

> *Then Ulla fair, she stepped ashore,*
> *And Odrhan took her hand . . .*

The poem, as she had recognised even then, was a dreadful bit of doggerel, and her grandmother was all too prone to recite as much as she could remember, filling the gaps with the story as she had been told it by Ellen, her own grandmother. She had given Libby the little sketchbook with Ellen's drawings in it and

25

Libby had solemnly copied them, and it had become something they shared whenever Libby came to stay, their very own legend. She would sit amongst the rocks below the landing at her grandparents' house, and make up different, more satisfactory endings than the official one, drawing pictures in Ellen's sketchbook and showing them to her grandmother.

The story, as she was told it, opened with Odrhan watching a sail approach the shore. The poem suggested that he had known it was a Viking ship, but Libby had always thought that unlikely. If he had, then why would he have stood there and watched it beach in the bay? He would have run away. Her grandmother had smiled at her reasoning. 'Perhaps so, my dear.'

There had been a woman, a wounded warrior and three faithful men on board, together with a stash of gold and silver. 'And what did Odrhan do?' Libby would ask, even though she knew.

'Odrhan was a good Christian man, my dear, so he took them in and tended to Harald's wounds and urged Ulla to become a Christian. But that night poor Harald died, and Ulla wept over him. The three men buried him next day and then they made off in the ship with all the treasure.'

'And left poor Ulla stranded!'

'That's right.'

'What happened next?'

Her grandmother had smiled, a little sadly, and shaken her head. 'This is where the story begins to unravel, my dear. My grandmother told it differently every time, and only one thing was certain: Ulla stayed with Odrhan and that winter she had a child.'

'Harald's child?'

Her grandmother had gazed out of the window towards the little harbour. 'When my grandmother first told me the story, she said it was Harald's, but as she grew more frail she insisted that Odrhan was the child's father, while other times she would grow fretful, saying it had really been the child of Erik, from whom they fled. Her mind had become very fragile by then, you see, and she was consumed by the legend, believing herself to be Ulla, left alone, deserted by God, and deserving of no comfort. It was almost as if she really felt the Norsewoman's pain and grief. And she would tell me the story as if she had never told it before, sometimes saying that murder had been done, sometimes that she was guilty, and sometimes even that she had killed a man, and she would cry piteously, calling out sometimes for Harald, sometimes for Odrhan. In the end she had to be confined to the house for her own safety.'

'Whose child do you think it was?' Libby had persisted, keen to have this matter resolved.

'We'll never know, my dear.'

She was too young then to appreciate Ellen's personal tragedy, and only later had she wondered about this strange obsession.

Libby woke next morning to the homely smell of frying bacon wafting up from the pub's kitchen. She dressed quickly and went downstairs to find a single table laid for breakfast and a plump woman sorting glasses behind the bar.

'I heard you on the stairs,' she said, and came over to switch on a heater beside the table. 'Were you warm enough last night?' Libby assured her that all had been fine and agreed to the offer of a full breakfast. It arrived a few minutes later and the woman stood over her, arms akimbo and curious. 'So what brings you here, at this time of year?'

Direct and to the point. Libby took a mouthful to give herself a moment. 'Just exploring, really, and having a bit of a break.' Time enough to talk about the excavation in the summer.

'And will you have a packed lunch then to take on your exploring?' the woman asked.

'That would be marvellous.'

Fortified by her mighty breakfast and with a packed lunch beside her, Libby drove back down the track to the coast. It was not yet nine o'clock. Best time of the day. Perhaps she need not have arranged to stay a second night after all, but could have left after lunch and driven through the night.

Too late now.

She bumped over the ruts in the road as it narrowed towards the coast and parked where she had done the night before, beside the manse, and went down to the beach. Emerald seas had replaced the dark waves of last night and she stood a moment watching the curls of waves roll in, row upon ordered row, over the sweeps of sand. What a place! She walked along the beach, sending knock-kneed shorebirds scuttling along the foamy edge ahead of her, jabbing their beaks into the sand, questing – If the weather was good, it would be idyllic this summer. Perhaps she would swim.

To get out onto the headland from the beach she had to scramble over barnacle-encrusted rocks, and she slipped on the treacherous green seaweed. Straightening as she reached the plateau, she stood with a hand on the tumbled ruin and saw that an early morning mist still hung over the water, thickening further out. It was all too easy to imagine a high-prowed ship making its way towards the shore. And Odrhan had stood right here watching it approach, not fleeing as he might have done.

And on that simple, unfathomable decision had hung all subsequent events. What an extraordinary thought.

She turned and looked back towards the dunes; even in daylight the mound was hard to spot unless you knew where to look. Such a pity they weren't allowed to do a survey and plot the landscape properly, but that, it seemed, was out of the question. From where she stood, the ruin on the headland appeared to triangulate with the mound on one side and the ruined church on the other. Paganism and Christianity joined, or perhaps divided, by Ulla's ness.

And Sturrock House, that bastion of authority, positioned across the divide.

She looked down at the jumble of stones at her feet. Odrhan's cell, if that was what it was, survived as only a few low courses masked now by nettles and grasses, the roof fallen in, its stones softened by moss and lichens. Was there any chance at all that they might be allowed to clear the debris and reveal the ground plan? It stood perilously close to the edge of the headland, so perhaps they could point out the continuing threat of erosion.

————

She walked down onto the other beach, disturbing more shorebirds which rose as a piping cloud to settle again a little further on, and she branched off into the dunes to examine the mound more closely. It lay in a little hollow between two sand dunes where, during the storm, the sea had carved a channel inland to gnaw away at its base, revealing it for what it was. She pulled herself uphill, grabbing handfuls of marram grass to reach a vantage point on one of the flanking dunes from where she could look down.

The exposed line of five large stones really did form a curve. But was it boat-shaped? Oval certainly.

She stood there, totally absorbed. And if it was a burial mound, as they hoped and predicted, who might they find? Harald, dead of his wounds as described in the legend? Or Ulla herself – the place was named for her, after all. It was not going to be Odrhan, that much was certain, not buried in a pagan—

'Are you alright up there?'

The voice seemed to come from nowhere. She looked up and saw that a figure had appeared on top of the opposing dune, a black Labrador at his heels. It was the man from last night, the one who had left the pub with his sons, dressed today in an old donkey jacket and wellington boots.

'Yes. Fine, thanks.' He seemed to expect more. 'I was miles away.'

His gaze sharpened as she pushed her windswept hair from her face. 'You were in the pub last night,' he said and, swiftly descending the side of his dune, he came up to join her, followed by the dog.

'And you came to collect your boys, and their fish.'

He gave a slight smile. 'Not the fish, thank God. But what brings you out here?' His directness echoed her landlady's, and the tone suggested that he had a right to ask.

'Just exploring,' she said, and instantly regretted it. Better to have introduced herself. If he was connected with the estate, then she would encounter him again in the summer.

He seemed to find her answer unsatisfactory. 'Exploring what?' he asked, and she remembered then that the older man in the pub had called him 'sir.' Oh God.

'My name's Libby Snow,' she said, distracted as the thought grew in her mind.

The man looked surprised, then briefly amused. 'How do you do, Libby Snow. And just to be tedious, might I ask again, exploring what? Coalbox!' He snapped his fingers at the dog, who was digging out a rabbit hole in the side of the dune, and it came to him at once. Coalbox? 'Technically you're on estate land, you see, so I'm within my rights to ask you.'

The words were mildly spoken and yet she felt wrong-footed. 'I'm sorry. You must be –'

'Sturrock,' he said.

Damn. The sand slid a little under her feet.

'I'm sorry,' she said. 'Let me introduce myself.'

'You just did – Libby Snow.'

'I meant, who I really am.' She was making a right mess of this. 'We've been dealing with your agent, you see, and I thought he might have told you my name. Which was why I told you –'

'It is an unusual name,' he conceded. 'And what were your dealings about?'

'The dig this summer.'

'Ah.' A frown appeared on his forehead, just a single vertical crease between his eyes, and it made his lean face austere. 'And what brings you here, now?'

'Just an opportunity to look around, really, do a bit of thinking, and planning. Getting the lay of the land.'

'Did you tell us you were coming?'

Was that the majestic plural? Dear Lord! 'Actually it was a spur-of-the-moment decision, and there was no need to disturb you.'

He continued to study her. 'So what's the meeting about next week then? As you're here now –' What meeting? She must have looked blank, and the frown on his face deepened. 'I have Professor Lockhart in the diary for Wednesday morning.' He paused; then: 'You must forgive my stupidity, but who exactly are you, Libby Snow?'

'His assistant.'

Perhaps he caught the bitterness in her tone, for his expression lightened. 'Crossed wires, eh?'

'Looks like it.' Damn Declan. When had this been arranged? And why –

The man was still regarding her with a disconcerting intensity. 'Is there anything unclear in the arrangements?'

'Not as far as I know.' And she mentally cursed again, realising that she'd have to tell Declan about this encounter. She'd no idea what he was up to, but she'd probably queered his pitch. As if things weren't bad enough between them.

'So you're all set?'

She made an effort to regain lost ground. 'Yes. I think we are, sir.' The 'sir' sounded unctuous and servile and she immediately regretted it. 'We're getting our team together and there'll be about six or eight students and me. And Declan – Professor Lockhart – will be here for part of the time.' He nodded, his eyes still holding hers. 'And, as we agreed with your agent, four or five tents for the students, a cook tent, eating tent, et cetera. Is that alright?' He nodded again, saying nothing. 'He suggested there was some flat land behind the manse we could camp on.'

'Aye. It's well-drained and quite sheltered there.'

'And we've sorted two chemical toilets,' she continued desperately. He must know that all this would have been covered, and could not possibly be interested, having delegated the whole thing. 'And we've fixed to take the students up to the youth hostel a couple of times a week for a shower.' She was talking too much, but how *did* you address a baronet in the twenty-first century? When you needed him firmly on-side – 'They'll be well-behaved, I promise you, and I'll be here all the time, although Declan – the professor – will come and go.'

'You're running the show?'

'Day to day. With a supervisor to help me.'

He started to move off back down the side of the dune, his hands thrust deep into his jacket pockets, but slowly and in a manner that seemed to assume that she would fall in beside him. His dog understood what was expected. 'Is there anything else?'

Coalbox probably had the right idea, she decided, so she walked beside him, pretending to consider the question in what she hoped was a professional manner. 'We'll bring stoves and gas bottles for cooking.'

'Yes.'

'And I've arranged for a bowser for drinking water.'

'Yes.'

'And we'll ship out all the rubbish when we go.'

'Of course.'

'And record and catalogue everything we find.'

'Naturally.' He stopped and turned to her. 'So is that it?'

'I think so.'

His expression was unreadable as he searched her face. 'And if I went back through the e-mails and agreements, I imagine I'd find that this had all been discussed, and agreed, some weeks ago.' He raised his eyebrows, awaiting her confirmation.

'Probably.'

'So what remains for your professor to discuss next week?' She began to feel bullied. 'He's been prepared to make all the arrangements through post and e-mail so far. So why bother to come up here now, do you imagine?'

'I'm afraid I've no idea.'

'And yet he sent you on ahead – 'The frown was back and his lips were a thin line as he continued to examine her.

'No. He didn't send me.' She maintained a neutral tone. 'I came on my own account. He doesn't know.'

He appeared not to hear. 'He's been very persistent, but you can tell him from me that if it's the headland he wants to talk about again, he's wasting his time and can save himself the journey. Same goes for the church.'

'The church?' They were not planning any work there, other than recording the early stonework, and that was more of a teaching exercise than anything else. 'You mean the building recording?'

'We're fine with that. But no trial pits, no sampling, no metal detectors. It's a plain and simple no, as it has been from the start. Our position has not and will not change, no matter who he sends up to make his case.' He looked her up and down in an infuriating manner. 'Perhaps you'll make that clear?'

She contained herself with difficulty. 'As I said before, he *didn't* send me. But I'll make sure he understands the situation.'

'Thank you.' He gave a brief nod and looked away at last, out towards the ocean. 'So if he wants to cancel his visit, he can give me a ring. It's a busy time, you see, what with lambing and calving starting.' When he turned back to her, the frown had gone. 'We can sort any other practical matters in the summer, I'm sure. Everything except the weather, that is. You'll have to take what comes.' Out to sea the sun had broken through the mist and along the beach there were now patches of dazzling white sand and the sea was a chalky pastel. He gave her a half smile and raised a hand to his forehead in a brief salute. 'So, I'll leave you to your thoughts again.'

'Thank you,' she said, and added another 'sir,' just for good measure.

At that he stopped and turned back. 'My name is Rodri Sturrock. Plain Mr, not Sir.' His eyes flashed with sudden amusement, unmistakable this time, and it transformed his face. 'I seem to have given you the wrong impression. My brother Hector is the Sir, but he lives in Norway and is rarely here. I'm his agent – and so, until the summer, Libby Snow. And I'll remember the name next time.' And he left her, following a narrow track that led to a gate in the wall which surrounded Sturrock House, the dog at his heels.

Given her the wrong impression, indeed! He'd made no attempt to correct her after her first obsequious *sir* but had let her toady on. Wretched man! She watched him disappear through the gate, imagining the smile still lingering. And so it was him that Declan had been dealing with, and the *Sturrock* signature had been his own, not that of the baronet after all. And judging from his manner, Declan was probably right in believing that the boss himself had had little involvement.

That thought brought her sharply back to Declan himself and to what he might be up to. There'd never been any discussion about the church, beyond the agreed recording work. Hector Sturrock, it appeared, was not the only one being kept in the dark.

———•———

Libby left the dunes and walked back across the soft sheep-cropped turf towards the church, rerunning the conversation in her mind, puzzled, and annoyed with both men. She stepped over the shallow stream to enter the little graveyard which encircled the church. It was picturesque, certainly, with broken stubs of mossy stones marking burials drowning in clumps of nettles and sorrel, long forgotten, while fresh daffodils and clutches of primroses brightened more recent graves. The church might have lost its congregation along with its roof, but the burial place still served the community, binding the generations together, transcending the dimension of time.

But what was so special here? She ducked under the stone lintel to cross a threshold raised by blown sand and entered the roofless nave, and found that there was a stillness there, a sense of a space set apart, defined by the four stone walls, and a pervasive earthy smell of soil and moss. The simple nave had been extended by an early-nineteenth-century chancel, and she glanced quickly around, reckoning the time needed to survey and record it. In all likelihood there had been an earlier building on the site, an idea supported by the fragments of associated sculpture, but Declan had never suggested that they excavate there to find out.

A patch of primroses lit a sheltered corner beside an ancient grave slab, its lettering obscured by lichens. What looked like a recent crack had split the corner off, detaching the carved stone hilt from the blade of a warrior's sword. Ideally all the stones would be lifted and conserved, though it would be a shame to move them, a sacrilege almost. Perhaps that was what Declan wanted to discuss.

She sensed movement behind her and turned. Nothing. A rabbit, no doubt, she'd seen plenty.

At the back of the nave, up against the wall, was the ornate nineteenth-century tomb of the third baronet and his lady, a lavish pastiche of classical and Celtic styles, displaying wealth rather than taste. She had taken a step forward when again she sensed movement behind her, and this time she saw a flash followed by sounds of a scuffle, then a giggle, and the two boys who had left the pub with their father jostled each other in the doorway.

'Stalkers!' she said.

They were dressed in jumpers, jeans and wellingtons, free spirits by the look of them. The younger boy giggled again, but his brother stepped through the doorway, his hands thrust into his pockets. 'Are you the lady who's coming here to dig this summer?' he asked.

'Yes, I am.'

He nodded, satisfied. 'Well, we've found stuff too.'

'Really! What have you found?'

'All sorts.'

The younger boy (Charlie, wasn't it?) stepped forward. 'It's up at the house. We'll show you. Dad says you're to come.'

Did he, indeed.

His brother frowned at him. 'No, he said to ask nicely if you would *please* come up to the house, and said he's putting the kettle on.'

Tea. That universal cure-all. An olive branch, perhaps.

'And then we can show you what we've found.' There was, of course, no way she could refuse, so she smiled her agreement. 'We'll spread it out on the kitchen table, while you drink your tea.'

The boy turned towards the entrance, clearly expecting her to follow; his father's son. Libby cast another quick look around the church, no nearer knowing what Declan had hoped to do there, then allowed herself to be escorted back across the stream.

The older boy said his name was Donald and he walked companionably beside her, asking her what they hoped to find in the summer, while his brother leapt from one grassy tussock to another, arms outstretched for balance, loudly proclaiming each successful landing. Uncomplicated, engaging boys. They led her to the wrought-iron gate through which their father had earlier disappeared and stood aside to let her pass. Well-trained too. The path divided inside the gate; one half headed off into the garden, but they took the other route along the inside line of the wall, through a dark tunnel of overgrown rhododendrons, until it reached an arch which led them into a cobbled courtyard flanked by what had once been stables and out-buildings. Sturrock House was some place.

'This way,' Charlie said, gesturing to a back entrance and pushing open the door. He went ahead of her, down a short passage, and she heard him call: 'We got her, Dad! She was in the church.'

'Boots *off*!' The roar shot him back out like a cannonball and both boys grinned at her, obedient but unabashed as they kicked their boots off against the step. 'I don't think he meant you,' said Donald kindly.

'But dare I risk it?' she asked, smiling back at him as she placed her shoes next to the two pairs of muddy boots.

He led her down the short passage where coats hung from a

row of pegs competed with an array of fishing rods, shrimping nets, shooting sticks, and the like, and through a door into a large square kitchen. The black Labrador came over to inspect her, tail thumping, but was called to order by Donald.

Rodri Sturrock was lifting a kettle off the Aga. 'Hello again,' he said, glancing to where she stood in the doorway before turning back to fill a brown teapot. 'Come in and have some tea.'

The boys crossed the stone-flagged floor and vanished through another door, and she could hear their voices off in another room. 'You sent for me,' she said, risking a dry tone.

He looked up sharply. 'Is that what they said?'

Not quite, but it had been implied. 'They said you were putting the kettle on.'

He grunted. 'Good. Milk and sugar?'

'Just milk.'

'I owe you an apology. I was unfriendly.'

'Duplicitous rather than unfriendly, I'd have said,' she replied.

He glanced at her again, an eyebrow raised, then seemed to consider, weighing the kettle in his hand before replacing it. 'No, I simply said my name was Sturrock; the rest was your assumption, which I chose not to correct. You were a stranger, you see, and wouldn't know any better.' He pulled up a stool and gestured her to a chair. 'Have one of these by way of reparation.' He pushed a plate of shortbread towards her. 'Alice made them yesterday. They win prizes, you know.'

She took one, considering the man. 'Do you often impersonate your brother?' she asked.

He took back the plate and chose the largest piece. 'I don't often have the opportunity,' he said, biting into it. 'But if strangers come poking about where they've no business, I let them draw their own conclusions. You did have business here, of a sort, but I couldn't have known that, could I?'

Not initially, perhaps, but she wouldn't split hairs. She still needed him on-side.

He raised his mug and regarded her over the rim with that same appraising look he had given her out by the mound. 'So your brother lives in Norway, and you live here?' she said, feeling that she should say something and looking around the sunlit kitchen. The scrutiny was unnerving. 'Very nice too.'

'I look after things for Hector.'

Like keeping archaeologists at bay, accosting visitors, seeing off nighthawks. A gatekeeper. And had he been here, looking after things, when the Ullaness chalice had been stolen? It would be insensitive to allude to it but she decided she would anyway, to balance the score. 'And I suppose you've had trouble with strangers in the past,' she said.

He took another drink. 'If you mean the burglary, that actually happened during one of Hector's visits. But since then we've had a van-load of likely lads with metal detectors sniffing around, treasure-hunting. So yes, we've had trouble.'

'And is that what you thought I was?'

'A likely lass?' He looked amused, briefly. 'You were studying the mound very carefully, you know.'

Fair enough, but she pursued him. 'I understand your brother's gamekeeper has a more direct way of seeing people off. Will he take potshots at my students if they wander around at night?'

The single-line frown reappeared smartly. 'I wonder where you heard that. Angus did *not* fire at them, he was ten miles away at the time visiting his mother, so I'd be grateful if you'd scotch that rumour.' He set his mug down. 'You saw him last night in the pub. A lovely man.'

Benign he certainly appeared, but Libby imagined the bearded giant might have a steelier side, and the glimmer in her host's eye gave confirmation. At that moment the boys reappeared, one carrying bulging carrier bags, the other a pile of shoe boxes. 'Good God,' said their father. 'What's all that?' The Labrador lifted its nose but decided to stay put.

'Where's my tea?' demanded the younger boy, obliquely eyeing the shortbreads.

'You don't like tea.'

'I do!'

'Wait. What are you doing?' Having deposited their burdens on the table, the boys were starting to tip out the shoe boxes. 'Stop!'

'But she said she'd like to see it.'

Wordplay seemed to run in the family, but she couldn't withstand the appeal in the boys' expressions. 'Of course I would. But maybe some newspaper on the table first – '

'Good idea. Go and get some.'

'And I *do* like tea.'

'Alright.' The man rose. 'Spread out some newspaper and keep all your loot on it, and I'll get you both some tea. And it's *one* shortbread each.'

These conditions met, the boys tipped out the contents of the first box and began spreading it over the table with wide sweeps of robust arms, cascading sand onto the floor. 'Give me strength,' said their father, turning back to watch, 'you've collected half the beach.' The boys ignored him, their eyes fixed hopefully on Libby.

It was a motley collection comprising mostly rusty metal, broken china and animal bones, but she felt that she must rise to the occasion. 'Let's group them first,' she suggested, 'stone with stone, bone with bone, metal with metal, and so on.' They set to, a couple of bright boys, she guessed, keener than many of her students. Her eye fell on two very fine chert blades, which she rescued from further abuse and set aside.

'Leave 'em to it, and have some more tea,' Rodri Sturrock said, refilling her mug. 'They've been out collecting stuff ever since they heard about the dig.'

'And before!' The older boy was examining a third chert blade, which he put with the others; a quick learner. 'There's been treasure found here already, you know,' he said, glancing shyly up at her. 'Real gold and stuff.'

'A very long time ago,' said his father.

The dampening remark earned him a frown. 'But there might be more. Like the dish thing that was stolen.'

The dish thing. Libby looked across at their father. Would she have to explain to *this* man about the cross? It was a daunting thought; he had an uncompromising air. 'There's been no news about it, I suppose?' she asked, and he shook his head, drinking his tea and watching the boys. She'd have to grasp that nettle sometime, but it could wait, at least until she heard back from Nan.

While his attention was elsewhere, she looked around the kitchen. It was old-fashioned and rather spartan but attractive nonetheless. An ancient Aga stood under the original fireplace arch with a tall coal scuttle beside it, filled to the brim. The cupboards and shelves were wooden, painted a pale grey and chipped, probably 1920s or earlier, while the long free-standing dresser looked older and the table bore evidence of scrubbing by generations of cooks and kitchen maids. The sink too was of the old Belfast type, with tall taps and wooden draining boards. There was a dishwasher, she noticed, and an electric hob but, other than an espresso machine, barely a nod towards modernity. The drying rail above the Aga was empty of clothing and a bleached tea-towel had been neatly folded beside the sink, while a striped butcher's apron hung on the back of a closed door. The room was almost severely uncluttered, with not a thing left out that had no purpose, testament to a formidable housewife. Alice the shortbread maker, and presumably his wife, must be a paragon.

'Is that what *you're* looking for?' Charlie asked, bringing her back to the moment as he cheerfully snapped together the mandibles of two different sheep, crocodile-style. 'The rest of the treasure?'

'Not treasure, as such . . .' She sensed his father's eyes on her. 'But the sea is starting to wash away that big mound, so we need to record what there is before—'

'Other people came looking for treasure,' the boy interrupted, 'with metal detectors, but *someone* shot at them and they haven't come back.'

'Charlie,' said his father.

'It's true!' the boy insisted.

'You know perfectly well that Angus was with Jennet that night.' The two boys exchanged grins and dropped their heads back to their task. Libby helped them sort while she drank her tea, glancing across at their father, who returned her a bland smile.

Eventually the boys stood back, indicating that their part in the exercise was complete, and she surveyed the results. They had done a good job but there was, at first glance, little of interest. Nails of all sizes, rusted and bent, the corroded spout of a metal teapot, a heavy iron cog from some sort of farm machinery, a bed or car seat spring, fragments of old china, and more chips of chert that she would need to examine more closely. Lots of animal bone, teeth, sheep horn cores . . . Then her eye was caught by a small dark stone, elongated and thin. It had a hole pierced in one end, like a pendant, and she rescued it, putting it to one side. Rodri Sturrock reached out his hand and picked it up to examine.

'Do you know the legend of Ullaness?' the older boy asked her, dusting the sand off his hands. 'It's really famous.'

'Only bits of it,' she replied, and sat back again. How had the legend survived here, she wondered, in the place of its conception? 'So tell me.'

And she felt a sort of wonder as she sat in the old kitchen and listened while the boys, their eyes large with conviction, told her much the same story that she had learned when she was their age, two thousand miles away. It was an erratic but drama-filled telling as the boys spoke over one another, squabbling about some details and backtracking as they remembered others; but in the telling they were continuing a tradition which stretched back over the generations, unconsciously doing their bit towards the legend's preservation.

'And years later Erik came back to find the treasure—'

'No! He came to find Pádraig.'

'Who's Pádraig?' she asked quickly, before the squabble moved the story on.

'The boy.'

'Which boy?'

'Ulla's son!'

They spoke in unison, in the same belittling tone, as if this was surely common knowledge; but here was a detail – a name – which had not survived the transatlantic journey, and she thrilled at the thought of what other nuggets might have been retained. 'And who was his father?' she asked, curious to hear their take on this disputed point.

'Harald, of course. The Viking.'

'Not Odrhan?'

Charlie looked at her. 'He was a *monk*!'

'Ridiculous suggestion,' agreed their father, leaning back in his chair.

'And not Erik?' she asked, ignoring him.

Donald answered this time. 'She was running away from *him*.'

'Ulla and Harald were *lovers*, you see,' his brother explained patiently, to his father's evident amusement.

'Yes, I do see,' Libby replied, not looking at him. 'Of course.'

And so to them at least that detail of the legend was unambiguous, and she wondered who had passed the story on. Women were usually the keepers of tales. 'How do you know all this?' she asked.

They misunderstood the question. 'Because Pádraig was hiding when Erik came and he saw what happened to Odrhan, so he ran away and grew up somewhere, and then he came back with lots of treasure himself and built the church, and told people what—'

'And that's how the legend started, you see,' Donald informed her gravely, 'and why the church is St Oran's, because of Odrhan and what he did for Pádraig.'

Odrhan. Pádraig. The names tripped off the small boys' lips as if they were discussing their neighbours, and, in a curious sort of way, they were. Neighbours separated from them only by time and made immortal by a story. She found the continuity deeply satisfying. They pronounced Odrhan with a lovely soft roll to the *r*, but her grandmother had said it differently, emphasising the flatter, broader *o* sound whereby Newfoundlanders made oxen into *aa*xen. And they pronounced Pádraig in the Gaelic way, not as its modern equivalent, Patrick. So Ulla's child had been named for Ireland's patron saint, had he, giving credence to the idea that the monk had, after all, converted her – or had he had the naming of the boy himself? In her grandmother's telling, Ulla's son had been a shadowy figure, while here both he and Odrhan had substance, kept alive by the retelling of the story.

Libby urged them to continue, but they'd lost interest, just as she had done, at the point where the legend morphed into a sort of biblical tale of a feral boy who had been taken in by good Christian souls, and who had returned as a man to build a church.

No, it was the drama of the earlier episode which had caught their imaginations, and which perhaps had ensured the legend's survival. Sex, murder – and a reckoning, just as Declan had said.

'Is there anything Viking here?' Donald's question brought her back to the task in hand.

'It's all very interesting,' she said, and wondered what these children made of it all as they pored over their booty. She pointed to the chert blades. 'Can you remember where you found these?' After some discussion they agreed that they had found them at the edge of the south bay, amongst the rocks just above the beach, near where she knew that Mesolithic shell middens had been found. 'They're the oldest things.'

'Viking?'

She shook her head. 'Much earlier.'

'Caveman?'

'Sort of.'

'Cool!' Donald examined them again, but it was clearly Vikings they were after, so she retrieved the little pendant-like stone. 'That's from Viking times. It's a stone used for sharpening blades.' This time the chorus of *'Cool!'* carried conviction and they began arguing about who had found it and where, and then shot off saying they would go right now and look for more.

'You've redeemed yourself,' their father said, sitting back again as the door slammed. 'A rabbit out of a hat. But how do you know?'

'By the type of rock, and the shape. And the wear.'

He nodded, apparently content with that explanation. 'And why do you bother?' He smiled slightly at her expression. 'With all of it, I mean. Digging things up?'

She was unprepared for that one. 'Curiosity, I suppose.'

'And so yours is a profession for the curious, is it? How quaint.' His smile was mocking. Did he hope for a rise? 'Why not just leave it all to disappear back into the sand and grass?'

'A sort of cultural compost?' she enquired, resolving to be unprovoked.

'Exactly.'

'So why let us excavate the mound? Why not just let the sea have it?'

'Fair point,' he acknowledged. 'I suppose I was intrigued.'

'As in curious?'

He laughed. 'And I thought something might be salvaged.'

'*You* did?'

He raised an eyebrow. 'Who else d'you think reported it?'

That was a surprise. 'I thought you weren't keen for us to come?'

'Hector certainly wasn't! But you were explaining your choice of career. Are you in it because you think we can learn from the past and avoid repeating the same mistakes?'

She wasn't, actually, but last night she'd felt time shrink around her to a point where the past was almost tangible. She decided to toss the question back at him. 'I take it you aren't.'

He looked out of the window as if considering his response, then shook his head. 'No. Not really. Every situation is unique, so there are no patterns to learn from.'

'In the broadest sense, surely –'

He shrugged. 'The very broadest, perhaps. But in the detail it's all down to individuals, and the choices they make.' Such as Odrhan's decision to go down to meet the ship rather than hide, she thought fleetingly. 'And people behave in unexpected ways.' He gestured to the little whetstone on the table. 'So how does finding bits like that help?'

'We can build the big picture from all the little –'

'But you can't get from there to the individuals, or their motivations.'

A man of fixed views, but this was an opportunity to get him on board. 'Maybe here, at Ullaness, we will,' she replied, picking up the little stone again. 'To some extent anyway.'

'How so?' he said, taking it back from her.

'Because of the stories that survive. That little stone might have belonged to one of Harald's men. And that mound might be Harald's burial place.'

'Hmmm.' He looked unconvinced 'But you'll never know who put him there, or whether the lovely Ulla was a convert or a whore. And that's the interesting bit.' He laid the whetstone back beside the other finds on the table and looked across at her.

'We'll do our best,' she replied, sensing it was probably time that she left, but as she began to gather herself he put out a hand.

'You were in the church when the boys found you.'

'Yes.'

'Is it in any way remarkable?' he asked. 'Other than for the ghastly tomb of my forebears?'

'There's a lot that could be done there . . .' she began.

'But you've no idea what your colleague might want to discuss?'

Were they back on this? 'No.'

'As you said before,' he remarked, smiling a little as if he read her mind.

She stood up. 'But one of those grave slabs is cracked, and the damage looks quite recent. Was that down to your nighthawks?'

'It was. Damn them.' He too rose.

'It's a remarkable collection of stones, you know. Have they ever been properly recorded?'

'No idea,' he replied. 'Probably not. Are you touting for more work as well?'

Goaded, she spoke without thinking. 'And if I was, is it you or your brother who decides?'

'Hector, of course,' he said, but there was a glint of amusement in his eye. 'And I guide his decision-making. I argued your case for you very hard.' She wasn't convinced, but he had headed down the passageway to the back door. 'And you're away now, are you?' he asked, over his shoulder. 'Back south.'

'I'm here another night.'

'So how will you spend the afternoon?'

'I'll continue to explore, if that's alright, and maybe go further along the shore.'

'Explore away while you can. There's some bad weather on its way.' He watched as she pulled on her shoes and tied the laces. 'Until the summer then, Libby Snow. And put some flesh on these characters for me.'

Chapter 5

The wounded man moaned softly.

Her name was Ulla, the woman said, and she watched Odrhan apply a poultice to his wounds, her face lit by the firelight.

She had bid the men bring the baskets into the shelter but there was no room for them. They would be safe outside, Odrhan told her. Few people came here.

They removed them again, all but one, forgotten in the shadows. It was only when Odrhan rose to fetch fresh water that he saw it. The fire's flame caught the glint of metal, and the richness of a precious stone. He bent to look more closely and his heart stalled.

As a boy he had been schooled at the white monastery beside Lough Neagh, learning to love a life of contemplation and prayer, and he had stayed there, serving at the altar. And on that altar –

He reached into the basket and drew from it the jewelled chalice he had last seen raised in supplication, blood now roaring in his ears.

'Sweet Jesu. How came you by this, lady?'

◄═ *Libby* ═►

Clouds were forming over the sea as Libby sat on the headland later that day, having eaten her sandwiches and explored the shell middens, and she watched the thin line of grey spread like an awning across the sky, and sensed the wind strengthening. She felt the first spots of rain, and they were falling fast by the time she reached the car. Please God it didn't do this in June!

She stared through the rain-streaked windscreen as the scene in front of her grew wild. It was dramatic, almost menacing, how quickly the sky darkened. There was nothing for it but to return to the pub, read a book and have an early night. Which would, in fact, be a luxury.

And later, as she lay in bed, book in hand, she listened to the storm raging outside. Rain was flung like gravel against the window and the ill-fitting frame rattled in the gusting wind. When was high tide? she wondered. It had been that fateful combination of tide and storm which had damaged the mound last time. She ought to have asked Rodri Sturrock if she could re-cover the exposed stones. Maybe she should nip down in the morning and check that all was well, and then e-mail him when she got home and suggest some temporary form of consolidation. He seemed a quixotic character, but it was easier to ask now that she'd met him.

It was still blowing hard next morning when she parked in the same spot beside the church. Ahead of her the sea was turbulent, each wave crested by a mane of spray blown back, and the distant view formed a single dark wash of grey. At least the rain had eased a little and it would require only a quick dash into the dunes to see the state of things, and then she'd be away.

She had to push hard to open the car door and the wind slammed it shut behind her as the hood of her jacket was blown back. She ran, leaping the stream, and made for the dunes, reached the mound and saw at once that the waves, driven by the storm, had again found a channel to its base. The flattened wet sand reminded her of a child's attempt to fill a sandcastle moat. Surely there were more stones now – she counted them: four, five, *six* . . . and then a seventh lying off-set, still half buried. There could be no doubt now that they'd been deliberately laid on a curve, and she felt a renewed buzz of excitement.

She went closer. The newly exposed stone, number six, was similar in shape and size to the others, another oval grey-white water-worn cobble. Stone seven, however, was smooth and dark, and of a fine-grained rock.

Except, she saw as she began clearing the sand away from it, it wasn't a rock, it was dried and cracked leather. The toe of a shoe.

Odd boots or shoes frequently turned up along high-tide lines, lost overboard and carried for miles by current and tide, or left behind by forgetful paddlers. This must be one of those. She gave it a little tug but it stuck firm, so she cleared away more sand, wondering what held it there.

Then the sand fell away and she had her answer.

She straightened and stood looking down at it, not believing what she saw. A discoloured leg bone jutted incongruously out of the top of it. She bent to inspect more closely, her breath coming fast and shallow. It was a boot, not a shoe, an ankle boot, warped and misshapen, old but not ancient, and the bone was simply bone, without flesh or sinew. Dear God! But a matter for the police, not an archaeologist. Rapidly she scooped up handfuls of wet sand and plastered them over the exposed remains, hardly noticing that the rain had come on again hard, driven by the wind, and she was soon soaked, and shivering.

Once bone and boot were covered, she turned and ran for the car, got inside, and pulled out her mobile. No signal. She started the car, thinking rapidly. She could phone from Sturrock House, Rodri Sturrock needed to know anyway, unless he had already gone for the day, or maybe his wife would be there. It was still early, not yet nine – she might catch someone, unless out on the school run. She could always go back to the pub, they'd know who to ring. She reversed the car, the windscreen wipers on full but barely keeping up with the deluge, and the wheels spun as she accelerated forward, then gripped as they found gravel, and she drove fast up the track. Dear God – somewhere she'd seen a turning which must be a drive leading up to Sturrock House, and she leaned forward to peer through the rain-drenched windscreen as the car bounced over the rough track. Just past that clump of gorse bushes, if she remembered correctly – and she swung the wheel hard to the left, into the drive and straight into the grille of the oncoming Land Rover.

Everything went blank. The airbag inflated but she'd forgotten her seat belt and was thrown sideways, banging her head hard.

The next thing she was aware of was Rodri Sturrock wrenching the door open. 'Of all the—! God, are you alright?'

'I think so –'

'She's bleeding.'

Two small white faces had appeared beside his, and he turned them swiftly away. 'No, you don't. Get your stuff and run back to the house. Tell Alice she'll have to take you in. And tell her to use the back road. Go on! Off with you – ' He turned back to Libby, reaching over her to pull on the handbrake, then briefly examined her forehead. 'Could have been worse. Sit tight a minute.'

Groggily she watched him go to the front and examine the damage, then return to the Land Rover. A moment later there was an awful wrenching sound as he reversed, and she felt her car strain forward, then release abruptly as the bumpers disengaged. He was right, it could have been worse, but sympathy looked as if it would be in short order.

'Alright?' he asked, opening the door a moment later, rain plastering his hair to his head. 'Out you get then.' And he swept her out and into the passenger seat of the Land Rover, which he reversed speedily back up the drive and into the courtyard of Sturrock House. He came round and opened her door. 'We'll sort your car later. Come on, into the dry,' and with a hand under her elbow, he steered her into the house. The dog, released from the back of the Land Rover, followed them in.

'You're drenched!' he remarked as he took her jacket, hanging it to drip in the passageway. 'How did that happen? Go and sit over by the Aga.' She was shivering uncontrollably now and only vaguely aware of him moving around the kitchen as she huddled close to the warmth. Next minute an ice pack was pressed to her forehead and she yelped.

'You make your mark, Libby Snow. I'll say that for you,' he said. 'Hold it there, and drink that.' He slid a mug towards her. 'You're going to have a stunning black eye.' He disappeared but returned at once, and she felt a blanket being draped around her shoulders.

She took a sip. Tea, hot and sweet and strong. It was good. 'Thank you,' she said. The fuzziness in her head was going but her voice sounded odd.

'D'you feel sick?' he asked, looking intently into her eyes. She shook her head, regretting it immediately, and he examined her forehead again. 'It's stopped bleeding. Vision alright?' She nodded more carefully, licked her dry lips, and took another sip, feeling the warmth reviving her. The shivering began to subside. 'What on earth were you doing tearing round a blind corner like that? And no seat belt! A second later I'd have hit you full-on. I thought you'd gone back south.'

The question kick-started her brain and she took the pack off her head.

'Keep it on,' he said.

'We have to call the police.'

He shook his head. 'They won't be interested –'

'Not for the car. It's the mound. There's a body in it. I saw a boot, and a leg –'

He stared at her. It sounded ridiculous, of course; he must think her concussed and rambling. The tea, however, was working wonders. 'The storm uncovered it. And it's not old, not ancient, the boot I mean, but not new, there's only bone, not flesh, and I covered it up again. With wet sand. I was coming to tell you, and use the phone.'

He continued to stare. 'Say all that again, will you, but slowly.' She did. Then: 'Are you quite sure?'

'Yes.' And she started trembling again.

He put a hand to her arm and gripped it for a moment. 'Alright, I believe you. But how do you know it's not ancient?'

'The boot. Wrong sort.'

He got up and went to the window, where the rain had again abated. 'I'll go and take a look. But first – ' He disappeared again, returning a moment later with a towel and a baggy sweatshirt with matching purple leggings. 'Dry your hair, and put these on. I'll be right back.'

Unsympathetic, perhaps, but good on the practical side. She clutched the blanket and drank the hot sweet tea, then carefully dried her hair, avoiding the lump which was rising on her forehead, before exchanging her wet clothes for the dry ones. They fitted well. But would their owner mind? She went over to the sink and squeezed the melted water out of the tea-towel, twisting the remaining ice into a corner and held it to the bruise again. Breakfast dishes had been hastily abandoned, she saw, presumably when Rodri's sons had brought their message, and the striped apron lay where it had been flung. But it had been Alice he'd referred to, not Mum.

She touched the side of the teapot. It was still warm, and she had just refilled her mug when a blast of cold announced Rodri's return. He strode into the kitchen, followed by the dog, his face grim. 'I'd hoped you were just concussed,' he said, making for the sink where he rinsed his hands, shaking them dry. Then he came and stood in front of her, peering at her head. 'How's the bang?'

'Fine. Did you cover it up again?'

He nodded, then went to set the kettle back on the Aga. 'I brought your car up too. The bumper's had it, and one of the headlights is smashed, but otherwise it's not too bad.' He picked up her discarded towel and briskly dried his own hair.

'Thank you, but oughtn't we –'

'The local garage is good, they'll sort it.'

'Yes, I'm sure they will.' Puzzled now, she watched him as he brewed another pot of tea, his mind clearly working, his expression intense. He made no move towards the phone but filled two mugs, ladling sugar into both, and pushed one towards her.

This would not do. 'I've got one,' she said, raising her mug to show him. 'And hadn't we better phone the police?'

He sipped at his tea, staring fixedly over the rim at nothing. 'Aye, we will,' he said, but made no move.

'Shall I? As I found it –' She rose and pulled out her mobile.

He raised a hand, still not looking at her. 'Just hang on a minute. Let me think.'

She sat again. If there had been flesh on those bones, she would now be suspicious, but what possible reason could there be for delay? Then he turned and fixed her with a sharp look. 'They'll wreck your site, you know.'

'I know.' She'd already thought of that, and the idea of the police hacking into the mound was sickening, but he was contemplating her in an oddly speculative way. Then abruptly he went across to the phone and tapped in a number.

'Fergus? Rodri Sturrock here . . . I'm fine, yes, well, sort of fine –' and he explained what had been found, concisely and to

the point. '. . . yes. Her name's Libby Snow. She's still here. In
my kitchen. No, she's not going anywhere, her car's had a bit of a
mishap. . . . Yep, she'll stay right here. And, Fergus? Will you do
me a favour and not say anything to anyone just yet? Until you've
seen it. Aye . . . No . . . That's right, I don't want that circus again.
Good man.' He put the phone down and turned back to her.
'Sorted.'

He came back and sat opposite her. 'But you're right, though,'
he said after a moment, 'that bone's been there awhile, and the
boot looks old-fashioned' – where was he going with this? – 'so
not a missing person. A recent one, I mean.'

'No.'

'But if word gets out, we'll have the press crawling all over us
again, like it was after the theft. First that, and now a body. Great.
You can imagine the headlines, can't you? And we'll get all sorts,
trashing your site and making my life hell.'

He sat there, brooding into middle distance, then looked back
at her. 'Unless . . .' She waited for whatever was coming '. . . unless
we can keep it quiet.' The morning was taking a very bizarre turn.
'I'm on good terms with the local police, you see, and the regional
hierarchy, and I'm wondering if I might persuade them to keep
this quiet and let you be involved in lifting the bones.' He paused,
his eyes on her. 'Under police supervision, of course. And then I
can pass it off as part of your project if word gets out.' He stopped
again, then asked: 'How long does it take flesh to disappear in
sand?'

From bizarre to macabre. 'I've no idea!'

'Thought perhaps you might.' He seemed lost in his own
thoughts again, then shot her another of his direct looks. 'So,
would you do it, if the police could be persuaded?'

This man liked to have things go his way, it appeared; but, in
fact, it wasn't a bad idea. She'd do as good a job as the police in

recovering the bones, better in terms of preserving the context and the integrity of the site. 'Are they *likely* to agree?' It seemed improbable.

'We'll find out.' He took the empty mugs over to the sink. 'How's the head doing?' he asked, over his shoulder.

It was spinning, but she could no longer distinguish between bruising, shock, and the extraordinary scheme that was evolving in the well-ordered kitchen – then suddenly the thought of Declan came into her mind. Oh God, she'd have to tell him! Panicked, she stood up: 'Wait! I'll need to ring in to work. And I ought to tell Declan, Professor Lockhart – '

'Don't.'

'What?'

'Don't tell your professor.' He took in her expression. 'Ring in sick, by all means, and tell them you've had a car accident, it's true after all. Or better still, let me. What's the number?'

Her head spun faster. 'No. I'll ring them.'

He didn't like that. 'I don't want *any* mention of what you found to get out.' The frown was back in place. 'They'll plague you with questions, you know. You'd much better let me do it.'

Again, he was probably right. If Glenda, the departmental secretary, answered the phone, it would be a full-on interrogation and the whole department would know within minutes. 'Well, alright, but tell them I'm OK and I'll be back in work tomorrow, or the next day. If the car's driveable.' She handed him her phone with the department's number on it. 'Do you think it is?'

'Let's do this first.' He punched the number into the house phone, and when he got through he adopted the tone of cool authority she'd heard on Declan's speakerphone, quite different from the one used a moment ago. He spoke quickly, describing the accident, exaggerating both the damage to the car and her injury. 'Neither she nor her vehicle will be in a fit state to drive down for a day or two. No . . . she's fine . . . We're looking after her and I'll get her to ring you. No . . . no . . . be sure to pass the message on, will you? Must go, we expect the police any moment . . . Yes, they're involved, but there's no need to alarm anyone. Thank you. Must go.' And he rang off. 'And so that's sorted too,' he said.

Well, after a fashion. 'Was it a woman with a Liverpool accent?' she asked.

'Yes.'

Glenda. And she could imagine the office buzzing. 'But you didn't tell her where I was.'

'I know. And I didn't give her the chance to ask.'

He seemed pleased about that. 'Whyever not?'

'Let's hear what Fergus says first. He'll be here in two ticks. Least said and all that.'

'She might try to ring back.'

'Number's withheld.'

'Or my mobile –'

'Don't answer it. Patchy signal.'

She stared at him. She was, in fact, cut off with no one knowing where she was. Except the police, she reminded herself. Could things get more peculiar! And Rodri Sturrock, with everything now arranged to his satisfaction, was calmly drying the two mugs on a tea-towel. He glanced across at her and took in the bemused stare. 'It's all alright, you know. We will look after you, like I said—' He broke off as another waft of cold air hit them and a young woman stepped into the kitchen, stopping at the doorway. 'Alice! Bless you. Were you on time?'

'Aye, more or less. Are you alright?' she asked, addressing Libby, taking in the sweatshirt and leggings. 'The boys told me what happened, and I saw your car. That's a cracking bump you've got.'

'It looks worse than it is.'

'I should hope so!' She was probably about Libby's age, late twenties, with fair hair pulled back into a high ponytail which swung jauntily as she came over to peer at Libby's brow. 'Ice,' she said, going over to the freezer.

'We've done ice,' said Rodri.

'Well, let's do it again. Have you taken painkillers?'

'No.'

'I'll get some. And that cut needs covering.' But as she pulled open a high cupboard, there was a knock at the door. 'Now, who'll that be,' she said, '*knocking* . . . ?'

'I'll go,' said Rodri.

'. . . no one *knocks*! I'm Alice, by the way. Purple suits you.'

'I'm Libby. Are they yours? I hope you don't mind.'

'Don't be daft.' The girl dabbed Libby's cut forehead with something which stung, and covered it with a dressing. 'That's better.' There was no time for more as Rodri ushered a middle-aged policeman through the door.

His aura of calm officialdom was very welcome. Rodri introduced him as Fergus McAdam and the man shook Libby's hand, enquiring about the accident and her injuries with a fatherly concern before accepting a cup of tea from Alice. He drank it as Libby explained about the planned excavation and what the storm had uncovered.

'Dear God!' she heard Alice exclaim behind her.

The policeman listened attentively as she spoke but made no comment. 'I'll need to take a statement from you,' he said, when she had finished, 'but just now I'll go and have a wee look. And I'd like you to come and show me what you did, clearing the sand away and such, if you can manage it?'

'Are you fit?' Rodri asked.

It was actually the last thing Libby wanted to do, but she had to say yes if the plan Rodri was hatching was to succeed.

Alice, who had been spreading her wet things on the rack above the Aga, stopped. 'She's not, and she'll get all wet again.'

'She says she is, and we've got more dry things,' Rodri countered, guiding Libby towards the door, from where he looked back at Alice. 'And not a word about all this to anyone, alright?'

'Angus?'

'I'll tell him myself.'

'Maddy?'

He nodded. 'Aye, but nothing to the boys. And I'll string up the pair of you if a whisper of it gets about.'

'Right,' Alice replied, apparently unconcerned by both threat and tone as she turned back to the wet clothes, leaving Libby wondering at the cut and thrust of their domestic bliss. The policeman, she noticed, was grinning.

In the passage Rodri tossed aside her still-dripping jacket and held out a waxed coat for her. 'Wear this,' he said. It was warm and must belong to Alice, but he was in the courtyard with the policeman before Libby could protest.

'Libby's in charge of the excavations this summer,' he was saying as she joined them. 'And she'll be running the show.' Technically, that was true, though Declan would take issue with the statement. She had the sensation of being carried along on a tidal wave.

It had stopped raining by the time they reached the mound, and Rodri brushed away the sand to expose the toe of the boot again, then stood back to allow Fergus to examine it. Now that the shock of discovery had passed, Libby was able to consider things more calmly, and she looked at it again. It was certainly not ancient, and was in fact very distinctive, a sturdy style with a low heel, and a strip of decorative tooling across the width of the toe. The sole, once attached by nails and stitching, had dried out and sprung away from the upper, and the layers of the composite heel had begun to separate. But what distinguished it was the fasten-ing, an off-centre row of holes opposite where there had once been buttons, one or two of which remained in place.

Rodri was watching her. 'What do you think?' he asked.

'It looks Victorian to me. And it's a man's boot, obviously.'

'So, what? A hundred years old?' Fergus asked.

'Maybe more.'

The policeman looked relieved. She suggested that she clear away a little more of the sand from the bone, just enough to see if they could glimpse the other leg lying beneath it, and he agreed. She worked carefully but it was an easy job, the damp sand just fell away. And then it hit her, in a sickening wave. Not nausea exactly, but an awful sensation, and she stopped, still crouching over the sand, remembering what her grandmother had said. Ellen, in her fragile later years, had wept, saying that murder had been done.

⊷ Odrhan ⊶

In answer to his question Ulla told a dreadful tale of summer raids and desecration, and in a red mist of fury Odrhan bid the woman go. 'And take that defiler with you.'

She stared steadily back at him. 'If we move him, he will die.'

'Then it is I who will leave.'

She said a word and his escape was barred by her followers. Blades flashed in the firelight. 'Stay, holy man,' she said, 'and attend to Harald's wounds and I will make you a vow. If he lives, I will pray to your god and seek forgiveness for my sins, and for his.'

He sensed the tension in the men behind him in the blackness. They would slay him at a word, as they had doubtless slain the gentle monks at the white monastery, his erstwhile companions. And he felt a great

fury swell within him. Ungodly, unforgiving. 'You will truly repent?'
he asked, and she nodded, her eyes not leaving his. 'And give your soul
to God?' She nodded again, but he knew that she would agree to any-
thing to achieve her purpose. 'Then I will cleanse the wound again,' he
said.

He prepared another poultice under their watchful eyes, but so in-
tent were they on what his right hand was doing that they did not see
how with his left he scratched at a grey-white patch left on the basket
by a passing gull. It was easy then to transfer the guano to the cloth,
wipe the wound, and repeat the process.

Within hours the man passed from quiescence to a burning fever,
and he tossed in writhing delirium while Odrhan prayed for the souls
of the murdered monks. From there the man sank into a deep coma.

By dawn he was dead.

➤ *Libby* ➤

'That's fine,' said the policeman. 'Let's cover it back up again. Do
you get many visitors coming down here, Mr Sturrock?' he asked.
'Dog-walkers and the like?'

But Rodri was looking at her. 'Are you alright?'

'Fine. Just the head,' she said.

He crouched beside her and helped her to cover the exposed
remains, answering the policeman over his shoulder. 'Not at this
time of year. And not in this weather.' He glanced at her again.
'Job done,' he said, and they both straightened. The sand would
dry fast now that the rain had stopped and the patch of disturbed
ground would soon be indistinguishable from the rest of the
mound.

Rodri led them off towards the house, talking intently to Fergus, and Libby turned to look back at the mound, then quickened

her step to catch up, half wishing that she'd driven straight home this morning as she listened to Rodri planting his scheme in the policeman's mind. 'She'll have to stay over while the car gets fixed anyway. The work here could be all done and dusted tomorrow if the weather improves. She's a professional after all.' But Fergus wasn't a pushover and courteously, but firmly, refused to make any commitment until he had discussed matters with his superiors. Rodri nodded, agreeing that of course he'd have to do that. 'But why not talk to Dougie first though, see what he says? If it's more than a century old, then the chances of making an arrest are a bit thin, don't you think?'

'Aye, maybe.' And that was as far as Fergus was willing to go.

Back in the kitchen, Alice was ironing. 'The kettle's on,' she said. It seemed that it always was, and Libby went to huddle close to the warmth of the Aga.

'Fantastic,' Rodri replied. 'Come through to the library, Fergus, you can use the phone in there. Will it be Dougie you'll be talking to, or Jenkins? I never know who deals with what these days.' The policeman was given no time to resist as Rodri ushered him through the door, calling over his shoulder: 'Bring some tea through to us, Alice, there's a love. And look after Libby.'

Alice turned the iron off. 'Oh God, he's in one of those force-of-nature moods,' she said as she filled the teapot, then carried two mugs through to the men. On her return she stopped in the doorway and looked across at Libby. 'God, you look awful! White as a sheet. Let me pull a chair up to the Aga. There now, sit.' And for the second time that day she was given a mug of tea so sweet she could hear her teeth howling. It was accompanied by an insistent offer of shortbread. 'Men. Honestly. I should never have let them take you.'

She hovered as Libby smiled her thanks and bit into the shortbread. 'He said you win prizes for these,' she said.

'Aye, I do.' There was a kindness and concern in the girl's eyes, and Libby decided that Rodri Sturrock was a lucky man. 'And for other stuff too. We're a good team here. Foodies. . . .' She went back to her ironing, saying nothing more, but when Libby looked up a moment later she found herself once again under scrutiny. 'There, you look better already. I was waiting for you to keel over.'

'It's just the cold, I think.'

'And the shock! Finding *that*, and then hitting the Land Rover. Not great, eh? The boys told me all about the dig this summer, but that sort of body wasn't on the cards, was it? Though I suppose you're used to bones.' She continued to regard Libby, but now with curiosity rather than concern. 'Or is it different if they're recent ones?' Libby had sometimes considered that point as she scratched away at ancient soils, intruding into times long past. 'Still a dead person, though. You mustn't let Rodri do his overbearing bit, you know, and he really should've taken you to the hospital with that head of yours.'

The men reappeared at that moment and Libby saw that the two mugs had been augmented by a couple of glasses, now empty. Alice repeated her remark, adding: 'She was as white as a sheet just now.'

Rodri gave Libby a sharp look. 'I'll take you in if you like. Of course I will.'

'I'm fine, really,' she replied.

'You've only to say. But take it easy the rest of the day, maybe have a nap, and you'll need an early night.' So an agreement had been reached, had it? His next words confirmed it. 'Fergus and his superiors feel it would be helpful if you could stay on for a bit,' he said, and gave her one of his direct looks. 'Could you do that? They're going to send a man over in the morning to take charge of things, and they'll take the bones away along with anything else that turns up. But they'd like you to expose the remains and they'll lift them.' Things moved fast with a force of nature behind them. 'Is that alright with you?'

And what could she say? It was, in fact, a good idea. She would notice things that they might miss, changes in soil colour and texture which could be vital, and she didn't want to think of anyone else doing it. 'Of course,' she said.

Behind her Alice made a quiet hrmph noise, which Rodri ignored. 'Well, that's settled then. And we'll see you in the morning, Fergus,' he said, and escorted the policeman to the back door.

Alice watched them go. 'You mustn't let him bully you,' she said. 'You can just say no. He can be a juggernaut when he—'

'Defamation of character, Alice, m'dear,' he said, returning in time to catch the last remark but seemingly unmoved by it. 'And of course you can say no. Think about it, and if there's anything you don't like about the arrangement, that's fine. Alright?' Libby nodded, remembering that sudden sense of horror and wondering at it; it had never happened to her before. Maybe tomorrow, after a good night's sleep, things would feel different.

'Good thing you decided to go and take a look,' Rodri continued. 'Imagine if some walker had found it! I'll have your car sorted out for you, by the way, to return the favour.'

'Thanks, but it is insured –'

'I wouldn't bother with that, we'll just get on with the repairs. And I'll make it right with your work. Your professor's coming up on Wednesday anyway, isn't he?' Oh God, Declan. She'd forgotten again. 'Will he keep quiet if I ask him? The show'll be over by then anyway, and if we get any snoopers tomorrow we can say it's preparation for the dig in the summer.' She could almost see his brain constructing a narrative which was broadly truthful, and which suited him. 'That's what you came up for, after all, wasn't it? And the police were there just in case –' Alice was folding a sheet behind him, and she made another little hrmph sound. He swung round to her, an eyebrow raised. 'Was there something?' he asked.

Alice simply snapped together the two corners of the sheet by way of response, and Libby said: 'That's all fine, but I'll handle Professor Lockhart.'

'Just as you like.'

'He'll find it all very odd, though, as he didn't know I was up here this weekend, and then all this.' In fact he'd be livid, upstaged and out of the loop. 'But first I need to ring the pub and get my room back.' Presumably the Sturrock estate would pick up the tab.

Rodri looked up. 'Oh, but you'll be—' He stopped, glanced at Alice, and started again. 'If you'd like to, you can stay here, we've plenty of space and the spare room's all made up. You'll be very comfortable, but I'll take you back to the pub if you prefer.'

'Much better, Rodri,' said Alice, and she left the kitchen, her arms piled high with ironed clothes, ponytail swinging. 'Well done.'

And at that Libby had to laugh and agreed she would like to stay.

Chapter 6

Alice had taken her across the hall into what must be the core of the old tower house and up an extraordinary carved staircase to a room off a galleried landing. 'Settle yourself in,' she said, 'and then come down for some lunch. Bathroom's through there,' and she left.

It was a lovely room, a corner room with two windows, one overlooking the garden, the other with views stretching out to the headland. Libby could see the stream with the ruined church and the manse beyond, once the focus of a scattered community. And she thought of Ellen going about her daily chores, escaping perhaps to step across the stream as Libby had done and walking out onto the headland. And if she leaned out Libby could just see the roofless cottages where Ellen might have lived.

She turned back to examine the room; the old-fashioned sleigh-style bed looked gloriously inviting. The door Alice had indicated opened into a bathroom which had doubtless once been a dressing room with a tiny fireplace, now dominated by a deep ball-and-claw-footed bath with an overhead shower arrangement. It was a triumph of Edwardian plumbing, but would she dare use it? There was a fine sink with a marble surround and a toilet with overhead cistern and chain, apparently in good working order. A little period piece. But everything was very clean, and Alice had put thick fluffy towels on top of the old radiator which was gurgling into life, and left a pink-striped dressing gown on the bed.

Rodri had brought up her bag and she surveyed the contents, thinking that what had seemed enough for a weekend was inadequate for a longer stay. She had a quick wash, in scalding water, tidied her hair, and went out onto the landing and took in her surroundings. The panelling on the walls looked very old but everything else appeared Victorian in date, and decidedly shabby, almost as if the house had settled into that time, and saw no way of moving on.

She examined the paintings on the staircase as she went downstairs: romantic highland scenes for the most part, many foxed and yellowing, interspersed with mediocre portraits, presumably of past baronets and their families. One of these took her attention, not so much for the individual, who was resplendent in full highland dress, but for the background. It encompassed not only the church with a high cross beside it but, by skewing perspective, the painter had included the headland, and out on the tip was Odrhan's cell, restored imaginatively into a small chapel. Libby peered more closely, and saw two figures standing beside it. Ulla, presumably, with fair hair cascading to her waist, and Odrhan, the monk, facing her and holding an improbable hook-ended staff.

Dear God –

She found her way back to the kitchen, drawn by the sound of voices. Rodri Sturrock had disappeared, but Alice was sitting at the table chatting to another woman and they looked up as Libby came in. 'All sorted? Rodri's gone to see a customer and then on to school for a football match. He says you're to take it easy, and I agree. This is Maddy. Maddy, Libby.'

'Hello,' said the newcomer, and Libby thought she had never seen such incredible green eyes, their colour sharpened by her red hair. 'I've been hearing about your day.' She spoke in a soft, lilting voice which proclaimed her to be a local. 'That bruise looks dreadful.'

'Rodri always drives like a maniac,' said Alice, 'so we'll blame him. Come and have some lunch. And I've lit the fire in the library so you can put your feet up in there afterwards. Maddy and me'll be heading for the dairy when we've eaten.' She bent to the Aga and pulled out a quiche which smelt wonderful. 'And we want your opinion of this. It's a new recipe.'

Foodies, Libby remembered her saying, and as they ate she asked about their business. What did they make? 'Everything,' Alice replied. 'At the moment we're specialising in butter, as well as smoked cheeses, smoked fish, and anything else we can think of.'

'And shortbread,' said Libby, with a smile.

'Aye, shortbread, and tatty scones and oatcakes. Bread and fancies. Jams and pickles. We're still working out what sells best. The big hotels are our mainstay, although other people are getting to know us and word's spreading. We were just at a big food fair, networking, selling too. Lots of new orders. We're partners, Rodri, Maddy, and me.'

Libby struggled to see Rodri Sturrock making jam, and said so. Alice gave a hoot. Maddy smiled and said, 'He's mostly tied up with running the estate, but he does the admin, and promotion.'

'And he shoots things,' Alice added. 'All the macho stuff. Rabbits, pheasants and deer, and we host rough shoots in season. Maddy's dad supplies the salmon and smokes it for us. We're a proper little cooperative and it's beginning to pay off.'

'Fantastic,' Libby said. 'How long have you been at it?'

'When did I move up here?' Alice turned to Maddy. 'Eight years ago?'

'Nine. When David was two.'

'Aye, nine. Time flies.'

When lunch was finished, Alice hustled Libby into the library, refusing point-blank to let her help with the clearing up.

She gestured to a low armchair by the fireside and pulled over a footstool. 'Go on, feet up, pamper yourself. I'll bring some tea through before we go off, and we're only across the courtyard if you need us. Get yourself settled.'

The fire looked inviting, but Libby stood where Alice had left her, looking around and taking in the extraordinary room. It was part of the later addition, and clearly designed when Scottish Romanticism was in high vogue. Oak panelling and bookshelves lined three sides of the room, the fourth being mainly filled by a large bay window overlooking the garden. A frieze of carved knotwork decorated the shelves and above them were panels depicting elongated birds with improbable legs carved in low relief. The plaster coving and ceiling displayed thistles and rowanberries in complex interlace patterns. Celtic revivalists had been furiously at work. Not to everyone's taste, perhaps, but when newly completed the room must have been quite extraordinary.

And it must have cost a fortune.

But these were more straitened times. The furnishings were worn and faded and stained plaster above the window suggested leaking gutters; the days of gracious living at Sturrock House, it appeared, were long gone. Through the window she could see a neglected lawn, a playground for the moles, while rhododendrons and broom spilled from the borders with unfettered abandon. Daisies too were doing well.

Her eye was caught by the brackets supporting the window seat and she bent to examine them. They had been carved into the stylised trunks of trees, each one uniquely gnarled, with spreading branches and carved foliage flattened to provide the seat.

'Blame the third baronet.' Alice appeared in the doorway, a tray of tea in her hands.

'What an extraordinary room –'

'Makes me feel like a hobbit.'

Libby laughed. Straightening, she saw that the upper panes of the windows had been painted. Some had heraldic devices but one showed a ship with a striped sail, another the headland on which stood a monk and a tall woman, their clothing blown by the wind as they watched the ship pulling away from the shore towards a crescent moon.

'It's Ulla, isn't it, and Odrhan?'

'Aye. They get everywhere. The barmy baronet went a bit over the top.' She set the tray down and Libby moved on to the second window, which showed Odrhan standing over a grave.

'Is he the one in highland dress, on the stairs?'

'And a daft expression on his face? Aye, that's the one. He'd a screw loose, if you ask me. Spent shed-loads of money turning the place into a Celtic theme park. These windows are famous, they tell me, so it's a good thing they aren't at the front of the house or they'd have suffered the same fate as the dining room ones.'

'Meaning?' she asked, but her eyes were fixed on the figure of Odrhan.

'Football. Cost Rodri a fortune in restoration. Now, are you going to sit yourself in front of that fire, or do I have to rope you down?' Libby went and sat, while Alice built up the fire. 'Good girl. And we're just across the way if you need us.'

She closed the door behind her and left Libby alone in the room, where the silence was broken only by the quietly ticking clock on the mantelpiece and the gentle sound of peat settling in the hearth. Even the ends of the fire irons had been forged into tall Celtic crosses, and the coal scuttle was thistle-shaped; the iron fireback proclaimed a coat of arms. No detail had been overlooked, and the room must have changed little from how it had looked a century ago.

She picked up her teacup and saucer, then looked back at the window with its depiction of Odrhan and was swamped again by a deep sense of unease. For there could be no mistaking the jewel which hung on his chest – a gold cross with a single central stone – identical to the one which had slipped from an envelope onto her lap just one week ago.

Chapter 7

If she had been allowed to choose, Ellen would have spent all her time in the library at Sturrock House. Polishing the carving along the edge of the bookshelves, she would run her eyes along the rows of leather-bound books with their gilded lettering wondering what mysteries they contained, and let her imagination run wild. It was a fault in her, her mother often said, her imagination, and she should learn to curb it. She smiled to herself and moved on to clean the leaded window glass, tracing the painted figures with her forefinger and picturing them as living souls. On dull days the scenes appeared heavy with foreboding, foreshadowed by what she knew of the legend's dark twists and turns, but on days like this when the sun streamed through the glass to light Ulla's yellow hair, the painted waves beyond the painted headland seemed to dance, and then Ellen's imagination broke its bounds. Her finger followed the outline of Odrhan's form where he stood looking at Ulla, the lovely pagan whom the ocean had delivered to his rocky retreat. Had he loved her? Ellen asked herself this question every day, moving aside the cushions on the window seat so that she could stand on it and reach to the glass horizon. She spat on her cloth and gently rubbed at the flow of Ulla's painted gown, and the vivid colours glowed like jewels.

And had Ulla learned to love the chaste monk or remained true to her dead lover?

Ellen had invented her own versions of the legend in which

she allowed Ulla to survive beyond the birth of her child. Some days she decided that Ulla had lived virtuously with Odrhan, raising Harald's child as their own, growing old and wise into her twilight years. But on others, guiltily, she wondered if the child was Odrhan's and if the monk had cast aside his vows and taken Ulla for his lover, though this would have condemned him to—

'Ellen! Are you still in here?' Mrs Dawson appeared at the door. 'And the fire's not laid! Look sharp, lass, or they'll be back and the room stone cold.'

She had forgotten.

Mungo Sturrock was returning.

She stepped down and hastily put the window seat cushions back in place. Murmuring an apology, she dropped to her knees beside the hearth and began sweeping the ashes from the grate.

She must be gone from here before he arrived, long gone.

'And when you've finished, take a duster up to Mr Mungo's room. If it's aired then you can close the windows, but don't light the fire until they get here. Check that the coal scuttles are full. And stop your daydreaming, girl.' With that, the housekeeper swept from the room.

Ellen worked fast now, panic quickening her movements. Avoiding Mungo Sturrock in the library was desirable, but it was vital not to get trapped in his bedroom. After last time, when he had cornered her there, she always checked his whereabouts before going to do his room, stoically risking censure from Mrs Dawson. If she complained she would not be believed – and anyway she would likely fare no better than Maria, a former housemaid. When the girl's waist had begun to thicken, her whole family had disappeared; some said they had been given passage to America, but no one knew for certain.

She glanced over her shoulder at the final pane of the painted window, which depicted the return of Erik, seeking vengeance.

Erik, she had long ago decided, must have been like Mungo Stur-rock, handsome but coarse in his ways.

Quickly she laid the fire, brushing the last bit of ash back into the grate as she lit it. There was wood and peat enough, but filling the coal scuttle would have to wait. She collected her dusters and left, giving the banisters a superficial rub as she hurried upstairs. And she could not confide in her mother either, knowing what she knew, and besides, her mother had enough to deal with. Ellen stopped and rubbed a little polish onto the newel post so that a smell of lavender and beeswax would cloak her neglect of the banisters themselves. And she nodded towards the portraits; their frames too would have to wait.

She reached the galleried landing just in time to hear the front door open, and then voices rose from the hall. Here already! She backed against the wall and stayed there a moment, her hands splayed on the panelling behind her, and listened, hearing the master's deep voice, and then Mr Mungo's drawl, but there was another voice too, a lighter tone, and she heard Mrs Dawson exclaim: 'Mr Alexander! Goodness me. How are you, sir?'

Ellen raised a hand to her heart. So both brothers had re-turned.

'I'm *well*, Mrs Dawson. And yourself?'

'Nicely, sir, thank you. I'll have your room aired at once. Is Ellen still in the library?' She heard the library door open as the housekeeper checked. 'No, but the fire is lit – ' Then Ellen heard Lady Sturrock's voice as her ladyship came out of the morning room.

'Alick, you dreadful boy! Why did you not tell us? Mrs Daw-son, have Ellen bring some refreshments – '

But Ellen must first be found! She glided soundlessly across the landing and into Mr Mungo's room, pulling the door closed behind her. She would be safe here now while they were all busy a-greeting each other, and someone else would have to bring them their tea. Rapidly she scanned the room, closing the windows and whipping her duster over the surfaces. Another quick check and she was done, out and away, the empty coal scuttle in her hand as she headed for the back stairs. So Mr Alick was back! She suppressed the little jump that her heart gave, and then paused. Wait – if she went down now, she might be in time to be sent to the library with the tray. She lingered, torn by indecision, until she saw that Fiona, the kitchen maid, was coming up the back stairs.

'Mrs Dawson's looking for you,' the girl said.

'Have you been sent to do Mr Alick's room?'

'Aye –'

'I'll do it.' Ellen thrust the coal scuttle at the girl. 'Fill this for Mr Mungo's instead. And then light his fire.' She gave the girl no time to protest but turned and went quickly back across the landing.

Mr Alick's room had been shut up for weeks and was airless, so she flung open the windows, pausing a moment to let the air cool her burning cheeks, then went to lay the fire. It would take the chill off, so she lit it; he might find it welcoming. The sheets could well be damp, so she turned back the covers and continued her dusting, her mind jumping from one thing to another as it did when she was excited. And then she stopped in the middle of the room to catch her breath, and looked around. What else could she do for him? It was a nicer room than Mr Mungo's, which seemed right, and being a corner room it had two windows, one overlooking the church and the manse, the other out towards the headland and the sea. If *she* had this room, she would sit by the window each night and watch the moon rise over the waves and imagine – She stopped. No time for that now. She went back to the dressing table and rubbed hard to bring a gleam to the wood.

Later she would come back and run the warming pan over the sheets and remake the bed.

Tam appeared at the door carrying a leather valise and a small trunk on his shoulder. He took them through to the dressing room, and when he had gone Ellen stood looking down at them. Mr Alick must be planning to stay a while then, a week or two at least – Ought she to unpack for him, or wait until she was told? She would dearly like to do him that service.

Then the door swung open and he was there, filling the doorway. 'Gosh! How truly splendid, a fire lit and my bed turned back. I've a mind to crawl straight in and sleep for a year.' He gave her his open, ready smile. 'How are you, Ellen?'

She made a little bob and dropped her head to hide her flaming cheeks. If Mungo Sturrock was Erik, then by the same token, in the dark solitude of the night, Alick Sturrock was Harald –

'I'm well, thank you, sir.'

– and she was Ulla.

It was a game she had invented in childhood, acting out the legend, and occasionally the two brothers had joined in. Alick Sturrock had had to double for both Harald and Odrhan as Mungo refused both roles, the one dying too early, the second a mere churchman. The boys' preferred part of the legend was Ulla's escape from Erik, and they would act that out using sticks for a prolonged sword fight, but it was never very satisfactory because Mungo was stronger and refused to let Harald escape with Ulla. He preferred to re-create the return of the vengeful Erik, but there had been no role there for her, Ulla being long gone. The boys had soon grown out of the play-acting, of course, scorning such childish folly, although the game had continued in Ellen's imaginings.

'And your mother?' Mr Alick asked her as he stooped to his valise. 'How is she keeping?'

'Much the same, sir. No worse, anyway. Would you like me to unpack for you?'

'That would be marvellous, though rather shaming.' He set the valise on the edge of the bed. 'I packed in an awful rush, you see, and just threw everything in. Still a disgrace, I'm afraid. Most of it needs a wash.'

That lopsided grin brought those less complicated days flooding back, days when there had been sunlit rock pools to examine and shrimps to be caught, and a helping hand offered over the seaweed. Children then, dismissive of class and status, with Mungo following, unwanted and complaining while she and Alick found joy in little things. It had all changed since then, of course, but she would have loved to laugh with Mr Alick as she used to do, and looked aside lest he read her thoughts. 'Shall I sort through it for you?'

'You're a treasure, Ellen,' he said, turning away to unbuckle the valise. 'But for now, somewhere there's a gift for Mama.' He began going through the contents, spewing them across the floor like a hound digging out a fox. 'Aha!' he said, pulling out a crumpled package, and then he looked down at the mess at his feet. 'Oh Lord, Ellen, you'd just tidied!'

And so she laughed with him anyway.

———•———

She left the room a moment later with a smile still on her lips, carrying an armful of washing, and stepped lightly down the back stairs. But once in the kitchen her stratagem came to naught: the laundry was taken from her and she was sent with a bucket of coals to the library, scolded for her earlier neglect.

She slipped in, keeping her head down to make herself invisible, mumbling an apology as she went over to the fireplace. There were just two occupants in the room: the master, who raised his eyes from his newspaper, said nothing, and returned to it; and Mungo Sturrock, sprawled in the other armchair. His eyes kindled when he saw her – his outstretched legs were blocking her route to the hearth but he showed no sign of moving them, so she muttered another low apology and he shifted them, but only slightly, forcing her to lift her skirts with her free hand and step across him. She sensed his eyes on her.

Hastily, clumsily, she filled the scuttle, and a piece of coal fell from the bucket and rolled onto the floor beside his shoe. Face aflame, she bent and reached for it, but he moved quickly to cover it with his foot, pinning it to the place where her fingers held it, and she pulled back her hand.

The master read on, oblivious.

'Allow me,' said Mungo, and he bent forward, his face close to hers, his eyes mocking. 'Fair Ellen,' he added in a whisper, and he handed her the coal as if it had been a jewel, then pulled out a handkerchief and began slowly wiping his fingers, as his eyes followed her retreat.

Chapter 8

Libby woke as a smouldering log split and fell into the hearth, and it was a moment before she remembered where she was. Looking up at the clock she saw that it was almost five; she'd slept for more than two hours.

It must be the stillness of the room.

She rose and stretched, marvelling again at the timeless quality of her surroundings, and thought of the curious circumstances of her being here. Then she picked up the tea tray and went through to the kitchen to find Alice alone there, lifting scones onto a cooling rack. 'You look better. Did you sleep?' she asked.

'I did. It was marvellous.'

'Good. Rodri'll be back soon with the boys, and Maddy's just finishing off. And I was thinking that you can have only so much tea so I've opened a bottle of wine.'

Maddy came through the door. 'I'm driving, remember,' she said.

'Aye, and I'm to be driven.' She gestured Libby to the table and sat down herself, three glasses dangling from her fingers and a bottle in the other hand. 'Rodri *said* I was to look after you.' She filled the glasses with a pale white wine and pushed a plate of brown bread and smoked salmon towards her. 'And that's left over from the food fair, so eat up. How much did we get done?' she asked, addressing Maddy.

They discussed butter orders and delivery deadlines for a

few minutes, revealing a process more complicated than Libby had imagined, and then they heard the sound of the back door opening.

'So!' said Rodri, from the kitchen doorway. 'I leave you alone for an afternoon and you plunder my wine.' He strode up to the table, picked up the bottle, and examined the label. 'Wretched woman. My best Sancerre.'

'Better get yourself a glass then,' said Alice. 'I liked the label.'

Rodri snorted. 'And we'll need another bottle, by the look of it. Hello, Maddy.'

Maddy smiled her quiet smile and gestured to the plate of smoked salmon. 'We're eating the profits too.'

'Worse and worse.' He turned to Libby. 'You look better.'

'Much better,' she agreed, then decided to align herself with the women. 'The wine is helping.'

He snorted again and then the boys trooped in, three of them this time, all talking at once, and she recognised the boy who had been with Rodri's sons that first night in the pub. He looked a year or two older than Donald, and was taller. But they were surely related? 'This is David, Maddy's boy,' said Alice, and the boy nodded politely at her. 'And this is Libby, who's going to have a shiner you lot can only dream of.'

All three boys grinned.

'How was the match?' Maddy asked, and the boys replied in unison. David, it transpired, had been goalie, Donald in defence, and Charlie a staunchly partisan spectator.

'It should have been six-four but I let a really stupid one in,' said David.

'Bad luck. Did they give you a hard time?'

'Not really.'

'But it was *offside*, wasn't it, Dad? We all saw it.' Charlie was clearly outraged. 'Shouldn't have been given.'

Rodri shrugged as he poured himself a glass of wine. 'Maybe not.'

'See! Dad says it was offside.'

'No. I said "maybe not."'

'Same thing.'

'It isn't.'

The argument continued in high good humour, neither side giving ground, and then it seemed to Libby that everyone was on their feet, talking over each other in cheerful confusion. 'The casserole's in the Aga, Rodri, and everything's in it, veg and all. Just dish up,' Alice said, as she gathered up her bag. 'And there's an apple pie on the top, keeping warm. Just one scone each, boys, and I'll murder anyone who makes crumbs. *One*, I said. I saw that. Put it back, Charlie, or you'll have none. See you in the morning, Libby, and make sure to get an early night.' Libby nodded, quite bewildered now. Who was staying and who was going? 'Don't stay up all night finishing off that second bottle.'

In the end it was Alice, Maddy and David who left, and the two remaining boys began laying the table while Rodri refilled the glasses. 'Is the head really feeling better?' he asked.

Had she completely misread the situation here? 'It's fine,' she said. But perhaps Alice was just out for the evening.

'Alice says she'll get a shiner,' said Charlie, as proud as if it had been his own.

'Aye, I heard her,' his father replied. 'Now, go and wash your hands and then sit up.'

School and football continued to dominate the conversation as they worked their way through Alice's casserole, and she sensed this was the norm. Rodri included her but his focus was on the boys, deftly checking manners and balancing opinions, drawing them out. Hands-on fathering.

No mention was made of the body.

'The referee was rubbish,' Charlie concluded as he scraped up the last of the gravy with a piece of bread. 'The one David let in was *definitely* offside and should—'

'Have you got homework, either of you?' their father interrupted, rolling his eyes at Libby.

'McFadden should have said something,' the child continued.

'*Mr* McFadden to you. Homework, I said. Who's got any?'

Both boys admitted to having some and were told to cut themselves some pie and go and get on with it. And when they had gone, Rodri turned to Libby. 'You slept, Alice said?'

'Yes, in the library. What a room!'

'Aye. Ossian made manifest; a flight of Romantic fantasy. Very trendy in its day and I do rather like the madness of it.' He began to clear away, waving her back to her seat when she rose. 'I'll put the pots in the dishwasher and leave the rest for Alice to do in the morning.' Lucky Alice. He angled the bottle over her glass. 'Top up?' She nodded, wondering what had happened to the boys' mother. But with that attitude to the division of labour, perhaps no explanation was needed.

'So tell me about the business,' she asked, and studied him as he explained again what the two women had told her earlier. He was somewhere in his mid- or late thirties, she decided, younger than she had first thought. When they had met at the mound yesterday (was it only yesterday?), he had looked hard-faced and austere, but she'd seen a different side to him during the meal. More humour, perhaps, and yet she sensed a suppressed tension which made him difficult to read. He was a coiled spring of a man, and might not be easy to live with, but Alice seemed able to handle him, and his sons clearly had his measure.

Something he said suggested he had once been in the army, and she asked him about it.

'I was a trainer at Aldershot for a while,' he said, 'and came

back here when the boys were small, just after their mother died.'
So that question was resolved, but he moved swiftly on. 'Hector
had married a woman from Trondheim who'd found life a little,
shall we say, *difficult* here, so they live in Oslo, an arrangement
which suited everyone.' She caught a dryness in his tone. 'When
my wife died I baled out of the army, brought the boys up here
and took over managing the estate for Hector. It's working out
fine, after a fashion. But enough of me,' he said. 'Tell me about
yourself.'

And so she did. Or some of it. She told him about her childhood in Toronto, fractured as it had been when her artistic mother
left her oil prospector father and went to live in New Zealand. It
had been a difficult time but, as her host had done, she stuck to
the bare facts, not dwelling on the sense of dislocation which had
characterised her adolescence. 'I moved around a lot after that. My
mother is English and my fixed points were a rather grim English
boarding school and my grandmother's house in Newfoundland.
Gosse Harbour. Sometimes my father came out, and those were
the best of times.' He kept his eyes on her as she spoke; they had
an oddly piercing quality and she could imagine a sharp brain
working behind them. The trick would be knowing what it was
doing. 'And then I decided to go to university here and study ar-
chaeology. The Vikings were the obvious research choice if your
life is in Britain and Newfoundland.'

'So no fixed abode, then?'

'Not really. Except for my job.' Which was alright, for now.
She'd made her choice when she let Simon go. And she'd had no
ancestral home to retreat to – but then again, Sturrock House was
his brother Hector's, not Rodri's.

She wondered if he minded.

He suggested that they take the remaining wine into the library, where he built up the fire before excusing himself to press

the issue of homework and bedtime. He had drawn the curtains and she saw that they too were old and faded, continuing the Celtic theme, and showing signs of needing repair. Perhaps his brother kept a tight grip on the finances; running this place could not be cheap.

'You've a lot going on,' she said when he came back and slumped into the other armchair. 'With the boys, and the business, and running the estate.'

He picked up his untouched glass. 'The estate is pretty full-time. Alice keeps house and sees to the boys, and she and Maddy run the business.'

'It's good to have a second income stream.'

He frowned at that. 'The business isn't part of the estate. We pay a token peppercorn rent for the dairy, and something for the Sturrock House branding, but that's it.'

'I see,' she said, but didn't really.

He glanced at her, and explained a little more. 'Hector will probably come back to live here one day and want to run things himself, and then I'll be out of a job. So the business is a safeguard for the future.'

'But where would you live?' None of her business, of course, but she was curious.

He answered readily enough. 'In the old manse. I bought it off Hector for a quid, so when he comes back, me and the boys will move there, once I've fixed it up. And Hector has no use for the dairy, so I imagine we'll carry on.'

He gave the hearth a long, hard stare and she took a sip of wine, wondering a little at the change of tone. It must be strange living in another man's house, even if he was your brother, knowing that at any time he might come back and boot you out. Difficult for Alice too.

Maybe that explained the tension.

His expression discouraged further probing, but she risked one last question. 'Has your brother got a family?' she asked.

'No.'

A question too far. Conversation flagged after that and her host seemed preoccupied. Then he looked up and snapped back into the moment. 'And so are you alright with what's planned for tomorrow? If you don't feel up to it, you must say so, and you can always just watch while the police do the work.'

'I'm sure I'll be fine.'

He considered her. 'You weren't fine this morning, though, were you? I suppose you don't often find bones wearing boots.'

She laughed, a little shakily. 'No. I sort of surprised myself. It . . . it was suddenly a dead man, you see, not a skeleton. All wrong . . .' And she felt an echo of that same dread feeling.

'Foul play.'

'Yes. Don't you think?'

Rodri looked back at her. 'I do, and Alice is probably right. I've bullied you into agreeing.'

Perhaps he had, but nothing was going to stop her now. One way or another she was hooked. 'I'll be fine once I get going.'

He continued to regard her, then his face cleared. 'And we can't have the police churning up your cultural compost, can we? It'll be an early start and I'm for turning in. I'll knock on your door when I wake the boys. And then tomorrow we'll take things one step at a time.'

Chapter 9

The storm had more or less blown itself out next morning when Rodri tapped on her door. From the window the ocean was steely grey, the waves still tipped with white against a blurred horizon, but at least it was no longer raining. Libby dressed quickly and went down to find Alice in the kitchen, where she informed Libby, in low tones, that she had been detailed to take the boys to school early before the police arrived.

What exactly did keeping house entail? Libby wondered.

The school run had only been gone ten minutes when Fergus arrived with another officer, who he introduced as PC Ranworth. 'He answers to Duncan, though,' he added with a smile, and they set off for the dunes.

The storm might be easing but it had left a lowering sky and a petulant wind which blew in cold gusts from the sea. They'd be shielded from it amongst the dunes, Libby thought, as they left the shelter of the garden wall, but she was mistaken. The wind, like the sea the night before, found many ways through the low, contoured landscape, whipping up little flurries of sand, and she turned her face away to avoid the sting of blown grains.

The police had brought bags, boxes, and other equipment, and they set themselves up as best they could in a sheltered spot, then discussed how to proceed while Libby took photographs of the undisturbed mound. It was agreed that she would uncover the bones while they watched, and would stop if she found anything significant.

Rodri had remained silent up to this point, listening attentively, but now he swung round to her. 'Alright with that?' he asked, and she nodded.

It was easy digging; the sand was light and dry on the surface and damp a few centimetres below, making progress swift. She would have preferred her own trowel to the cumbersome one she had been given, but the sandy soil fell away easily enough, and she was able to brush the light stuff off. Carefully she worked her way up the skeleton, following the femur until she reached the hip where the sand was slightly darker, having taken the stain of the decomposed flesh and clothing. Under the ball joint of the hip, she spotted a scrap of textile which she pointed out to the police, who carefully retrieved it with tweezers, placing it in an evidence bag.

This was alright, she decided as she got into her stride, just like any other excavation, careful methodical work where the same standards of good practice applied. They were joined after an hour by the keeper, Angus, who stood beside Rodri, but her audience remained silent and she was able to forget about them as she exposed the pelvis, the other leg, and the lower vertebrae before stopping to allow more photographs to be taken.

She straightened, easing the tension from her shoulders.

'Alright?' Rodri asked again, and again she nodded.

It had been agreed that she would expose the whole skeleton before lifting individual bones so that they could record how the body lay and, with photographs done for now, she carried on. Blanched bones, once a man, now a mystery – And that strange uneasiness she had felt the day before began to creep up her spine.

And then she encountered the first small finger bone.

'His hand must have lain beside his hip, elbow crooked,' she said, swivelling round to address the policemen.

'And the other one was squashed below, I suppose,' said Fergus, crouching beside her.

'Probably.' The hand had been in the flexed position when buried, and now was curled into an open fist. Once exposed, the disarticulated bones could easily fall apart, so she left a supporting block of sand beneath them, then carefully sculpted around it, following the ulna and the radius to the elbow. Other small scraps of textile survived; some were probably fragments of shirt, others looked more like tweed. And as she revealed first the well-developed humerus and then the scapula, she found her breathing quickening; she wasn't looking forward to the next stage. So far there had been no indication of cause of death, but what would the skull reveal?

But when she reached it, it appeared quite intact.

At least, what she could see was intact, although the head must have lain on its side, the face turned slightly downward into the mound. And that sense of uneasiness grew, mingled now with a guilty sense of desecration that she had never felt when excavating more ancient skeletons. It was some consolation to know that the police would have done it if she had not, and perhaps with less care.

Even so –

What she could see of the skull suggested the individual had regular features: a straight brow, and the cheek bones indicated a firm jaw. If she allowed her imagination full rein, she could see the man himself lying there, and she worked hard to keep her thoughts in check. Sooner or later they would discover how the man had died.

And then the sand shifted beneath the mandible and the jaw fell open.

She must have started. 'Take a break.' Rodri's hand was under her elbow, bringing her firmly to her feet. 'And have a sit-down.'

He led her to a grassy hummock, adding quietly, 'You're doing a fine job, but you can stop anytime, you know.' She met his eyes and saw real concern there, and found that she was glad to sit, her knees were stiff from crouching. 'Angus went to ask Alice to bring down some tea. She'll be here in a minute.'

She nodded, pressing down hard on her knees to stop them from trembling. 'It's just cramp,' she said. Then she saw that the policemen were bent over the skull, studying it with a sudden intensity. 'What have they seen?' she asked, looking up at Rodri, and he went over to join them. The sense of dread was heavy on her now. He returned immediately. 'A bullet?'

He smiled at her. 'Gold filling, upper left molar. Excellent dentistry.' She bent forward to stifle giggles at the sudden release of tension. 'Go on, have a good laugh,' he said, and then Alice appeared with a bright orange scarf wrapped round her neck and two thermos flasks tucked under her arm, mugs in her other hand.

'How's it going?' she asked.

Rodri took a thermos from her and poured tea, handing a mug to Libby. 'She's doing just fine.'

'Dear God!' Alice had gone to look over the policemen's shoulders. 'Poor soul. There's tea, you two, if you want it.' The men straightened and came over, nodding without comment as Alice pulled a half bottle of whisky from her jacket pocket and added a drop to each mug.

'Good lass,' said Angus as he took the bottle and offered it to Libby, but she shook her head.

'He was no pauper, then,' Fergus said as he and Duncan sat down beside Libby. 'Who could afford gold fillings a hundred years ago?'

Rodri shrugged. 'The gentry, rich tradesmen, some of the clergy, I suppose.'

'Thieves, racketeers, gamblers –' added Alice.

Angus offered another libation, which was silently accepted. 'Aye. The field's wide open.'

Or was it? Libby swallowed her tea, remembering again what her grandmother had said, then pushed the memory aside and reached for a thermos to refill her mug, shaking her head again at the proffered bottle. She needed her wits about her. 'Let's press on, shall we?' she said.

The wind was drying the exposed sand quickly now, and as she crouched again she could see that the little platform supporting the hand was beginning to crumble. She would have to work fast or it would all fall apart. It was not so easy to dig now as she had to lean across the exposed side of the skeleton, and she dreaded the whole thing collapsing. She built a second little cushion of sand to hold the mandible in place, and another to support the position of the cranium, then rapidly revealed the lower scapula, and investigated the position of the other arm. It was, as Fergus had said, squashed beneath the body. And the more she revealed, the less it felt like excavating bones, and the more it became a dead man, now shockingly exposed. There had been no attempt to lay him out with any dignity: he had simply been tipped into a shallow hollow scooped out of the side of the mound and covered where he lay.

Then two things happened in quick succession. She saw something metallic in the sand beside the ribs and, in reaching towards it, her elbow caught the sand cushion she had constructed under the clenched hand. 'Damn!' She pulled back as the finger bones slipped out of position. 'We'd better bag these up, I think, before—' And then she stopped.

The cascade of drying sand had collapsed the curl of the fist to reveal something once clasped there. 'What is it?' Rodri asked, leaning over her shoulder. The others gathered round.

She made no reply but carried on, carefully now. One by one

she picked up and bagged the phalanges. Twenty-seven individual bones in the hand, she told herself to steady her mind. And as she lifted the fan of metacarpals which were once the palm of a man's hand, she saw the flash of gold.

She stared down at it in disbelief, then picked it up.

Could there be two such?

'Wow,' said Alice. 'Is that a ruby in the middle?'

'A garnet,' she said, without thinking, and turned the object over, gently brushing the sand from the back, and then nearly dropped it.

The cross was identical in every way to the one her grand-mother had sent, except for the fact that this one was hallmarked, and its twin, nestled in the top drawer of her dressing table at home, was not. She turned it back over quickly.

Rodri shot her a look. 'Is it old?'

'Yes,' she replied, distracted. It was true. Sort of.

'How old?' he persisted, and made to take it from her, but Fergus was there with an evidence bag.

'We can worry about that later,' he said, taking it. 'Let's press on.'

Her mind was whirring now. This went deep, too deep, and she felt herself drawn in further – In a daze she turned back to the mound, and only then remembered the other flash of metal that had caught her attention, and scraped the sand away from around the ribs.

This time it was a bullet.

Chapter 10

They laid the dead man in a hollow between two dunes and Odrhan watched from the headland as the men set white stones around him in the outline of a ship. The woman laid his sword beside him, then lifted a string of beads from her neck and placed them on his chest. Odrhan stood, arms folded and scowling, but felt the first prick of conscience as she slumped forward, sobbing, over her lover's dead form. The men stood back a moment and then raised her to her feet, drawing her aside, and began covering the corpse with sand.

Ulla turned away, her head in her hands.

Once the mound was covered, the men went inland, returning with turves cut from above the strand line, which they placed on top. And all that time the woman stood and watched, and a sense of shame began to creep over Odrhan for what he had done.

The man had looked strong! He would have lived —

Then, as the sun rose to its zenith, Ulla's men drew aside to confer, and Odrhan saw them look towards him. He tensed as they approached, but they simply collected their baskets of stolen goods and went back down to the beach.

He watched them reloading the ship at the place where they had first come ashore. They were leaving! God be praised. The sand was now blindingly white, reflecting the sun, and he narrowed his eyes, seeing that the woman still knelt beside the mound. Suddenly she became aware of what the men were doing and called out, but by then the vessel was in the surf. She ran towards them, desperate now,

93

grabbing at the nearest man, but he thrust her away and she fell as the next wave hit her. Her garments became heavy with seawater and she reached out only to fall again as the men raised the ship's tan sail and it caught the freshening wind. It was soon yards from the shore.

And so for the second time Odrhan found himself staring back at the woman as she stood in the ebbing flow of the tide, and for the second time he found that he had no will but to go down to where she stood waiting for him, at the strand line.

⇥ Libby ⇤

Two hours later they were back in Rodri's kitchen. The skeleton had been exposed, recorded and lifted, and was now in plastic bags inside the boot of the police car, together with the finds.

Libby felt drained and shaken, and could only play with the bowl of broth that Alice had placed in front of her. The attitude of the two policemen had changed as soon as the bullet was found. Politely but firmly, she had been moved aside while the men completed the work themselves, but they had all seen the marks on the ribs where the bullet had entered the body from the back. 'Probably punctured a lung or hit the heart,' Fergus remarked.

Silently Libby helped them lift and pack the bones, her mind racing. She labelled them as carefully as she would have done in an excavation, and the task had steadied her enough for her to stop and scribble a few notes on the various deposits they had seen. A dark layer of soil suggested that the mound might originally have been covered by turves which had decayed and left a distinctive stain in the soil, and the makeshift grave had been dug through the turf layer. Maybe, just maybe, it had sealed an earlier burial. If the students were still to have a chance to excavate this summer, something which now hung in the balance, that observation might be useful.

There had been another little flurry of excitement when a steel cufflink had appeared beneath the wrist bones of the lower arm, and a little bit of sifting through the sand had produced its match on the other side. They might be marked, Fergus had said, and give a date of sorts. Perhaps he hadn't noticed the tiny cartouche on the arm of the cross, but it would be spotted once it reached the lab.

She needed time to think.

'Eat up, Libby,' Alice commanded from across the table, bringing her back to the moment. 'You've gone all white again.'

She smiled and picked up her spoon. 'This is delicious,' she said, making an effort, and feeling Rodri's eyes on her.

The policemen stayed only long enough to eat, eschewing the whisky bottle with a firmness which suggested their earlier enthusiasm for it was something to be overlooked. Stern duty had become the order of the day. With the rest of the equipment packed into the car, they were ready to leave. Rodri went with them into the courtyard and stayed there, chatting, while Alice began clearing away the dishes. Libby rose to help her.

'And that's how you make a living!' Alice remarked, as they stood together by the sink. 'I hope it pays well.'

'It doesn't, actually.'

Alice looked at her, curious. 'Doesn't it ever get to you, that sort of thing, stirring up bits of the past?'

'Not really.' At least not until today.

'And yet twice now I've seen you go a very peculiar colour. I was waiting for you to keel over.'

Libby smiled. 'I can't say I enjoyed finding that bullet.'

It was the cross, though, that had really shaken her. Two crosses, one on a dead man, the other taken by Ellen. What could it possibly mean?

Rodri came back into the kitchen, having seen off the police-men, and sat on a stool beside the dresser and looked across at her. 'So. Well done, Libby Snow. The lads were impressed; it wasn't an easy thing to do.'

She smiled slightly. 'What happens now?'

'It's wait-and-see time, but I'd better warn you that they're talking about wanting to clear the rest of the mound –'

'Oh no –'

'Aye. They're pretty well convinced that the body's too old to be of interest to them, but they need to be sure.'

Too old to be of interest. Could that ever be the case? 'I sup-pose they do, but if they decide to clear it, will you let me know, and I'll come up again and at least watch them do it? There has to be something else down there. Something ancient, I mean.' The thought of all that planning coming to nothing was too awful to contemplate.

'Of course.' He turned to Alice. 'Can you or Maddy collect the boys? You could feed them all here. I have to head off to see the bank. Hector's been in touch –'

'Not again!'

' – I was supposed to go this morning but with everything else it got forgotten. I'm sorry, Libby, but the girls will look after you, and I'll see you later. And your professor'll be here at ten tomor-row. We need to decide what to tell him.'

Declan. She'd forgotten again.

'I'll check on your car as I pass the garage.' And with that, he was gone.

Chapter 11

After lunch Alice suggested that they go to see work in progress at the dairy. And as Libby followed her across the courtyard, she wondered again about the strange ménage: the two women and the three such similar-looking boys. Whatever was going on here? But it wasn't her concern, she thought, as she watched the churns turning rich cream into pale butter, and stood by as Maddy divided it into portions, weighed it, and wrapped it in the distinctive Sturrock House packaging. 'We're developing a brand,' Alice explained. Sunlight shafted in through a high window and lit Maddy's red hair as she and Alice worked side by side. There was a pleasing calm to the place, a sort of contentment, and a continuity of use which was somehow satisfying. Next Alice showed her the old game larder which, in season, also served its original purpose. 'The smokehouse is a couple of miles away round the next bay. Angus's province.' Angus, it transpired, was Maddy's father, but there was no mention of her partner or husband. 'Now come and see the latest project.'

She led Libby back into the courtyard and through a gate into a small walled garden completely hidden from view. There were two old glasshouses built against the wall, one derelict, the other in use. 'We restored it last autumn, ready for this season.' Alice pushed open the door and Libby was hit by that loamy smell peculiar to hothouses, and saw rows of plant pots with green shoots already pushing through. 'All organic, of course.' The winding mechanism for the roof ventilation looked to be the same vintage as her shower fittings and, like them, still functioning. 'If it's a success, we'll start repairing the other one this autumn, then we might get a pay rise.'

A pay rise? It was flippantly said, and Libby was still considering what it might mean when Maddy appeared. 'Stewart from the Abbey Inn's on the phone with a big order. You'd better take it or I'll be late getting the boys.' Alice keeps house, Rodri had said, but did he mean quite literally? So what about the purple leggings and the dressing gown?

Alice left Libby to wonder and, as she surveyed the lost world of the walled garden, she felt the charm of it. As in the house itself, there was a sense of time standing still; it would still be recognisable to those who had once worked there, the gardeners, the stable hands, and the dairymaids who had provided service for meagre returns and a roof over their heads, but it was imbued with a new spirit. The garden had once supplied food for the household and now was making a living for them again. A big project. Impressive. Some of the old raised beds had been restored and planted out, but others were full of nettles and thistles, over-sailed by brambles and couch grass. A brick-built potting shed stood at the far end of the garden with an old wooden wheelbarrow, sturdy and still usable, propped against it. Rusting away in a patch of nettles was an old garden roller, and she wondered when the daisy-strewn lawns of Sturrock House had last felt its weight. She pushed open the potting shed door and took in the array of old clay pots, antiquated pruners and vintage tools. It was not only the ancient past which had resonance at Sturrock House – the Victorians had simply never left.

Determination and energy had gone into bringing the walled garden back to life, she thought, as she pulled the door closed behind her, and if this was the handiwork of Rodri and the two women, she took her hat off to them.

And all for another man's property, she thought, as she luxuri-
ated a little later in the deep bath, having decided not to risk the
terrifying shower – but the estate and the nascent food business
would surely be better run as a single enterprise, so why was it
not? She thought again of Rodri's cleft brow, and wondered –

There seemed to be endless hot water, presumably supplied
by the Aga, but having reached no conclusion to this puzzle she
dressed and went downstairs to find that Maddy had returned
with the boys.

The kitchen table was laid for six. 'You sit there, Libby. It's fishcakes and peas. That alright?' The fishcakes looked homemade and
tasted very much alright, and the peas, she was told, were frozen
from last year's garden produce. She ate and, as yesterday, listened
as the boys regaled them with the events of the day. Hands-on
motherhood too, even if that motherhood was partly surrogate.

Charlie fed titbits to the dog until Alice told him to stop.

'Sorry, Coalbox. No more.'

'Why Coalbox?' Libby asked him, but it was Donald who
answered.

'I said he was as sooty as the coal box when we got him.'

'And Rodri drew the line at Sooty,' said Maddy.

'Quite right too,' said Alice. 'But the name stuck.'

Coalbox looked up at her. Of course it had, in this curiously
eccentric household. She looked around the table and thought of
her own childhood, rootless and wandering, never long enough
in one place to feel grounded. How different for these lads, chatting away, unabashed by a stranger at the table, properly cared for,
whatever unusual arrangement it was that existed between the
adults.

Maddy was asking David about future football matches, and
he frowned as he tried to recall. 'We're away next, I think,' he
said, and his frown deepened. 'Or maybe that changed?' Then he

shrugged. 'I'll check.' His brow cleared, but not before Libby had seen an exact replica of Rodri Sturrock's frown, a single vertical line etched deep.

Oh!

But then, why not?

'Are you going to do some digging now?' Donald asked her, breaking into the thought. 'Now that your head's better.' The black eye had not, after all, developed into an object of envy, although the bruise on her forehead was still striking. The boys must wonder why she was still here.

'No. I'm just waiting for my car to be fixed, but I'll come back in the summer to dig.' So where did Maddy fit in?

'With tents and stuff?' asked Charlie.

'That's right.'

There was a noise in the passageway and he lost interest. 'Dad!'

The faces of all three boys had lit up. It might be an unconventional family, but it was a close one. She watched as the boys vied for his attention while the two women cleared away, and a cheery chaos again ensued. 'How was the bank?' she heard Alice ask in a low tone as Rodri went over to the Aga.

'Tell you later.'

'That bad?'

'Worse.'

And then somehow the chaos resolved itself and, like the day before, Alice and Maddy, with David, gathered themselves and headed for the door. 'Fishcakes, in the warming oven,' Alice called to Rodri. 'And the Abbey doubled their order.'

'Great stuff! See you tomorrow, then.'

They left and Rodri hustled the two younger boys along to wherever it was that homework was done, then retrieved his plate from the oven and came and sat at the table. He rose again to fetch the half-finished bottle of Sancerre and two glasses.

'Your professor has arrived,' he said, as he filled one glass and gestured an enquiry towards the other. 'I called at the pub for a swift half.' She nodded at the bottle, thinking she would need to fortify herself for whatever tomorrow would bring. 'He and his wife were just checking in.'

'His *wife*?' She held her glass, arrested by the thought of Dec-lan's wife, who was hardly the type to relish a sojourn in Scotland. In March.

'Leggy brunette?' he said.

Ah. 'Did you speak to him?'

'No.' He glanced at her as he chewed. 'You're not looking for-ward to this, are you?'

'Not at all.'

He sat back and contemplated her. 'I wonder why . . . Is he a pain to work with?'

'He can be difficult. He likes to be the one in control.'

'Don't we all?'

'So he won't like being upstaged and not knowing about all this.'

'I see,' he said. Then, with a smile: 'Well, trust me, Libby Snow, it's going to go well.' And for a moment he looked just like his younger son, then he switched subjects. 'Tell me about that cross,' he said, and her stomach lurched. 'It's something special, isn't it?'

'Possibly – ' ought she just tell him?

'It was familiar,' he continued, 'but I couldn't place it, and then, driving home, I remembered. It's on one of the library windows – I checked just now, the monk's wearing it.' She had been right about the brain behind those sharp eyes. 'I remember being told about it, it went missing decades ago. And now we know why.'

Except it wasn't quite that simple. And if she told him about the other cross, then she would have to tell him everything, and she wasn't ready to do that yet.

She lifted her glass and saw he was studying her from under his brows, his eyes narrowed a little. 'And that's one mystery solved,' he said, pushing aside his plate and leaning back again, filling his own with the last of the wine. 'Hector'll be pleased anyway.'

'I thought he wasn't interested.'

'If it's valuable, then he is. Very interested. And so is his lady wife.' There was an unmistakable dryness in his tone again. 'Very keen on their possessions, those two.'

'So losing the chalice was a blow.'

'Dreadful business,' he said, and his eyes remained on her.

She felt suddenly exhausted by the emotions of the day and needed to be alone, with space to think things through. Finding the copy of the cross had drawn her further in, linking her grandmother's stories very directly with whatever had happened here, something connected with Ellen, and still reverberating.

Had she really only been here two days? 'If you don't mind, I think I'm going to go up to bed –'

He continued his rather disconcerting scrutiny, then sat back. 'Good idea. And then we'll see what the professor has to say.'

Chapter 12

It was dusk by the time Ellen was released from her duties at Sturrock House. She slipped out of the back door, across the courtyard, down the drive, and then followed the track that led to the church, the manse, and her mother's cottage. Somewhere in a nettle patch she heard a corncrake's rasping call, and pulled her shawl close, looking back to check that she was not being followed. He would hardly trouble her tonight, though, newly returned, and with his brother here; they would be making a family evening of it. Then the corncrake, neck outstretched and furtive, scuttled across the path in front of her and disappeared into the undergrowth where, a moment later, it resumed its persistent harsh-toned wooing.

She stepped quickly over the stones in the stream. There were lights on in the manse ahead of her, and she saw a figure move across a window. Mr Drummond, the new minister. She had only spoken to him briefly, but her mother had said that he had called on her and was a good man, so Ellen thought well of him. Quietly spoken, her mother said, and sincere with gentle ways. They had prayed together, she told Ellen, and he had promised to bring her the sacrament and to lend her a book of sermons that she might enjoy. Sermons! Ellen had laughed, and her mother had laughed with her.

The door of the cottage creaked as she opened it and she saw her mother asleep in a chair beside what remained of the fire. The peat had burned into a bed of white powder and the house was cold. She hurried forward. Tam had promised that he would look in and make up the fire, but he must have forgotten in the hubbub of the arrivals, so Ellen threw aside her shawl and rolled up her sleeves. The pot which hung from a chain in the hearth was still half full. Had her mother not eaten today? Ellen had had no time to come home to make sure that she did – and then a thought clutched at her heart and she went quickly over to the still form in the chair and touched her hand. Stone cold. She circled the papery wrist and felt for her pulse, and found it, feather-light but regular, and she breathed again. Taking up her discarded shawl, she draped it across her mother's thin chest and gave her attention to the fire.

It was a good half hour before the warmth spread beyond a shallow arc in front of the hearth, and longer before the broth was hot enough to eat. By then her mother had roused and now sat, serene and uncomplaining as ever, and asked what news there was from the big house.

For once there was something to relate. 'Both Mr Mungo and Mr Alick are back. And Mr Alick brought a trunk with him.'

Her mother raised her eyebrows. 'But surely his studies aren't finished! He's not been away for many weeks.'

'Ten.'

Her mother looked at her. 'And did you speak with him?'

'A little. I was preparing his room when he came in.'

'And did you speak to Mungo Sturrock?'

'No.'

Her mother continued to contemplate her, saying nothing.

'Everyone was surprised to see Mr Alick, though, so it wasn't planned.' Ellen tasted the broth on the end of a spoon and, finding it hot enough, ladled some into a bowl which she took to her mother.

'We'll learn in due course what brings him back,' her mother said, taking the bowl from her and lowering it to her lap.

'Eat, Ma!'

'I will, my dear. I will.'

Eventually she did, but only a little, and then Ellen helped her to bed, propping her up as best she could so that her thin chest would not be wracked by the coughing which so weakened her. Usually at this time of day, once she had her mother settled and if the weather was fine, Ellen would walk out onto the headland and watch the seabirds dipping and rising over the waves or follow the groups of little shorebirds along the beach, their wingtips flashing white as they lifted from the sand. Just a few moments that she could call her own.

Only by agreement with Lady Sturrock was she allowed to sleep at her mother's house rather than with the other servants in the attics of Sturrock House; but the mistress knew of her mother's need for her and was kind. Lady Sturrock knew other things too and was a woman who had never shirked her Christian duty, taking on a responsibility that her husband would gladly have ignored. Not every woman, Christian or no, would have tolerated her husband's misconceived half sister living on her doorstep, nor given her daughter employment. Ellen scraped the uneaten broth from the bottom of the pot into a basin and put it to one side. She sometimes wondered if she was kept on at the big house as a reminder of the price of sin, but if so, then Mungo Sturrock had learned nothing. But she and her mother were ensured a roof over their heads, at least, and she knew what was expected of her. At no time was she to allude to kinship with the family but was to do her allotted duty, and then return home having earned sufficient money to put food on the table. They lived modestly, rent-free, a concession wrung from the third baronet by the previous incumbent at the manse, who had been determined to safeguard the wronged woman and her child. And, for as long as her mother lived, they could not be evicted from the cottage.

What would happen afterwards was something never discussed.

From the Sturrocks' perspective, it was fortunate that her mother's illness kept her confined indoors where her presence could be ignored, Ellen thought as she scrubbed the pan clean. She could never forget that Mungo and Alick were her half cousins, and that the master, lofty and remote in every way, was her kin, and sometimes she allowed herself to imagine that Sturrock House was something more than her place of employment.

Her imagination, her mother often told her, would be her downfall.

She put aside the cleaned pot and listened for a moment to the wheezy breathing that came from the bed until its rhythm told her that her mother was sleeping. Then she quietly opened the cottage door, stepped out, and breathed deeply, filling her lungs with the soft night air, and pulled the door closed behind her. She would just stand here a moment listening to the night sounds. The air was so still, windless, and the scent of peat smoke hung there. Somewhere a curlew gave its wild cry, tempting her further into the night, and she was torn, but with Mungo Sturrock at home she would not risk the headland tonight, in the dark.

'Ellen?' Her heart leapt in panic as a figure emerged from the blackness and her hand went to her throat. 'Is everything alright?'

It was Mr Drummond, the minister.

'Your mother? Is she unwell?'

'She's asleep, sir, and I was just taking the air.'

He came closer and she could see his features, softly lit by the oil lamp inside the croft window. Strong, earnest features, confident yet kind. It was a good face. When she had first met him he had seemed a little distant, but tonight he seemed inclined to linger. 'I've seen you sometimes walking out on the headland in the evenings,' he said.

'I like it there.'

'And on the beach.'

'Yes.'

In the darkness he seemed less of a minister and just a man. Perhaps he was lonely at the manse with no company other than his housekeeper, and always needing to be solemn and godly, set apart from the flock he served.

Still he stood there, looking at her. 'I like to watch the seabirds,' she said, for want of anything else, 'and to think that it's always been the same there. Nothing changed.'

'Since Odrhan built his little chapel,' he agreed, 'and for aeons before then.'

She considered this, then asked: 'How long is an aeon?'

He laughed, but it was a kindly laugh, not mocking. 'It is a long time, an age, but unmeasurable.' Her puzzlement must have showed because he added, 'Maybe as much as a thousand years.'

'So long! It seems too much.' She spoke half to herself.

'For what?'

'I can't imagine such a stretch of time.'

He smiled in the darkness. 'Do you think those times feel closer or further away?'

'Closer. Like something still remembered.'

He stayed silent, then said: 'Perhaps that's what a legend is, a memory preserved over many generations.'

She liked that idea. 'How many?' Few people would ever speak to her about the stories of Ulla, but this man seemed to know things.

He hesitated. 'If a man's lifespan is fifty years, then . . .' He paused again, calculating. '. . . maybe as much as twenty generations.'

'Twenty! And we can only remember back to our grand-parents.'

'So that's two. But they can remember back another two, making it four, and so on, reaching back into the past, an unbroken chain.'

The thought delighted her. 'To Odrhan. And Ulla.'

'That's right.'

'And yet his house is just as he left it.'

He gave his soft laugh again. 'A little tumbled-down, though.'

———————

It was a few days later, on a rare half day off, that Ellen encountered the minister again. She had left her mother reading the promised book of sermons and had picked up her shawl, determined to take some exercise before the rain came. There would be no incentive to linger today, no chance to sit as she loved to do with her head resting on the stones of the ruin, eyes closed, drinking in the warmth of the sun, glad to escape the prevailing sense of despair which now attended thoughts of her mother – But she would make for the headland anyway; there would be no danger in broad daylight.

No danger perhaps, but there was a chill wind coming off the sea, and it carried with it the scent of rain; it might be May but it felt like winter still. She stepped across the stream, her skirt brushing the clump of yellow marsh marigolds which grew on the far side, and followed the track along the ridge to the headland. Out to sea the clouds hung low, darkening the surface of the ocean, and she pulled the shawl over her head. When she reached the end of the causeway she clambered up the barnacled rocks and stepped onto the little plateau, and then stopped.

A figure was sat there on a boulder, hunched over, head down and apparently writing. Mr Drummond! How strange. He gave a start when he saw her and started to rise, but in his confusion he knocked over a tin of pencils at his feet and his hat, released from under his bent knees, blew away, taken by the wind.

Ellen gave chase and rescued it from the edge of the rocks just as the wind lifted the rim, before it was lost forever. She wiped it dry with her handkerchief and handed it back to him with a laugh and a smile, then bent to help him reassemble his unruly belongings.

'Thank you, Ellen,' he said.

'I startled you.'

'A little!' he said, laughing too. 'I'd been thinking about Ulla and then suddenly there you were.'

'You thought I was a ghost!' The idea of being mistaken for Ulla was most gratifying.

He pulled a face. 'My dear girl. I was simply engrossed in my drawing.'

She looked down at the discarded notebook, which had landed face-up beside a measuring rod and a ruler. 'What is it that you are doing, sir?'

'I'm recording the ruin before it is lost to the sea,' he replied.

She looked about her. 'Will it be lost?'

'I think so. One day.'

'But you said it's been here for – for an aeon! Why should it be lost now?'

'Not now, perhaps not for many years, but come and look.' He beckoned her to the edge of the little plateau where the turf over-hung the rocks and pointed to where a clump of grass and soil compacted with roots lay below them. 'See there? That must have fallen this winter. And how much fell the year before, and the year before that, going back all those thousands of years? Once the headland was much bigger, I think, so in another thousand years, what will be left?'

She stayed silent, remembering the storms which battered the coastline in the winter and how far the sea could reach into the dunes. One night it had reached the wall which surrounded Sturrock House. 'Will it reach our cottage?' she asked him.

'Not in your lifetime,' he replied, with his gentle smile.

'And even if it did, and if it washed the headland away, the legend would still survive, wouldn't it?'

'Perhaps.'

'So you know of the legend?' she asked, probing a little. Perhaps he knew more than she did; he was a learned man.

'Sir Donald has lent me a book his father wrote, setting it all down as a poem.'

His father, the third baronet, her grandfather. Did the minister know that too? If not, then he soon would, the gossips would make sure of that. She knew the book he meant. 'Mr Alick showed it to me.'

He looked surprised. 'Can you read, Ellen?'

'As well as you can.' Stung, she frowned at him.

'Forgive me, I meant no insult,' he said, then added, 'If you came to the manse, you could look at it again, if you like.'

'I've no need of it,' she said, piqued by his assumption of her ignorance. 'I've learned the poem by heart, and I've known the legend since the day I was born.'

He looked at her as if reassessing his idea of her. Out to sea the dark veils of rain seemed to have been blown south of them, and beyond them now were patches of bright blue. Perhaps it would stay fine after all.

'Then, if you will, tell me the legend as you first heard it.'

He gestured to the rocks and she hesitated, then sat, fastening her shawl in a knot between her breasts, and he sat opposite her, a little apart, on the tumbled stones of Odrhan's cell, and prepared to listen. And so, with the sound of the waves and the wild birds as a backdrop, she told him the legend of Ulla as it had been passed down to her from her mother, and her mother's mother, down the chain of generations.

When she had finished, she said: 'The poem tells parts of it differently, but Odrhan must have loved Ulla, don't you think? To have cared for her and then for her child? He *must* have loved her. Even though he was a godly man and ought not to have done –'

He contemplated her a moment, then bent to collect his belongings. 'God's love comes in many forms, Ellen. And as a godly man, he would certainly have loved her.'

'But *only* as a godly man, not a lover?' Ellen persisted, not thinking to whom she was speaking.

He made no reply, then said, 'You've given this a lot of thought, I see.' He pulled the strap tight on his bag. 'And it is a powerful legend, I grant you. But for us the central message is that Odrhan tended the wounds of a pagan sinner, like a good Christian should, then he taught Ulla to love God. And through him the son of pagans learned Christian ways, and he, a misbegotten child, returned to build the church which still serves this little community.'

A misbegotten child. Would he speak thus if he knew her mother's history?

'But perhaps the child was Erik's son, not Harald's, so not misbegotten,' she said. Despite her illegitimacy, her mother *knew* who her own father was.

'Perhaps.'

She felt a sudden urge to provoke him. 'Or Odrhan's?'

'Does the legend tell us that?' he asked, unprovoked and gently reproving.

'No. But some people say it could be.'

'Some people like to shock.' This last was said with a smile and a light tone as he got to his feet. 'The poem *suggests* that it was Harald's son, although it could have been Erik's, so perhaps you are right.' And the poem was written by a man who was an adulterer himself, she thought. 'Now, tell me, what do you like to read?'

And so they left the headland together and picked their way back along the causeway, he with his satchel slung across his shoulder, she with her shawl drawn tight, and at the beach they parted.

Chapter 13

Libby overslept next morning, having lain awake for hours in the night considering what she ought to do about the cross, and thinking about the whole strange situation.

She went down to the kitchen and Rodri greeted her briefly, gesturing to where breakfast had been left out before turning to Alice at the sink. 'Bring the professor through to the library when he arrives, will you, and we'll require coffee. Full-on pitch. OK? Come through when you've eaten, Libby.' And with that, he disappeared in the direction of the hall.

Alice watched him go. 'Right,' she said, then: 'Will your prof come to the front door or the back?'

'The front.' There was little doubt of that.

'Right. I'll find a clean pinny.'

Libby ate her breakfast. Full-on pitch? Whatever it meant, Alice was lifting down what looked like very fine china from a high cupboard. She had somehow interpreted Rodri's requirements and was fulfilling them in her no-nonsense manner. Libby ate quickly, keen to get into the shelter of the library before Declan arrived and the storm broke.

Rodri looked up from his desk as she entered. 'I imagine the police might expect some sort of formal report from you, you know, while it's fresh in your mind.' He was more smartly dressed this morning, she noticed, more county set, and had somehow put a distance between them.

'I made some notes –'

'Yes, I saw you. Why not run up and get your notebook, and make a start? I cleared a space for you to work.' He nodded towards a side table where a laptop was open at a document headed *Recovery of bones and artefacts from Ullaness: police report*, and then gave his attention back to his papers. Puzzled, she went and fetched her notebook, sat at the table and began looking through it, secretly watching him as he wrote away at the great desk, cool and detached, and wondered what had brought on this changed manner.

The long case clock in the hall had just finished chiming ten when the front-door bell sounded. Libby swung round in her chair, but Rodri continued writing, not lifting his head. She heard voices, recognising Declan's; then there was a deferential knock at the door and Alice entered. 'Professor Lockhart is here, sir,' she said, in low tones. 'Shall I show them in?' She was wearing an immaculate white apron and had put her jaunty ponytail into a neat bun. It transformed her appearance.

Whatever Rodri Sturrock might be paying her, it was not enough.

'Ah. Yes, by all means.' He snapped the lid onto his fountain pen and stood, coming round to the side of the desk as Alice ushered the visitors in, and he held out his hand. 'Good morning, Professor. Good morning, Mrs Lockhart.'

'Good morning, and it's good of you to see us. But let me—'

'A good journey, I hope?' he interrupted smoothly. 'You know Libby Snow, of course.'

Libby had stayed seated outside their line of vision, but at Rodri's gesture Declan swung round, and went white. She had never before seen him knocked off balance.

From white his face suffused with colour. 'Libby – ?' It was all he could manage.

'Hello, Declan. Hello, Caro,' she said. Caroline Albertino was looking almost as shocked as Declan. She was, as ever, immaculately turned out in black, the leggings and a tight-fitting top showing her form to great advantage, and black provided a striking contrast to her ashen face. Libby glanced at Rodri and saw a spark in his eye which suggested he'd known damn well that the woman he'd seen with Declan wasn't his wife. A half smile passed briefly over his face, and she began to understand.

Power games.

'Let me get you some coffee,' Rodri said, and turned an old-fashioned bell handle on the wall. 'Do have a seat,' he said. Alice reappeared, and he barely glanced at her. 'Coffee please, Alice, for our guests.'

'Yes, sir.' For a moment Libby thought Alice was about to bob a curtsy and spoil everything, but she resisted. This was teamwork! Libby dropped her head to hide a smile.

Rodri gestured Declan and Caro to the two armchairs beside the fire and pulled forward a worn leather winged chair for himself which gave him the advantage of several inches' height. He then crossed his legs and gave them a courteous smile. 'Now, tell me what brings you here.' He had not, she noticed, suggested that she join them, which was fine by her. From here she could watch, fascinated.

Declan was struggling to sit up straighter in the squashy armchair. 'First, let me introduce Caro Albertino, who is, in fact, my research student, not my wife –'

'I do beg your pardon,' said Rodri, nodding towards Caro, who said not a word.

'She's a part of the project, you see –' Declan continued. Was she? This was news. He flung a glance in Libby's direction as if reading her mind, and his face hardened. 'But, forgive me, why on *earth* is Libby Snow here?' Then he addressed her directly. 'I was told you'd rung in sick on Monday, after some sort of accident? No one knew where you were.' His eyes studied her bruised brow, which fortunately had yet to fade.

At that moment Alice pushed open the door carrying a loaded tray and upstaged them all with her fussy arrangement of little tables and enquiries about milk and sugar as she distributed cups and offered shortbreads, and took the force out of Declan's challenge.

'Her car had the worst of it,' Rodri replied for her. 'I hit her going rather fast out of the drive to get my boys to school on time. Just there will do.' This to Alice. 'She got away with a bang on the head which we thought might be concussion, but she insisted she was alright and refused to go to the hospital.' Rodri Sturrock, she was learning, handled facts robustly, and then dared them to protest. 'Thank you, Alice, that will be all for now.' He turned back to Declan. 'But, as I told whoever I spoke to in your department, we insisted on her staying quietly under observation here. It was the least we could do.'

Until, that was, he persuaded the police to let her excavate a body –

'We'd no idea she was *here*, though.' Declan sent another baleful glance in her direction.

Rodri raised his eyebrows. 'Did I not say? Surely – but you see, there's rather more to explain than a vehicle collision.' He paused, his expression severe. 'But first I must ask that you both treat what I tell you as strictly confidential, in fact I must insist upon it. It's now a police matter.'

And Libby sat back and listened as Rodri succinctly explained the events of the past two days, from her discovering the bones to excavating the skeleton, briefly referring to her role in advising the police, and to her valuable contribution, a commendation judged to a nicety, neither meagre nor gushing. 'I'm indebted to her as, indeed, are you, because if the police had been let loose on the mound, there'd have been little left for your students to work with this summer, don't you think?' He waited for Declan to concur, which he did, briefly. 'As it is, Libby is now compiling a report for the police, but she tells me she was also able to record some useful archaeological observations. Is that not right?'

'Yes,' she replied, and he carried on, making no reference to the possibility of the rest of the mound being cleared. Nor did he mention the cross.

When he had finished, Declan gave her a wooden smile and she watched him struggling for words. 'Well. How extraordinary! And who'd have imagined . . . But it's a Victorian body, you say?'

Rodri nodded, deferring to Libby.

'Probably,' she said. 'On the basis of some cufflinks and the boots, and some scraps of textile. And a gold filling in his tooth. The police have taken everything away.' Since Rodri hadn't mentioned the cross, neither would she. Time enough later to explore the reasons why.

Declan was just about managing not to appear hostile, and then he asked the inevitable question. 'But why were you up here in the first place?'

She'd rehearsed for this one. 'I'd a free weekend and thought I'd come and have a look at the site and do some planning.'

'But everything was planned, and agreed!'

'That's exactly what I said myself when I came across her in the dunes,' said Rodri. 'I assumed, of course, that she'd come up in advance of your own visit today, but she said not.' He regarded Declan politely, his crossed leg bouncing gently. 'Which brings us nicely to the point of it?'

It was masterfully done, and she watched Declan calculating quickly. He'd had no time to recover from the morning's quick-fire shocks, and now he had no choice but to explain his intentions with her sitting there listening. And if Caro had been brought up to charm Rodri into cooperating, then she wasn't playing her part. Libby watched her colleague re-evaluating his approach while Rodri sat there and let the silence lengthen.

Declan made another attempt to sit up straight. 'All this has driven everything from my head. So, yes, to business! I brought Ms Albertino up to meet you because her current research is very relevant to the Ullaness project.' He looked at Caro, but she showed no sign of contributing beyond a tight smile, so Declan continued. 'It involves gathering data on the use of space in these early churches, and investigating how function changes through time.' Rodri glanced briefly at Caro too. 'Internal divisions within churches have, of course, inevitably been modified over time as buildings were extended, or liturgical practices altered, or as interiors were used for elite burials. Small chapels get carved out of larger spaces, and then re-absorbed, and so forth.' Rodri remained silent as Declan continued, his face expressionless, and Libby wondered fleetingly what he made of it. 'New ground-penetrating techniques mean that there is no longer a requirement to disturb deposits at all, other than inserting short probes which—'

'May I stop you there, Professor.'

'Please call me Declan.'

'Thank you. But are you thinking that the estate might change its mind regarding work in the church?'

Declan hesitated, foiled by the direct question. 'It would very usefully complement the survey work, and the excavation, and in no way impact upon deposits inside the church. I realised that I hadn't previously explained what we want to do, so I wondered if Sir Hector might consider the more detailed proposal that Caro has put together.' He turned at that point to Caro, who pulled a thin file out of her elegant handbag and handed it to him, confirming to Libby's mind that it had been intended that she would

do the pitch. Declan passed the file to Rodri, who glanced at it,
read the cover and then placed it on his desk.

'Thank you. I will draw it to his attention,' he said, and folded
his hands.

Declan looked briefly annoyed and made one final assault. 'I
quite understand that, as his agent, you act on his behalf, and are
very much in his confidence.' Then he seemed to change tack and
gave a laugh. 'And given that, I thought that if, by carrying out a
little trial, we can convince *you* that we will in no way compromise
the church, then –'

' – then maybe I'll persuade my brother?'

'Your brother?'

'Why, yes.' Rodri looked surprised. 'I'm Sir Hector's agent, but
I'm also his brother. Had I not made that clear?'

It simply wasn't Declan's day. Rodri swiftly and smoothly drew
the interview to a close, offering more coffee which he knew would
be refused, assuring Declan that he would certainly consult his
brother while expressing his concern that he and Caro might well
have made a wasted journey. 'And I'd suggest that you take Libby
Snow back with you now, but she has this report to complete, and
I think her car repairs will be another day. Monday should see her
back at her desk, though, assuming her head is alright.' He barely
glanced in her direction as he said this. 'But may I stress the complete embargo on publicity concerning last week's discoveries?' He
included Caro in a stern look. 'So far very few people are in the
loop, and the police will not release information until they're ready
to do so. I feel sure you can persuade whoever needs persuasion
that Libby's absence is due entirely to the accident. Nothing else.'

He rose, giving his guests no option but to do likewise. Libby
also stood but remained where she was as Rodri ushered them
to the door. 'Have you thought of doing your trial work on St
Brides's Church, Carrie?' she heard him say. 'It's much the same

date and size. Just outside Brindsay, about twenty-five miles southwest of here. Tell them I sent you.' Caro murmured some inaudible response. 'So, we have an interesting summer ahead, Professor, and all being well you'll see Libby back with you on Monday.'

Declan nodded her a curt goodbye. 'Come and see me when you get back, won't you?' he said, and the tone did not augur well. And then they were in the hall, where she did not follow, and she heard the front door open. A moment later it closed behind them and voices faded as Rodri, now all courtesy and attention, escorted them to their car.

She sat back feeling as if she had been under the wheels of the Land Rover, rolled out flat, impressed by Rodri's performance and not a little amused, although Declan, out-manoeuvred, would now be impossible to work with.

A moment later Rodri returned. 'Why's he so keen to work in the church?' he demanded from the doorway, that distinctive frown on his brow.

'I've no idea.'

'He had another go at me in the courtyard. Even the bait weighed in at that point.'

'The bait?'

'Well, she was, wasn't she? I'm not a fool.' He picked up his cup from the desk and swallowed the last of his coffee. 'And she's not Italian.'

'No.'

'But her husband is?'

Libby hesitated. 'Yes.' Caro had, after all, been wearing a wedding ring.

'Hmmm.' He began gathering up the cups. 'I didn't think she looked like a wife. Well, not his, anyway.'

'Aren't you rather leaping to conclusions?'

'They checked into a double room.' His tone boded ill for the work in the church, and he began collecting the dirty cups.

'Oh, let me do that, sir,' Alice simpered as she came through the door with a tray.

He laughed. 'Alice! You were wonderful.'

'It'll cost ye.'

'Don't I know it,' he said as she piled the tray high and backed out of the door.

'Full-on pitch?' Libby asked when she had gone.

He had picked up the file Declan and Caro had left and was thumbing through it, the frown still on his face, but he looked up at her words and gave a grin. 'It's a technique we developed for the more pretentious of our clients: playing to their vanity. Some like the idea of dilettante landowners indulging themselves in the food business, and we let them think it's just that. They'd screw us if they knew how desperate we are for orders.' He went back to the file, pausing once or twice to absorb particular pages. 'And it took the wind out of your professor's sails a bit, don't you think?'

'But why did you want to, particularly?' Rodri Sturrock was difficult to read, but intriguing.

'He's been as persistent as a wasp, and I don't like the type. Nor do I like faithless women.'

'It was unforgivable to call her *Carrie*, though.'

A little smile appeared and he tossed the report aside. 'Shall we go and see if your car's ready?'

'You just said it'd be another day –'

'Did I?'

'And shouldn't I finish this report for the police?'

He looked at the table as if he had forgotten what she'd been doing. 'Do you know, Libby Snow,' he said, with a lilt and a smile, 'it was just an idea I had, but if they'd wanted a report from you, they'd have said, don't you think?'

———

In the Land Rover she looked across at him as he drove, still trying to fathom the man. His moods were as changeable as the weather, a blaze of sunshine one minute, storm clouds the next, and behind those intelligent eyes that persistent tension. And a determination that things would go his way, every move purposeful. Not, perhaps, a man to cross. But gone now were both the lordly manner and the laughter, and he seemed to have retreated into himself.

He became conscious of her scrutiny and glanced across at her. 'That went alright, didn't it? From your point of view?'

After a fashion. 'Yes, but he'll be hell to work with now.'

He looked at her again. 'Hadn't thought of that. Sorry! Bit of a prima donna, is he?'

'He's a showman, and the project's his show.'

'His, or his and the bait's?'

'She's new on the scene.'

'Thought so.' They drove on, climbing away from the coast. 'So how did you get hitched up with him?'

She turned her face to the window. There'd never been any danger of getting 'hitched up' with Declan, and his efforts in that direction had scarred their professional relationship. When she had first joined the department she'd found him supportive, giving her free rein to go for funding and allowing her the responsibility of planning for the summer. Soon, however, she'd realised that he was simply idle and had just offloaded the donkey work to her, limiting his own input to dealing with the Sturrock estate and signing off as director of the project. And then he had made a pass at her at a party, pulling her outside ostensibly to discuss the application. Declan Lockhart was not used to rejection and their relationship had plummeted. If the paperwork had not already been sent in, he would probably have struck her name from it, and now the summer seemed blighted.

Rodri glanced at her, awaiting an answer. 'I just applied for the job,' she said, 'and got it.' He made no response and she changed the subject. 'So will you send the file on to your brother?'

'I'll tell him I have it, summarise its contents, include my own recommendations, offer to forward it and await a response.'

'And?'

'I won't get one.' The exasperation was impossible to miss.

'Has your brother lived abroad for long?' she asked, after a while.

'Donkey's years. And he spreads himself about – Norway, France, Italy.'

'Does he come home often?'

'No.' The response was curt, with the subtext to drop it, and so they continued in silence. After a mile or so they turned off down a narrow single-lane road which wound its way through rough grazing land divided by old stone walls, many of them tumbled into mossy heaps. Sheep wandered through openings where gates had long stood open, sagging on rusty hinges, bound with brambles. Was this still estate land? she wondered. Making it pay its way must be a challenge.

Rodri drove fast and carelessly, causing her to wonder if the accident had not been wholly her fault after all. 'You didn't mention the little cross we found,' he said. 'I thought you would.'

She was taken off-guard. A pulse started in her throat, but Rodri kept his face forward. 'I was following your lead.'

He acknowledged that with a half nod and said nothing more. She turned her attention back to the view from the window, and rehearsed again the arguments that had gone through her head last night. If she told him what lay hidden in her chest of drawers, she would have to tell him about Ellen, about what her grandmother had told her. And if the cross *had* been stolen from Sturrock House, then she was branding Ellen a thief. She needed more time to think it through, and to hear back from Nan.

The road wound its way uphill round tight bends and blind corners which gave awesome views over great sweeps of land, climbing ever higher until they reached a little plateau which opened up a wider landscape broken by small lochans, then dropped downhill again to skirt the edge of a narrow sea loch. An old stone jetty stood by the shore and beside it were the rotting remains of a timber wharf festooned with seaweed. A handful of fishing boats lay askew on the low-tide flat, their mooring ropes stretched to rusty iron rings on the jetty, trailing ribbons of kelp. Several kayaks had been pulled up above the tide line, and beyond them along the shore were three stone buildings. One, judging by its shape, had once been a chapel and looked as if it had recently been reroofed. The other two were traditional cottages, and both had curtains at the windows.

An old caravan stood beside one of them and Rodri parked in front of it. 'I'll see if anyone's at home,' he said, and she watched him tap on the front door of one of the cottages, then push it open. A moment later he emerged with Angus, and beckoned her to join them in front of the caravan. 'Would this be any use to you in the summer?' he asked, gesturing to it. 'If we can get it shifted down to the site.'

A dry roof, somewhere to keep paperwork, or wet-weather tea breaks. 'It would be fantastic.' If there was still to be an excavation, of course. But why the sudden helpfulness?

'It's in better nick than I remembered,' he said, kicking the tyres. 'Is it roadworthy, Angus?'

'We'll get it that far,' he replied.

'That's sorted then.' And then they were back in the Land Rover again and away, with a nod and a wave. He drove on to where the track petered out and there was space to turn. 'Alice lives there, next door to Angus,' he remarked, as they drove back past the cottages, 'with Maddy and David.' So that's another piece of the jigsaw, thought Libby, but she still didn't think she had the whole picture, and wondered again about the single-line frown on David's forehead. 'And the old Free Church is now our smoke-house, newly roofed. Good that, don't you think? Hellfire and damnation reduced to premium oak – smoked salmon.'

She laughed. 'It's a lovely spot. Isolated, though,' she said, especially for a growing boy. There had once been other houses, she saw, ruined shells now vanishing into nettle patches and gorse, thick-walled structures, some with gable-end chimneys, and one with sagging roof timbers surviving, still supporting patches of rotting thatch. But the community was long gone.

'If you asked David, he'd not have it any other way,' Rodri replied, with his unnerving habit of reading her mind. 'Which is just as well, all things considered.' He left it at that, and her eyes swept the inlet where a pair of oystercatchers had lifted off, piping their alarm, to settle on a rock on the far side. 'And my lads love it down here. They can walk round from home in just half an hour, following the shore.'

My lads. Not including David? 'And do they?'

'Aye. All the time.'

They drove back up the single-lane track and eventually rejoined the wider one which, a couple of miles further on, connected with a main road, and Libby recognised this as the point where she had turned off on her journey north. But now they turned the other way, and a few miles further on they came into a larger community which had a garage fronting onto the road. And there, parked to one side, was her car.

'Looks like it's done,' she said, as Rodri pulled up alongside.

A man came over to them, wiping his hands on an oily rag.

'All sorted, Mr Sturrock,' he said. 'Good as new. And the front brake pads were wearing so we replaced them while we were at it.' He nodded towards Libby. 'You need them sharp round here.'

You did indeed. 'Thank you,' said Libby, swinging her bag off her shoulder. 'And so what do I owe you?'

But the man looked at Rodri. 'You said to – '

'That's right, I did. We'll have a bite next door first and collect it after.' Rodri gestured to the adjacent pub. 'Is the Land Rover alright where it is?' The man nodded and returned to his garage while Rodri headed towards the pub, leaving her to follow.

———

The place was simple and unpretentious, and Rodri was no stranger there. Several people greeted him, some addressing him respectfully as Mr Sturrock, others as Rodri, and the landlord with a cheerful familiarity. 'What'll it be?'

Libby waited until they'd ordered drinks and sandwiches and settled themselves at a corner table before tackling him about the repair bill, but he waved her words aside. 'I told you I'd sort it. And it's done now, so leave it.' He took a drink, dismissing the subject. 'I want to ask you more about this ground-penetrating equipment. How accurate is it?'

That was a surprise. 'Are you changing your mind?'

'I need to give Hector the facts.' He smiled blandly and took another drink.

Briefly she described the various techniques, then added, 'Declan will be delighted that you're considering his proposal.'

'Don't raise the man's hopes.'

The landlord arrived with the sandwiches and stayed chatting for a moment. When he had gone, Rodri turned back to her. 'So, is Libby short for Elizabeth?'

'No. Liberty.'

'Liberty! Unusual.' He tried it out. 'Liberty Snow. Sort of Quakerish, or New England.'

She hesitated. Was this an opening she should take? 'My grandfather was a New Englander.'

He bit into his sandwich. 'Tell me more.'

'There's not much to tell. He went north and settled in a little fishing port called Gosse Harbour, on the east coast of New-foundland, north of Trinity, and married my grandmother. I spent a lot of the school holidays with them there.' She watched his face carefully, but the mention of Gosse Harbour got no reaction.

He continued chewing. 'And so what brought you to Ullaness, Liberty Snow?' She found that she wanted to tell him. 'Just the profession of the curious?'

'More or less. I saw the field school job advertised and I knew a bit about the site, and the legend, so I grabbed the chance.'

He took another bite. 'Exciting stuff, eh?'

'Definitely.' But something still held her back.

'It's strange, you know – ' he said, contemplating the fire for a moment, then continued, 'you grow up with old stories for as long as you can remember, and believe they're simply personal to you, or your family or your place in the world. Just some local tale, something no one else knows or cares about.' He looked back at her. 'I was a grown man before I realised that the Ullaness legend was known beyond the area, or that there was interest in it. Hector started collecting references to it once when he was laid up, and found that there's all sorts written about it – but I suppose you already know that.' He took another bite and chewed thoughtfully. 'I was amazed, but at the same time it felt a bit intrusive, which is nonsense, of course. No one can lay claim to little private bits of the past.'

'Is that how you see the excavations, as intrusive?' And she thought of all those clauses spelled out in the contract: *No recovered finds, of any and all types of material, will be taken off the estate without written consent from the Agent. Any objects loaned for study will be returned, undamaged, within a period agreed with the Agent. All objects remain the property of the estate. . . .* It was, in part, this uncompromising tenor which made her reluctant to raise the subject of the cross. Was it Rodri who had insisted on those clauses, or his brother?

'A bit. Not so much now. You've got me interested.'

Something in his tone made her look at him, but he was chewing steadily, his expression unreadable.

'And what happens if your mound produces something of national interest?' she asked, to fill the moment.

'That'll be for Hector to say.'

'Will it?'

He raised his eyebrows. 'Of course.'

'Won't you try to – what was it you said – *guide* his decision-making?'

She had meant to tease, but it fell flat and his face hardened. 'If you find anything of national interest which has value, it won't be me doing the guiding, it'll be Laila.'

'Laila?'

'Hector's wife. If you find anything like the chalice, then Laila'll be over here like a shot.' He gave her a twisted smile. 'And it would rather beg the question of ownership, don't you think? Same with that bloody chalice. It was swiped from some monastery, if the legend's anything to go by, and then buried out on the headland. In fact it was stolen *twice* before it arrived here, once by Erik the Viking, and then nicked from him by his brother. And then lifted again last year. A holy relic, stolen three times, and once worth killing for.' He stood up and gave a wry smile. 'Damn thing would have been better left in the ground, composting nicely. Shall we go?'

Chapter 14

Oliver Drummond sat at his desk in what served as both dining room and study, and stared into middle distance. He was finding it difficult to concentrate; his mind kept returning to the conversation he had had with Ellen Mackay, out on the headland. How she had startled him! He had been ruminating, with some bitterness, on the theme of the power of lovely women to blight lives, and that thought had brought him to Ulla. Her charms had apparently captivated two brothers, disastrously for both if the legend was to be believed, but he also wondered how the celibate Odrhan had fared in the encounter; clergymen never seemed to come off well in dealings with the fairer sex.

And then Ellen had arrived and touched on the very point. 'But he loved her only as a godly man, not a lover?' she had asked, implying that godly love was a lesser, not a greater thing. And he thought briefly of the provost's daughter, who had apparently felt the same, and then put the memory aside.

He should have chided Ellen for such words, of course, but they sprang from a naïveté that was childlike, almost fey. How charmingly unaffected she was! She might be able to read, but she was uneducated, rather susceptible, perhaps, with thoughts unchecked. And had she any idea how lovely she was? He allowed himself a moment to contemplate her blue-green eyes. Where had she sprung from, he wondered, to be so well-favoured, so delicate and fine-boned?

But the poor girl must live in a state of constant anxiety if what he understood of her mother's illness was true, so small wonder that she took refuge in daydreams. And that, he supposed, was what he had been doing himself, musing on what he had read in Sir Donald's book, trying to separate the facts from the romantic embroidery of the would-be poet baronet. No Byron he! Out there, though, beside Odrhan's cell with water on three sides, it was all too easy to dream, suspended in time and space, with just a narrow causeway connecting the headland to the shore. Odrhan had chosen his site well, and Oliver felt himself very much in sympathy with the man, a missionary amongst the godless.

And then Ellen had appeared as if from nowhere, and expressed such unexpected ideas! The past was not lost, she had implied, just rendered invisible by the passing of the years; a sentiment with echoes of the pagan.

He pulled out the drawing he had made of the little oratory and studied it again. It was now little more than a pile of tumbled stones overgrown with thistles and nettles, but he had begun to discern a shape to it with courses built up by overlapping the stones towards a rounded roof, long since caved in. Had no one, in all these years, thought to ask what might be inside? He felt a thrill at the thought.

It would not be too great a job, surely, to shift the fallen roof stones and find out.

He sat, the sketchbook open before him, and stared out of the window. So far his duties had been light, his flock few in number and dutiful. Not godless, perhaps, but indifferent, and he was cynical enough to realise that his main purpose here was to provide support for Lady Sturrock, a good Christian woman, thoughtful of the tenants' bodily needs and mindful of their souls; but he was learning that his presence brought resentment from other quarters. Resentment, and contempt –

He glanced across at the clock above the fireplace and put the sketchbook away, schooling his mind to the matter of his sermon. This evening he had been bidden to the big house for dinner and there would be no time later to complete it.

———•———

Following his arrival two months ago, Oliver had eaten several times at Sturrock House and found it something of an ordeal, compensated for, however, by the excellence of the food and wine. Would it be beef tonight, he wondered, as he selected the best of his shirts, ideally accompanied by a good rich claret? Fatted calf, perhaps, to greet the return of the Sturrock sons. Alexander Sturrock's arrival had, he understood, been unexpected, and was for some reason contentious, so would he qualify as prodigal? Oliver considered the word as he dressed; as it embraced both the concept of repentant return and that of reckless waste, perhaps both sons, in their ways, could claim the fatted calf.

So it might be beef, then. He could only hope.

He dressed carefully, sponging a mark off his trouser leg. The Sturrocks usually dressed for dinner, but they seemed not to expect it from him, which was just as well. It was hard enough to make ends meet without unnecessary expenditure on smart evening clothes. His shoes, at least, he need not blush for. He kept them for such occasions, wearing stouter footwear to tramp the local paths and roads.

He left the manse and stepped carefully, mindful of them as he made his way across the stream and up the track towards Sturrock House, avoiding the marshy patches and thinking that it would be more difficult to do so on the way back, after dark.

He went through the garden gate and up the gravelled path to the front door, where a lantern had been hung to light his way. Sir Donald Sturrock greeted him as he was ushered into the drawing

room. 'Ah, Drummond! Come in, and for God's sake bring some
leaven to the party. You know Mungo, of course, but you've not
met my younger son, Alexander. I rely on you to talk some sense
into him.'

Oliver shook the proffered hand and felt an instant liking for
the open-faced young man who stood smiling before him. He
resembled his mother more than his father, with fine regular features and intelligent eyes, and he grimaced at his father's words.
'How d'ye do,' he said. Then Oliver bowed to Lady Sturrock and
greeted her elder son, who was sat at his ease beside the fire.
Mungo nodded in return.

Lady Sturrock, an elegant lady in her early fifties, patted the
seat beside her. 'How are you, Mr Drummond?' There was no sign
of Miss May Sturrock, Sir Donald's ancient aunt, sister of the
late baronet, who seemed to reside somewhere in the shadows
of Sturrock House. Usually when Oliver came to dine she was
present, and he had found conversation between the four of them
heavy going, but tonight he sensed a more pressing tension in
the air.

Mungo contemplated him with bored indifference while
Alexander asked, in a friendly manner, where he hailed from. 'I
grew up in Cumnock,' Oliver replied, 'though lately I have been
in Glasgow completing my studies.'

'You hear that, Alexander, *completing* his studies,' his father
remarked, handing Oliver a glass of whisky. It was a drink he ab-
horred, but he took it.

'Perhaps the church would suit Alick rather better than the
law,' drawled his brother.

Alexander Sturrock ignored him. 'I was in Edinburgh, though
I spent time in Glasgow too,' he said, continuing to address Oliver. 'Such a city of contrasts, don't you think? Abject poverty and
yet amongst it all such a flowering – '

'A flowering!' his father scoffed. 'My son has seen fit to pack in his studies, Mr Drummond, just a year before completing them, and chooses instead to *flower* as a writer.'

'No, Pa, a poet. He will flower as a poet,' Mungo corrected him, and Oliver glanced at the younger son with some sympathy but could think of no way of offering support. Alexander Sturrock, however, was viewing his assailants with amusement, and his eyes connected for a moment with his mother's. Was there indulgence there? he wondered.

'I shall keep myself by teaching, as well as writing,' the young man said.

Sir Donald's expletive was covered by Lady Sturrock's calm voice: 'And he has come home for a spell to think matters over.' Yes, Alexander Sturrock had an ally, and Oliver was glad of it.

At that point the door opened and May Sturrock slid soundlessly into the room, so frail a form that she seemed transparent. Oliver rose, but the old lady made no acknowledgement of his presence other than a slight dismissive gesture as Lady Sturrock bid her a good evening. Alexander rose to bring her chair closer to the fire and she sat, saying nothing, and stared ahead with the vacancy of extreme old age.

At dinner, Oliver found himself seated beside Alexander and opposite Mungo and Miss Sturrock. Sir Donald and his wife sat at either end of a table more lavishly set than usual with the crystal sparkling and an abundance of well-polished cutlery which indicated an extra course. A candelabra blazed in the centre. Perhaps the fatted calf had indeed been slaughtered! Oliver's stomach rumbled in anticipation.

As the soup was being consumed, Lady Sturrock remarked on the recent bad weather which had wrecked two of the fishing boats, with lives only narrowly saved. 'How are the families doing, Mr Drummond, do you know?'

'Robbie MacDonnell was worst hurt, but he's improving. His leg was badly broken and his shoulder damaged, and his wife is determined that he'll not go to sea again.'

Sir Donald grunted, gesturing for the hock to be served. 'And what does she propose he'll do instead?'

Oliver hesitated; this was not a fence to be rushed. 'Perhaps there will be work on the estate, sir – '

'Will he remain crippled?'

'I'll have a basket sent over tomorrow,' his wife said, and gave Oliver a smile. 'It was good of you to visit them, for they are not regular church attenders, are they?' Not at his church, Oliver thought as the fish course replaced the soup, but very regular at the Free Church three miles away. Like so many.

'They are God's creatures nonetheless, aren't they, Drummond?' Mungo Sturrock shot him a glinting look across the table.

Oliver sensed boredom behind the goading, as well as a general contempt for his ministry, and he had encountered the same attitude from the young man's father, but Sir Donald at least had the courtesy to hide it. He returned Mungo a tight smile, saying nothing, and applied himself instead to the poached cod which was thick and succulent, superior in every way to the tasteless flounders his housekeeper provided, and the conversation moved on. As he scraped the last morsel from his plate, he became aware that Mungo was watching him: 'And we can thank the Lord that at least some of the boats were able to bring home their catch, eh, Drummond, whichever church they attend.'

His successor at the manse in years to come would have a hard time of it when Mungo came into the baronetcy, Oliver decided.

Handsome and brawny he might be, but Mungo was seemingly a young man without compassion or understanding. Confident and contemptuous. On the occasions when he did attend church, he made a point of yawning through the sermons, and Oliver had to try hard not to dislike him.

At least it was beef that was subsequently brought to the table, well cooked and plentiful. Conversation dragged, however, and Oliver, fortified by a claret which surpassed expectations, decided to put his idea to the test, a toe in the water, so to speak, and addressed his host: 'Tell me, sir, has there ever been any investigation of the ruin on the headland?'

Alexander looked up. 'Odrhan's chapel?'

'I was looking at it this afternoon.'

'Whatever for?' asked Sir Donald.

'Curiosity, sir. Such an ancient site, and it would, perhaps, be worth examining it more closely. Clearing the fallen stones, perhaps, and looking at the shape of the place. There would be interest in Edinburgh –'

'I can't imagine why.'

'Well, I can!' Alexander put down his knife and fork. 'What an excellent idea, Mr Drummond. I shall assist you. Who knows what we might find.'

'Bones.' May Sturrock spoke the single word between tiny mouthfuls.

'Bones, Aunt?'

'Some fell out during a storm years back, when half the headland was washed away.'

Alexander looked across at Oliver, eyebrows lifted. 'Human bones?'

'Aye.'

'Perhaps there was a burial ground out there,' said Lady Sturrock, and Oliver saw the opportunity slipping away.

'Any graves encountered would not be disturbed,' he reassured her.

Miss Sturrock spoke up again. 'It would be a bad thing if you did, for there are those who believe the bones were Ulla's.'

Alexander paused, his fork half raised. '*Ulla's!* Really, Aunt? Why have you never said?'

Miss Sturrock viewed her nephew through rheumy eyes. 'You never asked.'

'Well, tell us now! Why Ulla?'

Oliver looked at the old woman, remembering his conversation with Ellen, and thought of the time span encompassed by Miss Sturrock's memory, stretching back perhaps eighty of her ninety years – links in a far-reaching chain. Nowhere near enough, of course, but she was worth hearing.

'It was said Odrhan buried her there,' she said, 'beside his cell, where he could watch over her, and pray.'

'Who said?' asked Oliver, drawn in, and accepting a second helping of potatoes.

She shifted her gaze to him. 'Folk said.'

Folk. The tellers and keepers of tales. And he had an image of the chain forged by the retelling reaching back into a lost past, preserving precious pieces of knowledge. 'A little gold cross was found at the same time, with the bones,' the old woman added. 'Odrhan must have placed it with her.'

'Did it come from there? I didn't know.' Alexander looked across at him again, his eyes sparkling. 'I've not looked at it for years. Is it still in the library, Mama?' His mother nodded. 'I'll show it to you, Mr Drummond, after dinner. And we'll go out there tomorrow, shall we, and take a look?' And then an idea seemed to strike him. 'Maybe I can write about the legend, develop it into an extended poem. Like Macpherson did – a new Ossian!'

His father snorted into his glass. 'So that's it, is it? Cobbling together some old nonsense and hoping to live on the proceeds? You'll more likely starve.' He wiped his mouth with the back of his hand. 'And besides, you're too late, your grandfather was ahead of you.' He addressed Oliver. 'What do you make of the book I lent you, Drummond?'

'It's very informative—' he began, but Alexander cut across him.

'It's hideous stuff! Romantic bilge with no attempt at a factual account.'

'Can a legend ever be factual, my dear?' asked his mother.

'Mr Drummond and I will find out, Mama, starting tomorrow.'

'Mr Drummond has his duties.'

'And shouldn't be concerning himself with pagan ladies anyway,' Mungo added, sitting back and twirling the stem of his empty wine glass. 'Especially not lovely ones who lead holy men astray.'

Oliver decided to let that one go but opened his mouth to refute any concerns about neglect of duties. Alexander, however, was before him again. 'It's a thought, you know! We've accepted the portrayal of Ulla as in Grandpapa's dreadful poetry, but perhaps she was really a sort of Eve figure, offering temptations –'

'Alick, really!'

'Wait, Mama, and consider. We can't know what actually happened, can we? We're just told that Ulla arrived here with her lover, a beautiful pagan, fleeing the husband she had wronged, then was abandoned here when Harald died. And what does Odrhan do?'

'Seduces her,' said Mungo, who had gone to the sideboard and was carving himself another slice of meat, 'if he'd any sense.' His father gave a snort of amusement, his mother a click of annoyance.

'You're a fool, Mungo Sturrock,' said his aunt.

Everyone ignored her, and Alexander continued: 'If the accepted story is correct and Odrhan *did* convert her, though, and thereby saved her soul and so forth – '

'And a blasphemer.'

That statement too was ignored and Alexander carried on: ' – having already, with true Christian charity, tended the wounds of her dying lover–'

'Probably finished him off to clear the field.' Mungo came back to the table.

Alick laughed. 'Perhaps so! And we'll never know whether Ulla really did convert or not. What had she to gain, after all?' Only eternal salvation, thought Oliver dryly, but was this the moment to say so? 'Anyway, Odrhan had the last laugh as he could bury her as a Christian regardless, and bring up Harald's child in the faith.'

Oliver opened his mouth to speak, but this time Mungo interjected: '*Harald*'s child? I may be a fool, as my beloved aunt remarks, but not so great a one to believe that Ulla and Odrhan spent their time together studying the Good Book. First woman he's seen for months? Ha! The child was his. What d'you think, Drummond?'

Oliver saw that two pink spots of annoyance had appeared on Lady Sturrock's cheeks, and he returned Mungo's look steadily. 'No version of the legend I have read suggested that was the case.' And yet had not Ellen raised that very question? *'But did he only love her as a godly man, not a lover?'*

'And you won't, because that's the point,' Mungo returned. 'The church created a winsome tale of a holy hermit tending a pagan's wound, a converted sinner, and a redeemed infant just to hide the fact that Pádraig, their great patron, was conceived by a monk and a harlot during a wild summer of carnal—'

'That is *quite* enough, Mungo!' Lady Sturrock rose to her feet. 'Sir Donald, if you do not think of the courtesies due to our guest, let alone my own and your aunt's sensibilities, then I do.'

'Sit down, m'dear,' her husband said, waving her back to her seat with an ill-disguised smile. 'Mungo, you go too far.'

Chapter 15

→ Libby ←

A week after returning from Ullaness, Libby was in her tiny office making lists of equipment needed and worrying about project finances when the phone rang.

'Libby Snow?' The voice was unmistakable, and she found herself pleased to hear it. 'Rodri Sturrock here. I've just had Fergus on the phone. Word's come down from on high that they have to clear the rest of the mound to look for further evidence.'

'Damn –'

'I did what I could, but Fergus has to obey orders.'

She looked down at the lists in front of her – now just so much waste paper. 'When will they start?'

'Tomorrow morning.'

'Oh God.'

'The only concession I won from them was that you could be there to observe. Will you come? We'll keep some supper for you.' Right now? A force of nature, Alice had called him. 'I sold them the idea on the basis that you'd recognise what was ancient and what wasn't and save them time. No promises that you'll be allowed to dig, though, Fergus went all vague at that point.'

'I'll have to speak to my head of department.'

'Is that Lockhart?'

'No. George Buchanan. Above him.'

'I'll speak to the man. Give me five minutes.' And he rang off. She put the phone down and sat there, absorbing the blow.

She should tell Declan, she owed him that much . . . Then she thought of the morning when she arrived back at the department: 'Whose fucking project is this?' he'd said, having first shut his office door. 'What were you doing up there, going behind my back?'

'Like I said. Just taking a look.'

'Why?'

Because it was a place that had been in her consciousness since childhood, a place which had a deep resonance, a place she had had to see. But that was not for Declan. 'I'd no intention of getting in touch with the estate, it just happened. A good thing too, or there would be no project left, would there?' Then, as payback, she added: 'Besides, what I do with my weekends is my own . . . affair, same as you.' That little pause silenced him, but now she had an enemy, rather than a colleague – and she owed him nothing.

———

Two hours later she was on the road, heading north. By the time she had gone to find George Buchanan, Rodri had already spoken to him and got him on board. 'Any help we can offer you, let me know. I suggested that one of the postgraduate students go with you but he said no, just you.' He paused a minute, then continued in an expressionless voice: 'I'll square all this with Declan, of course, when he finishes teaching.' By which time she would be on her way; George was a good sort. As she turned to go, he added: 'Mr Sturrock said he'd discuss the summer with you. So if you have ideas how we might keep six or seven students occupied in a way that'll let us hang on to that grant, I'd be grateful. He sounded like a reasonable man.'

She had left the building, stopping only to collect some basic equipment just in case, then drove to her flat, threw some clothes into a holdall, and set off. Another seven-hour drive, she calculated, plus stops, and she phoned Sturrock House to tell them she was on her way. No reply. School pickup probably. She left a brief message saying she hoped to be there soon after eleven.

Reasonable, was he?

In fact it was almost midnight by the time she pulled off the main road and plunged into the labyrinth of smaller ones which led out to the coast. Tiredness was jagging at her nerve ends as she negotiated the bends and twists in the narrowing road. Eyes, eerily lit by the headlights, stared back at her from the verges, sheep for the most part, but once she was sure it was a fox. A different world . . . Then, around a tight corner she had to brake hard, skidding across the road to avoid three deer which bounded out in front of her. Dear God! She watched them disappear into the blackness as her heart rate slowed.

The journey north had given her time to consider this new development. And as she drove her concerns about Declan had faded and been replaced by a growing sense of excitement at returning to Ullaness. The place had, on many levels, got under her skin. Something might yet be salvaged for the summer, and somehow she would find a way of explaining about the cross, and maybe learn more of Ellen along the way. She'd thought of writing to Rodri but sensed he would view that as cowardly – and found that his good opinion mattered.

This time when she saw him, she would tell him.

Then, out of the darkness, she found herself in the small community of Oran Bridge, and saw the pub's window softly aglow as she passed it. Almost there – a mile or so further on she turned into the fateful entrance to the track up to Sturrock House and, as she swung into the cobbled courtyard, she was struck by an odd sensation of homecoming.

Rodri must have been listening for her and she saw him framed at the back door even before she had turned off the engine. He came over and opened the driver's door. 'Hell of a thing to ask you to do. Alice was furious.'

The question of Alice had also occupied her thoughts.

She got out to stretch her cramped legs while he opened the boot and took out her bag, and stood for a moment viewing the assortment of equipment. 'You travel hopefully, Liberty Snow.'

'Always.'

The question of Maddy too, for that matter.

He shut the boot lid and ushered her through the back door. 'I can promise you nothing, but come in and have some food.'

The kitchen also felt familiar, and there were good smells coming from a pan which simmered on the Aga. Coalbox wagged a tail in greeting as Rodri ladled the pan's contents onto a plate which he put in front of her, together with a piece of mealy bread. 'Food. And then bed. We can talk tomorrow.'

'Will the weather be fine?' she asked, between mouthfuls. A day of torrential rain might give them a stay of execution and allow her to plan a little.

'Sunny and warm,' he replied. 'And they'll be here at eight.'

'Ooh! Early start. I'd like to go down to make a record before they begin, and draw a plan.'

He nodded. 'Sunrise is about five-thirty these days.'

'I'll set an alarm.'

'Right. I'll take your bag up. Same room.'

———

Dawn was already lighting a milky blue sea when Libby pulled back the curtains next morning, and a thin mist was lifting from its surface. The headland seemed to float there, disconnected from the shore.

She dressed quickly and went down to the kitchen to find Rodri at the Aga stirring porridge. He looked up as she came in. 'Tea's in the pot. Mug over there. Help yourself.' They ate in silence and then drove in her car down to the end of the track, parking as close to the mound as possible, and together they shifted the equipment she had brought into the dunes.

'You give the orders,' Rodri said. 'Just tell me what to do.'

He was efficient and practical, holding the ends of tapes as she plotted the outline of the mound, shouting out measurements as she hastily planned, somehow knowing instinctively what she was trying to achieve. 'Not bad for a beginner,' she said when they'd finished. 'And at least we've got a decent record of it.'

'Just in time,' he said, nodding to where a car was pulling up beside Libby's.

A look of consternation crossed Fergus's face when he joined them and saw the equipment lying beside the mound. 'I'm afraid –'

'Don't worry,' said Rodri. 'I explained, and we've not moved a single grain of sand, just made a drawn record.' Fergus nodded, and after a brief discussion work began.

Libby found it hard to watch from the sideline and turned her attention to what she could usefully do. Something must surely be retrievable. She'd brought down a sieve, and the policemen agreed to shovel the sand into a heap so that she could sieve it and retrieve any small items. Rodri watched her for a moment, then drove her car back up to the house to collect more buckets so that they could work as a team.

Almost at once their work was rewarded. Scraps of corroded iron began to appear.

'What was it?' Rodri asked.

'Impossible to say without X-raying it, but it suggests there is something else in there.'

Rodri met her eyes. 'Great,' adding softly, 'so we need to get them to stop, right?'

'Ideally, yes.' But as work progressed, it became increasingly clear that the mound was far from undisturbed. The dark stain which she believed to be decayed turves was not, as she'd hoped, a constant feature, but was confined mostly to the edges of the mound, and there was evidence that it had been cut into. And then a shout went up from one of the policemen and he straightened, holding something. A revolver. The smoking gun –

Her stomach turned over at the sight of it.

For a moment she had forgotten the reason that they were here, and the discovery brought work to a halt.

The man held the gun between finger and thumb as if fingerprints might have survived the century, and she saw that it had a short barrel and a distinctive chequerboard pattern on the grip. 'A Webley, by the looks of it,' the policeman said. 'The early RIC model.'

'Do we have a date?' asked Rodri.

'Around 1860. They became standard police force issue after the Royal Irish Constabulary adopted them, and pocket gun of choice for anyone who wanted one. The early models used .442 Boxer cartridges.'

'Consistent with the bullet?' Fergus asked.

The man nodded. There was an almost audible release of tension, and Rodri looked across at her, one eyebrow slightly raised. 'So does that close the case, gentlemen?' he asked.

But he had been too hasty and Fergus shook his head. 'There might be something else.'

Libby seized the opportunity to explain her thoughts about the turf layer. 'I think the whole mound was turf-covered once, and if I could just spend a moment cleaning the surface, we might get a better idea – ' Fergus agreed, and she went to work before he could change his mind.

It didn't take long for the situation to clarify. Her rapid cleaning demonstrated that if there had been a turf layer, it had been cut through along one side, and whoever had then robbed the burial mound had done so with careless abandon. And since the Victorian body had been found in the upper layers on the *other* side, these must have been two entirely separate events, divided, perhaps, by centuries.

She explained her reasoning to the police who, now that official duty was no longer so pressing, seemed as intrigued as she was. Slowly and subtly command of the operation shifted to her, helped along by Rodri's careful nudging. The police now stuck to the side from which the man's bones and the revolver had been recovered, while Libby worked along the other side, and Rodri continued to sieve the sand. After a further half hour, he called her over to examine the sieve's contents.

'Are these human?'

Small bones lay in the bottom of the sieve. 'Yes. Hands, by the look of them.'

She looked up and met Rodri's eyes. 'Better stop again, lads,' he said. 'There's someone else in there.' But these bones were bleached clean, shell white, and looked quite different to those lifted before.

'But older, much older,' she said.

Fergus came across to look and seemed convinced.

Alice came down with coffee, greeting Libby like an old friend, and they paused to drink it, then carried on, and those few bones were quickly followed by others. A collarbone, then a femur, and then ribs, one by one. Each was carefully bagged and recorded. The sound of a vehicle reached them, and Rodri looked up. 'Delivery, I expect,' said Alice, and returned to the house. The next find got everyone excited. It was part of a sword hilt with the blade snapped across six inches down its length. 'Your Viking?' Rodri asked.

'Could be,' Libby replied, feeling increasingly anxious. They should stop now or there would be nothing left. What a travesty! It was followed by more small fragments of iron, a pin which once fixed clothing in place, garment hooks – all confirming that the mound had once contained a much earlier burial.

Then suddenly, a reprieve. 'There's nothing for us here, boys,' Fergus said, straightening and leaning on his shovel. 'We'll hand over to you, Libby. And if Mr Sturrock doesn't mind, we'll—' He broke off, as Rodri was no longer listening but stood frozen, staring ahead, his gaze fixed on a figure that had appeared on the path from the house.

A woman in city clothes was carefully picking her way down towards them.

'I'll be right back,' he said, and went to meet her, stopping at the edge of the dunes. They stood talking for a moment, and then the woman turned and went back up the path towards the house.

Rodri returned, his face expressionless, and silently helped to pack up the equipment and take it to Libby's car. When he was out of earshot, she heard one of the policemen mutter, 'That was her ladyship, wasn't it?'

'Looked like it,' agreed Fergus, and Libby watched the woman disappear through the garden gate.

Rodri slipped into the passenger seat beside Libby a moment later, and confirmed the matter. 'My sister-in-law has chosen this moment to drop by,' he said quietly.

'From Oslo!'

He nodded. 'That's what she said.' Then: 'So was that your Viking, do you think?'

'What was left of him, yes.'

'Him?' He seemed distracted. 'Oh, yes – the sword.'

Earlier Libby had heard Rodri invite the policemen back to the house for a bite to eat when they were done, and when they entered the kitchen Lady Sturrock was seated at the kitchen table, her chin resting elegantly on the palm of her hand. Alice was beside the Aga with her back towards her.

'Ah!' said the woman, raising her head and smiling. 'All finished? But how exciting this is! I told Alice to make everyone a warm drink and prepare a little food.'

'Aye. She did,' said Alice, turning to set a teapot on the table, and Libby noticed two high spots of colour on her cheeks. 'And there it is. What'll you have, Fergus? Andy?'

Libby noticed Rodri briefly touch her shoulder as he passed and saw Alice respond with a quick smile. 'For those who've not had the pleasure, let me introduce my sister-in-law, Laila. Lady Sturrock – ' He introduced the policemen, who grunted and nodded. 'And, Laila, meet Libby Snow, archaeologist in charge.'

'Oho! How fascinating. And what have you found?'

Did she know about the body recovered a week ago? Rodri had surely told his brother, but Libby decided to play it safe. He was back into coiled-spring mode. 'It looks like it was once a burial mound, but it's been robbed out—'

'Robbed!' The woman looked quickly over at Rodri. 'Not again!'

Libby hastened to correct her. 'No, no. In the past, centuries ago. The bones and artefacts are all jumbled up. All there is left is a sword—'

'A sword!' the woman interrupted again. 'How marvellous. I must see it!'

She thought she heard one of Alice's little hrmph noises, but it was Rodri who responded: 'Just a rusty bit of metal, Laila, broken off below the hilt. No jewels, no gold.'

Laila Sturrock bestowed a sweet smile on Libby. 'But so interesting for you, my dear.'

'Yes,' said Libby. The woman was perhaps ten years her senior, maybe more, it was difficult to tell. Everything about her was immaculate and she emitted an aura of creamy elegance. And wealth – Libby could only guess what her outfit must have cost. Not a single blond hair was out of place and her complexion was as smooth as satin, but she did not belong in this spartan kitchen, and its atmosphere of well-being had been altered. She sat, almost regally, at one end of the table, speaking kindly to the suddenly taciturn Fergus, presiding over events, and making it clear with every gesture that she had the right to do so. The policemen did not hang about once they had finished eating but rose, making their excuses, and Laila Sturrock rose too and shook their hands, thanking them graciously. Rodri stood by watching her, saying nothing, and then followed the men out.

She turned to Libby and held out her hand. 'And thank *you*, my dear, for helping us with all this unpleasant business.' So she must know about the body. 'Have you far to go?'

'Libby's staying here,' Alice stated. 'As Rodri's guest.'

The woman's mouth opened in a perfect O and her eyes surveyed Libby again, more speculatively this time, and she smiled. 'But how nice,' she said, and sat down again.

Rodri returned to the kitchen. Taking the last of the bacon sandwiches from the plate, he sat down at the far end of the table, opposite Laila. 'Well, isn't this is a delightful surprise,' he said, and bit into the roll.

If Laila heard the irony she didn't show it, but just smiled her sweet smile again. 'Hector asked me to come if I could, so I changed my flight to travel via Glasgow and hired a car. Then I'll fly back to London before I head home.'

'When?'

His tone was barely civil, and she didn't answer. 'What news is there of the other body?' she asked instead. 'Hector is most concerned.'

'Is he? Why?'

'What a question!' She raised her eyebrows in polite incredulity, and rolled her eyes at Libby. 'A man is found murdered and buried on the estate, and you ask why Hector is concerned?'

'As I said in my e-mail, the body's over a hundred years old. And we found the probable murder weapon today, a nineteenth-century revolver. But we've learned nothing else.' He chewed the rest of his sandwich and swallowed. 'I told Hector I'd keep him informed, and if he is so concerned, why hasn't he rung me?'

'So do we know who it is?'

'No.'

Libby stood, uncomfortable in the increasing tension, but Rodri put out a hand. 'We need to talk.'

'Yes, I know, but for now I'll just walk back down to the mound, and have a think.'

She was aware of Laila Sturrock watching her, her oval eyes sliding from Rodri to her and then back. 'We too must talk, Rodri.' And to Libby: 'I'll not keep him long, my dear.'

———•———

Libby had no real desire to go back to the mound, but needed an excuse to leave them. The set-up here got more bizarre. Rodri, after their first meeting, had been nothing but friendly and helpful, in stark contrast to his manner just now which had been brusque to the point of rudeness. The wind still blew cold on her face as she left the shelter of the garden and went down to the dunes. And familial ties apart, wasn't his sister-in-law, to some extent, also his boss?

She went over to the mound and stood staring down at the ravaged site, trying not to dwell on what might have been. The wind was already drying the newly disturbed surfaces and soon their activities there would be nothing more than a few new humps and bumps, lost amongst others in the sand. They had recovered fewer than half of the bones from the disturbed burial, and no skull, but the size of the well-developed humerus and the sword fragments all indicated a male burial. And that gave rise to the inevitable question: Were they the remains of the legendary Harald, brother of the warlord Erik, and lover of his wife? Could there really be such a close tie-up with the legend?

She lifted her head and gazed out towards the headland. It wasn't hard to imagine the scene: the men bearing Harald's body down from Odrhan's cell, with Ulla following and the monk too perhaps. The following day, the legend said, the men had left, having no reason to stay only to serve Ulla, a woman powerless without her man. Had they returned to Erik, or set out to pursue their own fortunes taking the gold, leaving Harald there amongst the dunes?

She left the mound, drawn again to the headland, wondering where Ulla herself had been laid to rest. And then her thoughts moved forward in time to when the legend became entangled with another story. The body of the other man must connect with Ellen's story, but how—

She heard movement behind her and Coalbox bounded forward, pushing his nose into her hand. 'So,' said Rodri, as he climbed over the rocks. 'Did we find Harald, do you think?'

'I was just wondering.'

He came and stood beside her. 'And who decided to hack into his mound and pull him apart?'

'That too.'

'At least you can comfort yourself with the thought that the mound was already disturbed.'

'Cold comfort, but yes. Although I've no project now.'

He gave her a sideways look. 'Says who?' But then his attention was caught by a small fishing boat which had appeared from around the headland, trailing a cloud of gulls as it cleaved through the choppy seas. It gave a short blast on a horn and someone raised a hand. Rodri raised his in return. 'It's Angus,' he said. 'He's taken the lads fishing.' Three heads appeared above the side and three arms waved back. 'They're well off out there,' he added softly, 'and they'll stay over.'

'Because of the digging?' she asked, but suspected it was not that.

His answer was oblique but seemed to confirm the thought. 'Laila leaves in the morning, but we'll have her company tonight. A shame, actually, because there're some papers I wanted to show you, some of the stuff Hector assembled. They'll interest you, I think.' She nodded, registering the fact that he didn't want to discuss them in front of Hector's wife.

Nor, apparently, did he want his children under the same roof.

Then he swung round and looked about him at the tumbled stones of Odrhan's cell. 'And what about all this, then?' he asked, tapping a rock with his toe. 'What would you do here?'

'Make a proper plan for a start, then clear the stones and −' But he'd lost interest again and was looking back towards the house that he called home, and that Sturrock frown was back between his brows.

Dinner that night was awkward. Alice had left them a meat pie which Laila picked at, remarking how thick and solid British food was, and how hard on the digestion. Rodri remained coldly polite throughout, engaging Libby in conversation while fielding Laila's questions about the boys' whereabouts and her persistent enquiries into how his food business was doing.

'Are you making money yet?'

'Some.'

'We must review the rent for the dairy then.' It was playfully said, but Libby saw the muscles in Rodri's jaw tighten. 'I never understood this word *peppercorn*.'

'You don't need to. It's between me and Hector.'

'I will ask Hector to explain. And we really should talk about bringing the business under the estate management since you use the Sturrock House name, after all, and—' She jerked aside as Coalbox padded over. 'Oh, that dog! Take it away, Rodri, it's licking my shoes, and I can feel my asthma coming on.'

Coalbox retreated to his basket. 'Asthma? That's new, isn't it?'

'I've always suffered with it. Have you forgotten!'

'Probably.'

Libby grew increasingly uncomfortable as the meal progressed. Laila alternated between an unconvincing charm and calculated goading, Rodri between sarcasm and silence. There was bad blood here, and it was a relief when they had finished and Rodri got up to clear the plates away.

'When will the boys be home? I haven't seen my nephews at all,' Laila asked, with a little moue of disappointment.

'They're staying over with Maddy and Alice. *David* asked them.'

'Then I shall miss seeing them!'

'I'll tell them you were asking.'

She gave him a look, then shrugged. 'Oh well, next time. Now, where can I find cardboard, and some sort of padding?'

'What for?'

'To wrap the painting, of course. I told you.'

Rodri came back to the table. 'You're surely not thinking of taking it as cabin baggage? Even if it isn't a Nasmyth, it deserves better treatment than that.'

'How else will I get it to London?'

Rodri ran his fingers though his hair. 'Why this sudden need to have it authenticated? It's hung there minding its own business for decades. More wine, Libby?' He leant across the table to fill her glass.

Laila was not deflected. 'But we *must* know for sure, of course we must! Hector's certain it's a Nasmyth.'

'Hector's deluded. It's a copy.'

Laila turned to Libby. 'Do you know anything about paintings, Libbee?'

'Very little,' she replied, keen not to be drawn in.

But there was no escape. 'Then come and I will show you.' Laila sprang to her feet and took Libby by the wrist, pulling her half-playfully into the library, where she halted in front of a landscape painting Libby had admired earlier, a soft highland scene with sweeping mountains and a threatening sky. 'There, is it not fine! And my husband believes it to be the work of Alexander Nasmyth, although sadly it is unsigned.'

'Awkward –'

'And so the only way is for a specialist to decide, don't you think?' Rodri appeared in the doorway and leaned against the door jamb, wine glass in hand. Laila threw him a coquettish smile. 'I shall enlist Libbee to my side.'

Libby was not inclined to be enlisted. 'But does it matter, unless you want to sell it? Or insure it, I suppose.'

Rodri raised his glass to his lips. 'And last time that didn't end so well, did it?'

Laila went and sat in one of the low armchairs by the fire. 'Are

you bringing the wine through for us all, or just your own glass?'
She gestured Libby to the other chair. 'Such a bad host! Come
and sit with me, my dear. I am so glad that you are here. You
know, I expect, what he is referring to?'

Libby could guess. 'The chalice?'

'Just so.' Laila pulled a face and curled her legs up into the
chair with effortless elegance. 'We think that someone connected
with the insurance company was behind it, or that one of them
spoke to the wrong people. We'd just had it valued, you see, for
insurance purposes.' Rodri reappeared carrying the wine bottle
and two glasses, and gave her a wry look. 'And then, just days
later, someone broke into the house, smashed the cabinet, and
took it, *before* we had completed all the documents.'

'How dreadful.' Libby took a refilled glass from Rodri, and
glanced up at him.

'We were all away at a wedding when it happened,' Laila continued, 'so someone must have known the house was empty and
seized their chance – it was valued at more than half a million!'

'And not insured – ' said Libby, though its value lay not in
pounds.

'And not insured,' echoed Rodri, handing a second glass to
Laila. 'Though if it had been, you'd have been suspected of nick-
ing it yourselves.'

'We were! Or at least, Hector was,' Laila replied. 'Have you
forgotten? That stupid policeman suggested he'd had it stolen to
order and taken out of the country to avoid an export licence or
some such nonsense. Hector was furious!'

'An outrageous slur,' agreed Rodri, but something in his tone
sent a flicker across Libby's mind and she glanced at him. Did he
believe that *was* what had happened? This quarrel went deep.

She finished her wine and went up to bed as early as she felt
she could, pleading fatigue, leaving them free to argue further if

they so wished. At face value, Laila was avarice writ large, but who was in the wrong here? 'Rodri sows,' Alice had said during the meal Libby had eaten with her and Maddy, 'and Hector reaps.' But then again, was he not within his rights to do so?

———

By next morning the quarrel was far from played out, and when Libby left her bedroom and came out onto the landing she heard raised voices and retreated hastily. But curiosity got the better of her and she crept forward again to listen.

She could hear Rodri's voice quite clearly. '. . . so, get him to ring me and tell me himself. That's reasonable, isn't it?'

'I've already said! I *cannot* reach him in Dubai. How dared you remove it. . . .' Laila spoke quickly, clearly in a high passion, and her next words were lost.

'Like I said, when I *do* hear from him, I'll package it up and have it couriered down to whatever gallery –'

'No! Tell me where it is! It's not yours to—'

'And it ain't yours either, sweetie. It's Hector's.'

'What's Hector's is mine!'

'Yeah? Get him to tell me that.'

That suggestion could only further infuriate her, and it did. 'I will call the police instead and report it stolen.'

'There's the phone.'

'Oh *yes*, but you have everyone round here in your pocket, don't you!'

His response was lost as a chair was scraped back on the flagged floor. Then Laila's voice came again. 'You seem to think your position here is secure –'

'Believe me, I never do.'

' – you live rent-free, you spend half your time on your own business –'

'Wrong.'

' – your children treat this house as if it was their own home.'

'It is, while I live here.'

'But that could change.'

'At Hector's say-so, not yours.'

'I will speak to Hector.'

'Do that. And tell him I'd like to speak to him too.'

The woman hurled further fury at him, but the sound diminished as she went down the passage to the back door. Libby returned to her room and carefully pulled the door closed behind her, and through her open window she heard the sound of a car engine starting up and then fading as Lady Sturrock drove away.

She sat on the edge of her bed, rather ashamed of her eavesdropping. But had Rodri actually hidden the painting from her? How extraordinary.

When enough time had elapsed, she started downstairs and found him standing looking out of the kitchen window, his hands thrust into his pockets and his back to her. He turned and bid her a neutral good morning, looking like a man who had not slept. 'Help yourself to whatever. No porridge, I'm afraid.'

After a moment he came away from the window and brought the teapot over to the table, filled two mugs, and sat down opposite her.

'There's muesli somewhere. Or toast.'

'I'm fine.'

'Have something. I'll make toast.' He got up again, restless as a caged animal and then stood silently over the toaster, then brought the plate over and pushed the butter towards her. 'So what are your plans now?' he asked, and sat again.

There were dark rings round his eyes. 'There's nothing more I can do here, so I'll get on my way.' She wanted to raise the question of the summer, as well as tell him about the cross, but this hardly seemed the time.

'It's Friday.'

'Yes –'

'Have you things fixed for the weekend?'

'Not especially.'

'Then why don't you stay?' There was nothing flirtatious in his manner, nothing other than a straightforward suggestion, and yet she was unsure how to respond. 'Frankly, I could do with the company,' he continued, leaning back in his chair and contemplating her. 'Even a small dose of my sister-in-law plunges me into the depths of gloom. I could go round to the girls and vent to them, but I'd rather not.' He paused. 'I expect you heard the barney we had just now.'

'Yes.'

'Laila would liquidate the entire estate given half a chance and undo everything I'm trying to achieve. And besides, the Nasmyth was my father's favourite.'

'The Nasmyth? I thought Hector was deluded?'

He smiled, an unrepentant smile, and a spark lit his eye. 'Not on this occasion. My mother had it checked out, as Hector no doubt dimly remembered, and he must have told Laila.'

'So . . . ?'

'So what? Hector has never told me he intended to sell it. If I'd let her take it away today, that's what would have happened. Authentication, my arse. And it wouldn't be the first time; a charming French ormolu clock went the same way a couple of years ago. So it's in the game larder, up in the rafters, safe and sound.'

He got to his feet. 'I don't actually believe Hector knows about half the stuff she's filched, so I've no scruples about thwarting her little plans, having no more conscience than she has. So will you stay the weekend?'

With a man with no conscience? She hesitated for a moment, then realised that she wanted to. 'Yes. I will.'

He nodded his satisfaction. 'Good.' He began clearing the breakfast things away while Libby ate her toast and swallowed her tea. Was the man never still for a moment?

'The things Laila said,' she began, watching him. 'Those threats –'

'Laila specialises in threats.'

'Could she really cause trouble for you? And the boys?'

He shook his head. 'Hector'll not throw us out. He's a decent bloke at heart. Idle, self-indulgent, drunk half the time, but decent. Drives me mad, but he stepped up to the mark when my wife was killed and offered us the chance to come back here. But he always gives in to Laila, anything for an easy life. Afghanistan wrecked him.' He paused. 'And Laila knows my weak spot.'

'The boys?'

He nodded. 'She's none of her own, you see.'

'So you keep them out of her way?'

'Better all round.' He waved a dismissive hand. 'But enough of Lady Macbeth. Come through and let me show you something.'

He led her across the hall into a room she'd not been in before. It too was part of the Victorian addition and matched the library in size and layout, bearing witness to the hand of the third baronet. A long dining table occupied the centre, its surface protected by a thick dark-green cloth over which were strewn books and papers. A dozen or so dining chairs were all wedged along one side, suggesting it was some time since this room had been used for gracious dining. An office-style swivel chair was drawn up on the other side in front of several box files with an empty mug beside them.

'I got this lot out after you were here last time. I'd not looked at them for years.' He pulled a box of papers towards him. 'They're more or less as Hector abandoned them, after his little burst of enthusiasm.' He began lifting papers from it while Libby looked around her, taking in the room. Faded wallpaper covered the walls, depicting thistles and rowanberries like the plaster ceiling in the library, and below dado height was more wood panelling, lighter-hued here and more pleasing, and once again some of the windowpanes had scenes painted on them, repaired presumably after the ravages of football. 'See what you make of these,' he said and unrolled a sheaf of papers, weighting the curling corners with books and the coffee mug.

Her interest was immediately aroused. The papers were dog-eared and tatty and covered with neat drawings in faded black ink complete with measurements. It was unmistakably the headland, with Odrhan's cell at the end of it, and she leaned closer and saw little notes and sketches in the margins. 'There was more headland in those days,' Rodri remarked, and she nodded, examining the exquisite elevation drawings of the cell with walls standing several courses high. It had been drawn from all four compass points, each aspect carefully labelled: *View looking north. View looking west. View looking . . .* and she paused at the view looking east. The entrance to the cell, and much of the centre was filled with the dome's fallen blocks.

'Fantastic,' she said.

'Dated too.' He pointed to the corner, where the same neat hand had written *12th May 1890. O.D.*

'Who was O.D.?'

'Not a clue,' he replied, and she bent closer to read the tiny handwriting in the margin. Rodri passed her a hand lens.

She took it and read out loud: *'Probably originally of domed form and corbelled construction in the manner of the Irish Monasteries of the Early Period. This would be consistent with the view currently held that this ruin is the small house described in the Legend as belong-*

ing to the hermit Odrhan.' She looked across at Rodri. 'So O.D. was chasing the legend too.'

'Looks like it.' He removed the top drawing to reveal the next. It was a plan rather than an elevation, and depicted the cell as a rough oval; from the contours, Libby could see how much of the headland had eroded away in a century and a half. She picked up the hand lens again to read the tiny lettering. The same word was written in three separate places. *Bones? Bones? Bones?*

She looked up to see that Rodri was watching her. 'Bones –' she said.

'Could be sheep bones, of course.'

'I don't think he'd note sheep bones –'

'Nor do I.'

She bent to the drawing again, creeping over it with the hand lens as she searched for something more, but there were no further annotations other than *rocks, turf, sand.* And then her eye was caught by something, not a word but a symbol beside one of the *Bones?.* A tiny splayed-arm cross, and a further question mark beside it.

'Another grave, perhaps, eroding away at the time. What do you think?' Rodri asked.

Libby straightened, her brain working furiously. 'And now long gone.'

He released the edge of the drawing and it rolled back up. 'Well, open the other boxes. There's more.'

Chapter 16

In their haste to get away, the men had left behind the basket in Odrhan's cell, but he saw it as soon as he brought Ulla up from the shore. First he draped a sheepskin around her shivering form and built up the fire, then he tipped the contents of the basket onto the floor.

And he stood, consumed with fury at the sight of jewelled clasps ripped from books he had once known and cherished, silver dishes and bowls as well as the chalice from which he had taken the sacrament. And then the final insult, the gold cross once worn by the abbot himself, its central garnet the colour of blood.

He turned to Ulla. 'Who stole these things?'

She looked back at him. 'Erik and Harald. Last summer. But we brought away with us only what was Harald's due, no more.'

'His due!' Odrhan raised his hand to strike her, but she did not flinch. 'Lady – May God forgive him, for I cannot.'

➳ *Oliver* ➳

Alexander was before him to the headland next day, coat flung aside and sleeves rolled up, and had already moved several of the stones. 'Good morning, Oliver!' the young man cried out as he approached. He had declared in the library last night that the formality of address was tiresome and unnecessary. 'I've made a start.'

'So I see,' Oliver replied. At least he had managed to complete his drawing of Odrhan's cell in its pristine state, from all four angles, before his companion had begun his work. Alick, as he had been told to call him, was clearly going to be enthusiastic rather than scientific in his approach. Oliver pulled out his notebook and wrote the date, ready to record further discoveries as they were made. Things looked set to move fast.

'We ought to record everything we—'

'Absolutely! But just for now I'm clearing the rubble off the top. We'll make a pile of it over there.'

There was nothing to do but join in, so Oliver stripped off his own jacket, folded it, and placed it beside Alick's discarded tweed. Then he too rolled up his sleeves and started moving the stones of the collapsed roof. Some of them were small and easily shifted, others required the two of them working together, and as the sun rose they began to sweat. But physical work made a pleasant change from the spiritual, and the silence between them was companionable. Once, when Alick paused to wipe his forearm across his brow, Oliver took the opportunity to do a quick sketch, pointing out that they had reached a portion of intact wall.

'You're right,' said Alick.

'So we should leave that as it is, and I'll draw it.'

'Righto. Lord, it's thirsty work, ain't it? I left word that someone was to bring us a drink halfway through the morning, and a bite to eat. Then we'll have a break.' Oliver just had time to complete his sketch before Alick was back at work with an energy he could only admire.

'No treasure yet,' he remarked as they staggered under the weight of a larger stone.

Oliver smiled. 'Were you hoping for some?'

'At least another gold cross or two.'

After dinner last night, Alick had cut short the ordeal by port with the gentlemen by filling two glasses and taking Oliver to the library, giving only the briefest apology to his father. Once there he had pulled the library ladder along its rails until it reached a shelf in the corner. While he ascended it, Oliver had looked around the magnificent room with its rich hues and dark panelling, and the shelves of leather-bound books. He ran his eye enviously along them, seeing works old and new which charted the rise of civilised society, a collection he feared was wasted on the present baronet and his heir. Perhaps Alick Sturrock would make better use of them.

'Aha! Here we are.' Alick had descended the ladder carrying a small carved wooden box, which he placed on the desk. A complex interlace pattern adorned the outside of it, and he lifted the lid, unwrapping an object from a covering of chamois, and passed it to Oliver. The fire had burned low and the room was still and cool, the silence almost reverential, and the metal warmed in his hand. 'Splendid, isn't it.'

'Quite remarkable.' Four equally splayed arms, each carefully decorated, came together in the centre where a single deep-red stone was set. Carefully he turned it over and examined the back and saw how it had been worn, on a thong or chain.

A thousand years ago Odrhan himself must have held what he was holding now, and Oliver marvelled at the thought, conscious of a great upwelling of emotion towards the man who shared his calling. It was a bond he sometimes felt out on the headland as daylight faded, an empathy with the man, a man of God, living out there, alone and more dedicated than he could ever hope to be.

'Just imagine. Odrhan himself might have worn it,' he said. 'And then given it to Ulla, if your aunt is right about finding it with the bones.'

'That's true! Or else it was Viking loot swiped from some monastery.' And as if in recognition of such dark deeds, the lamp on the desk had guttered and died, and the stone in the centre of the cross had seemed to dull.

⇁ *Odrhan* ↼

Odrhan tried to explain to the woman about the holy books with their wondrous illuminations and beautiful lettering which proclaimed the word of God. He showed her the fragments of vellum which still adhered to the ravaged bindings, railing at the sinfulness of their destruction, and her finger slowly traced the curving lines of the designs as she listened to him, but she said nothing.

For days after Harald's death she had hardly spoken nor eaten, subsisting only on water or a thin gruel that he coaxed her to eat. He feared for her. And though he did not pray for forgiveness for himself, he prayed for Ulla with a fervour that made him light-headed.

Then one day he came upon her sitting cross-legged in his cell threading the abbot's cross onto a thin leather cord, and he grabbed it from her. 'No! You shall not wear that. Not until you can truthfully say that you have repented. You promised me that you would give your soul to God!'

'And you promised that your prayers would save Harald. Yet Harald is dead.'

He had looked back at her, then turned away, unable to meet her eyes. 'Then let us pray together for the salvation of his soul.'

She gave him an odd, narrow smile. 'Do you imagine he would care for that, holy man?'

⇁ *Oliver* ↼

Alick wiped a sleeve across his brow and went to sit a moment on the pile of stones. 'Rumour has it, you know, that my grandfather funded his building works at the house from the proceeds of treasure found under the church.'

'*Under* the church?'

'At the east end, when the chancel was being built, hard up against the wall. God's providence, he called it, but it's been kept pretty quiet, just in the family, you know, in case the church authorities made a claim. He bought off the minister with promises of a new church roof, and spent the rest on the house, and on his own ghastly tomb.'

'And the treasure itself?'

'Melted down and sold, I suppose. Talk to my aunt, she'll remember the old stories. Pity we can't get her up here to point out where those bones were found, but we could take her those drawings you made, see if she remembers.' Then he gave Oliver his open, engaging smile. 'I can't tell you how pleased I am to find you here, Oliver. This is a desert, you know, Mungo and Pa haven't an intellectual thought between them and there's so much I'd like to discuss with you. I don't plan to stay long, mind you, I want to get back to Edinburgh. It's just throbbing with new ideas there, it's such— Oh look, splendid! Tea.'

Oliver turned and saw Ellen clambering over the rocks behind them, carrying a basket, and Alick went forward to offer a hand, taking it from her.

As she rounded the edge of the ruin, she stopped, aghast. 'Whatever are you doing?' she said, a hand on her breast.

'We're excavating, m'dear. Like that German fellow did at Troy. Did you read about that, Oliver? Extraordinary discoveries. And he was following a legend too, wasn't he? Homer, I believe. Just think what we might—'

But Ellen was staring at the pile of stones in dismay. 'But this is a *holy* place!'

Alick pulled out a metal flask and two mugs and examined the basket's contents. 'Scones too! Splendid girl. We are being meticulous, don't you worry, and Mr Drummond is recording each stage, and we've agreed that no burials will be disturbed so there's no—'

'But what about the spirits? You're disturbing them!' The girl shot Oliver a reproachful look. 'Why are you allowing him to do this?'

'It was his idea, actually.' Alick had filled the two mugs and passed one to Oliver, adding cheerfully, 'All in the name of scientific enquiry.'

'But you mustn't!'

'Whyever not, m'dear?' Alick sat on one of the boulders and grinned at her, and Oliver was struck by the familiarity with which they addressed each other. 'We're being very respectful.'

'There were bones found here.'

'Do you know precisely where, by any chance?'

'Some say they were Ulla's bones!' So that was not just Miss Sturrock's fancy then, Oliver thought.

'Or Odrhan's,' Alick suggested, seemingly unaware of Ellen's stricken expression.

The girl had clasped her arms about her. 'Whoever it is, this is their resting place and they should be left alone. How can you be doing such a thing! Don't you *feel* the wrongness of it?'

She looked truly shaken, and Oliver felt a twinge of unease. He remembered their previous conversation and her flights of fancy; he had thought her simply naïve and credulous then, but suddenly realised that he had no idea how the locals regarded the headland. He should have considered –

He was still searching for the right words to reassure her when he heard someone else clambering up the rocks. 'Is this a private picnic, or can anyone join in?' Mungo Sturrock asked.

'Only two mugs and the last scone just went,' his brother replied, taking it and biting into it.

'Perhaps the good Ellen would go back for more,' Mungo suggested, his eyes sliding between them and lingering on the girl. She looked away and gave no reply.

'Refreshments are for the workers, and we neither want nor expect you to assist,' said Alick. Ellen began collecting the mugs. Oliver sensed that she was anxious to be off, but Alick took his back and refilled it, offering the can to Oliver.

'Any gold doubloons yet? Pieces of eight?' Mungo asked.

'Not a one.'

Mungo sat down on the rocks and seemed inclined to stay. 'If I can't join in, then I'll watch.'

'I wish you wouldn't.' Alick drained the mug and packed it away in the basket. Ellen, eyes down, picked it up and left without a further word. 'You're a distraction. Go away.'

Oliver saw that Mungo's eyes were following her departure. 'Perhaps I will,' he said, 'but if I do, what's to stop the two of you sharing the spoils between you, and cutting me out?'

'Risk it,' said his brother.

Mungo laughed and rose, surveying their handiwork. 'I suppose I must,' he said, then added: 'I count on you, Drummond, to do the decent thing.' Oliver watched him go, feeling a swelling of unease, and decided to keep a lookout for when Ellen might reappear on the sand at the end of the causeway.

'Ellen's always been a bit superstitious, you know, and very keen on the legend,' said Alick, 'so you mustn't mind her. I'll smooth things over when I see her next.'

'Do you see her often?' Oliver asked, still watching for her. 'At the house, I meant.'

'Ah, yes –' And then he saw them both. Ellen was walking fast along the shoreline, half-running, as much as the basket would allow, head averted, with Mungo beside her. Oliver went and stood at the highest point on the headland, where he would be silhouetted against the skyline.

'What's the—' Alick climbed up and joined him, and then, seeing where Oliver was looking, said in tones of repulsion: 'Oh God! Not Ellen, Mungo, you goat – 'Their movements must have caught his brother's attention; Mungo looked in their direction, and they saw him fall back while Ellen ran on, head down, towards the gate in the garden wall.

'What do you mean?' Oliver asked, though he could guess.

Alick gave him a chagrined look. 'Mungo can be a bit of a nuisance, sometimes, with the housemaids. Bit of a ladies' man. Always was. After last time, though, he swore – and, dammit, Ellen's practically family.' He turned to look at Oliver, a lock of hair blowing across his face. 'You know about that, don't you? About her mother, I mean. Mrs Mackay?'

'It seems I don't.'

Alick looked embarrassed. 'Poor woman's a by-blow of my grandfather's. Not her fault, of course, and it's all rather awkward, really.' He began kicking at the pile of stones, glancing at Oliver and then away again. 'What must you think of us? *He* was a dreadful old goat by all accounts, saw himself as some sort of medieval overlord who could do as he pleased in his little fiefdom. Pa's had his moments too, from what I gather, but not on the estate, Mama would never forgive him if he did, so when Mungo got one of the housemaids in trouble there was a hell of a fuss. Pa bought off the family and they left, but Mama was furious, threatened Mungo with all sorts. He promised her it wouldn't happen again.'

Oliver looked back at him. 'And you think he's bothering Ellen?' He had enjoyed this morning, the chance to cast aside the mantle of his ministry, but he felt it settle heavily again.

'No, no.' The denial was unconvincing. 'He's just being a nuisance.'

A nuisance. Oliver continued moving the stones, tight-lipped now and angry. Goading the minister was one thing, but making unwelcome advances towards an unprotected girl was quite another. Especially a girl like that, half fey and with her head in the clouds. The matter needed handling with tact, but with resolve.

The incident had taken the joy out of the morning, and once the centre of the ancient structure had been revealed, the two men paused and looked at it. 'It's sort of rectangular,' said Oliver.

'With rounded corners.'

The middle of the structure, once its floor, was now visible in places, but neither of them suggested that they went any further. Oliver got his notebook out again and they took some measurements, which he jotted down beside his simple sketch, intending to expand it later into a measured drawing. Ellen's distress at what they were doing had somehow transmitted itself to him, and he began to wonder if they were justified in going any further. Alick had gone quiet too, ever since they had seen his brother in pursuit of the girl, and the incident hovered, unremarked, between them.

Then Alick said with sudden ferocity, 'We used to play together as children, you know, with Ellen, and with the other tenants' children too. But Ellen mostly, because she lived so close. And then her father was lost at sea and her mother took ill and couldn't work, and so Ellen had to find employment. Mama took her on at the house, which was rather marvellous of her, I think, and then things changed between us. They had to, of course. She was always such a bright little thing, weaving her stories, but neither fish nor fowl, caught between the big house and the tenantry. It's been hard for her and her mother, and I'm not sure that my grandmamma did them a favour, really, insisting they were given that cottage; they'd have been better moving away. But with Ellen's father dead, they at least had a roof over their heads. It's been a bad business all round –'

Oliver looked gravely back at him. 'For which Ellen must not suffer further.'

'I'll speak to Mungo.'

'Do.'

And he would speak to Ellen himself.

———

Two days passed before Oliver had his chance. He was returning home on the rough track which connected Ullaness to the next bay, having visited the injured fisherman's family again. It had been an uncomfortable experience; he had been treated with courtesy, but with distance, and he was not sure that his visit had been welcome. The man's leg had been set but was giving him a distressing amount of pain, and it would be some time before he was fit for any sort of work. What, he wondered, might be the best way to persuade Sir Donald to give the poor fellow some sort of employment? If successful, Oliver might win these people's trust, although success could serve to further underline his close association with the estate. But something would have to be done, and soon. Oliver had taken them some food of his own and would mention to Lady Sturrock how much another basket would be appreciated. The weather was closing in again and it was cold for May, more like November, and the air was heavy with imminent rain.

He looked up then, and saw Ellen standing stock-still in the middle of the road ahead of him, backlit by the sun, and he was struck again by the loveliness of her. 'I came to find you,' she said.

No wonder she had caught Mungo Sturrock's eye.

He went up to her, and spoke quietly. 'And I wish to speak with you, Ellen.' He was reminded suddenly of the painted glass in the Sturrock House library, and of the figure of Odrhan confronting Ulla. 'Let us walk back together.'

Ellen did not move. 'You must put those stones back, Mr Drummond.'

Her words surprised him. 'Ellen, I promise you, there's—'

'Some places ought to be left alone! That's a special place and should not be disturbed.' She looked about her anxiously, as if the wind that shook the yellow gorse and sped the clouds across the skies was driven by a malign hand. 'My grandmother says the same. And others too –'

Her grandmother? Surely – but she must mean her father's mother, a local woman, steeped no doubt in heathen mythology. He adopted a chiding tone: 'Ellen, as a Christian you ought to know better. Excavating the ruin is not desecration, and it's entirely appropriate that we are furthering our understanding of the early days of Christianity.'

Her chin went up. 'Ulla was a pagan –'

'Whom Odrhan converted.'

'Some say she died a pagan, cursing him.'

What nonsense the girl's head was filled with! Oliver began to lose patience. 'I've never heard that said! Not in the book I read.'

'It's what people say, though. And writing it in a book doesn't make it true.'

Oliver contemplated the fierce creature who stood scowling before him. It was a reasonable point, and Alick was right, she was a bright little thing, but ignorant, and with such an imagination she was prey to foolish fears.

But was she equally attuned to earthly dangers? 'Does Mungo Sturrock make a nuisance of himself, Ellen?' he asked abruptly, using Alick's bland words but confronting the matter head-on.

Her face changed colour. 'What's been said?' she asked, stepping away from him.

'My dear girl!' He put out a hand, but she backed away, so he dropped it. 'Nothing has been said. I simply observed the other day that you seemed to be running from him, and I wondered. He has something of a reputation – ' Her colour began to return to normal. 'You can speak in confidence to me, Ellen. Does he make advances?'

She was silent for a long time, looking down at the track. Then: 'Sometimes.'

'Did he do so the other day?'

'He tried.'

'Have you told anyone?'

'No.'

'Not Mrs Dawson?'

'No!'

She was not making this easy, but he needed to know more. Just how serious were these advances? 'Does he try to kiss you?' Silence. 'Does he . . . touch you?' More silence, and then a brief nod.

Oliver felt anger rising in him, but kept his voice quiet and calm. 'And what do you do?'

'I get away quickly, and hide.'

Dear God! But what else could she do? 'You must endeavour never to be alone with him, Ellen. Do you understand?'

She gave a sort of despairing laugh. 'But I've my duties in the house, sir. I can't pick and choose.'

'I shall speak to Mrs Dawson myself.'

'No!'

'Whyever not?'

'I don't want trouble, and I'd not be believed. Maria wasn't. And Mr Mungo is Mrs Dawson's favourite.'

Maria? Was she the girl Alick had spoken of? He regarded Ellen with growing concern. 'But you cannot be expected to put up with—'

'I'm alright as long as Mr Alick is at home.'

This was a surprise. 'How so?' he asked.

'Mr Alick wouldn't let anything happen to me.' Her face coloured again, and Oliver was worldly-wise enough to recognise that this was for quite different reasons. Different, but really just as bad, and he recalled their easy manner with each other. Did the poor girl fancy herself in love with him? He thought back to his conversations with Alick, but there was nothing in *his* tone or words other than a friendly, and detached, concern.

And yet, with Mungo in lustful pursuit and Alick cast as hero, Oliver feared that between them these two brothers could do Ellen real harm.

Chapter 17

Libby and Rodri spent the rest of the afternoon sifting through the papers, working opposite each other at the old dining table, exchanging few words. Occasionally they drew one another's attention to something, or got absorbed by a newspaper clipping or some other item, and occasionally Libby would look up and find that Rodri was watching her –

The other drawings that he had shown her had been equally fascinating. They were in the same hand and depicted a plan of the ruin with the centre cleared of fallen stones. It too had been carefully measured and annotated, and proved that the ruin had once been cleared. Might it be possible, she wondered, to persuade Rodri to let them clear it again and maybe, just maybe, put a test pit in the centre? She glanced across at him, head down again absorbed in one of the ledgers, and decided to bide her time.

The papers offered a treasure trove for a social historian, she thought as she waded through old household accounts, lists of game bagged on various shoots, badly written letters from tenants begging for leniency, and gilt-edged invitations from other gentry families. 'Someone should catalogue this lot,' she said, as she pulled over another box. 'It's extraordinary. But what was your brother looking for?'

'Treasure.' She laughed, then saw that he was serious. 'He was convinced there'd be something which would lead him to a hoard of Viking gold.'

'But no luck?'

He gave a twisted smile. 'No. It kept him occupied, though. He was in bad shape, poor bugger, invalided home from Afghanistan with a massive hole in his leg, and his head messed up from things he'd witnessed there. My mother dragged out all this stuff to try to keep him off the booze.'

'Oh.' What else could she say?

He pushed his chair away from the table, crossing one leg over the other, and twirled his pen on the green cloth, staring down at it.

'When was this?' she asked, after a moment.

'Eleven years ago.' He went on staring at the table, still spinning his pen.

'But he's made a full recovery – ' she said.

'Has he?' Rodri's tone was bleak, and she thought she'd blundered, but after a short silence he answered her. 'His injuries healed up pretty well, but he started having periods of depression, interspersed with fits of riotous joy or reckless fury – and always the booze. And then Laila. The two constants in Hector's life. Laila and the bottle.'

She opened the next box file, saying nothing, and began to sort through it. This was a troubled house. Then Rodri made an exasperated sound and rose, going over to stand by the window, hands deep in his pockets again, and stared out at the neglected garden. 'I should have let her take the damn painting,' he said, as if to himself. 'It's a small price to keep her on board. God knows what she'll tell Hector.' Still Libby said nothing – it felt too much like intruding. 'Wretched woman. She never fails to get a rise out of me.'

He stood there for a long time, saying nothing; then, still with his back to her, he said: 'So treasure was what Hector was looking for, but what he got was Laila and an addiction to whisky, despite my mother's best endeavours.' He didn't seem to expect an answer but continued to look out of the window where starlings jostled and bickered on the path. Then he swung round to her. 'And what is it that you're looking for, Liberty Snow?'

The sudden shift took her entirely by surprise.

He was looking intently at her, the frown back in place. 'There's something, isn't there? More than just the dig. And I think it's time I understood. So, let's start with this.' He shunted a piece of paper across the table towards her. It was a page of the same yellowing paper as the diagrams of the ruin, and on it, drawn with the same meticulous care, was the chalice, and beside it the cross, drawn front and back and annotated: *Discovered on the headland?* No hallmark.

'That's it, isn't it? The one we found.'

It was and it wasn't. 'Not exactly,' she said, after a moment.

'Quite.'

She looked up and saw that his expression had darkened, and she felt her own face flush. 'You saw the hallmark,' she said.

'You thought I hadn't?'

'I wasn't sure.'

The Sturrock frown deepened, but he looked perplexed rather than angry. 'What sort of an answer is that! Twice now I've seen you go white as a sheet over those bones, and you a professional! And then your expression when you found that cross. Not thrilled, as you might well have been, but almost horrified. I know what Laila's all about, but not you. And I've been wracking my brains to imagine.'

She knew then that she should have spoken earlier, not waited to be wrong-footed like this. She started to pack the papers back into the box, giving herself time to think. But where to begin? Then he straightened and went over to the mantelpiece and extracted an envelope from behind the clock and put it in front of her.

'And while we are at it – explain that.'

She picked it up, cursing herself for not having had the sense to talk to him before this, and pulled out a letter. It was dated 13th March 1893.

Dear Lady Sturrock,

It is with the deepest regret that I write to inform you that I have once again failed in my endeavours. A passage was certainly booked and I thought that I had traced him, travelling with a woman, to this little township, but the trail has gone cold. Several couples from Scotland have settled here in recent years but none fit the description that you gave me, or bear your son's name, and no one can cast any light on the matter. I will return to St John's and take a passage home, then come to see you, but unless you have new information I fear there is nothing more that I can do, but I remain your obedient servant,

John Robinson
Gosse Harbour, Newfoundland

Gosse Harbour. She lowered the letter.

'You mentioned that place the other day.' He came round to the end of the table, watching her face. 'Yes?'

'Yes. I did.'

He nodded. 'Right. Well, suppose we go and make some coffee, Liberty Snow, and you can explain to me why you're here.'

———

She'd had no time to prepare, no time to shape her own thoughts into something which made sense. But then nothing ever had . . . She followed him into the kitchen, the letter still in her hand. There were too many trailing ends, too many unknowns, and now this letter . . . But central in her mind just now was the know-ledge that she had priceless property belonging to the estate in a drawer back home in her flat. And she ought to have told him so.

Silently Rodri made the coffee, assembling mugs and milk which he set on the table. Then he gestured to a chair opposite and sat. 'Gosse Harbour,' he said. 'I looked it up, tiny little place.'

Libby sat and reached for one of the mugs. 'And as good a place as any to begin, I suppose. Just four hundred people, and shrinking. Mostly old folk, but it was bigger once, before the fishing finished.'

'And you spent your summers there, you said.'

'Christmas too, a few times. It's a special place, and my grand-mother still lives there. She's ninety-five.'

With a long memory, and a head full of stories. Still living in the small clapboard house where she had been born, supported by a community who revered her. A natural story-teller whose reminiscences had brought alive a vanished world of topsail schooners and dories, of seal hunts and hunger. She had seen bodies brought ashore from ill-fated Atlantic convoys, and watched the death of a fishery which had been the people's lifeblood. And she had absorbed it all with the calm acceptance which defined her. The thought gave Libby strength.

Rodri's eyes were still on her. 'So she must have been born when? Nineteen-twenties?'

'1917.'

'At Gosse Harbour? Or somewhere else?'

'At Gosse Harbour. It was she who told me the story of Ulla and Odrhan, and of this place.'

'Really?' He sat back and hooked an arm around the back of the chair. 'Go on.'

'And she learned it from her own grandmother, Ellen Mac-donald.'

He gestured to her coffee mug. She drank half of it, and he filled it from the pot. 'And so who then was Ellen Macdonald?'

A crazy lady, a mad crone, a demented old woman who had gripped her granddaughter's hand and told her that *she* was Ulla and that murder had been done. Libby swallowed. 'She used to live here, in a cottage beside the manse.'

She had his full attention, and he gestured to the letter Libby had placed on the table. 'The woman who was travelling with a Sturrock son, I presume?'

'I suppose so. But I hadn't known that bit.'

'Which bit?'

'The Sturrock bit.'

He glanced at her, as if deciding whether to believe her, then pulled the letter towards him and looked at it again. 'Some time before 1893, it would seem.'

'Yes.'

'So what happened? What's the story?'

'I don't really know.' He looked sceptical. 'But that sort of answers your question. I'm here to try and find out.'

'But for some reason you didn't say? I wonder why – But go on.' And she found herself wondering too why she hadn't. Was it only the cross, or had the way her grandmother spoken of Ellen's later years somehow transmitted to her a sense of her own unease? 'They presumably didn't marry, this Ellen and the Sturrock man? Or was she Sturrock before she was Macdonald?'

'No – at least, I don't know. As I said, the Sturrock connection is new –' And would take some absorbing.

'Did he leave her?' Rodri persisted.

'I don't know that either. She was only ever Ellen Macdonald in my grandmother's stories.' Libby looked down and traced the grain in the wooden table, noting the cuts and chips where knives had scored the surface over the years. Had Ellen once sat here, where she now sat? But even if Ellen's avowal of murder was true, and that she had a part in it, the crime was long past having consequences. Her own possession of the cross, however, needed explaining, and now was the time.

She began in a rather disjointed way. 'She simply told me that Ellen came from Scotland, from here where she'd been in service, and that she brought the legend with her. Nothing about who she came over with. As a child I loved the legend, but as I got older Nan told me other things too.' She hesitated, then continued, 'She'd lived with Ellen when she was a child, you see, although it was her grandfather, John Macdonald, who really looked after her. He was the schoolmaster in Gosse Harbour.'

'A Scot too, I presume.'

'Yes, I think he was.'

'Go on.'

Libby got up and walked over to the window; if she was going to be anything like coherent, then she couldn't be hurried. 'Ellen was unstable, my grandmother told me, considered crazy by the standards of the day, and there were long periods when she never left the house. I suppose she had some form of dementia.' She paused again. 'When I got the job on the dig here, I wrote to tell my grandmother, and she sent me some of the things that had once been Ellen's. Amongst them was a sketchbook . . .' She hesitated again.

'Keep going.'

Rodri had brought the drawing of the cross and the chalice with him, and it lay on the table in front of him. Libby went and sat again and stared down at it. It had to be said: '. . . and with it, tucked inside, was the gold cross. That one. The real one.' His eyebrows went up at that, but it was easier now she'd started. 'She said Ellen used to wear it on a chain around her neck, and when she died it was put away and everyone forgot about it. Nan thought I'd like to have it.' Thousands of pounds' worth of eighth-century antiquity wrapped in bubble wrap and popped in the post. She could still remember the shock of opening it. 'I don't think she had a clue what it was.'

He was staring at her. 'And where is it now?'

'In a drawer in my flat.'

'Good God!'

Then, to her astonishment, he gave a shout of laughter. 'Was *that* it? And so, Liberty Snow, you've been concealing stolen property.' The tension had gone out of him and he rocked back on his chair, clasped his hands behind his head, and contemplated her with an odd smile.

'I should have told you.'

'I'm still wondering why you didn't.'

'Just as you said – it's probably stolen property, and I didn't understand how it got there. I've written and asked Nan if she knows more, but she's not replied. Ellen must have taken it, I suppose. It's very valuable, you see.'

'Then don't tell Laila.'

His reaction was totally unexpected. He looked genuinely amused, and there was a new warmth in his eyes. 'What are you planning to do with it?'

'That's just it. I'm not sure what to do. It's awkward –'

He gave another laugh, letting his chair come forward. 'I'll say! Imagine the headlines: "Archaeologist Hides Priceless Stolen Antiquity Amongst Her Knickers." Not great, eh?' He leaned forward, elbows on the table and his chin on his hands, and contemplated her.

'There's more,' she said.

'I thought there might be.'

'It's as bad – worse, in fact.'

'Go for it.'

In some ways this was just as difficult. 'My grandmother said Ellen was always strange, prone to fits of wild anguish – panic attacks, I suppose we'd call them now – and increasingly so as she got older. Her husband had to fight off the authorities who wanted to put her in an institution, and by the end of her life he kept her virtually under house arrest, locked in for her own safety.'

'Poor woman.'

'My grandmother said she became obsessed by the legend, and believed that *she* was Ulla. I'd written it off as some sort of dementia, but one of the things she said was that she'd seen murder done, and was to blame. A man had been killed.'

His expression sharpened. 'What man?'

'Harald, she said.'

'*Harald!*'

'But if she was telling the truth, I suppose it could have been –'

' – a well-shod gent with a gold filling in his tooth.'

Chapter 18

Ellen began to feel hunted.

It was not her imagination, she was sure of it. Mungo Sturrock, finding life dull, had taken to stalking her. He was doing it in such a way that gave her no grounds for complaint, had she the intention of making one, but it was relentless. Usually she was able to elude him, doing her chores in the library first thing in the morning while he slept, then slipping into his room while he ate breakfast, and only entering the drawing room when she knew for certain that he was not alone there. Once she had miscalculated and met him at the door of his bedroom. 'Leaving so soon, Ellen?' he had said, and she had held the chamber pot in front of her as a shield, meeting his look and ready to tip it on him.

He had laughed that time, and let her pass.

By contrast she would linger in Mr Alick's room, hoping that he might return there while she was cleaning or making the bed. Sometimes she was rewarded, and then she would dawdle, rearranging his silver-backed hairbrushes and collar box, polishing the bedposts and dusting places newly dusted while talking to him on all manner of things. She lived for such moments.

The day after she had met Mr Drummond on the road home, she found Alick in his room and backed out as she had been taught to do, but slowly, hoping –

'Come on in, Ellen. Don't mind me. I'm just off,' he said.

She went over to the bed and began making it while he stood

184

at his mirror, adjusting his collar, and looking at her through the glass. 'How are you, Ellen?'

She addressed his reflection, saying what was uppermost in her mind: 'I told Mr Drummond yesterday that you should stop what you are doing at the headland. It's wrong to disturb that place.'

He swung round to her. 'They're only old tumbled stones, you know. Nothing fearful.'

She shook her head at him. 'Things feel unsettled there now.'

He turned back to the mirror, still wrestling with his collar stud, a little frown on his forehead. 'Do you think so? But if Mr Drummond has no concerns, then neither should you.'

'*He* thought I was a ghost!'

Alick swung round again with a laugh. 'Really?'

'And that was before you started shifting the stones. He thought I was Ulla.'

'Did he say so?'

She hesitated, trying to remember exactly what the minister had said. 'He said he'd been thinking about Ulla and then looked up and saw me, and I could see he was startled. So Ulla's spirit must be there still.'

'This is child's stuff, Ellen! You've let your imagination run on –'

'But everything happened to Ulla out on that headland. You know that. Her lover died there, her child was born there, and she herself might be buried there. It had all settled, but you disturbed it again.'

He was staring at her in a strangely intent way, and she felt that at last she had his attention. 'How extraordinary,' he said. 'What are you suggesting?'

She wasn't sure. He cocked his head on one side and waited, and then: 'Are you suggesting that things which happened there have somehow left their mark on the place, seeped into the soil, so to speak? And we've released them, like a gas?' She shrugged, not quite understanding him. 'What an extraordinary idea! I wonder what Oliver – Mr Drummond – would have to say to that! I must ask him. You know, I went to a lecture once – but never mind. Is it a question for the church, or for a psychic, I wonder?' He seemed to have forgotten her. 'It's not what the church would have us believe, of course, like so much,' then he met her eyes through the mirror and smiled. 'But you mustn't be fearful, you know, Ellen. Whatever happened there, it was hundreds of years ago, and it can't hurt you.'

Her fears diminished with his smile. His complexion had caught the sun since he had been working outdoors, and the laughter lines seemed more pronounced, ageing him a little perhaps but making him more handsome than ever. 'But time passing doesn't change what happened there.'

He came away from the dressing table and sat on the side of the bed. 'No – but supposing that the past *can* seep into the soil like you say, I wonder – does its presence decay over time like flesh on bones?' He paused. 'Or is it as timeless and eternal as the soul, and so beyond mortality?'

'I don't know,' she said, wishing that she was not so ignorant and could understand him better.

'Years, after all, are only numbers. Time is a continuum, but is it linear or coiled in cycles? This lecture I went to . . .' He had lost her again, but she liked to listen to him when he talked like this, spinning ideas in her head like the flat pebbles he used to skim over the water when they were children, and when life was sweet and simple.

→→ *Odrhan* ←←

Little by little his prayers were answered and Ulla began to speak to him. Harald had been her first love, she told him, but had been forced to relinquish her to his older brother, who took her as wife. But Erik was impotent, she had discovered, and beat her as if the fault was hers. Her life was made unbearable, so she and Harald had conspired together to leave. 'He had always loved me, and he was a good man.'

From fury Odrhan's feelings had swung to remorse and then to pity, and from there to an emotion he did not recognise.

At first he had slept outside the cell, rolling himself in hides. It mattered not where he rested because the anguish of guilt robbed him of sleep. But as the weather worsened she insisted that he sleep indoors, though he stayed close to the entrance as if modesty was served thereby.

She still visited Harald's grave, and would take long walks along the shore, returning at sunset as he grew anxious. Once he had gone looking for her and came upon her swimming, and he had stood and watched her lithe form, his pulse racing, ashamed but unable to move.

And, as summer faded and autumn storms battered the walls of Odrhan's cell, the warmth of the fire drew him further in, and Ulla smiled at him more.

⤞ Ellen ⤝

Next morning, as Ellen cleared the ash from last night's fire in the library, her mind turned again to what Mr Alick had said, and to the troubling idea of the past seeping into the soil. *Was* that what she had meant? She wasn't sure, but the image of a gas released into the air was troubling. She went over to the painted window and saw how the low sun, filtering through the moving branches outside, seemed to shift the folds of Ulla's gown and lift her hair, while counterfeit swells rose beneath the painted ocean. Could the past really live on?

She was so engrossed in the thought that she failed to hear the library door open, and then quietly close. 'Run to earth at last,' a voice said, and she spun round.

Mungo. He was leaning against the door, his hands deep in his pockets, surveying her alarm with amusement. 'You've been very adroit at avoiding me, m'dear.'

Trapped.

'The fire,' she said, gesturing wildly towards it. 'I'm here to light the fire.'

His eyebrows rose to mock her. 'Oh, sweet Ellen, that's already done –'

'No,' she said, and panic lit tiny sparks behind her eyes. 'But I'll do it now.'

The smile he gave her was a dreadful parody of his brother's, and fear set her heart thumping. She went quickly to the fire and took the matches from behind the clock. Her hand shook as she struck one, knowing that he was watching her; it went out, and the second did the same.

Mungo held his position by the door, barring her escape. 'Allow me to assist,' he said as she let a third match fall.

Lazily he heaved himself off the door.

'No!' she said, fumbling frantically with the matchbox, striking another, which she dropped with a cry as the flame licked up at her fingers.

'Poor finger,' he said, coming towards her and taking her hand. She tried to pull away, but he lifted her scorched finger to his lips, and next moment it was inside his mouth, hot and wet.

'Let me go!' she said, trying to pull away.

He held it tight. 'But you've not lit the fire.'

'You do it.' She threw the matchbox at his face. He released her hand to catch it while his other arm encircled her waist.

'Be nice, Ellen!' he said, and pulled her towards him, sealing her mouth with his.

She could not breathe. Tobacco, hard lips, and his tongue, like that other time. Every sense revolted, but instinct told her not to struggle, and she went limp and heavy in his arms, feeling his muscles tauten to support her. She let her head loll away from him. 'Ellen?' Then, 'Oh, for Christ's sake!' He began to lower her onto the settle beside the fire, and as he did she twisted in his arms, as lithe as a seal leaving the rocks, and ducked under his arm. As she did her elbow caught the side of his nose and she saw blood spurt as she fled, and she heard him swear as she slipped through the door. She sped across the hall, looking neither right nor left, making for the door leading into the servants' passage, and so failed to notice Alick Sturrock on the stairs. He looked after her in astonishment. 'Ellen?'

But she did not hear him, so she did not stop.

⇒ *Oliver* ⇐

Oliver sat at his desk, tapping the end of his pen against his teeth, and stared out of the window, suffering the anguish of remorse; if only time could somehow be rewound. And the suggestion had been his! He groaned out loud. Several of his congregation had stopped him in recent days and expressed their disapproval of the work at the headland. Others shook their heads, warning him of the risks of disturbing what ought not to be disturbed, or made oblique comments about how uncommonly harsh the weather was, how wild the seas, glancing up at him from under lowered brows. He had gone from amusement to irritation with such ignorance and then arrived at the guilty recognition that he should have considered more fully the sensibilities of his largely uneducated and superstitious flock. But by then the damage had been done.

The best way to put the matter right, he had decided, was to address it directly in next Sunday's sermon. He would take the opportunity to explain to them something about the early Irish monks who had brought the teachings of God to Scotland's rocky coast, while gently scolding them for their un-Christian belief in malevolent spirits, and so allay their fears. But, he thought as he ran his fingers through his hair, the task of combining a history lesson with a rebuttal of mysticism was proving difficult.

A sound outside the door interrupted his deliberations and he looked up, recognising the cheerful tones of Alick Sturrock. 'I'll show myself in, Mrs Nichol, no need for ceremony.'

Oliver rose as the door opened. 'Alick! The very man. Come in, and help me.'

Alick strode in, tossing his hat onto a side table. 'Of course. With what?'

'My sermon.'

He grimaced. 'Ah. Then I am very much *not* your man – '

'Mrs Nichol, some tea, please, if you would be so good.' He gestured to a seat by the fire. 'Tell me, Alick, has anyone expressed concerns to you about our work on the headland?'

His visitor dropped into a chair beside the sluggish fire. ''Fraid so, and Mama told me people have approached her too.' He paused. 'And Ellen spoke to me again. Said we should put the stones back.'

'She waylaid me too and said the same' – Oliver settled into the other chair – 'and told me that people were talking. I thought I'd try to reassure the congregation in this Sunday's sermon and explain – '

'What will you say?'

'That a belief in malevolent spirits is at odds with Christian teaching.'

Alick gave him a quizzical look. 'What about Lucifer and his henchmen?'

'That's quite another thing.'

'Is it?'

Mrs Nichol tapped on the door and entered bearing a tray of tea and scones, and Alick leapt to his feet to clear a space on a side table. 'Scones too. How splendid!' The old housekeeper beamed a smile and withdrew.

Alick's gaze followed her departure. 'Do you have anyone else in service here, besides Mrs Nichol?'

'No –'

'She's looking much older these days.'

Oliver laughed. 'Is she? Well, I don't take much seeing to, you know.' He rose to pour the tea.

Alick took a cup from him, and Oliver saw him surveying the bleak room, noting the patch of damp under the window and the threadbare rug on the painted wooden floor. 'Perhaps not – but even so.'

Oliver smiled. 'My wants are simple and easily satisfied. Now, to return to Lucifer, he is—'

'You should have someone else,' Alick interrupted, speaking quickly. 'Besides Mrs Nichol, I mean. Someone younger, to help her. Ellen Mackay would be ideal, you know, she's a quiet, pleasant girl, and Mama could spare her.' Oliver paused, his teacup half raised. 'She'd be close to her mother's cottage then, and could pop in now and then and keep an eye on her.'

'Is there concern about Mrs Mackay?' Oliver felt a pang at the thought of neglected duties, but his guest was avoiding his eyes.

'The poor woman grows frail, I believe.'

Oliver contemplated him, saying nothing. This sudden concern seemed forced, rehearsed even. 'My dear fellow, I neither need nor can support another servant.'

'I can persuade Mama to cover the cost, I know I can.' There was a determined set to Alick's jaw, and Oliver realised that this was the real reason for his visit; he could imagine what lay behind it, although a direct reference seemed inappropriate.

'Have you spoken to Ellen about this?' he asked, probing a little.

'Lord, no. Not until I'd sounded you out . . .' Alick seemed suddenly to warm to his theme '. . . and it strikes me we ought to make you more comfortable here. Some more help, some work on the house – you've some rot in that windowsill, I see – and there must be some surplus furniture in the big house which would make this place more homely. Ellen is very nice in her ways, you know, and would bring a woman's touch. And she'd still go home in the evenings, of course, to sleep,' he added, 'and care for her mother. It's barely a stone's throw away, and if she doesn't go out onto the headland in the evenings –' He stopped, then continued on a divergent tack: 'There are plenty who could fill her role at the house if we find ourselves short. Give it a try, why don't you?'

So Ellen's safety had become a concern, had it? Mungo must be making a more serious nuisance of himself. *Mr Alick wouldn't let anything happen to me,* Ellen had said, and it seemed that she was right.

'I will consider it,' Oliver said, in a neutral tone. Whatever else was at stake, Ellen must be protected. 'If Lady Sturrock agrees.'

'She will. And now, tell me more about this sermon of yours.'

———•———

Oliver remained beside the fire for some time after Alick had left, not troubling to repair it as it burned low. Then he lifted his head and looked about him, seeing the room as Alick must have seen it, stark and cheerless. For himself, he barely noticed. Once, perhaps, the old manse had had pretensions of graciousness, though on a scale befitting its purpose and just sufficient to reflect prestige back to its patrons at Sturrock House while remaining well short of rivalling them. But that had been before the Free Church had lured away most of the congregation, rendering the manse something of an anachronism.

And its occupant largely irrelevant.

He knew perfectly well that he owed his position here to Lady Sturrock's connections, a thinly disguised patronage of the type which had lain at the root of the Disruption that had split the church a generation ago. But such matters now raised indifference rather than ire amongst the community, the larger part of which simply slipped past St Oran's Church on their way to the overflowing Free Church built by the labours of their fathers over on the next bay. His own congregation, outside the family and servants, numbered barely a score.

He rose and went to stand at the window, looking out towards St Oran's. Had the church really come to the end of its purpose after so many centuries? He felt his failure to woo back the errant congregation very personally. Since his arrival they had tolerated but largely ignored him, until the ill-judged excavations had attracted their censure, and caused widespread offence. And now Alick was offering to press for improvements to be made to the manse! Oliver recognised that this was sparked to mask a need to provide protection for Ellen, rather than by real concern for his personal comfort, and of course he was perfectly ready to provide the necessary sanctuary. What Alick had failed to consider, however, was how this arrangement, combined with improvements at the manse, might raise eyebrows and invite comment. His congregation already saw him as an adjunct of Sturrock House, partisan to the estate's interests, and detached from the realities of their lives and woes.

He turned back to his desk and looked moodily at the notes he had been assembling for the sermon, and felt his earlier enthusiasm for the theme evaporating. Alick had been amused at the thought of him discoursing on the early Irish fathers and their missionary role. 'But it will make the point that Christianity was brought by wise and devoted men like Odrhan,' Oliver had insisted. 'A man who was prepared to tend the wounds of his enemy and convert a fallen woman, and who died protecting a child of pagan parentage – '

'It'll be that pagan element they worry about,' Alick had said, with a smile.

'What do you mean?'

'Us stirring it up.'

'What nonsense!'

'Is it? Ellen said *you* mistook her for Ulla's ghost.'

Alick's smile was suddenly too much like his brother's, and Oliver felt his face flush with annoyance. 'She simply startled me. I was absorbed in my drawing. But there must be *some* way of convincing people that their concerns are not only groundless but wrong-headed.'

When Alick spoke again, the mockery had gone, and Oliver received a troubling insight into the workings of his friend's mind. 'The problem is, of course, that you're seeking to replace one mythology with another. You tell them not to believe in spirits, and yet you require them to believe unquestioningly in the *Holy* Spirit. You reassure them that there are no malevolent spirits, but the church teaches them to fear Satan. It's not that they are ignorant people, my friend, but rather that they will see the inconsistencies.'

Oliver had been more deeply shocked than he showed. 'Christian teaching cannot be compared with folklore and mythology!'

'At one level, both are stories, are they not?'

Oliver shook his head as he reran their conversation, and began gathering his papers into a heap, angry enough to burn the lot and recourse to some fiery sermon written by a firebrand predecessor, promising everlasting damnation to disbelievers, but something stayed his hand. Alick, it appeared, was questioning not simply his choice of career but, more fundamentally, his own faith, rejecting Christian teaching along with a study of the law, and his parents' wishes. If so, then Oliver's duty was plain. He had listened sympathetically to Alick's woes regarding his studies, but a loss of faith required a sterner approach – and Alick, he was fast learning, was prepared to argue such matters.

He slumped back into the chair, weary suddenly and filled again with self-doubt, not for the first time questioning his own calling. Was he any more suited for the ministry than Alick was for the law? Or was this malaise simply from being here at Ulla-ness, undermined and in a false position, little more than a lapdog to Lady Sturrock? What good was he doing here? Not only was his brand of Christianity rejected by the common people, he now had to confront superstition from his flock and atheism from his patron's son!

How much worse could things get?

Chapter 19

They returned to the papers in the dining room, but the mood had lightened.

'What we need now, Libby Snow,' Rodri said with a slow smile, 'is to find an account of the theft, and then I can have you arrested for harbouring stolen goods.' He pulled another box file towards him. 'A new incentive.'

'It's Nan you'll have to go for,' she replied, responding to the smile. 'Are you prepared to persecute an old lady?'

'To the bitter end.'

But they found little else of interest. Concerns over household expenditures, final demands from tradesmen, a poacher sent to Inveraray gaol, a vacancy at the manse, repairs needed to the gutter. 'Some things never change,' Rodri muttered. 'I wonder if Angus might know something – better still, his mother, Jennet. She's maybe our best bet, sharp as a pin, and as old as the hills.' Then he glanced at the clock. 'You coming with me to collect the lads? We can talk as we go.'

He drove fast as before, and the Land Rover bounced over the uneven ground. 'Did Ellen have other children?' he asked, as they sped along. She felt relaxed now, and it was good to be able to discuss Ellen with him, to get another perspective.

'No. Just the one son, and he went to the bad. A handsome tearaway, my grandmother said.'

'Probably a Sturrock then. Keep going.'

196

'He disappeared when Nan was just five, so she never knew him. Her mother took to the bottle after he left and fell over the harbour wall one night.' And Libby thought again of the wooden house overlooking the bay where small boats rode at anchor, their high prows lifting on the waves, weighed down by the outboard motors on their stern boards, and by loss. 'So my grandmother went to live with her grandparents, but by then Ellen was like a wraith, she said, thin and fragile, and in a world of her own.' She remembered Nan's words: *'She'd drift around the house in a vague sort of way and whenever the weather was fit she'd take her shawl and set off to the point and stand there staring out to sea. Folks said my father had grown up wild, with his drinking and his women, because he was starved of her love, but she might have been made of crystal, the way my grandfather handled her—'*

'Come back from wherever you've gone.' Rodri's voice returned her to the moment. 'You said that Ellen used to live in one of the old cottages, and worked at the manse. Your grandmother told you this?'

'Yes.'

'Then we should be able to track her down. Jennet might know, or there might be something in those papers about who lived in the cottages and paid rent.' He drove fast, every bend and twist as familiar as the lines on the palm of his hand. The sheep seemed to anticipate him, leaping aside as the Land Rover rounded hairpin bends, and he raised a hand to vehicles which pulled into passing places as they approached. 'But I still don't understand why you didn't tell me about the connection,' he said as they hurtled over the potholes. 'You could have stayed quiet about the cross.'

Why had she not? So much had happened since their first encounter that she was no longer sure. 'I needed to get a feel of the place, and the Sturrock estate had not been welcoming.'

He glanced across at her. 'No?'

'No.' They drove on in silence.

'Better now, though?' Again that sidelong look.

'It's improving. But then we found the body.'

'And you remembered what your grandmother had told you.'

'And worried about what else we might discover.'

'So did I.'

She looked at him. 'Meaning?'

'I thought you'd find treasure, and then Laila would flog it, and it would be gone.'

This man was full of contradictions. 'Was that why you didn't want us coming to dig?'

'Partly, yes, and Hector took some persuading.'

'Still smarting over the chalice, I suppose.'

'That and a natural indolence. I actually think it was Laila who decided the matter – seeing potential cash.'

They drove on in silence until they came out from under the shadow of the trees at the head of the estuary and turned onto the small road leading to the cottages where Angus and the women lived. And as they followed the line of the shore, she saw two figures down at the shoreline throwing stones at a floating branch.

Then a third appeared from behind a boulder and joined in.

Rodri stopped the Land Rover, and lowered the window and sat a moment, looking at them. 'That's what really matters, you know, those lads, and giving them the best chance. And holding things together here, if I can.' He watched them a little longer, then put two fingers to his lips and let out a piercing whistle.

Three heads jerked round, and the boys abandoned their sport and came tearing towards them, leaping over mooring ropes and fish crates to arrive panting at the side of the Land Rover, eyes asparkle.

'We're having a cook-up.'

'Alice tried to ring but you'd already left.'

'We can stay, can't we?'

'Libby too.' This from David, with a shy smile.

'And can we take the kayaks out?'

'Beyond the bay . . .'

Rodri put up a hand and the babble ceased. 'Yes to the cook-up. Yes to Libby too. Yes to the kayaks. Usual rules apply. No to beyond the bay.'

'But if *you're* here?'

'And Angus is on his boat – '

'Although he's stripping down the engine just now,' David added.

'Thank you, David. The voice of reason. Usual rules apply or it's no to the kayaks. Got it? Now, shift yourselves so I can go and park.'

The boys turned and pelted back down the beach towards the kayaks, satisfied with the deal, and Rodri started the Land Rover again, driving off to park beside the caravan that had been promised for the dig. 'You OK with that?' he asked as he pulled on the handbrake. 'Cook-up means sausages cooked on the beach, Angus in charge.'

'And the usual rules?' Rodri was holding things together pretty well, it seemed to her, and the boys were robust and lively. Grounded and secure.

'That's for the kayaks. Life jackets at all times and not beyond the mouth of the estuary without an adult. One day I'll have to weaken, but not yet. David could manage it, and maybe Donald. But not Charlie.'

Alice came out of the cottage as they left the Land Rover. 'I just tried to phone you,' she said.

'I heard.'

'And you'll stay?' He nodded. 'Lady Macbeth gone?'

'Aye. Now what?' David was running back towards them with the air of an emissary.

'Why don't *you* come out with us, then we *could* go beyond the rocks.'

'Great idea,' said Alice. 'Go stress-busting, Rodri.'

Beyond the rocks a flock of terns was diving, flashes of white against an indigo blue. The sea was calm, and Libby could see that he was tempted. 'Don't stay because of me,' she said, 'I'll just sit here.' And drink in the loveliness of it all.

'Off you go, man! How often do time and weather allow?' Alice gave him a push, and David, encouraged, grabbed his arm and pulled. A cheer went up from the watchers on the beach, and then there was a mad scramble for life jackets and paddles, and four kayaks were lifted down to the water's edge.

Alice stood beside Libby and watched them pull away from the shore. 'Do him good,' she said. 'Tea?' When was Alice without it? Libby thought, and followed her into the cottage.

The room they entered was not large but was as neat as a pin. No clutter, the walls painted in pastel shades and hung with watercolour paintings, all seemingly by a single hand. Libby recognised the bay and the old jetty, but there were also places she didn't know. The paintings were skilful and executed with an eye for the soft colours of dawn and the drama of evening. Alice or Maddy? she wondered, but somehow she knew it was Maddy.

'So when did her ladyship leave?' Alice said.

'This morning.'

Alice gave a satisfied nod. 'Good. It usually takes Rodri a day or two to recover, so the kayaking should help.' There were questions Libby badly wanted to ask. 'Maddy's out, but she'll be back soon,' she called from the kitchen. 'She's gone to see her grandma.'

Angus's mother? Their best bet.

Alice reappeared with two mugs a moment later, passed one to Libby, and picked up a pair of knitting needles. A colourful garment in a complex cable pattern was in progress, and Libby complimented her on it. 'And are the paintings yours too?' she asked, gesturing at the walls.

Alice shook her head, counting stitches under her breath. 'Maddy's.'

'They're very good.'

'Aye. She's brilliant.' She lowered the knitting to take a sip of tea. 'What did Laila want, do you know?'

'Something about a painting.'

'Oh, aye. Which one?'

'A landscape in the library.' Should she be telling Alice this?

'The Nasmyth? And did she take it?'

'No.'

She began knitting again. 'So where did Rodri hide it?'

Libby laughed at the casual question. 'Has this happened before?'

'Oh, aye, it's cat-and-mouse every time. But usually we have some warning that she's coming and can put things away. Hiring a car and coming out of the blue is a new one. Must be getting desperate.' She switched needles and carried on. 'As long as he didn't stick it in the freezer, that's fine. I found a silver snuff box there once, and a pair of candlesticks. She's got a habit of grazing on small items, has Laila, but if she's moved on to paintings we're in trouble.'

Libby looked at the petite figure opposite her, knitting busily away. *We're a good team*, Alice had said, that first day. Then curiosity got the better of her. 'But strictly speaking, aren't the things hers?'

'Rodri takes the view that they're Hector's, and unless he hears from Hector himself nothing leaves the house, but milady has a

handbag like the Tardis and Rodri hears less and less from Hector. Except through the bank, of course, demanding more money.'
Alice lowered her knitting again, her face sharp now and fierce. 'So
we knit and we paint and we make butter and we wrack our brains
to think how on earth we'll survive when Hector decides to come
back and live here. We've got roofs over our heads, at least, because
Rodri made Hector give Angus and Maddy tenancy of these cottages for life, rent-free, when Maddy came back with David. But
we do need an income.'

The questions were multiplying, and increasingly Libby needed
to understand. 'Came back from where?'

Alice looked up. 'He has told you, hasn't he?'

'I'm not sure –'

'David's Hector's son. Can't you tell, the boys all look so alike?'

So that was it. 'I'd noticed, yes, but I . . .' She stopped.

Alice continued knitting and chuckled. '. . . drew the wrong
conclusion? No, no – not Rodri's. Though Rodri's a father to all
three lads, and makes no difference between them. He'd do anything for those boys, David included.'

'Does Hector never see him?'

'No. The Ice Queen can't deal with it, having none of her own,
and Hector's a weak man.'

'Poor David.'

'Poor Hector, more like, it's him that's missing out. David's
doing fine. Between them Angus and Rodri make sure he's not
over-mothered, but David's his own man these days. He's grand.'

It was beginning to come together, this odd ménage. 'Rodri
told me he'd move into the old manse if Hector comes back to
live, and run the business from there.'

The needles clicked away. 'Aye, and that'll not be easy.'

'If the brothers don't get on, wouldn't he be better moving
away?'

'Rodri leave Ullaness?' She shook her head vigorously. 'He'll not do that again. Disaster from start to finish last time, apart from having the boys.' Alice seemed to sense the next question and spared her the need to ask. 'He left in a fury and married the first woman he met, stupid man. She was killed in a car accident, years ago, but it was ages before he told us she'd been with another man that night, both stoned out of their minds when they drove into a wall. She was as bad a deal for him as Laila.' Laila? What did she mean? 'Twice bitten was Rodri, but the lads are brilliant, a real credit to him. So he came back, and now his whole world is here, everything he cares about.' She switched needles and the clicking continued. 'No, it'll be Hector who suffers if he decides to return, he knows perfectly well he's not wanted.' Alice's voice had hardened again. 'And he'd have to face Maddy, and David. And Angus,' she paused, 'as well as Rodri. He simply hasn't the guts. Have you ever read *The Master of Ballantrae*?'

'No.' Libby was lost again.

'Durisdeer all over. Two brothers in love with the same woman. The older leaves the estate in his brother's care and then bleeds it dry. Except in Hector's case, he took the woman when he went. It's a great read. Try it.' Alice gave her a slanting look, taking in her stunned look. 'He hasn't told you that either, has he?'

'I don't think he can have.'

'No, I suppose maybe he wouldn't. Laila came here as Rodri's girlfriend' – Alice watched for her reaction – 'then dumped him for Hector. She was a stunner by all accounts and Hector's a self-centred soul with his brains in his balls, so he let Laila squeeze Maddy out, egged on by his stuck-up mama, and not a thought for Rodri, and they got engaged. Maddy's got her pride and didn't tell Hector she was pregnant and went to Glasgow, where we met. When Rodri came back and found out he took himself off and married his bimbo, the fool. It was a right old mess. Apart from the me and Maddy bit, of course.' There was the sound of a car pulling up outside, and Alice looked up. 'Speak of angels,' she said, and got to her feet.

Maddy came through the door and smiled at Libby. 'Hello! You're still here, how lovely!' And she gave Alice a quick hug and a kiss, and the last piece fell swiftly into place.

'How was Jennet?' Alice asked.

'Good. I said I'd bring her over for supper soon.' She nodded towards the window. 'I see the kayaks are out.'

'Aye, Rodri's with them.'

'It'll do him good.'

'And we're having a cook-up, so I've thawed some sausages and put jacket potatoes in the oven. What else should we have? Excuse us a minute, Libby.' So for Maddy, at least, whatever had been damaged by Hector had been healed by Alice.

A few minutes later she heard a shout and a burst of laughter as a kicked-off welly flew past the window. 'You break that window, my lad,' came Rodri's voice, 'and I'll hand you to Angus for a thrashing.' And then the room was full of life and chatter, and Rodri looked across the boys' heads at her and smiled.

———

Half an hour later they all trooped down to the pebble beach laden with food and drink. Just a little way above the strand line Libby saw a simple round hearth with fire-blackened stones, encircled by boulders worn smooth by countless tides. A jumble of pebbles, shells, and coloured fishing floats brought by ocean currents lay spread amongst the seaweed like pieces in some abandoned game.

Angus called out to the boys, who were down on the beach collecting driftwood, and they came running, arms full. The fire was already lit. 'How long are you staying?' Alice asked her as they stepped over the rocks, avoiding the slippery seaweed as they transported trays of provisions down the beach.

'Until tomorrow. Back to work on Monday.'

'But you'll be coming in the summer still? For the dig?'

To dig what? she wondered. 'I'm not sure.'

'She will be,' said Rodri as he passed them, his arms full of bottles. 'We sorted, then? Who's cooking?'

'Why does food cooked outdoors always taste so good?' Libby remarked, wiping her fingers on a patch of turf. It had been a riotous meal, with Rodri and Alice sparring with each other and teasing the boys, who gave back as good as they got, and Angus chuckling while Maddy tended to the food and laughed at them all. But the boys were now back down by the shoreline skimming stones across the still waters of the bay, leaving the adults around the fire, their faces aglow. Not quite the conventional family, Libby thought as she surveyed them, but it was working very well, and she felt its strength. The three boys had Alice and Maddy, a quixotic father/uncle, and a shared grandfather. Better than many kids these days. A good team.

'The spice of adventure,' said Rodri. He looked relaxed now, that drawn expression softened in the evening light; the foray out on the ocean had done him good.

'And you're starving by the time it's cooked.' Alice reached for a bottle of beer.

Rodri laughed. 'That too,' and then he turned to Maddy. 'You visited Jennet today, Angus said. Is she up for visitors?'

'Aye, she'd like that.'

'Good. I thought I'd take Libby to see her first thing tomorrow. We've got some questions and I'm hoping her memory is long enough.'

Angus had settled into what looked like his regular seat amongst the rocks, his back resting against a smooth boulder, and he was nursing a beer. 'Long enough for what?'

'Old scandals, past transgressions. Gossip, rumour. Jennet's forte. We were looking through some old papers and found one which suggests that a Sturrock man ran off with a local woman sometime in the 1890s, then disappeared, and we wondered if there might be a tie-up with the body in the mound.'

'Tell Jennet about the body and everyone will know by lunch-time,' said Alice.

'I wasn't planning to.'

Angus was looking back at Rodri. 'Old tragedies, then,' he said.

Rodri paused, then flipped the top off a beer bottle and looked up. 'Aye. Do you know something?'

Angus shook his head. 'No, I don't. But it was a tragedy if it ended with a man's death, whatever else it was. The only scandal I remember was about a minister who disappeared, but they said he'd been thieving and went off with a woman. The manse hasn't been occupied since. But you knew that!'

'Did I? Then I'd forgotten.'

'Do you know when that was?' asked Libby.

Angus shrugged. 'Not really. But old folk still spoke of it when I was a lad. Gossip like that has an energy of its own, and it takes its time in fading.'

Or becomes the stuff of legends.

'Will Jennet know about it?' Rodri asked.

'She'll know the same gossip,' said Angus, 'and maybe some more details, but I doubt she'll know a date. What else did the letter say?'

Rodri told her, making no reference to Libby's connection, though he looked across the fire at her as he spoke, and she saw that he was leaving the matter to her. Somewhere along the line she had started reading his thoughts too . . . And she watched the circle of faces, shadowed now by the fading light, a small but tight-knit family making a success of lives fractured by others. And so she told them, not about the cross, but about her grandmother and Gosse Harbour and the stories she'd been told. Alice sat forward, eyes bright, and even Angus looked interested.

'So it was meant!' said Alice with an air of satisfaction when she had finished. 'I knew, right from the start, that – '

'Oh Lord.' Rodri groaned and got to his feet. He picked up a piece of driftwood and began poking the fire. 'We'll not hear the end of it now. She's convinced that everything is "meant," what-ever "meant" means. There's a wacky side to our Alice.'

'Aye, maybe.' Alice continued undaunted: 'But some things in this life *are* meant to be. Like me and Maddy. It was no accident that Libby came here and that it was she who found the body. Remember how white she went? She's a sensitive.'

'I'm not sure that I am!' Libby said, but there was something very endearing about Alice.

'If Alice says you are, then you are, so get used to it,' said Rodri, and he gave her his slanting smile. 'They used to burn her sort at the stake, you know.' He stretched out on the beach again, leaning back on his elbow. 'And old ways are good ways.' Angus chuckled, and Maddy put an affectionate arm around Alice and gave her a squeeze.

But she was unstoppable. 'I read a book once which—'

'Don't read, Alice,' said Rodri. 'Just make butter. Lots of but-ter. And shortbread. And knit.'

Alice lobbed a pebble at him. 'You'd do well to listen, Rodri Sturrock, and seize your chance.'

'Shut up, Alice.'

Libby felt her cheeks grow warm.

'Nonsense aside,' said Angus, staying on topic, 'this business gets complicated. We've a body and no local tale of a man missing, which is strange in itself. And now we've a missing Sturrock man who went to Canada, and from what Libby tells us, he took a woman from here with him.'

'Except that Lady Sturrock's envoy didn't find them,' said Alice.

Angus shook his head. 'But they were there nonetheless, if their descendants are.'

He was right, of course. But Libby's grandmother had said nothing about a man coming with Ellen.

'Perhaps the Sturrock man left her, came back, and was murdered,' Maddy suggested.

'Or perhaps,' Angus continued, 'they heard someone was asking questions and hid, not wanting to be found.'

'Well, you wouldn't, would you? If you'd killed a man.' A chill silence followed Alice's words.

It was what Libby hadn't wanted to admit could possibly be true. And she wondered if she would have to tell her grandmother this, or if she could let it lie.

'Maybe not.' Rodri looked across at her. 'And yet, as Angus said, there's no record here of a man being killed, or his murderer being looked for, just of a mother searching for her son.'

The silence resumed; then Alice sat up. 'I've just had a thought. If Libby's descended from some Sturrock man, then she's kin and maybe it's Libby who ought to be living in Sturrock House, not Hector at all. So you can be *her* agent, Rodri, and you'd not chuck him out, would you, Libby?'

The tension broke with laughter, but Libby was glad of the darkness. 'That might depend – '

Rodri got to his feet. 'On what, I wonder?' he said, looking down at her. 'And I'll tell you straight, Liberty Snow, only the male line inherits.'

'Time *that* was changed,' muttered Alice, but her words were drowned out by Rodri's ear-splitting whistle as he summoned his offspring back from the shore.

———•———

As they drove home to Sturrock House, the two boys plugged into earphones, Libby turned to Rodri. 'About the summer –'

'Yes?'

'There's hardly anything left of the mound now, so I'm not sure that we'll be back.' It pained her to say so, but it was true. Unless –

He glanced across at her, then back to the road. 'You've still got the building recording in the church.'

'Yes, but that won't take long.'

'And you spoke of doing a general survey, with little trial pits.'

'You said no to that.'

He kept his face forward. 'And wasn't there something about shell middens, and putting the site in a wider context?'

'The estate said it would sanction no other work.'

The corner of his mouth twitched. 'My instructions were to do what I thought best,' he said as they took a hairpin bend at speed.

'In that case, the ruin on the headland would bear further investigation, don't you think?'

'An excellent idea.'

And again, that smile. Just a smile, but it was enough, and Libby settled back into her seat.

Chapter 20

Ellen was pleased with her new situation. Life at Sturrock House had become a game of hide-and-seek, and she had sensed a careless determination in Mungo when he had cornered her in the library. As long as he had nothing to occupy him, he would pursue her, of that she was certain. She was also in no doubt that it was Alick who had orchestrated the move to the manse, and her one regret about being here was that she would see less of him.

The painted scenes in the library which fuelled her daydreams would also be lost to her, though every detail was now etched in her mind, and she had glanced across at them as she listened to Lady Sturrock explaining about the changes. 'Mrs Nichol is plagued by rheumatism,' her ladyship had said, 'and will welcome some assistance. We must see that Mr Drummond is comfortable so that he can attend to his duties, and your mother will be close by so you can be easy on that score too.' Something in her ladyship's tone, and in the searching look that she gave Ellen, suggested that Alick had been forthright in giving his reasons for the move. Nothing was said, of course, so she had bobbed a curtsey and left.

Mrs Nichol had been surprised by her arrival, having had no warning of it, but welcomed her nevertheless, and they had sat at the kitchen table and discussed how best to divide duties between them. There was little heavy work but the old housekeeper confessed herself glad of some help with it, and matters were soon settled. One of Ellen's first tasks had been to prepare a tray of tea for her new master, and she had laid it carefully, choosing a cup and saucer that was not chipped or cracked, and taken it through to him in the study. He had risen when she entered, as if she was a visitor rather than a servant, and greeted her kindly.

'I hope you'll be happy here, Ellen.' He too had given her a searching look. 'And you must feel free to go across to your mother's cottage whenever you wish.' She guessed that he knew the reason behind the move, and wondered why the thought brought on a feeling of shame. 'And I trust you'll be happy and here you will be safe,' he said, confirming the matter.

He had given her a gentle smile of understanding. He was a good man and she was grateful for the refuge.

It was a shock, therefore, when she went to answer a knock at the front door the following morning and opened it to find Mungo Sturrock standing there, his eyes mocking her. 'Good morning, fair Ellen. Is your master at home?'

Mr Drummond had just left, and too late she realised that Mungo must have known this. 'No, he isn't.'

She made as if to close the door, but he stepped forward, filling the doorway. 'It's customary in these circumstances, you know,' he said, forcing her to give ground, 'to invite a caller in to wait, and a well-trained housemaid would also offer some refreshment. Must you be schooled in your duties, Ellen?' He looked beyond her to where the housekeeper had appeared. 'Good day, Mrs Nichol, I understand the minister is out, but I'll await his return. Ellen was just offering me some tea.'

Mrs Nichol, oblivious to the tensions, nodded vigorously. 'Of course, though I'm not sure how long he'll be, sir.'

'I've all the time in the world. Run along now, Ellen, I'll find my own way.'

Ellen returned to the kitchen, tight-lipped and angry, and

began assembling tea things on a tray. A cracked cup would do for him. Surely here, though, of all places, he would offer her no assault. 'Not that cup!' Mrs Nichol protested, flustered by Mungo's unprecedented appearance. 'And no scones made.' She bustled about, finding a starched linen tray cloth in a drawer. 'Whatever can Mr Mungo want with the minister, I wonder?' Ellen remained silent and rolled up her sleeves ready to begin cleaning, hoping to avoid taking the tray through, but this was not to be. 'Make yourself tidy, my dear. I will hold the door.'

When Ellen entered the room, Mungo Sturrock was coolly examining the papers on Mr Drummond's desk, but he left them and came over to the fire as she set the tray down on the side table. She straightened to find him once again blocking her route to the door. 'Tell me, Ellen, does your new position please you?'

'It does, sir. Excuse—'

'Mr Drummond decided he needs two servants to look after him, did he?' He let the remark hang there. 'What a finicky fellow he must be. Although I believe my brother was the one who espied the need.' She made another attempt to get round him but he side-stepped her, keeping his distance but not letting her past. 'Very considerate, my brother, don't you think?'

'Your tea is there, sir, and if you'll excuse me – '

'In a moment. Tell me a little about your duties here. What is it the minister requires of you that the good Mrs Nichol cannot provide?'

From somewhere she found the strength to answer him. 'It pleases you to torment me, Mungo Sturrock, but people are wise to your ways and – '

'What ways are those?' He moved a step closer, filling the space between them, but still made no attempt to touch her, his eyes searching her face. 'Have you been carrying tales, fair Ellen, and blackening my good name?'

'You've no good name! No one has forgotten Maria.'

'I have.'

'Let me pass.'

'You've not poured my tea.'

'Pour it yourself, and may it choke you.'

At that he laughed. 'It's your spirit, Ellen, which makes the chase so delightful, even at the cost of a bloody nose.'

She pushed past him just as the door opened and Mr Drummond entered. From his alarmed expression, she saw that he had been told of his visitor. 'Thank you, Ellen. That'll be all,' he said, and held the door open for her to make good her escape.

⊷ *Oliver* ⊶

Mungo Sturrock returned to the fireside. 'Good day, Drummond. Ellen invited me in to await your return and has just brought me tea, though she's neglected to pour it. Why not ring for another cup and join me?' He dropped into the chair beside the fire and crossed his legs, entirely at his ease.

Oliver went over to the tray, filled the cup, and handed it to Mungo, but remained standing, fighting his outrage. He had glimpsed Mungo crossing the stream and it had occurred to him that he might be heading here, so he had swiftly returned. 'What can I do for you, sir?' he said.

'Two matters,' Mungo replied, then paused and looked pained. 'But I can hardly unburden myself with you standing over me like this. Pray, do sit down.' Oliver sat. 'That's better. Are you sure you won't ring for a cup?' Mungo looked very out of place in the stark room, large and brazen with self-confidence, and Oliver declined. 'Firstly, I'm sorry to have to report that there is upset amongst the tenants about the work you are doing out on the headland.' He looked gravely at Oliver, but there was mockery in his eyes. 'This worries me and I should be pleased to hear how you plan to resolve the situation.'

Oliver ground his teeth. 'We intend to bring the work there rapidly to a close.'

'You relieve my mind –'

'And the second matter?'

'More delicate still, I'm afraid.' Mungo Sturrock lifted his cup and sipped at the tea, looking at Oliver over the rim. 'It concerns my brother. May I speak in confidence?'

Oliver would have cheerfully knocked the cup from his hand, and his teeth with it. The man was the very devil. 'Go on,' he said.

'It is a serious business, minister, and one that gives me deep concern. I fear that Alick is beginning to question his Christian faith.' He paused, his eyes holding Oliver's in false communion. 'Mama will be devastated, you know, if I am proved correct –' He leaned forward in a parody of intimacy. 'Has he disclosed to you, Mr Drummond, that he's recently joined the Psychic Society?' He hadn't, and Oliver must have failed to hide his surprise as Mungo sat back again, satisfied with his reaction. 'I thought not. Worrying, isn't it? My parents, my mother in particular, would be most upset to learn of this, so I have brought my concerns to you. What ought we to do, Mr Drummond?'

Damn the man's insolence! And damn Alick's stupidity in telling him. But what could he say? 'I will consider the matter,' he replied.

Mungo said nothing for a moment, enjoying Oliver's discomfort. Then: 'You will forgive me saying, Mr Drummond, but as a minister, my brother's spiritual well-being is not only a concern for the family but is central to your duties. My worry is such—'

Oliver got to his feet, holding himself in check with difficulty. 'You choose to mock, sir. I know my duty, and you have previously made clear your views on my ministry. I am perfectly well aware of what really brings you here.' Mungo's eyebrows went up at that. 'You saw me leave this morning, I know you did, so your motive for calling was to pursue a course from which you had been diverted.'

Mungo sat back apparently well-pleased at having provoked a response. 'And what course would that be, minister?'

But Oliver had had enough and said, with as much dignity as he could muster: 'You have finished your tea, so you must excuse me. I have work to do. If you wish to speak to me again, I will arrange to meet you in the church.'

Mungo chose to look outraged. 'Am I to be denied the comfort of your ministry, Mr Drummond?'

'You do not seek it.'

'But what of my brother's immortal soul?'

'I've said all I intend to on that subject.'

'And so I am barred from the manse?'

'Yes.'

Mungo seemed to consider this a moment, then got to his feet. 'You'd do well to remember your position here, minister, and to whom you owe it.' He spoke mildly, but the pretence of affability slipped a little.

Oliver reached out and rang the bell. 'Mrs Nichol will show you out.'

Oliver found himself shaking as the door closed behind Mungo, and he went to sit behind his desk, spreading his palms on the surface to steady himself. The look on Mungo's face as he turned at the door suggested a foe undefeated, retreating only to regroup; and his mischief now had the added spice of resistance – Dear Lord, could the man find no better occupation! Perhaps Ellen would be safer away while Mungo was at home, but where would she go? And there was her mother to think of . . . But how on earth was he to convey the message to Mrs Nichol that the baronet's heir was not to be admitted? It must be done, though, for whatever else happened Ellen must be protected. He considered the matter a moment. The only sure way would be to issue a general embargo on visitors being admitted to the manse in his absence. But that would hardly do! How could he turn away his tiny flock should they come to him in need? It would be disastrous, compounding the view that the minister considered himself above his fellows. Damn Mungo Sturrock! And damn those wretched undertakings on the headland which had exposed him to censure, leaving him vulnerable. The sooner that he and Alick could draw matters to a close there, the better.

It was only later that he remembered the second of Mungo's spurious reasons for his visit, and found time to wonder what company Alick Sturrock had been keeping.

Next day he strode out from the manse to meet Alick at the headland, resolved to bring the work there to an end, and to finding a way of exploring where Alick's intellectual curiosity had led him. Somehow he must do this without divulging that Mungo had come to the manse, still pursuing Ellen, and spreading his poison. He sensed that telling Alick might inflame the situation.

He arrived to find that once again Alick was there before him, sleeves rolled up and at work. He looked up and hailed Oliver as he approached. 'I made a start,' he said. 'It is a floor, I'm certain, or whatever served as floor. Beaten earth really. Glorious day for it, eh?' And he continued heaving the last of the stones aside, apparently oblivious to anything other than the work in hand.

'We must finish here today,' Oliver said, straining as he helped Alick lift one of the larger stones. 'If it doesn't finish us first.'

Alick laughed. 'You do very well, Oliver,' he said, and they worked together in companionable silence for half an hour until they had cleared the rest of the interior and revealed a surface of compacted earth. Oliver straightened and wiped the sweat from his brow, conscious again, despite everything, of the satisfaction of physical activity.

They agreed to have a break and sat together on the rocks, looking out over a clear blue sea. Alick lit his pipe, offering it to Oliver, who declined it. 'It's fascinating, don't you think, all this interest in what we are doing here.'

Oliver looked at him in astonishment. Had the discord not registered with him at all? 'Fascinating, perhaps, but regrettable. We've upset people.'

'So I hear. But there was never any talk of the place being haunted until we started, you know. No phantasms at dusk, no weird lights glowing on the headland.'

'I should hope not.' But here was his opening. 'These things interest you, do they?' he asked. 'Phantasms and the like?'

If he had been expecting evasion, he was mistaken. 'They do! Very much. Fascinating stuff. And here on our very doorstep we have an ancient legend which we've never really given a thought to, and now, suddenly, there's widespread concern that we are disturbing something which has been biding its time in the ether, or lurking in the soil. The legend had just lain there, dormant, but apparently a part of everyone's deep psyche, and now it's suddenly alive again, and still with the power to stir up a fuss and move their emotions.'

'Rubbish,' Oliver replied, 'it's simply folklore that everyone's suddenly remembering,' but Alick's words disturbed him.

'And what is folklore?' Alick leaned back on his elbow and looked out to sea as if considering. 'Somewhere beyond gossip and memory, stretched over time. And with a kernel of truth embedded in the centre.'

'Perhaps. But that kernel is lost in the tangle of fantasy.'

Alick continued to stare out beyond the waves, his eyes unfocussed, then looked back at him with a twisted smile. 'And yet, minister, you ask us to believe in something very similar, do you not?'

'What do you mean?'

'Christianity.'

'That's quite different – '

'Is it? The church tells us a set of stories and asks us to believe in them, so why not other stories too? Does one preclude all others?'

'The teachings of—'

'Why not simply accept that there are things beyond this material world which we cannot understand?'

'But that surely is the basis of all Christian teaching,' Oliver replied, 'of Christian faith!'

Alick looked out to sea again and drew on his pipe. 'Ah yes. Faith – '

He had spoken in tones of deep scepticism and Oliver looked back at him, bewildered and concerned, uncertain how best to proceed. Mungo's anxiety for his brother's soul was counterfeit, but Oliver's duty was clear.

He tried for a lighter tone. 'Faith, the Bible tells us, is the substance of things hoped for, the evidence of things not seen. Hebrews 11:1 . . .' he began, but Alick continued his seaward gaze and Oliver faltered.

'The evidence of things not seen,' Alick echoed after a moment. 'Do you never question it yourself, Oliver?' he said, and looked back at him with an expression so open and honest that it was all Oliver could do not to admit to very real doubts, not only of his own faith but of his fitness for his current role. But that would never do! Alick looked away again, taking his silence for denial. 'Forgive me, of course you don't.'

His pipe had gone out and Alick took some time relighting it, and carried on speaking as he did. 'But bear with me a moment, if you will. I value your views, my friend, and who else is there in this benighted place with whom to discuss such matters? I joined the Psychic Society, you know, and it's eye-opening stuff. Really makes you think.' So Mungo was right about that too! 'A lot of it is clearly fraudulent, of course, but if you tell me a man's soul transcends death, why cannot I also believe that his spirit might linger on earth?'

'Are not the spirit and the soul one thing?'

'Do they have to be? And anyway, could not that same soul-spirit remain earth-bound by *choice*, or even by necessity? If earthly matters are unresolved.'

'Alick! This is child's stuff.' For an intelligent man, his friend could be extraordinarily naïve. 'There is no circumstance in which—'

'No, listen. Treat me like a child, if you like. Suppose a man did evil all his life and then as death approached he did a good deed and craved forgiveness – would his soul-spirit be admitted through the pearly gates?'

'God forgives those who repent –'

'Splendid! And supposing that he lived a fine and godly life and did one ghastly thing, then died before he could repent or put things right, what then? Eternal damnation?'

'We cannot know who will be saved and who cast out. Only God—'

'Exactly! We cannot know. And there you have it. There are things that are unknown – things not seen – and it is only by scientific enquiry that we begin to understand them. If things are ordered, as we believe them to be, and purposeful, then they must be observable. And many things that have been observed and reported have been dismissed as rot. Blind bigotry! Faith alone is not enough anymore, don't you see! We must be allowed to make enquiries into these things unseen, Oliver, even though it goes against the grain.' Oliver tried to interject, but there was no stopping the man. 'It wasn't so very long ago that we were burning alive those who challenged Christian teaching, but we've moved on from there, surely, and need to take stock and be allowed to question the things we've been told we must *not* question.' He made a large, expansive gesture, scattering tobacco and ash from his pipe. 'We must question everything! The people here are not credulous savages to be told what they must believe and what to discount; they hark back to an older wisdom. One we have lost –'

'I told you there was cause for worry, Drummond.'

Mungo Sturrock had come up silently behind them, and both men swung round at his voice.

'God, Mungo. You gave us a start,' said Alick, and then he frowned. 'What d'you mean?'

But Mungo ignored him and began examining the area they had cleared. 'I saw you out here, but I'd understood you were packing it in. That's what you said, wasn't it, Drummond? Still no gold or silver? Or have you secreted it all away somewhere?'

'Cause for worry about what?'

Mungo continued to ignore him and stood looking down at the surface of beaten earth. 'Unless it's buried beneath the floor, of course.'

Alick turned to Oliver, scowling. 'What's he been saying?'

Mungo shifted his attention back to them, his eyes mocking Oliver. 'But how tactless of me, minister! We spoke in confidence.'

Oliver looked from one brother to the other and opted for the truth. 'Your brother is concerned about your immortal soul, Alick, and the company you keep.' Mungo looked surprised, then amused at his directness. 'He paid a call to the manse yesterday, with the spurious excuse of wanting to see me, having assured himself first that I was out. He came to bait poor Ellen, of course, then proceeded to bait me –'

Alick was on his feet and had swung a punch, catching Mungo, and Oliver, quite unprepared. It connected with Mungo's jaw, and the man went down like a stone and landed on the pile of rocks they had just cleared, out cold, and Alick stood over him, breathing hard. Then he glanced across at Oliver. 'Why didn't you tell me this?'

'You ask me that now!' he retorted, and knelt beside Mungo's prone form, putting a hand on the man's heart; to his relief, he found a good strong beat. 'Help me lift him off these rocks.'

But Mungo roused as they tried to do so and shook them off. He sat forward, looking up at them and scowling, his fingers exploring the place where Alick's punch had landed, his eyes very dark. 'That, little brother, was a mistake.'

'You go near Ellen Mackay again, and so help me God . . . !'

'Why would God help you! You deny his authority, I heard you say so.' Mungo brushed aside Oliver's offer of assistance and got unsteadily to his feet, wiping a hand across a bloodied lip, and leaned on the ruin for a moment. 'So Ellen has a champion, has she? Two, perhaps.' His glance flickered towards Oliver. 'What a honey pot the girl has become. But which of us will have her first, I wonder?'

Alick went for him again, but Oliver got between them. 'Enough! Both of you. Mungo, be off. *Enough*, I said,' as they squared up to each other.

Mungo, perhaps because he had injured himself in his fall, or perhaps his purpose was served, backed off with a laugh. 'Go in peace then, brother, but stay sharp.'

Alick stood beside Oliver and watched him go. 'You should have told me!' he reiterated, his face set hard. 'Why did you not?'

'To prevent what just happened! Your brother likes to provoke.'

'Damn him. And poor Ellen! He must be *made* to leave her alone.'

Oliver hesitated, but knew he must speak. 'Alick. Forgive me, but is there something between you and Ellen, because if so . . .'

'There isn't.'

'No?'

Alick turned impatiently aside. 'Only a fondness, and a concern that history doesn't repeat itself.'

But is that not what history does? Oliver thought bleakly. It repeats itself over and over again, as each generation fails to learn, and is doomed to suffer again in the learning. And looking at Alick's set expression, he wondered again which of the two brothers offered the greater likelihood of destroying Ellen's peace of mind.

Chapter 21

Back in the kitchen of Sturrock House, Libby left Rodri making crisp recommendations regarding homework while she retreated upstairs to pack. When she came down ten minutes later, a lively discussion was under way. 'But *when*, Dad? When I'm ten?' asked Donald.

His brother scented discrimination. 'That's not fair – and he can't go on his own even when he's ten, can he?'

'You both did well today, but you know how quickly—'

'I could go with Davy, though, couldn't I?' Donald persisted. 'When I'm ten, he'll be twelve.'

'Dad!'

Charlie's cry was that of outraged siblings the world over, and Rodri rolled his eyes at Libby. 'It's not a numbers game, it's when you're safe, and that's not yet. And your swimming needs to improve. A lot. Both of you.'

'I can swim across the bay.'

'Homework, I said.'

'So can I, almost.' Charlie looked as if he was spoiling for a fight.

Rodri put a hand on his head. 'Just be content with the bay this summer, unless someone's with you. High tide or incoming. You know the rules. And I repeat, homework?'

'Done.'

'Fine. So who's for a walk before bed?'

From the way the boys ran for their jumpers, this was a welcome suggestion, although there were still muttered grumblings as, bonded by a common grievance, they headed for the door. 'Coming?' Rodri asked Libby, eyebrows raised.

They went out through the old front door, down the steps, and along the mossy garden path to the gate, and from there out across the dunes, making for the headland, the boys casting leaping shadows as they ran on ahead. And she thought of how she used to rise early as a child to watch that same sun appear over the horizon on the other side of the ocean. The shadows were long then too.

Donald fell back with a question. 'Did you go kayaking in Canada? On the open sea, I mean.'

She shook her head. 'No, too dangerous. Squalls come up from nowhere and then the waves are huge. Even the fishing boats had to dash to shore sometimes.' Donald absorbed this unsatisfactory response and ran off to rejoin his brother. 'Straining at the leash,' she remarked.

'Don't I know it.' Rodri watched his sons as they went down onto the beach where they wrestled cheerfully in the sand, venting their frustration like puppies. 'But thank you for that. They think they're invincible at that age, and Davy being two years older sets the bar. Donald's a sensible lad, but Charlie hasn't a clue. And anything Davy can do, they have to try.'

She hesitated, then said, 'Alice told me that he's Hector's son.'

'Didn't I – ? I thought I'd said. Aye, though Hector's barely ever seen him.' He drew in a long breath. 'He's losing out big time, Davy's such a good lad, but I can't get past Laila.' They had diverted from the route to the headland and he led her instead to the mound, which had already shape-shifted into a natural form with sand covering the curve of stones. No one could have guessed what had been there. 'How long to clear the rest?' he asked.

'A day, two at most, for two or three students. Even sieving every scrap of sand.' And they had maybe ten students signed up to come.

He grunted. 'And the stonework survey of the church?'

She calculated quickly, two students per wall, exterior and interior, going slowly. 'Two or three days, maybe four.' Then added, 'And another day if we do a geophysical survey like the one—'

'Forget it. Waste of time,' he said, and moved off in the direction of the headland. 'And surveying the rest of the bay?' he asked over his shoulder.

She looked around her, rapidly calculating what needed to be plotted and drawn: the contour lines, the church, the manse, the house, the headland. Was he reconsidering? But why not the geophysical work? 'We could do it in a couple of days.'

'Say three.'

By now they were on the causeway going out to the headland. He turned back and offered a hand over the slippery rocks as they climbed up to the small plateau, where he stopped and looked down at the fallen stones of Odrhan's cell.

'And what would you do here?' he asked.

She thought again of the drawing they had seen that morning; nothing would be lost by removing the tumble of stones again and seeing what, if anything, remained intact below. 'Ideally we'd expose the original shape again, plot it, photograph it – and maybe dig it.'

He said nothing more for a while but fixed his gaze on the two boys, who were now busy rolling two fishing floats down the dunes, scouring the sand where the floats came to a halt before staggering back up the dunes with them to repeat the game, lit by the rich light of the low sun. 'And what will you find?'

'Who knows – ? But O.D.'s drawing suggests that there were bones found on the headland.'

He nodded. 'Hmm. Letting you loose out here is a bit of a risk, though.' She was beginning to recognise that dry smile, and warmed to it.

'Why so?'

'I'm not sure I could deal with another body.'

Out to sea the sun's disc slipped below a wash of charcoal which had spread above the horizon, and the shore darkened.

'No guarantees at this stage, I'm afraid,' she said.

A moment later the sun reappeared and lit the ragged edge of cloud, and hung there suspended for a glorious moment before it began its final descent, setting the clouds and sea aflame.

'I suppose I'll just have to chance it.'

———

Jennet lived in a neat whitewashed cottage in a small community a few miles inland from Oran Bridge, and they were on her doorstep early next morning. Rodri drummed his knuckles on the door, opened it, and called out: 'Jennet? It's Rodri.' Libby heard a faint response and he beckoned her in.

The door opened into a low-ceilinged room which seemed to serve as both kitchen and living room, and in a high-backed chair pulled close to the fire sat a woman with a halo of white hair and bright eyes the colour of Maddy's. She rose as Rodri entered and allowed herself to be enveloped in a great hug, peeping round him to smile at Libby. Libby smiled back and came forward to take her hand. The old lady barely reached Libby's shoulder and it seemed quite inconceivable that Angus, that great bear of a man, was her son.

Rodri introduced them. 'Jennet, this is Libby Snow who'll be running an archaeological dig on the estate this summer. Libby, this is Mrs Cameron, but everyone calls her Jennet.'

'And you must too,' said the woman with a bobbing smile. 'A dig, eh? Well, well. Will you have some tea?'

'Aye, but I'll make it,' said Rodri.

Jennet gestured Libby towards a settle beside the fire and asked her where she was from while Rodri filled the kettle and set it on an electric ring. Libby told her about the university town where she now lived, but spoke also about Gosse Harbour and her father's family, watching for a response. There was none, other than a polite interest, but the old woman was examining her carefully.

Rodri passed round mugs of tea, then settled himself down on the settle beside Libby and came straight to the point. 'We've come to dredge your memory for scandals, Jennet.'

'Scandals!' Her eyes seemed to grow sharper. 'You know them as well as I do, Rodri Sturrock.'

He gave a wry smile. 'Old scandals, *mo chridhe*, scandals that you heard as a child.'

The old lady turned to Libby, her eyes bright and alive. 'He's no more right to be up at the big house than you have, you know. Now, there's a scandal, if you like! Sturrocks only came after—'

'No! Not as far back as that, you incorrigible woman.'

'It's true! Sturrocks *took* the land . . .'

Rodri groaned. 'Alright, we'll deal with this first. The estate was confiscated after Culloden and given to the Sturrock family, along with a baronetcy, as a reward for loyalty to the crown. Jennet claims descent from the family who were thrown out and never for one minute lets me forget it. By her reckoning, Angus should be sitting where Hector now sits.'

'And so he should. And then David after him.'

Libby smiled at the old woman. So much ferocity in so small a frame!

'Let's argue that out again another time, shall we?' Rodri said, with a fond smile. 'But for now, tell me instead if you ever heard anything about a Sturrock son running off with a local woman.'

The old woman slurped at her tea, then wiped her lips carefully with a handkerchief before setting down the cup. 'But that was years back,' she said.

Libby felt a jolt of excitement and Rodri leaned forward. 'So you do know something?'

The old lady looked from one to the other. 'Only what everyone knew.'

'And what was that?'

But the old woman seemed to go off on a tangent. 'The old laird fathered children on everyone except his own wife.'

'Which old laird?'

'The fifth baronet. Between him and his puny wife, they'd no children who survived them. He buried four infants, or was it five? And that was why your grandfather inherited, because they couldn't find his brother.'

Rodri and Libby exchanged glances. 'His brother? Who was his brother?'

'The one that ran off. The one you asked about!'

Rodri rose and filled their mugs from the old brown teapot, and then sat again. 'Tell us about this brother, Jennet,' he said.

'It was years before I was born, but folk still spoke of it. Alexander, he was, and he ran off with my mother's cousin, Ellen Mackay . . .'

Ellen – Libby caught her breath. 'You're *related* to Ellen?' she said.

The old woman nodded, then looked back at Rodri with eyes

grown suddenly hard. 'Ellen Mackay's mother was Kirsty, and she was the old laird's bastard. The third baronet. Nothing changes, does it? Well, Kirsty married my mother's uncle, Samuel Mackay, and Ellen was their child.'

The room seemed to close in on them as time contracted. Old scandals, Rodri had said, old transgressions, still remembered and repeated, the essence distilled over time and preserved by the telling and retelling. So somewhere, through the twists and turns, Libby was related to this old woman, and to Maddy, and to David. And Rodri . . . ? This woman who sat opposite her in her high-backed chair was of her own grandmother's generation and came from the same ancient stock. And suddenly the connection that had brought her here felt strong, and real.

'And she ran off with this Sturrock man?' Rodri asked.

The old woman nodded. 'So they said. She was very lovely, by all accounts, even though she was just a housemaid in the big house – instead of living there as she should have done.'

'In the big house, not the manse?' Libby asked.

'Maybe it was the manse, I don't know, my dear. Some said it was the minister who'd run off with her, others said he'd been caught thieving and forced out.'

'So *two* men disappeared around the same time?' Rodri frowned and glanced across at Libby. 'When was this?'

The old woman chuckled. 'I can't remember what year it is now, never mind that far back. But it was long before I was born, and I'm ninety-two.'

'And who told you all this?' he persisted.

'Everyone! The old folk still spoke of it, gossip like that had a life of its own when there was no television or anything else to talk about. And then the old laird died and they couldn't trace his brother. If they had done, then your branch of the family would still be farming in Perthshire and the likes of Hector Sturrock would not have—' She broke off, her lips working. Two patches of colour had appeared on her cheeks and her eyes had grown needle sharp.

Rodri raised his hand but spoke gently. 'I know, I know. Let's stick to old scandals, Jennet.' She sniffed angrily. 'So no one knew what happened to the minister, or to Alexander Sturrock?'

She shook her head. 'They might have done, but I don't. He was a good man, they said, worth ten of his brother. Same they say about you.'

Chapter 22

The call from her father came out of the blue.

Libby had been back at work for a few weeks following her return from Ullaness and was in her office marking essays when the phone rang. Her father rarely called her, and never during the day, so as soon as she heard his voice her heart lurched.

'It was all very peaceful,' he said. 'She just slipped away in her sleep. Best we could hope for.' Libby put down the phone when he'd finished and stared out of the window at the horse chestnut tree which was now bedecked with blossom, overwhelmed by the sudden void.

Rapid arrangements had then to be made to get herself released from her teaching commitments and booked on a flight to St John's in order to reach Gosse Harbour in time for the funeral. The dig would be starting in just over a week, but all the preparation work had been done. It would be tight, but she had to get there. Nothing mattered as much as that.

She'd had intermittent contact with Rodri over the weeks, agreeing modifications to the arrangements for the summer, redefining the scope of the work. He'd been businesslike, still demanding that the details be spelt out, but obliging. Declan had tried to wrest back control of the project but Rodri had handled him skilfully, still refusing any further work in the nave of the church but agreeing to most other suggestions, keeping him sweet but dealing mainly through Libby.

'What's his problem?' Declan had demanded after failing again to persuade him to let them do a magnetometer survey inside the church. 'Ask him, why don't you, since you're so damn friendly.'

And so she had. But she was met by silence at the end of the phone. Then: 'Tell the good professor that I don't want the dead disturbed.'

'Really?'

'I don't have to give him a reason.'

'No, but –'

'And Libby . . .' He paused. 'The day we first met, you told me there had been shots fired at metal-detectorists caught in the churchyard.'

'That's right, and you said it wasn't Angus.'

'It wasn't. But how did you know about it? The shots, I mean?'

She thought back, trying to remember. It was surely Declan who had told her. 'Declan.'

'And who told him?'

'I don't know. Shall I ask?'

'No.'

'You surely aren't suggesting that –'

'I'm suggesting nothing, but I'm confirming, yet again, that there will no below-ground survey done in the church. No electrical resistance survey, no GPR, no magnetometer survey, no conductivity survey. No nothing. Understood?'

'You've been swotting up.'

'Aye.'

To what purpose? she wondered, then asked: '*Were* shots fired at the nighthawks?'

There was another silence at the end of the phone. 'Allegedly,' he said, and she could almost see his smile.

But all that had been blown away by her father's news, and

when she rang back two days later to tell Rodri about the funeral, there was a different sort of silence. 'I'm sorry,' he said. 'It's a sad time for you.'

'Yes.'

'She'd had a good innings. Isn't that what people say?'

'Yes.'

'But it doesn't help, and she leaves a hole, eh?' It was the right sort of comfort.

'A huge one.'

'And we'll learn no more from her.'

'I thought that too.' A vital link in the chain had snapped, and all that would survive now would be filtered by her own memory, the details lost, the nuances distorted. And she thought of Jennet and remembered the fierce looks and her tone as she spoke of the past, and thought that it was more than words that told a story. It was the voice itself, the gestures, the shaken head and the smile. All that was gone now, and that part of Ellen's story, the New-foundland part, was diminished, a pale echo of the truth that she herself would pass on.

———————

And she wondered again, as she stood at the Gosse Harbour church door three days later, if one day perhaps she would tell her own children and grandchildren how she used to go out with the fishermen and describe the size of the lobsters and crabs they brought back, the whales they saw off the headlands, and the sculpted icebergs which drifted past the entrance to the harbour, calved from sea ice hundreds of miles away. And would she tell them about her grandmother and her grandmother's grandmother and the legend she had brought across the ocean, unwittingly re-shaping it just as the sand had reshaped the mound they had dug into at Ullaness? She too, after all, was a link in that chain.

She turned back as Nan's neighbour touched her shoulder and expressed condolences. It felt as if the whole community had turned out for the funeral, and the little church overflowed with goodwill. One after another the people had come up to her, some strangers, some known from years back, bringing anecdotes as if they were tributes, small threads in the fabric of her grandmother's long life, and Libby thought again of the richness of the collective memory. But it was fragile. Only strong stories survived.

She stood beside her father for what seemed like hours, gripping his hand, as people filed past, and waited for the coffin and then followed it up to the little cemetery on the hill, while the sun blazed in a cobalt sky and the wind swept the hillside, scooping up the old woman's departing spirit. Her father was an undemonstrative man, but he was clearly moved as he watched his mother buried beside his father. Her grandfather had been a cheerful man who had died fifteen years earlier, and Libby paused a moment, remembering digging bait with him and then sitting for hours beside him on the wooden stage catching crabs. And on the other side was Ellen's grave. Just a simple stone stating her name, Ellen Macdonald, date of birth and death, and those of her husband, John Macdonald, who had survived her by many years. And she wondered a moment about him, realising that she knew nothing beyond the fact that he had been a schoolmaster, and had cared deeply for Ellen. Rodri had remarked that the name had a ring of anonymity about it, and perhaps he was right, but that too was something she could never know. Had Ellen Mackay once been Ellen Sturrock, and if so, at what point had she become Ellen Macdonald? And with which man had she borne a son?

When the will was read, Libby found that the house had been left to her. 'It was that or sell it,' her father said, and from the smile on his face she saw that he had known. 'I talked it over with your grandmother and we didn't think you could bear to see it go, not yet at any rate. Nor, strangely enough, could I, for all that I couldn't wait to get away when I was your age.' And she had smiled at him, knowing that there was still no place in his busy life for a clapboard house perched on a remote rock, a hundred miles from nowhere. But perhaps there might be in hers. 'Do with it what you will, Libby, and maybe one day I'll come and take my grandchildren crabbing.' He had left immediately after the funeral with the intention of returning later to sort through the contents of the house. Libby had shaken her head when he suggested they travel to the airport together, and resolved instead that she would sleep that night in the house. Neighbours had offered their own spare rooms, anxious at the thought of her being alone there, but she had refused, grateful but determined. That night, with her grandmother's spirit so recently flown, she would sleep in the room where she had always slept and pretend, just for that one night, that the old lady slept in the room next door.

Chapter 23

⤖ Libby ⤖

She left Gosse Harbour next day and flew from St John's to Heathrow, where she had a two-hour wait for her connection. The airport was busy, but when was it not? And as she sat there, sleep-deprived and weary, still coming to terms with her loss, she stared at the myriad of people who streamed past: scruffy students, businessmen, exotic figures in flowing robes, exhausted families, and uniformed guards, armed and alert. Then the flow parted for a moment and she looked beyond to see a woman, slender and immaculate, buying perfume across the way. Libby's gaze sharpened, and then focussed. Surely not. It couldn't be . . . But the woman raised unnecessary sunglasses in order to count her change, and Libby saw that, incredibly, it was, without a doubt. Laila Sturrock, as sleek as a cat, smiling and gracious as she paid for whatever it was she was buying, her blond hair falling forward as she put her purchase in her bag. Libby watched her put her sunglasses back in place and glide away, to be lost in the crowd.

The encounter was soon forgotten, and she arrived back at her flat and hit the ground running. Just two days to get the rest of the gear together, double-check all the arrangements about tents, toilets, water, and so forth and then set off north, still fighting jet lag and an emotional numbness. The former must be worked through, the latter postponed. It would be good to talk to Rodri, explain her sadness, and she somehow felt that he would understand.

She arrived to find that he had been true to his word: the old caravan had been moved down to the site and now stood in a sheltered spot behind the old manse. She walked around it, thinking that, given the forecast, a solid roof was going to be a godsend. The students had been arriving all day, many doubling up in cars to get here, others finding tortuous bus routes, and they were now cheerfully erecting tents and establishing themselves. Only eight had come in the end, making a company of ten with herself and her supervisor, Callum Lewis. He was a dependable young man doing postgraduate work, a rock, and Libby had been very relieved when he had agreed to come, stipulating only that his girlfriend came along too.

She watched them from the window of the caravan, in T-shirts, shorts and boots, spraying each other with insect repellent, a mixed bag of ability and attitude. The wind was providing riotous entertainment as tent fly sheets billowed like colourful spinnakers until cooperative effort secured them to the ground. Callum was supervising the erection of a sturdy army surplus tent, which would double as an eating and cooking tent and for finds cataloguing on wet days. 'Not that I expect there will be many finds,' she had said to him, 'and we're going to have to stretch the work out to make this meaningful training. We'll clear the mound first and start the building recording and wider survey work, and then, if we still have time, we'll tackle Odrhan's cell.'

'Fine. No worries,' he had replied.

No worries. If only that was true! The worries were hers, though, not Callum's, and she was ready to get started. But where was Rodri?

She left the caravan and glanced towards Sturrock House, but the path to the garden gate remained empty. She'd expected that he would come down when they arrived, but he hadn't. Off for the day perhaps . . . Then she saw the truck with the portable toilets lumbering down the track and hurried across to greet it.

'Can we build a bonfire on the beach?' one of the students asked as she was showing the driver where the toilets were to be placed. 'There's plenty of driftwood about.'

'And dried cowshit,' said another.

'We'll have to ask,' she replied, glancing again up the path.

She put up her own tent a little way from the others to give an illusion of privacy, something she reckoned would be in short supply these next two weeks. Once her mat and sleeping bag were unrolled, she was done; the car would serve as storage and wardrobe, the caravan for overflow.

She stuck her head out, thinking that she heard the sound of a vehicle fading as if it had turned off into the courtyard, but still no one appeared.

She'd left a phone message telling Rodri that she was back home and that everything would go ahead as planned, following it up with an e-mail this morning saying that she was on her way. He hadn't responded to either, and in the confusion of last-minute packing she hadn't noticed. But now it seemed odd. The door to Sturrock House had been locked when she had gone up there earlier, and that too was unusual. She looked again towards the path to the house, but it remained empty, and she began to wonder if something was wrong. And where were Maddy and Alice? A food fair maybe, and perhaps Rodri was with them. The possibilities were endless, but she was conscious of disappointment.

Perhaps she'd not heard a vehicle after all.

Once the camp was set up, she took the students to see what remained of the mound. It had settled back into the dune landscape, just another sand-blown hillock, and the stone setting was now invisible. And as she described the various discoveries that had been made, she kept an eye on Sturrock House and saw that an upstairs window had been opened, but still he did not come.

She led the students out onto the headland next and they stood in front of Odrhan's cell while she told them about the work that was planned, and thought fleetingly of the night she had stood beside Rodri and watched the sunset. She made reference to the legend but not, not yet anyway, to the drawings that she and Rodri had pored over in the dining room. And, wafting away a cloud of midges which had risen from the turf, she led the students down to the church, wondering again about Rodri's determined embargo.

It was not until they had finished eating and the light was fading that he came. She was in the food tent sharing a beer with the students, conscious of a vague inexplicable unease, when he appeared at the open flap, bending to peer inside.

Straightaway she knew that something was wrong. His face looked drawn and weary and that distinctive frown was etched deep. She rose. 'Rodri! Come in and meet everyone. This is Mr Sturrock, who has made all the arrangements for us to be here. Meet Callum, who –' He nodded, unsmiling, at her various introductions, and then asked if they had everything they needed. The students murmured a polite assurance, which she confirmed.

'Good. Well, the weather'll be fine tomorrow at least, and beyond that who knows,' he said, and turned to go.

'It's OK if we build fires on the beach, isn't it?' the student who had approached her earlier asked with a casual drawl.

Rodri turned back, and the frown went deeper. 'No. Actually, it's not OK.' The student coloured, recoiling at the tone. Rodri glanced at Libby, and gave a tight smile. 'I'll come down in the morning and see how you're getting on.' And with that, he was gone.

Libby stood a moment, staring at the blank space, and then went after him. He was already striding up the path that led to the garden gate, but he turned when she called. 'I'm sorry about that. There'll be no fires.'

'Good, they make a mess.' He paused. 'I barked, didn't I?' And there was a shadow of his ironic smile.

'It won't hurt him.'

For a moment she thought that he wasn't going to tell her what was wrong. Then, abruptly, he did. 'Laila's back. I just collected her from the airport.'

So that was it. 'The Nasmyth?' she asked.

He gave a short laugh and turned away. 'If only . . . Look, let me know if you need anything, won't you? I'll come down in the morning.' He raised a hand briefly and strode off towards the gate in the garden wall.

———

It was left to Alice to explain.

They had been at work for a couple of hours next morning when she arrived with a laden basket and greeted Libby with a hug and a smile, but her eyes were clouded too. Even her ponytail had lost its bounce.

Libby called a tea break and pulled her aside. 'Gannets, aren't they?' Alice commented as she watched shortbread, scones, and other fancies being rapidly consumed. Then: 'Has he told you?'

Libby nodded. 'Laila's back.'

Alice paused. 'And the rest?'

'What rest?'

'Hector's fired him. He's got three months to pack up and leave.'

'*What!* No!' She stared back at Alice. 'Because of the Nasmyth?'

'No. But Hector's coming back to live here, and plans to take over running the estate himself. And her ladyship's finally expecting. They want to raise the child here, she says, so Rodri's got to get out. They want us out of the old dairy too, but we're going to fight that when Hector gets here.'

'Oh, *Alice!*' This was truly a disaster.

'And Hector didn't even have the decency to tell Rodri himself, just sent a letter through his lawyer. It's that as much as anything that's gutted the poor man. After all he's done holding the place together while they bled it dry.'

It wasn't just the dairy, but the walled garden, the restored hothouses, the raised beds, the glue which bound them all together. It wasn't unreasonable that his brother should want to come back and to raise their child here, but why behave like that? The reality for Rodri was brutal. How much, she wondered, was Laila's spite?

Three months was nothing.

Alice was looking up at the manse with a bleak expression and expressed the same thought. 'It'll take more than three months to get that old place in order. And the man has no money! Hector let him live rent-free but he paid him a pittance. And Rodri's poured every bit of it into the business.' And whatever would it be like for them going forward, living here, right on the doorstep? Alice lifted her chin. 'But we'll manage. We're a team. Between us and Angus we've space enough to give them a roof till it's done, and we'll move foodie operations into the old cottages beside us if we have to. Angus has started work on one already.' Then she gave Libby a hint of her old smile. 'And we'll have that old caravan back when you're done with it. We'll be needing it.'

Chapter 24

Folk from the scattered settlements used to bring food for Odrhan, but they rarely came now. At first he had kept Ulla hidden, and he would meet them instead at a place where there was a flattened rock behind the dunes. He raised a wooden cross there to encourage this practice, but people came less frequently. Ulla must have been seen and judgements made, but he found that he did not care.

Gradually he forgot a time when Ulla had not been there. She became his soul-mate and his comfort, helping him to gather wild berries and harvest the rough crops he had planted in sheltered places away from the shore. She would make flat bread and smile at him as she tore into it with her white teeth.

And as her waist swelled, she grew even more lovely, a wild rose in full summer bloom.

➤ Ellen ⟵

Once a week, usually on a Friday when Mr Drummond was visiting his flock or thinking about his sermon for Sunday, Ellen would walk the three miles across the ridge which separated the two bays and visit her grandmother, who lived in a cottage beside the long estuary. Mungo Sturrock had not repeated his invasion of the manse, and Ellen had begun to feel settled there and safe.

'The man needs an occupation – ' she had heard Mr Drummond say to Alick during one of his frequent visits.

'I think Pa is seeing to that, so Mama must have said something,' she heard him reply.

And the two men had assured Ellen that the work at the headland was finished and that the stones would soon be restored, so she could be content about that too.

She walked slowly, listening to the birdsong and savouring the balmy summer air. Mr Drummond was a kind and considerate master, and her duties were light compared with those at Sturrock House. It was a lonely life for him, she had come to realise, and he seemed pleased to have her company, breaking off his work to talk to her and to ask after her mother, thanking her for her efforts, his eyes following her with a kindly warmth. He encouraged her to go across to the cottage two or three times a day, and they laughed about having a bell wire rigged up across the path so that her mother could call for her. Life had developed a calm rhythm, and Ellen was happy.

Alick called frequently, and if Mr Drummond was out he would linger and talk to her, and it was almost like when they were children. Once he came when she was pegging out the washing and he stayed for a while, handing her the pegs, running after a shirt that blew out of her hand and caught on a thistle, returning it to her with a grand gesture. She smiled at the memory as she lifted the latch on her grandmother's door and went in.

The old woman had lived in the cottage all her life and was a very great age, but she was spent now, confined to her chair beside the hearth with her memories. Ellen loved to hear the stories of times when Sturrock House was more of a castle than a house, before the third baronet had altered things, and today had been no different. The old stories had come out again, delivered between noisy slurps of tea. Tales of folk hiding in the heather, of houses burned, crops ravaged, and cattle driven off. Hard times and good times, and Ellen had listened patiently, feeding her morsels of scone sent by Mrs Nichol wrapped in a square of linen, thinking that it might be the men who drove events but it was the women who kept the tales of them alive.

When it was time to leave, she tucked the square in her pocket and kissed her grandmother. 'I've made up the fire, and Annie will be in later to help you to your bed.' And with that she departed, leaving one bedridden old lady for another.

It was warmer outside than in today, she thought, as she pulled the cottage door closed behind her and stood a moment looking up at the sky, a cloudless blue. The wind had dropped enough for the land to absorb the sun's warmth, and her shawl slipped to the crooks of her elbows. Tomorrow it might rain, so best enjoy it now, and she looked down the estuary to where the fishing boats rode at anchor on a turquoise sea. They looked bonny, mirrored sharply by their reflections, and she sensed that little pause there was when the bay was full just before the tide turned and began to ebb away, exposing rank seaweed and leaving the boats awkward and askew.

She started homeward. On either side of the rough track there was a riot of yellow and purple vetch; buttercups grew amongst a miniature forest of silken meadow grasses and sorrel. Behind the verges the gorse was ablaze, and sheltered spots hid the last of the primroses and delicate bluebells. Could there be a place more lovely than this when early summer had the land in thrall! And there was not a sound except for the occasional cry of a gull in the skies above her and the drone of bees passing from flower to flower. The air was heavy with fragrance, the sweet-sour fecundity of spring.

Ellen climbed to the top of the rise, slightly breathless from the heat, and stopped to feel again the warmth on her face, and just for a moment she allowed herself to forget that her mother lay hollow-eyed and listless awaiting her return – then she continued on along the old drove road to where it dipped down towards a stream. A small bridge spanned the water there, and the track rose again before its final descent into Ullaness. Something moved ahead of her, disappearing into the shadows, a deer perhaps come down to drink.

Downstream of the bridge a clump of trees overhung the water, and this made for a sheltered spot, a cool place of dappled sunlight and leafy shade. And just out of sight the stream narrowed to drop as a thin veil of a waterfall and fed a small pool flanked by yellow iris. One or two of them had probably already opened, she thought, and decided she would stop there a moment and rest, and so she left the track.

Climbing over mossy boulders, Ellen followed the waterfall down, passing under low branches where the air was sweet and the shadows darkened. Twigs and cones crackled under her feet as she continued to a place where the undergrowth opened up, letting in the light, and there was the pool, sunlit and clear, hidden from view.

She stood a moment, savouring her solitude; then she knelt on the mossy turf beside a clump of marsh marigolds which cast their golden light on the water and loosened her hair, letting it fall forward. Looking down at her reflection, she allowed herself to imagine for a moment that it was Ulla who looked back, her image rippling just below the water. Surely she must have found this place, and come here; Ellen could almost sense her presence. The little waterfall made a gentle sound as it fell to the pool, and beside it the fiddle-heads of new bracken gave off a humid, peppery scent, while above her a blackbird gave its liquid call. She would stay here, hidden, just for a moment, and let the quiet and the peace and the sense of timelessness give her succour.

Perhaps it was Ulla herself who had drawn her here.

After a moment she bent forward and splashed the cool water onto her face, cupping her hand to drink. Then she sat on a boulder beside the pool and pulled off her shoes and stockings, hitching her skirt to her knees, and stretched her slender legs to the water. The gasping cold was followed by an almost painful bliss as her hot feet found relief, and then, leaning forward, she cupped her hand again and began washing her lower limbs. Remembering the scrap of linen in her pocket, she dipped it in the water, squeezed it, and lifted her hair, rubbing the cloth along the arch of her neck, and closed her eyes in luxurious pleasure before letting her hair fall back. Had Ulla come here to bathe? And perhaps to grieve for Harald, lost to her forever. The blackbird ceased its song, and around her the woodland grew silent. She wetted the cloth again, squeezed it, and then unbuttoned the front of her blouse, delighting in the cool water on her throat –

A fish jumped in front of her, and she opened her eyes, seeing widening circles ripple across the pool. A fish, in so small a pool! She shut them again. Another plop sounded, but her eyes stayed closed and slowly her feet traced swirling circles of their own, the reeds silky against her skin.

A third pebble landed just in front of her. 'My God, nymph, you put on a good show,' and Mungo Sturrock stepped out from where he had been hidden in the deep shadows, his voice not quite his own. Ellen leapt from the boulder, fumbled for her shoes and, not finding them, turned to flee barefooted.

But with a single stride, Mungo crossed the stream and clouds dimmed the sun.

⊷ *Oliver* ⊷

'Ellen's mother is poorly this morning, sir, and Ellen has asked leave to stay with her,' Mrs Nichol said as she brought Oliver his breakfast next morning. 'Quite tearful she was.'

'Oh dear! Poor Ellen. I will call by later this morning.' There could be little doubt that the poor woman was fading. She hardly left her bed now, and Ellen had been backwards and forwards to the cottage these last days, her face increasingly strained. The old lady's passing could not be far off.

And what then?

Ellen must leave the cottage, that much he knew, but at least she now had a place here; already he could not imagine the house without her. He would listen for her light footfall in the mornings, and knew a great delight when he heard her singing or humming as she sometimes did when she swept the hall. She was happy here and blooming! He took a mouthful of porridge and ate thoughtfully, not able, not in the daylight hours anyway, to admit where, in the hours of darkness, his mind had begun to wander. But there would be time enough for such thought, and for now the sweetness of it brightened his days.

A loud knock disturbed his reverie, and a moment later the door was flung open and Alick Sturrock exploded into the room. 'Oliver! Forgive me, but you'll have to come. It's an absolute outrage!'

'My dear fellow—'

'Bloody Mungo. He's wrecked everything!'

'Whatever do you mean?'

'Up at the headland. He's dug up the floor and found bones. There's the most almighty outcry! Someone came up to the house at first light protesting to Papa, thinking we'd done it, so I went back with them to have a look, and it's a complete shambles. Bones everywhere. God knows what he thought he was doing! And then I found he'd left me this, curse him.' He thrust a sheet of notepaper into Oliver's hand.

Before you, little brother! I leave the remains to you and Drummond.

'And now he's gone off, leaving a pile of bones and a hell of a mess for us to clear up. Mama is furious, and people are gathering up there.'

Oh God. 'I'll come.'

They left the house together and made for the headland, where Oliver could see a collection of a dozen or so people, dark clothes flapping in the strengthening breeze. Dour looks and murmurs of disapproval greeted their approach, and the group fell back to expose the results of Mungo's handiwork. 'It's a sacrilege,' one voice said, as they passed.

'Aye, there was no reason for it –'

No. No reason. Nor had there been reason behind what appeared to have been frenzied digging over much of the floor of the little cell. It had been hacked into with neither care nor caution, and the garden spade that had been used still stood propped up against the pile of rocks. Beside it lay something else, the bones presumably, now covered discreetly with a sheet.

A member of his own small congregation stepped forward. 'This is not right, minister.'

'No,' Oliver said, returning him a direct look. 'It isn't. And it should not have happened.'

'So why'd you do it?' a voice jeered from the group.

How to phrase their defence? Oliver had no particular desire to protect Mungo Sturrock, but he knew that he must consider the reputation of the family. 'I did not do it, Mr McBeath, nor did Mr Alick Sturrock. It was done overnight by . . . someone.' He caught Alick's eye and read approval. But how many more of Mungo's transgressions must he cover up? 'It was a dreadful thing to have done.'

'But you began the business!'

Oliver looked at the sea of faces and felt the heat of their animosity. Dear God, how he had failed them! He recognised members of his own congregation, their faces angry and troubled, but there were also people he barely knew, those who attended the Free Church, people who were pugnacious and outspoken. The matter could hardly be worse. He spoke loudly above the discordant mutterings. 'Our interest was purely in the history of the structure. We'd no reason to believe that there was a burial here.' Though perhaps they should have expected it, and, if truth be told, they probably would have dug up the floor themselves in the next day or so, albeit in a more controlled and careful manner. But on encountering the bones, they would have had the decency to stop, and the sense to keep quiet.

'You should have known better, minister.' The man spoke again, louder this time, confident that he had the group behind him. 'This place should never have been disturbed!'

His hostility seemed to arouse Alick's indignation. 'Why not? This was a *scientific* enquiry.'

'And what have you learned, Mr Sturrock, that we did not know before?' This came from a big man, a stalwart of the Free Church congregation, a man who had standing in the community.

There was really no answer to that, and Alick made a poor fist of it. 'We've learned about the shape of the structure . . . its size . . . and –'

'And what, young sir?'

Oliver stepped in to rescue him. 'This travesty was not of our doing, Mr McClure. The work began as a simple considered matter of enquiry which has been . . .' He wanted to say *desecrated* but the word would rebound against him. '. . . violated by a thoughtless individual, or individuals, sometime last night. But let me remind you that these bones, though they are to be respected, are *ancient* bones, and the soul is long departed.' There were more mutterings but Oliver pressed on. 'They will be reburied today, I promise you, and with due reverence. I will conduct a brief service and say prayers here which everyone is welcome to attend –'

'And you'll put the stones back as they were!' someone shouted from the back.

Oliver glanced briefly at Alick, who gave a slight nod. 'And the stones will be put back as they were.'

'And what if the bones are those of a pagan?' the Free Churchman asked.

Alick really would have done well to stay silent and let Oliver handle the situation. 'Do your prayers only intercede for those who have heard the word of God, Mr McClure?' he asked.

There was sharp intake of breath, followed by an expectant silence. It seemed that the sky darkened above them, and the man's voice carried like the distant growl of thunder. 'Meaning what, young man?'

Oliver saw with dismay that Alick was ready to take him on. He was more used to caps being doffed and to unquestioning respect than to confrontation, and perhaps the man had probed too deep. These were ideas that he and Alick had wrestled with, but this was neither the time nor the place to explore them. 'Gentlemen—' Oliver began, but Alick spoke over him.

'Meaning that if the bones are those of a pagan, ignorant of your god, then is the soul bound for hellfire, sir, regardless of virtue?'

Another shocked silence followed, and Oliver tried again. 'This is not the moment to—'

'You speak lightly of hellfire, Mr Sturrock.' Alick's adversary had grown red in the face and ignored Oliver's intervention. 'And who is *your* god, if different to mine?'

'I ask only if a pagan is undeserving of your prayers?'

'Alick, for pity's sake!' Oliver hissed, and moved in front of him, determined to close the debate, as there was now a groundswell of dark mutterings and angry looks. 'We need not discuss this now, gentlemen, and given the place the bones were found, it can be assumed that this person *was* a Christian. Even if that was not the case, our prayers must try to intercede for the soul of the departed. Now, who amongst you will volunteer to make a simple box which will serve as a coffin? I will cover the cost myself, and I believe the estate will supply the planks.' Alick gave a curt nod in answer to Oliver's glance.

Gradually the group dispersed, by no means satisfied, but there was no further reason to stay. Alick's adversary looked as if he would like to say more, but someone tugged at his sleeve and he went with the others. Eventually there was only himself, Alick, and the man who had volunteered to make the box left on the headland. Tentatively they lifted the sheet to assess the dimensions needed, and then the man departed.

'Phew!' said Alick, when he was out of earshot. 'That was nasty.'

Oliver watched the group walk along the causeway in twos and threes, still locked in discussion. A pair of ravens passed overhead, crying out a protest of their own. 'I don't imagine we've heard the last of it.'

'I should have stayed quiet.'

'Yes. You should,' said Oliver, then squeezed his shoulder. 'And one day soon, my free-thinking friend, you and I must talk. But for now let us see what damage your wretched brother has done.'

He lifted the sheet from the bones and reviewed the sorry pile. Judging by the length of the leg bone, they were of a man, a tall individual, and Oliver moved them gently aside to look at where the skull lay, and offered it a silent apology.

'There's a leg missing,' said Alick, 'or part of it anyway. Look –'

He was right. The arm bones appeared to be all there, and the rib cage, with some ribs freshly broken, together with a multitude of small bones and two upper leg bones but only one lower one, much cut about and broken.

'We can't bury the poor beggar with half a leg missing, can we?' said Alick. 'Must still be in the ground. I'll take a look.' Alick's spirits revived quickly, it seemed. He picked up the spade and, with an enthusiasm which made Oliver wince, began sifting through the sandy soil, digging into the remaining undisturbed patches. Oliver watched, biting his lip, as Alick came across other small bones which he set to one side. It really did feel like a desecration now, and his parishioners had every reason to be incensed. Thank God they had seen fit to depart.

'Aha! It's here.' Alick stopped digging and began pulling out a long bone.

'Wait!' cried Oliver. 'Get the soil off it and then follow it down. We need to collect the foot bones too.'

'Righto.'

This was appalling! But at least Alick had slowed down and was now using a flat stone to scrape away the surrounding deposit until he reached the bones of the foot. 'Hand me something, will you, my hat'll do.' And so the bones were decanted into the crown of Alick's hat, and the matter descended into a black farce. Please God that none of the people returned! 'You know what, I bet Mungo didn't get the other foot either. I'll have a look while I'm here.' Still in his crouched position, Alick began scraping again at the soil. Then – 'Hello! There's something else.'

Oliver peered over his shoulder and saw what appeared to be a ring of metal some eight inches in diameter still buried in the soil. Despite himself, he felt a jolt of excitement. 'Go carefully!'

'Here, you'd better do it. I'm more of a bones man. I'll shift over and keep looking for the other foot. Use this.' He pulled a penknife from his pocket.

Oliver took it and began carefully scraping the soil away from the centre of the ring. Gradually it revealed itself to be a bowl of metal, the colour of dull steel, except he saw that it was not steel – He cleared the sandy soil from around it, following the edges down into the soil. Then his heart started to pound. His blade hit something partway down the outside of the bowl and he stopped – a protuberance of some sort, perhaps the setting for a precious stone. He continued clearing the soil from around it, and by the time he reached the point where the base of the bowl should be, he was certain what he was dealing with, and there indeed was the column of the pedestal, and below it the base.

'I've got the other foot. Mungo's a careless—' Alick pivoted on his heel but stopped as Oliver lifted the ancient chalice, for such it was, and held it up. For perhaps a thousand years it had lain there, a masterpiece of craftsmanship, finely wrought of silver, set with precious stones and trimmed with gold, a holy vessel which had once graced the altars of a re-emergent northern church. 'My God!' said Alick.

'My God, indeed,' said Oliver, and they both stood and stared at it.

And then a sudden thought made Oliver's hands tremble. He set down the chalice and straightened and went back across to the pile of bones and looked again at the skull. It lay where Mungo had placed it, staring back at him. He bent and, placing a hand on either side of it, gently lifted it, straightened, looked for a moment into the empty eye sockets, and then tilted the brow towards him.

And he saw what Mungo had perhaps failed to notice or to understand, saw not the rounded intact cranium but fractured bone and a long clean cut, a wound such as that made by the descending blade of a heavy sword.

Chapter 25

Odrhan grew anxious. Often he would find Ulla down by Harald's mound, her shawl clasped around her thickened form. Her time was fast approaching and he saw that she was frightened. Their only regular visitor now was old Morag, who came down to the shore to gather shellfish, and when he expressed his concern Ulla had raised a hand. 'Morag will come to me. All is arranged.'

He spoke again of Christ's love and urged her to pray with him.

'Your God did not save Harald,' she said, and Odrhan was consumed again with guilt and remorse.

'I pray daily for his salvation,' he said, with truth, 'and for your safe delivery.'

But she had given him a cool look and addressed him as she had in the early days. 'And if your prayers fail again, Odrhan, you must bury me with Harald, and I will take my chance with the old gods.'

The weather changed during the day and became overcast, the air heavy. Part of the survey equipment refused to work, causing frustrating delays, and although the mound, where work was being focussed, produced more bones, everything seemed to confirm that it had been heavily disturbed in the past. A few scraps of iron and two amber beads were the only other traces of the individual once buried there. The students, perhaps picking up on her mood, seemed downbeat too, wondering loudly how they would recharge their phones. Batteries for the laptop and survey equipment would become a concern as well; in planning the summer, she had thought she might ask Rodri for help in such matters, but that now seemed impossible.

She was bent over the data recorder, swiping the midges away and cursing, when Rodri appeared, his face no less drawn, but he managed a smile. 'How's it going?' he asked, coming to stand beside her.

'Fine, apart from this bit of kit. Nothing much to show yet except more disturbed bones and a couple of beads. Scraps of iron.'

He nodded. 'Well, if anything needs charging, bring them up to the house.'

She looked at him. 'Is that alright?'

'Aye.'

'Don't let the students hear you or they'll all be clamouring to charge their phones.'

'They can use the sockets in the dairy, after hours, boots off, one at a time.'

'No, really –'

'That's my electricity, not Hector's.' He paused, then: 'Alice told you, she said.'

'Yes.'

'It had to happen.' His face was devoid of expression and she had no idea how to reach him. The shutters were down.

'Three months, Alice said,' she probed gently.

'The baby's due in October and they want us out before then. I'm sorry about your grandmother. Funeral went alright?'

'Thank you. Yes.' She wanted to tell him about the house, how she had felt, how she had seen Ellen's grave, slept in Ellen's house, but that was impossible now. The man looked gutted.

'Good,' he said, and squeezed her arm; then, like Alice, he turned to look at the manse, surveying the windows devoid of glass, the rotten frames, the clumps of bracken sprouting in the broken gutter. Starlings darted in and out of a hole in the roof. The planks which had been nailed across the door, she noticed, had been removed.

How would the boys feel about the change?

And David.

'Laila tells me it needs pulling down, so I'm bringing a builder to have a look tomorrow before she plants that idea in Hector's mind,' he said, moving off.

'She wouldn't –'

He shook his head. 'Hector and I made a deal.' But was the deal backed up with deeds and documents? She daren't ask.

Then she remembered something and put out a hand to stop him leaving. 'Wait, please.' She ran back to the car and retrieved the package she had brought with her. 'It's the cross,' she said, handing it to him.

He handed it straight back. 'I don't want it, it's yours. There's no record of a theft, so the Sturrock lad must have slipped it in his pocket on his way to Canada and given it to Ellen. You'd no need to be worried.' He made to move off again.

'But I can't suddenly declare I have it! Please take it, for safe-keeping at least.' She thrust the package into his open jacket. 'It ought to be in a museum.'

'Give it to a museum then.'

'They'll ask questions. I had wondered . . .' she faltered.

'Go on.'

She felt her face colouring, hating the duplicity of it. 'Well, I wondered if I gave it to you, could you just "find" it again, inside an old book or in the back of a drawer, and then give it to a museum? It would be . . . neater.'

'But life isn't neat, Libby.' He explored her face for a moment, saying nothing, and then his expression hardened. 'And aren't you forgetting something?'

'What?'

'There'd be no need for Laila to flog the Nasmyth if she could sell the cross.'

She stared at him. 'But if there was a fuss about finding it, stuff in the press, she *couldn't* just go ahead and sell it then, could she?'

'Laila makes her own rules. And she's already said she won't put up with the old kitchen and the vintage plumbing, and they'll be selling every damn thing they can to pay for it all.' He stared at his feet for a moment, then looked up at her again, an angry blaze in his eyes. 'So follow your conscience, Liberty Snow, that way you sleep easy at night.'

———

Next morning the recording project in the church began, but there were blustery downpours to contend with and frequent retreats to the cook tent and caravan required. By lunchtime, however, the skies cleared, waterproofs were shed, and the smell of sun cream mingled with that of insect repellent. Rodri arrived with a builder and, with a brief nod to Libby, they went across to the old manse and disappeared inside.

Then the students sieving sand at the mound called her over. They'd found a larger lump of metal, more solid, and the shape suggested it might be part of the sword Libby had found previously. 'More bones too,' Callum said, 'a clavicle, ribs, and vertebrae, but still no skull. And another bead, a carnelian this time. Hello, who's this?'

Libby looked up to see Laila Sturrock coming down the path towards them, wearing navy-blue trousers and a loose white top, immaculate as ever, and she raised a hand when she saw that Libby had spotted her.

'Libbee!' she called as she approached, implying an intimacy well wide of the mark. 'So, you are here, and your students are here, working hard, and the sun is shining and all is well.'

'It's Lady Sturrock,' Libby quietly informed Callum, and she heard him pass the news to the others.

'So, show me what you have found.' Laila reached them, breathless but glowing, a hand on her midriff, and she scanned them all with a blazing smile. Callum picked up the finds tray and brought it over to her.

It was just as well that he did so, because at the sight of her Libby's brain had frozen.

'Not much, really,' Callum said. 'Just this bead, which is nice, and some possible sword fragments.'

Her brain kicked back in, and she began calculating furiously. What was it Rodri had told her? She'd not taken it in – rapidly she reran the conversation. Laila's child was due in October, and it was now June, which meant that Laila was already five months pregnant.

Hence the bump.

Not large yet, but a very definite bump.

'Has Rodri told you our wonderful news?' Laila soon tired of scrap metal and chipped beads and came over to Libby, speaking in the low voice of a confidante.

'I can see for myself.' Libby forced a smile. 'Congratulations.'

Laila looked complacently down at her midriff, smoothing her top over it. 'I had my suspicions, my hopes, when I was here before, but Hector and I have had so many disappointments that

I had to be sure before I said anything. And Hector, of course, had to be the first to know.'

Libby looked back at her. 'Of course. When is it due?'

'*He*, not it. We asked when we had the scan because I just *had* to know. I was given the date of October twelfth, but babies are so unpredictable.'

Libby was fighting her disbelief. Either that bump had grown in the last few days or – 'Do you feel it – him – moving yet?'

Laila hesitated, but only for a moment. 'My mother always said that I was a lazy baby,' she said with a smile, 'so sometimes I think so, but maybe it is indigestion.'

It was simply not possible. 'And you'll be here when he's born. The eighth baronet, on home turf.'

Laila gave her a brilliant smile, then added, 'Sadly, no, not here. He will be born in Norway. I feel more comfortable there, you understand, and the hospitals are better. And Rodri might need a little more time to arrange his own affairs.' As she spoke, Rodri and the builder emerged from the old manse, deep in discussion. Rodri looked briefly in their direction and then away again, and the two men walked up the track towards the builder's van, where they stood talking. Laila's eyes narrowed. 'He's quite mad, you know. That place needs pulling down. It is not a good building anymore.'

'But it's his own place,' she said, and then wished she hadn't.

The woman looked back at her. 'Is that what he told you?'

The builder drove off and Rodri came towards them, stopping a moment to talk to Callum and admire the blade fragments; then he strolled over to them, poker-faced.

'Did he also tell you that you are mad?' Laila asked with her lilting smile.

'Useful stuff.'

Laila put her hand on his arm. 'But you won't start any work

until you hear from Hector, will you?' There was something behind the sweetness that was not sweet, and Libby saw Rodri's face
darken.

'You know what you said yesterday about charging equipment?' she said quickly, and tried to catch his eye. 'Could I bring
my laptop and one or two other things up to the house tonight,
do you think?'

Laila answered for him. 'But of course! Come now. I will get
Alice to make us tea.'

No way. 'Thanks, but we need to keep going. Maybe this
evening?' She gave Rodri a steady look. 'I won't get in the way.
Perhaps best in the library or the dining room, away from dust
and grease?' She saw him register the look, and a flicker crossed
his features.

'Come about eight, when we've eaten.'

'But how ungracious, Rodri! Come and eat with us. You must,
as *my* guest if not his. You can leave your students for one evening,
surely, and your equipment can be charging while we eat.'

———————

Libby went over and over the calculations in her mind as she
headed up to the house that evening, the equipment in a rucksack
on her back, and she reran the image of Laila in Heathrow. It *was*
her, there was no doubt of that, she remembered seeing the mole
on her left cheek when she had lifted her sunglasses. Sunglasses!
She'd forgotten the sunglasses. Why wear them if not to pass
unrecognised in case of a chance encounter? And she had been
model-thin, wearing a close-fitting dress. Whatever she was up
to, Libby was positive that there had been no bump.

It was Laila who opened the door to her, which was a nuisance, but she ushered her through to the kitchen where Rodri
was standing over the Aga.

'Give those things to Rodri,' Laila said, 'and he'll set them to charge.'

'Thanks, but I think I'd better do it myself.'

'So do I.' Rodri came over and took the rucksack from her. 'Come through to the library. Keep an eye on those pans, will you, Laila? Keep stirring or the sauce will catch.'

He led her through to the library and set the laptop down on the desk. 'What is it?' he said, and suddenly it seemed so improbable, so incredibly offensive. And what if she was wrong? 'Make it quick.'

There was no going back. 'I don't believe she's pregnant.' He stared at her, and she ploughed on. 'I saw her, just a few days ago, in Heathrow, and there was no bump. She was wearing tight-fitting clothes. And sunglasses.'

'Sunglasses?'

'She took them off. It was her.'

He continued to stare, then shook his head. 'You saw someone who looked like her.'

'No. It was her.' She was certain, but she was also now terrified by what she was saying, and by his expression. Dear God, she had better be right.

He shook his head again, his eyes not leaving hers. 'Impossible.'

The door was pushed open and Laila entered carrying a tray with three glasses on it, one of them containing orange juice. Libby bent quickly to plug in the battery, while Rodri did the same with the laptop. 'I removed the sauce,' Laila said, 'it was done. And what is impossible, Rodri?' she asked as she set the tray down, looking from one to the other.

Libby said the first thing that came into her head. 'I was asking about digging inside the church. If we finish the other work, I wondered if Rodri would reconsider.'

Laila settled herself in one of the low armchairs and gave her a limpid smile. 'Surely nothing is *impossible*. And now that I'm here, you must ask me! Please take a glass.'

Libby took one. 'Of course, I hadn't thought. If we get good weather and get finished, then perhaps I might discuss it with you.'

'No, no, discuss it now. Please!' Laila flashed a smile towards Rodri. 'Because the day after tomorrow, I must return home.'

'So soon,' he murmured.

She sent him another smile. 'There seems to be an endless stream of check-ups once a woman is over thirty-five. I don't suppose our grandmothers had to put up with such things.'

'But then a lot of them died.'

His words were followed by a cold silence, and Laila turned back to Libby. 'What is it you want to do in the church?'

Libby sipped her drink and considered. She was tempted to say they wanted to dig out the nave and put in a dance floor, just to see what she would say. 'Perhaps some below-ground survey to start with, and then go from there.'

'There can surely be no objection to that!' Laila turned to Rodri, who was staring down into the fire, one hand on the mantelpiece.

'What?' he said, not moving. 'No, none at all.'

'Then please feel free to go ahead. I will inform Hector.' Laila bestowed a gracious nod. 'What will you hope to discover?'

Libby found herself parroting almost exactly what Declan had said when he'd sat in this room earlier in the year, improvising where there were gaps in her knowledge, and Laila pretended to listen, flicking an occasional look towards her brother-in-law where he still stood motionless, gazing down. Perhaps she thought he was sulking, but Libby knew otherwise.

Then abruptly he straightened, and Libby saw that she was

right, recognising that spark in his eye. His force-of-nature look, Alice had called it, except that now that force was being carefully controlled, restrained –

'You know what, Laila,' he said, looking down at her glass. 'We should open a bottle of fizz. I've been so astounded by your news that we've never actually celebrated – and since Libby is here too. A small glass will do you no harm.'

Laila opened her eyes wide as Rodri left the room. 'Well!' she said, lifting her shoulders in a gesture of elegant incredulity. 'That man is full of surprises.'

Yes, and so beware.

He returned a moment later with three champagne flutes and a bottle which he opened with some style, aiming the cork into the fire where it set off a shower of sparks and shrieks of protest from Laila. He filled the glasses, passed them round, and raised his own. 'To the next baronet, and to you, Laila. And, of course, to Hector.' Libby raised her glass, murmuring her thanks, and then Rodri set his glass down. 'And, dammit, I've not congratulated him either. That's really bad of me.'

He went over to the phone on the desk. 'He's not at home, Rodri,' said Laila. 'I told you –'

He put down the phone 'Of course, Dubai again.' He pulled out his mobile, scrolling down to find the number. 'They're, what, about three hours ahead? So, it's about nine-ish there, and if I know Hector he'll just be warming up for the evening. But hopefully still coherent.' He put the phone to his ear, and waited. 'Hello, Hector? That you?' Libby was watching Laila's face, but her smile never wavered. 'Damn, it's gone to voicemail.' He left a brief message of congratulation, asking Hector to phone back, and then punched in a message as well, and smiled at them both. 'Drink up, Libby. You too, Laila, it really won't do you a bit of harm.'

'What is your husband doing in Dubai?' Libby asked, because Laila was looking at Rodri in a puzzled way.

'Trade delegations,' she said, shifting her attention back to Libby. 'I never really understand what he does, but he has a role as facilitator between governments and various companies.' She flashed an arch look at Rodri. 'His brother thinks he just opens the bottles and pours the drinks, but I think it is rather more.'

'Did I say that? Scurrilous of me,' Rodri remarked, checking his phone.

'He's probably in a meeting, or at some dinner,' said Laila, watching him.

'Yeah. So let's eat too, shall we?'

He called the boys from wherever they had been, and they all went through to the kitchen. Laila insisted on accompanying them to wash their hands while Rodri dished up the food. The boys slid silently into their seats, joined a minute or two later by Laila. Conversation flagged, and the boys eyed their aunt with the instinctive wariness of young creatures. What had they been told? Libby wondered. In an effort to draw attention away from Rodri, who sat silent and distracted at the end of the table, she described what they had discovered at the mound, and the boys were enchanted by the idea of the sword.

'It might be the sword that cut Odrhan's head open,' Charlie speculated.

'No, stupid!' his brother retorted. 'If it's Harald who was buried there, then Odrhan probably helped to bury it.'

'But doubtless it cut other people's heads open.' His father seemed to spring back to life, and pushed a bowl of beans across the table. 'So don't fret.'

'How many, do you think?' Charlie asked Libby. 'Heads, I mean.'

'Dozens, I expect,' she replied. What was Rodri up to?

Laila pulled a face. 'Not over dinner, please.'

She was ignored. 'They had axes too.' Charlie made a two-handed downward chopping gesture, which earned him another rebuke. 'You might find one of those too.'

'Maybe. And we haven't found the skull yet,' Libby remarked.

'Haven't you?' the boys chorused, enthralled by the idea of a headless corpse.

'Someone disturbed the burial years later, you see, and—'

'It was Erik! He came back. The legend says so.' Donald had put down his knife and fork with a clatter.

'Donald –' But Laila held no sway here.

'Erik came back, killed Odrhan, and then dug up Harald. It must have been him, and he hacked off his head and—'

'Please!'

Laila had put her hands over her ears and appealed to Rodri, who simply added: 'And Erik's abandoned son bore witness to it all, so the legend says.'

A little silence fell.

'Clear the plates, lads, and bring on pudding. Tart, with whipped cream. OK with you, Laila?' He sat back and picked up his phone to check it. 'Aha! Message from Hector. *"Thanks. Yeah, great news, eh. Will ring from Oslo. Madness here."* When is he back, Laila?'

She shrugged. 'In about a week, I think. But plans change all the time.'

He nodded, that odd spark in his eye more intense now; he punched another message into his phone, then slipped it into his pocket.

A thought suddenly occurred to Charlie. 'Does Uncle Hector like kayaking?'

Laila looked surprised. 'I expect he does, I know I do. We

used to fall in and out of kayaks all day when I was a child on the fjords.'

Donald scented an advantage. 'With a grown-up there, I suppose?'

'No! My sister and I used to go for miles down the fjord, we'd make a picnic and be out all day.'

Donald turned to his father. 'Dad – '

'Forget it.'

'Dad won't let us out of the bay by ourselves, even on flat calm days,' Charlie remarked in a casual tone, avoiding his father's eye.

Laila gave a little smile. 'Ah, but Rodri, how will they ever learn?'

'Yeah, Dad!'

'Drop it, I said.' Something in his tone got through, and the boys rolled exasperated eyes at each other. 'And hop it. Homework done?'

The boys left, grumbling, and Laila offered to make coffee. Libby was anxious to be off now, having said what she had to say, and the atmosphere had become impossibly strained. She too rose to go, making the students an excuse.

'They'll be fine,' Rodri said. 'And there's something I want to show you. I'll get it and check the charging too. Stick around. Laila makes a mean coffee.'

'What a strange man he is.' Laila laughed as he left. 'Sunshine and showers.' He was gone for several minutes, and as he came through the door Libby caught a grim expression which he rapidly replaced by a rueful one.

'Sorry, Libby, but the laptop charger was switched off at the socket. My fault. Did I show you this?' He handed her a book they had looked at last time she was here. The mad baronet's poem. 'Take it with you, it's a proven cure for insomnia.' She took it and sat down again.

The boys reappeared to say good night, still giving their father dark looks, and he went off with them while Laila poured the coffee. 'He is too protective of those boys,' she remarked, then shrugged. 'They mean the world to him, of course, and I expect I will be just the same . . . Will you carry the tray through for me please, Libbee. I will join you in a moment.' Libby went through to the library, set the tray down, then went over to her laptop, which was, as she half expected, fully charged.

Rodri appeared in the doorway. 'How's it doing?' he asked, glancing over his shoulder.

'Won't take long,' she replied.

'Splendid,' he said, and went over to the tray. A moment later Laila slipped in behind him.

They took their coffee to the fire and a silence fell. A log moved in the grate, and Rodri enquired politely what work they would do the next day and Libby gave him a very full, and tedious, answer, filling the space. Laila looked bored, but Rodri's eyes were very much alive.

He pulled his phone from his pocket. 'Ah. Hector again. *"Looks like it's going to be an all nighter."* You know what, Laila, Hector really ought to drink less.'

She shrugged. 'I have tried to stop him.'

'Tell him it's bad for the baby.'

She laughed, a lovely sweet laugh. 'I will.'

'Laptop charged yet?' he asked a moment later with a nod which conveyed the fact that it was alright for it to be charged now. What on earth was he up to?

She went over to the desk and made a show of looking. 'Yep. Fully charged.' She hesitated. 'So I'll be off. Thank you for supper.' Presumably he would escort her to the door, if not back to the camp, and explain what was going on.

'It was our pleasure. Rodri will help you carry the things to the campsite,' said Laila.

'That's kind –'

'But there's no need. I know,' he said swiftly. 'An independent soul, is our Liberty Snow.' He handed her the laptop and battery with a bland smile. 'Laila will see you out, and I'll go and see the boys are settled. Early start tomorrow.'

Chapter 26

~~◆ *Ellen* ◆~~

Ellen saw from the window of her mother's cottage that people were gathering out on the headland. Earlier she had seen Alick walking swiftly towards the manse, and a moment later he and Mr Drummond had come out again and set off to join the group on the headland. Something must have been found there.

But she would not go to see. She would not leave the cottage, would see no one, speak to no one, thankful only that her mother was too spent to notice her distress. She was dying, and all that Ellen wanted was to die with her.

Ravens were nesting in the trees above the cottage, skittering on the roof like dark spirits, and she had lain listening to their harsh cawing as they mocked her. They knew what had happened, for she had glimpsed them circling above her in the clearing beside the pool, after he had gone, and now they had come for her mother.

But she felt nothing. Only numbness. And somewhere, shame. She would not think of what had happened. Not the struggle, nor the weight of him, and the pain –

– and then the threat.

~~◆ *Six weeks later, Oliver* ◆~~

It seemed to Oliver as he walked back home in the fading evening light that his superstitious parishioners could fairly claim that their prophesies had come true. Trouble stalked their little community. An outbreak of influenza threatened his flock; it had already carried off two old people and others were suffering. Ellen's mother had been in the ground for six weeks, and already a new family had moved into her cottage. Ellen now occupied a room in the manse's attic and went about her duties like a biddable wraith. For a while he thought that the influenza had caught her too and had watched her carefully, eventually concluding that her pallor and low spirits were attributable to grief rather than illness. Thank goodness he could provide a roof over her head. There might be talk, of course, although Mrs Nichol lived in, but his credit was now so low in the community he could not afford to sink further. He sensed a coolness even from Lady Sturrock.

He kicked a stone that lay in his path. And that coolness would turn arctic if she knew that the thought of marrying Ellen Mackay now dominated his daytime thoughts and kept him awake at night. He had already given her ladyship reason enough to have him removed from his position: a dwindling congregation, a desecrated grave, and an alienated community, and taking his housemaid to wife would doubtless seal his doom. And without a living, how could he support Ellen?

But she was so lovely, and now so lost, and his heart went out to her. If only for her sake, he wished that he had never suggested the work on the headland, for it seemed to have fed her strange obsession with Ulla's legend, warping and twisting her mind so that it had become a fear in her. She would jump at the slightest sound, her eyes round with alarm, shrinking hollow-eyed into the shadows if he addressed her, the bloom quite gone from her. And there seemed no way to reach her.

And then there was the chalice, burning a hole in his conscience. Alick had told him to say nothing but to keep it in the manse until they had time to consider what was best to do. It lay wrapped in a clean cloth, hidden in the deepest of the desk drawers, a constant worry and reproach. The thought that it was Odrhan's grave that had been desecrated haunted Oliver, unsettling his nights, and filled him with an overwhelming sense of shame and wrongdoing. Whoever had laid the holy father to rest had meant him to remain there at peace.

And at peace he had been until Oliver Drummond had taken it upon himself to propose that they investigate, and the devil of it was that because of all the furore they could tell no one of this extraordinary find!

A larger and even more disapproving crowd had gathered for the short service of prayer when the bones were reburied in the floor of the desecrated cell, and he had bestowed what dignity he could upon the occasion. On his return to the manse, he had learned from Mrs Nichol that Ellen's mother had breathed her last with only Ellen beside her, and he had gone to her at once but had been unable to reach the eldritch girl who had sat, tearless and distant, his words of comfort passing over her head. His failure had felt complete, and the shame of it would haunt him forever.

Alick Sturrock had started coming more regularly to the manse since then, and Oliver very much valued his company. He too was seeking sanctuary, he said with his wry, beguiling smile, out of range of his mother's censure and his father's tongue. 'Set against a career as a respected lawyer, that of grave robber sits ill with Papa,' he said. As, Oliver imagined, did upsetting the local tenantry.

Oliver too had suffered a humiliating interview with Lady Sturrock. Defence would have been difficult had not Alick told her beforehand that the desecration had been Mungo's handiwork, not theirs. 'Nevertheless, Mr Drummond,' she had said, 'the work was under your aegis and the upset caused is far out of proportion to the knowledge gained.' This was undeniable, and Oliver could only apologise again, trying not to think of the chalice which resided, undeclared, in the drawer of his desk.

⇢ Ellen ⇠

More and more Ellen found herself drawn back to the headland, the one place she could find solace. There were signs still of the recent disturbance there, the marram grasses trampled flat and newly exposed surfaces on the stones bare of the bright lichens and slow-growing mosses. Yet this was the place she came to dull her grief and hide her shame, where her senses were numbed and where she could inhabit another time.

Bones had been found, she had heard folk say. Human bones. But whose were these? The old folk said that Ulla's bones had been found years back, buried with a golden cross. But it was Ulla's presence she felt here.

⇢ Odrhan ⇠

Ulla's pains began the night of the next full moon.

She cried out, and Odrhan went running for Morag, blessing the moon for lighting his path. Morag came, but slowly, panting as she stopped for breath. 'Peace, holy man,' she gasped, her hand on her heaving bosom as he urged her on. They could hear Ulla's cries as they rounded the bay, and as Odrhan ran on ahead, the moon slid behind a charcoal cloud.

He burst through the entrance and took her hand, seeing her lips were bloodied from where she had bitten them.

'Promise me, Odrhan,' she said, as the pain subsided, 'that if I die, you will bury me with Harald.'

He looked over his shoulder. Where was the woman! 'You will not die, Ulla! Morag is here.'

She gripped his hand as the pains came again. 'Swear to it, and if I live I will turn to your god.'

He heard Morag panting outside. 'Ulla! I –'

'Promise me, Odrhan. On your soul!' Ulla's eyes were wild with pain and fear. 'Or I will curse you.'

And so, not because of the threat but to calm her, he laid his hand on her brow. 'I promise.'

⇥ *Ellen* ⇤

'Ellen!' She had half risen before she recognised the voice and sank back. Alick. He climbed over the rocks and came towards her. 'I thought I saw you heading this way. It's good to see you out and about, and you're looking better. There's colour in your cheeks!' His fair hair blew across his forehead and his eyes were kind. 'It'll get easier, you know, Ellen, as you grow accustomed, and she was very peaceful in the end.'

'How can we know that?'

He looked surprised. 'You were with her, were you not?'

Of course, he meant her mother. But her mother belonged to another world, one she had shut away, and she hung her head. 'I thought you meant Ulla.'

He stared at her. 'Ulla? My dear girl, why would I mean Ulla?'

She looked down at the tumbled stones. 'I feel her very close when I'm here.' And she felt her pain.

'Oh, Ellen, my dear, this is just your fancy!'

'It isn't.'

He contemplated her a moment, then sat on a boulder opposite her. 'So tell me then, what exactly is it that you feel?'

'Only that. It's as if she is here, as if they are all here, invisible, but just behind a veil. Ulla and Harald. Odrhan –' and Erik, but she would not say his name. How could one brother be so kind and one so cruel?

'And only in this place?'

She shrugged. 'Sometimes in others places too.' Like in a hidden spot below the drovers' bridge where sunlight shafting onto the pool had beguiled her to her fate. She wanted to tell him how she had seen Ulla's reflection. And not heeded the warning.

'At any particular time of day?'

'No.'

'I see you here in the evenings quite often. Is the feeling stronger then? In the fading light?'

She frowned. So many questions. 'No –' He was peering at her in a rather disconcerting way, but she had his full attention. 'Mr Drummond said some prayers over the bones, didn't he?'

'Yes, he did. That's right. People were upset, you see –'

'But Ulla might have died a pagan.'

'*Ulla* might have, but –'

'So what happens if prayers are said for a pagan who doesn't want to go to heaven?'

Alick pulled a wry face. 'That question sort of came up on the day the bones were found, but we managed to skirt around it. It's one for Oli—for Mr Drummond, not me. The efficaciousness of my prayers would be frankly questionable anyway. I'm not convinced about the reality of heaven and hell' – he gave her a conspiratorial smile – 'but don't tell Mama, or she'd say I was a pagan too.'

'And are you?'

It was a simple, direct question, but he laughed. 'Well, *atheist* is the word that's used now.'

'Atheist.' She tried out the unfamiliar word. 'And it means pagan?'

'Not quite. A pagan believes in gods other than the Christian God, while an atheist . . .' He paused. 'Well, an atheist believes there is no God.'

No God? His face had taken on a serious expression as he watched the gulls wheeling and diving. But where, after all, had God been that day below the drovers' bridge? She looked at him, uncertain. 'And that is what you believe?'

He did not answer at once. 'I believe in something beyond the physical,' he said at last, and his eyes followed the gliding flight of a fulmar as it skimmed past on powerful wings. It had a nest in the dunes, she had seen it go there earlier, changing places with its mate. 'And I believe in the enduring spirit, if not in the immortal soul.'

She felt excitement stir. 'You do?'

He turned back to her. 'I've heard people discussing such matters in Edinburgh, and you know, Ellen, there are so many things that are unexplained that there simply *has* to be something in it. Such a lot is just dismissed as bunkum, but that denies what science is showing us every day. And we are just at the beginning! There are unseen forces all around us, you know.' His enthusiasm was infectious, and she listened, her lips parted. 'Take magnetism for example, and electrical currents. They exist but we can't see them, and yet they've *always* been there awaiting discovery, like invisible waves, in the invisible ether. Evidence of things unseen! And they say that voices can travel hundreds of miles on these unseen waves, so maybe thoughts can do the same. Don't you think? And there can't be thoughts without something thinking 'em. And so if you take away the dimension of time, maybe these somethings survive.' He was talking quickly and she struggled to keep up with him. 'Let's call them spirits, shall we, released from their physical bodies, still here, all around us, just as you say, invisible behind a veil.' She stared back at him, understanding very little but feeling a strange surge within her as she listened. 'We have to open our minds to these possibilities even where they challenge our cherished beliefs, and that includes antiquated notions of heaven and hell. Perhaps once the spirit is free from the body, it is indestructible.'

His last sentence leapt out at her. 'So when I feel that Ulla is close to me, what I'm feeling is real?'

'Why not? I don't *know*, of course, but it could be. That's what's so fascinating about it all, and we have to keep asking these questions.'

Ellen's mind was in a whirl. 'And so when I feel her in me, as part of me, that's real too?'

The light in Alick's eyes changed and sharpened as if he was only now seeing her. 'You feel her *in* you?'

'I think I always have.'

He frowned a little, and his gaze slid away from her. After a moment he spoke again, but in a different tone. 'Look, Ellen, these are just ideas, you know. There's a lot of research still needed as no one really *understands* these phenomena. For goodness' sake, don't go off with the idea that I've said you're possessed or Mr Drummond would have my scalp.'

The radiance in her died. 'But you just said that maybe the spirit can survive. And if it can survive, perhaps it can inhabit – '

Alick got to his feet, and smiled a little oddly. 'Look, Ellen, I get carried away. Don't mind me too much. These things fascinate me, you see, but I had forgotten that for you just now, this is not the time, after recent events – '

Panic jagged through her. 'You *know*?'

The bafflement on his face brought her halfway back to reason. He meant her mother again, and for a moment the pain of loss penetrated the icy barrier and reached her heart. And she turned away, saying nothing. 'Are you alright, Ellen?' he asked, and she nodded, not meeting his eyes, and he held out his hand. 'Let me walk you back to the manse, then. And really, you know, don't take much account of what I said, will you. Listen to Mr Drummond instead, he's a good man and you can trust him, you know.'

⇥ Odrhan ⇤

There was a hollow outside Odrhan's cell filled with a sandy soil where marram grasses and sea thrift had taken root, and he worked all day, in numb despair, making a place for her. When he reached bare rock, he stopped and gazed out over the steel-grey ocean with unfocussed eyes. It had been a promise made only to calm her.

Morag had taken the child, a boy, and would find a nurse for him.

He went back into the cell and gathered her up, holding her close, and then laid her there on the unyielding rocks where he could watch over her, and pray. He took the cross from around his neck and placed it on her breast, and looked his last upon her beauty. A promise broken, aye, but he had to consider her soul.

God, he knew, would be merciful and take her to his bosom.

But for himself, he was lost, and cared not. All that was left to him now was to stay close to her, and pray.

Chapter 27

Libby expected that Rodri would come down to the site in the morning and explain, but he didn't; the path to Sturrock House remained empty. He was clearly up to something but she'd no idea what, so there was nothing to be done other than get stuck into work and await developments. Work helped, but her sense of unease grew as the morning wore on. The students had uncovered all of the stone setting at the mound and proved that it was indeed a long oval. 'Boat-shaped,' said Callum with a satisfied smile as he finished photographing it. At the beginning of the year that in itself would have made the whole project worthwhile, but now she merely nodded. The mound might go a long way to encapsulating the legend of Ullaness, but there was more hidden here than old bones and ancient wrongs.

It was midmorning when she looked up and saw Laila on the track walking briskly towards them, and went on alert. What now? She went forward to meet her before she got within earshot of the students. 'Good morning, Laila –'

'Where is Rodri?' Her face was hard and angry.

'I've not seen him this morning.'

'No?' She looked disbelieving. 'But you know where he is.'

'I'm afraid I don't.'

Laila made an angry dismissive noise. 'There's no one at the house. He's not answering his phone or replying to messages. No

Alice, no boys, and only *this* on the kitchen table.' She thrust a piece of paper at Libby. 'So where is he?'

> *Called away. The boys are with Maddy and Alice after school and will stay there until I get back. Alice will pop along sometime to see you have all you need.*

She handed the note back.

'Called away!' Laila almost spat at her. 'He said nothing about it last night.'

'Perhaps something came up.'

'After ten o'clock at night?'

Libby spread her hands. 'I've really no idea. He said nothing to me.'

Except, *early start tomorrow*, she remembered suddenly, accompanied by a steady stare. That sharp brain had been busy scheming as he stared into the fire last night. But doing what? And then she realised he had known that Laila would come asking these questions, and wanted her to be able to look the woman in the eye and say, with truth, that she knew nothing.

She turned back to find Laila viewing her with cold suspicion. 'He must have told *someone*. And he sneaked out early, taking the boys. Far too early for school. Where did they go?'

'To Alice and Maddy, he says.' Like a fox moving its young out of danger, and she remembered his expression that time during Laila's last visit when they had stood on the headland and watched small hands waving from Angus's fishing boat.

'The lesbians! And do I now have to wait until Alice chooses to come to work?' Laila turned to go. 'And how will I get to the airport in the morning? Rodri was going to take me. It's an early flight.'

'I expect he'll be back.'

But where was he?

'Yes. Because he is *employed* to be here.'

But not for much longer, she thought, so why care? 'Perhaps it's estate business he's gone to,' she offered.

'Or a woman, more likely. Did you think of that?' Spite briefly curled those lovely lips; then Laila turned and went swiftly back up the path.

Callum strolled over to her. 'Problem?' he asked, his eyes following Laila's retreat.

'Not for us. Come on, time for tea break.'

———————

Alice appeared at lunchtime with another of her baskets, and the students circled her like greedy gulls. 'Go on, take it away. Off you go,' she said, and pulled Libby to one side. 'Where's he gone?' she asked.

'I don't know.' But she'd come to the conclusion that the exchange of text messages last night was pivotal to Rodri's disappearance. Hector must have told him something that he hadn't read out. But for now she would keep quiet about it. Better so. 'I really don't.'

Alice explored her face a moment, then nodded. 'Angus said he arrived just after five this morning with the boys, bundled them into the cottage with instructions that no one was to let them out of sight, other than at school, until he got back. But he didn't explain. Normally I sleep over if he's going away, but he'd said nothing. Just left a message for me to go and see if milady needed anything. Other than a slap, that is.'

'Did he tell Angus when he'd be back?'

Alice shook her head. 'A day or two was all he said. And he's not answering his phone.'

'Laila goes back tomorrow –'

'I know! And she's spitting like a scalded cat. Got me to order her a taxi in case he's not back in time to take her. Tried to tell me I had to take her until I pointed out that I work for Rodri, not her. I just loved saying it!' She laughed and the tension broke for a moment; then she gave Libby a direct look. 'He's up to something, isn't he?'

'I think so, yes,' she replied, holding the look.

'Something big?'

'Perhaps.'

'Then there'll be no stopping him.' Alice had lost something of her jauntiness, and just for a moment she looked fearful. 'Angus said he kept telling him to watch over the boys, all three of them, and to keep them out of Laila's way until he got back. I don't like it.'

⊷ *Odrhan* ⊶

Odrhan watched the boy run down into the waves, squealing with delight, sending up sprays of water which caught the sunlight, and he smiled. Pádraig was a happy child, and an unexpected joy. When Morag had brought him back, newly weaned, Odrhan had protested, but she had shrugged, saying that they had enough mouths of their own to feed.

Odrhan had grown thin from self-neglect since Ulla died, his hair and beard long, but he had taken himself in hand when the child returned. He named him Pádraig and taught him to love God, describing his own boyhood in Ireland, and had shown him the wondrous chalice. And as the boy grew he told him about Harald, who had died a pagan, and about Ulla, his mother, and how she had turned to God in the end and found comfort there.

He almost convinced himself that it was so.

And he and the boy grew close.

⟶ *Libby* ⟵

It was hard to focus on work after Alice left, but with the students now engrossed in their own parts of the project Libby was able to spend the afternoon simply going between the mound, the church, and the surveyors, giving at least the appearance of being engaged. Surely Laila offered no threat to the boys, how could she! Libby crossed the little stream, back towards the church. And if Rodri was worried, he wouldn't leave them for long, and even if he wasn't answering his phone he'd be receiving messages, so if there was an emergency they could reach him.

But Alice had looked fearful. And Alice knew him well.

What on earth was he up to?

'Libby!' Callum called from the mound, and she saw him beckoning. She went over. 'Skull fragments,' he said.

Libby pulled her trowel from her back pocket and crouched down and saw that he was right. Distinctive curved fragments of bone had appeared in the sieve and there seemed to be a concentration of them in one patch of sand, well away from the other bones. 'Keep going,' she said, and straightened.

At the end of the hour they had recovered most of the skull, and Libby stood looking down at the finds tray. It was going to take conservators hours to reconstruct the many fragments and make a skull from them, but it didn't take a bone specialist to recognise the force of the injuries it had sustained. If this indeed was Harald, then his cranium had been smashed by a mighty blow, and a cut mark through the upper vertebrae showed where the head had been severed from the body. But all this, if she was right, was postmortem, and probably post-burial. In other words, someone had dug the poor soul up and then wreaked fury on the remains.

It was a sickening thought, and somehow served to heighten

the current tension. 'Bag it all up,' she said, 'and go carefully through the rest.'

———————

In the middle of the afternoon Alice was back, and again dragged Libby aside. 'You'll have to come up to the house. Laila's hysterical.' She dropped her voice. 'It's about the students.'

'The *students*?'

'I don't know what, but you'll have to come, or she'll be down here making a scene.'

That would never do, so Libby followed Alice back up the track. 'She's quite bonkers, you know,' Alice said, over her shoulder, 'and she's bloody well packed up another one of the paintings just out of spite. Then she went upstairs to get the rest of her stuff together and two minutes later came storming back down ranting about the students being in the house.'

'But they weren't! I said two of them could charge their phones in the dairy over lunch, if they asked you first –'

'Aye, and they did, and I told them to use the kitchen sockets, it's cold in the dairy.'

'So what happened?'

'She wouldn't say. Just told me to get you up there fast.'

Oh God. And one look at Laila's face was enough to see that this was serious. She was pacing the floor with her phone to her ear, but she slammed it down on the table as Libby entered. 'Those kids who were here this morning. What are their names? I'm calling the police. They've taken everything – passport, credit cards, money. Left me with a pile of loose change and a plane ticket for Oslo tomorrow, for a flight I cannot now take.'

Libby stared at her. 'But why do you think one of my students took them?'

'It was all there last night.'

Last night –

'Perhaps you moved them somewhere else,' Alice suggested, looking from Libby to Laila.

'Don't be a fool, girl.'

Libby went and sat down, buying herself a little time to think. Last night . . . How did Rodri expect her to handle this one? It was clearly his doing. Far from wanting Laila gone, for some reason of his own he wanted her stranded here. 'You're making a very serious allegation,' she said.

'Yes,' Laila snapped back. 'And so I shall ring the police.'

'By all means.'

Laila stopped pacing, arrested by Libby's calm compliance. 'You must search their tents first, of course,' she said.

Libby looked back at her. 'I doubt if any of my students are stupid enough to steal a passport, cards, and cash and then stuff them into their sleeping bags and hope no one will notice.' And fail to take an expensive phone at the same time; Laila seemed not to have remarked that oversight. 'Where was the stuff?'

'In my room. In my handbag.'

'And where was *your* bag this morning, Alice?'

'Where it is now.' Alice gestured to the counter where her bag was in plain sight, lying half open.

'Then you'd better check it too.' Alice gave her a swift look, went across to her bag, and tipped out the contents. She picked up her wallet and made a play of counting the bills and checking the cards.

'All fine.'

'So why risk going upstairs and robbing you instead?' Libby asked, and Laila glared back at her. 'Are you quite sure Alice isn't right, and you didn't repack it all somewhere?'

In the end there was a sort of stalemate. Libby agreed to go and question her students while Laila said she would go through her things again, with Alice's help, even though she declared it to be pointless.

It could be only a matter of time before she worked out who the culprit was. As Libby left, Alice came close and murmured: 'Rodri?' and Libby gave a nod and a shrug. 'Oh God.' Alice's eyes widened; then she turned back at Laila's sharp summons.

Back down at the camp, and in response to Libby's carefully casual questioning, the students all denied having gone anywhere except the dairy and the kitchen, and she left it at that. Callum raised his eyebrows, but she shook her head and said nothing more. A little later she told him simply that something had gone missing at the house but that she knew the students weren't involved, and work resumed with a minimum of fuss. If Laila *did* contact the police, she could now truthfully say that questions had been asked. The ball was back in Laila's court. Alice, she felt sure, was woman enough to deal with whatever was happening up at the house, and would play her part with style. *We're a good team*, she had said. But when the team leader abruptly absented himself without explaining the rules of engagement, it was a nerve-wracking experience.

At the end of the day Alice's little car appeared at the end of the track, and Libby went over to speak to her. She got out and leaned against the door, her eyes alive with merriment. 'Oh, but is she *cross*! Quite beside herself. She's decided that Rodri must have taken them.'

'I thought it wouldn't take her long. Has she called the police?'

'No. She's giving him until tomorrow to come back and explain himself and, if not, then she will. But she's brought forward his eviction date to August, and says he can't have the manse.'

'Can she do that?'

'Not without Hector's say-so.'

Libby thought swiftly. Alice deserved to know something of the truth. 'I think this is something to do with Hector,' she said, and told her about the messaging backwards and forwards which had somehow electrified Rodri. But of her suspicions regarding Laila's pregnancy she said nothing.

Alice listened. 'Dear God, what a pair! And why the cloak-and-dagger stuff? What's Hector up to?'

'I thought they were barely on speaking terms.'

'It's not been good and got worse this last year, but Maddy said they were close when they were young, just normal kids like Donald and Charlie. Then that woman came between them and messed up all their lives. Rodri's told you all this?'

'Some of it.'

Alice gave her a slanting look, but there was a smile in it. 'The man's so buttoned-up! Hector and Maddy had had a thing going, off and on, since childhood, and when Hector got her pregnant neither of them knew straightaway. His leave finished and he went back to fight but came home wounded soon after, and it all went pear-shaped. Maddy had never been good enough for precious Hector so having him immobilised in the house suited Lady Sturrock very well. Just imagine! The keeper's daughter? No way. So Maddy was kept at arm's length, and Hector, to be fair, was so stoned on medication he was out of it. About then Rodri brought Laila home to meet the family, and the lovely Laila realised she'd hitched herself to the wrong brother and became Hector's devoted nurse. Lady Sturrock thought she was an angel.'

'Poor Maddy.'

Alice smiled a complacent smile. 'But lucky me, eh? Maddy realised she was pregnant and took off, terrified of what Angus would say, though she'd no worries on that score, the silly girl. Anyway, she came to Glasgow, where we met.' She paused. 'And lucky Rodri too, escaping the Ice Queen's clutches. Hector and Laila deserve each other.' But it had left a legacy of resentment that went deep. 'And Laila hates the very thought of David, poor kid.'

'Were Hector's injuries – '

'Leg and chest. Don't know about the bits in between. Don't want to.'

Perhaps that accounted for the false pregnancy, though surely there were simpler ways! Or did inheritance have to follow the bloodline? Libby wondered how far Hector was involved in the deception. The text messages Rodri had read out had been cordial enough, but there must have been something in them which had prompted his disappearance.

And she found herself wondering how long it took to fly to Dubai.

Chapter 28

Damn Alick Sturrock! Oliver sat back in his chair as Ellen shut the study door behind her, and dismay was replaced by anger. How *could* he have said such things to her! Oliver got to his feet and went and stood at the window. Two ravens were tearing at the remains of a rabbit, squabbling and pecking at each other as they bounced around the corpse.

'You're looking a little better today, my dear,' he had said, when Ellen had brought him a tray of tea, noting the dark rings under her eyes and the translucency of her skin. He tried again to reach her through her aura of grief. 'Ellen, I feel sure that your mother would not have wanted you to grieve overlong.'

'No, sir.'

'She was a good person, a gentle soul.'

'Yes.'

It was not a promising start, but he had persevered. 'And you can draw comfort from the thought of her, looking down on you from heaven –'

She had straightened at that and given him an odd look. 'But how can I *know* that, sir?'

'My dear Ellen! She was a good woman, a godly woman. How could it be otherwise?'

She looked strange and fey, almost wild. 'Do you mean that her *soul* is in heaven?'

He replied with studied calm: 'Yes, that is what I mean.'

'And her spirit?'

'Her spirit?'

'If her soul is in heaven, can her spirit still be here in the . . .' She paused as if struggling for the word. '. . . the . . . the ether.' Oliver had frowned, wondering where she had learned it. 'Though I don't feel her around me, like I do with Ulla.'

This obsession with Ulla was becoming unhealthy, and he wondered if her mother's death might have affected her mind. He tried for a reproving but gentle tone. 'This belief in spirits is misguided, Ellen. Christian teaching tells us—'

'Should we not question it?' A suspicion began to enter Oliver's mind, and was quickly confirmed. 'Mr Alick says—'

'Stop there!' He spoke with enough force to make Ellen jump. So while he had been tiptoeing around Ellen's sensibilities, Alick Sturrock had become intimate enough to talk of spirits and the ether, had he? And had he, Oliver, saved her from the physical assaults of Mungo Sturrock only to have his brother corrupt her mind? 'I can well imagine what Mr Alick has been saying, but I tell you this, Ellen, he has got in with a bad group of people, misguided people, intellectuals who would undermine centuries of teaching and learning, and cast doubt on the word of God.'

But Ellen's face had adopted a stubborn expression. 'People ought to question those teachings, though, and Mr Alick says that scientists can actually *hear* the voices of spirits.'

'What?'

'From hundreds of miles away.'

'Ellen –'

'And he says that perhaps spirits can exist forever, like a sort of gas, so Ulla's spirit could still be here. And Harald's.'

Oliver had swallowed hard. If he was to win this battle, he must remain calm, and his words must carry authority. 'Mr Alick is confused in his own mind, and it is high time we spoke together on these matters. I've been meaning to – ' but had not found the courage to confront him, valuing his friendship too much. 'Listen to me, Ellen, you must disregard what he has told you and – ' But she was staring out of the window, beyond the dunes towards the headland, and he saw that he had lost her.

'Mr Alick said that he's a new sort of pagan. He gave it a name.'

Oliver supplied it through gritted teeth. 'An atheist?' She nodded. 'But you are not an atheist, Ellen, you are a good Christian.'

'Did Ulla really become a Christian, do you think, or did she remain a pagan?' Oliver groaned silently. What went on in the girl's head! 'Harald was a pagan, and she had loved him dearly,' she continued, and he began to see where her thinking was taking her.

'Yes! And Erik was a pagan too! A violent, murderous man.' At that, her face had drained of colour and she had gripped the side of the desk. He had risen and gone to her, putting out his hand, but she had stiffened like a cornered animal, so he dropped it and sat again. 'Enough now, Ellen. No more talk of pagans and spirits. Grief has unsettled your mind, my dear. Say your prayers. They will help you and we will speak again, but first I will talk to Mr Alick.' And somehow resist the un-Christian urge to throttle him.

Oliver grabbed his hat and coat and left the house. In this at least his duty was clear; he must tackle Alick robustly and should have done so much earlier. What was the man thinking! Expounding intellectual nihilism and placing such doubts in the mind of a susceptible girl, recently bereaved. It was entirely reprehensible! Poor Ellen! And yet, and yet – Honesty compelled him to admit that jealousy was also fuelling his fury, and he paused, rocking perilously on a stepping stone midstream, before leaping to the opposite bank. Ellen, who barely said more than yes sir and no sir to *him*, had apparently engaged in profound philosophical discussions with Alick, absorbing his nonsense like a heron swallowing a frog.

And it was Harald the pagan, he observed, not Odrhan the godly, who had been cast in the role of hero.

He stopped at the thought, and laughed out loud. But how absurd! Dear Lord, he was becoming as bad as Ellen. The thought calmed him, and he slowed his pace, realising that he could hardly march up to Sturrock House and accuse Alick of corrupting his housemaid without creating something of a stir. He paused beside a low mound amongst the dunes and looked out to sea where a cloud bank was forming. And better, of course, to put together a coherent argument first, one that would not sound fusty and prosaic.

And one that he himself believed in.

'Oliver!' He turned at the call and saw that his quarry was coming through the garden gate, his hand raised in greeting. 'I was coming to see you.'

Anger flooded back at the sight of him. 'Then well met, as I was coming to find you. Let's walk, shall we?' And he turned towards the shore.

'By all means. Look, I've been thinking about the chalice –'

'Another time. It's Ellen I want to talk about.'

'Ellen?'

'You've upset her, damn you! In fact, you've been entirely irresponsible. What did you think you were doing, discussing spirits when her mother is not yet two months in the ground? She's quite bewildered by it all.'

Alick winced. 'Oh Lord.'

'Yes. Quite!'

'I'd not upset Ellen for the world.'

'Well, you have!' Oliver snapped back. 'Filling her head with nonsense about spirit voices that can be heard over hundreds of miles . . .'

'What?'

'A new sort of pagan, are you? Good God, man!'

Alick was staring back at him, mouth agape. 'I was talking about telegraphy and radio waves.'

'And did *she* know that?' Oliver rounded on him. 'I knew it was your doing when she mentioned the ether. Did you imagine that the theories of Maxwell and his ilk would be in any way comprehensible to her? Just the thing for a girl like Ellen. Yes, you might well look aghast!' Oliver felt his anger boiling over. 'A little learning is a dangerous thing, Pope said, and shallow draughts intoxicate the brain. Well, Ellen's mind was already drunk on this wretched legend and straining under the burden of her mother's death –'

Alick's distress was almost ludicrous. Then he turned and looked out towards the headland, adding in chastened tones: 'She seemed to think it might be Ulla's bones that Mungo dug up.'

'What! *Why?*'

'I didn't try to correct her because then I'd have had to tell her about the cleaved skull, and I thought that might be worse.' Oliver hissed his annoyance. 'She thinks she's possessed by the spirit of Ulla, you see.' Alick spoke quickly, like a child wanting to get the worst off his chest.

Oliver looked at him over his shoulder in contempt. 'And who put the idea in her head!'

'Not I! We simply met out on the headland. She was just sitting there, looking so damned miserable, so we sat and talked for ages. I only wanted to comfort her. Oliver, we've known each other since childhood! I'm fond of her.'

Oliver remained silent. Then, with a deep reluctance, he said,

'That's as may be, but I suggest that you tread carefully.'

'Meaning what?' Hauteur returned to Alick's voice, and Oliver was reminded of Sir Donald.

'Meaning that having cast herself as Ulla, she needs little encouragement to see you as Harald.'

Chapter 29

Libby banned the students from going up to the house next day and they saw nothing of Laila, or Alice. Instead, that evening a shuttle of cars got everyone to the pub and, by agreement with the landlord, phones and laptops were recharged there while pints were pulled. Libby took hers to the corner of the room where the locals made space for the students, smiling her thanks as she wove her way through the tables. It was good to be away from the camp where the presence of Laila in Sturrock House seemed to hang like a menacing cloud. As far as Libby knew, no taxi had come to collect her, and so by now she would have missed her flight. Who knew what would happen next, but Libby sensed that things were coming rapidly to a head.

A commotion at the bar drew her attention, and the intensity of student noise suddenly increased. And then she saw why.

Declan.

He had emerged from the door leading to the stairs up to the bedrooms and was now being greeted enthusiastically by the students, for whom he was soon buying a round. She watched him scan the room until he found her, nod briefly, and then turn back to the students. She'd have to go over and talk to him, of course, and keep up the appearance of common purpose. But Declan, on top of everything else! She gave him a minute or two to come to her, and then wove her way back through the tables to the bar. He turned as she approached. 'Going well, I hear,' he said, but coldly.

'As well as can be expected, but the mound has been pretty well destroyed.'

'Callum said.'

'But it's still a useful—'

'You've not started at the headland, I understand,' he interrupted. 'Why not?'

His tone was aggressive, but she answered calmly. 'We needed to finish other things first. But I thought we'd start there tomorrow.'

'Dead right we will. I'll be down first thing and set things up there while you tie up the other loose ends. It's potentially the most interesting part of the site – besides the church.' He hesitated, then gave her a calculating look. 'I hear that Lady Sturrock is in residence, and Rodri Sturrock isn't.'

'That's right.'

'Good.' She knew what he was thinking, of course, but he'd soon learn that Laila had other things on her mind. 'I'll be down straight after breakfast,' he said, and turned back to join in the students' banter.

It was almost dark by the time everyone had been shuttled back to camp. The western sky was drained of colour, leaving the horizon a smudged line of pale shades fading into a dark sea. She parked her car, depressed by the thought of Declan, and was getting the laptop from the boot when she caught a glint of metal in the darkness. The Land Rover. It was parked up close to the old manse, half-hidden in the shadows. He was back! But parked here and not at the house . . . She scanned the camp, then went over to the caravan and looked inside. Empty.

But she knew where he would be.

Stopping only to collect a torch from her tent, she left the students on their way to the food tent for a last drink, and picked her way carefully along the causeway. Light still lingered in the sky, but darkness was creeping over the sea as the world became monochrome. She scrambled up to the plateau, the torch in her hand, and saw him, seated with his back against the walls of Odrhan's tumbled cell, his elbows resting on bent knees, staring out to the horizon.

He turned his head as the beam from her torch found him. 'Libby? Good. I hoped you'd come.' And in the dying light she saw how drawn his face was, how tired. He gestured to the space beside him and she sat. 'Is everything alright here? I've not been up to the house yet.'

'Everything's fine. Though Laila's in a fury over her passport and money.'

He gave a mirthless laugh. 'She would be, but I couldn't risk her following me.'

They sat in silence. Was he going to explain? 'You went to Dubai?' she prompted. But could he have been there and back so quickly?

'Oslo. Hector's in Norway. He's never been in Dubai.'

'Oh.'

There was a longer silence. 'Hector's dying,' he said, and his voice sounded thin and strained. 'Three months, the doctors said, six if he's lucky. He's in a private hospital. Been in and out over the last year attempting to dry out. Hopeless case. As soon as he gets out, they told me, he backslides. Every sodding time.'

He turned his head away from her and a light breeze ruffled the hair on his forehead, covering the frown which now seemed permanently etched there. 'I'm sorry,' she said, and put a hand on his arm. Without turning back, he closed his own over it, and kept it there.

'Not as sorry as I am,' he said, and then, after a moment, 'I've been so blind.' He fell silent again and she said nothing. He would tell this story his own way, or not at all.

Eventually, he did.

'I've known Laila was a bad lot for a long time,' he said, 'but not that she was wicked. Every damn e-mail I've had over the last few months has been from her, masquerading as Hector or Hector's secretary, deliberately driving the wedge between us.' He let out his breath in a juddering sigh. 'Every demand for money has been instigated by her, made to look as if it came from him. He's been in this hospital more or less continuously since March, just about the time she came here to cash in the Nasmyth, a virtual prisoner, from what I can gather. The doctors kept trying to send him home, but she'd told them he was violent and begged them to keep him. She has his credit cards, passport, e-mail passwords, everything – and she's been smuggling drink in to him there. He's so bloody stupid he thought she did it from kindness.' He dropped his head and stared down at the grass between his knees.

'And the pregnancy?' she asked.

His shoulder shook slightly before he replied. 'I asked him about it, and just for a moment I saw such a blaze of joy on his face . . . Then his eyes went dead and he said it wasn't his, and that it was unlikely to be true anyway, and told me why.' He stopped again, for longer this time. 'And then he started to put other things together in his head,' he continued in a flat tone, 'and so I've spent the last two days destroying the one thing he had to cling to, his love for that worthless woman.'

He raised his head and gazed out over the dark ocean, and then bit by bit the story came out. He'd caught a flight to Oslo and gone straight to Hector's house to find it locked and empty. A neighbour had come out, and when he told her who he was the woman assumed that Laila had sent him to collect things to take, imagining her to be at the hospital. 'Such a *lovely* lady, the neighbour said.' He'd gone along with the story and she'd let him in using the key she held for them.

Once inside he had rifled through their papers until he'd found bills from a private hospital, located in the mountainous area between Oslo and Bergen, and he'd set off to go there.

'But how did you know to go to Oslo, and not Dubai?' she asked.

'A hunch,' he said. 'That night – when was it? – two nights ago, it suddenly occurred to me what was happening. For weeks now, every time I tried to contact Hector I got a text or e-mail back, never a call. And they were brusque and brief, cold and impersonal; either he was busy or off somewhere with some trade delegation and didn't want to be bothered by estate matters. He'd tell me to just deal with it, and then demand more money be sent through to him. I'd taken offence, as I was meant to do, seeing myself exploited and deliberately distanced, so I contacted him less and less. All part of Laila's little plan, and Hector, away up in the mountains, didn't have a clue.' He paused. 'And then that night, after what you said, it hit me what might be happening, so I put it to the test. You saw me ring him and leave a voicemail message and then text him?'

'Yes.'

'And a little later she left the room, and, hey presto, I got a text message back from Hector. A surprisingly genial one. I replied to it, letting her see that I'd done so, and when she could, she slipped away again. Same thing happened, I got a reply. So when you and she were sorting coffee in the library, I went up and looked in her handbag. Two phones. His and hers. And my message flagged up on the screen of his.'

'Oh God.'

'Half of me thought he was dead already.' He paused for a long moment, his jaw set hard, as if reliving the moment. 'But

I needed to find out, so I took her passport and cards, gambling on getting away before she found they were gone. I had to know she was out of the game for a while.' He stopped again. 'And I couldn't tell anyone, you see, in case I was wrong.'

Libby sat in silence, staggered by Laila's calculated cruelty. 'And so the fictional baby is her insurance in case Hector dies?'

'Not in case, when. I can't begin to tell you the mess he's in. Liver's shot to hell, the doctors said, kidneys starting to fail and other stuff. It's just a matter of time – and when he died, who was going to challenge his grieving widow over the paternity of her child?' He stopped again, staring back down at the ground. 'So once Laila had established to the world, and to me in particular, that she's pregnant with a son, the sooner Hector died the better, as that bump of hers has got to grow. These next weeks were going to be the hardest part of the charade. Once he was dead, she could simply flee somewhere, distraught with grief, for the requisite number of months, and then emerge triumphant with the next baronet who even now some surrogate mother is presumably cooking up for her. Laila is not to be underestimated.'

Libby sat, stunned, while she absorbed this. 'But why didn't she get pregnant herself? Surely that would have been easier.'

There was another long silence. 'She couldn't. And besides, she had to be *not* pregnant when she visited Hector and the doctors, and pregnant for me and, after he died, for the rest of the world. A tricky act to keep up, but she was playing for high stakes, and Hector, hanging on to life as he is doing, must have been a worry to her. They're broke, I gather, all washed up, and I dread to think what her next move would have been. He has hefty life insurance cover, he told me.'

She felt a sudden chill as a zephyr blew across the surface of the sea, and she watched a night bird flying over the waves, low and fast.

'So then I had to get back here to tell her the game is up, and watch out for the boys. And David.'

His sudden fear was tangible, and she touched his arm again. 'The boys are fine,' she said, 'and they have Angus and Maddy and Alice looking out for them.' What could Laila possibly do to them? 'They haven't been here at all. Alice has, though, and she's borne the brunt of Laila's temper.'

He gave a short laugh. 'Alice is a trooper, bless her.'

'So what happens now?' Somewhere out at sea a gull's wild cry was snatched away by the wind.

'I'll go to the house and confront her.' She caught a glint in his eye, sharp as a blade. 'And then she can strip off whatever it is she has strapped to her belly and give an account of herself. But not tonight, I don't trust myself tonight.' He paused, and she sensed him struggling to restrain a passion so strong – 'I'll sleep in the Land Rover and tackle her in the morning.'

That, she was certain, was a good idea, for the look in his eye was murderous. 'She said that if you weren't back by today, she'd report the theft to the police.'

'Good. I'd like Fergus to hear all this, the sooner the better.' He rubbed the heel of his hand into his eye, and she saw exhaustion replace menace as he turned back to her. 'And I've got you embroiled in this ghastly mess, Libby. It's not where I want to be with you. I'm sorry.'

She looked away. The words and the tone reached beyond the moment. But it was not for now, and would not spoil for waiting.

'Don't be,' was all she said. Then: 'And there's no need to sleep in the Land Rover. I can shift a few boxes and you can stretch out in the caravan. There's a spare sleeping bag in there.'

He got up and reached a hand down to her. 'Right. I'll do that.' He pulled her to her feet and together they walked back along the causeway. The camp was in darkness now, the last of the revellers having retired to their tents, and they went silently across the chilly dunes, through the campsite to the caravan. Libby shifted the finds trays and boxes from the couch and retrieved the sleeping bag.

'Will you be alright?'

He smiled at her. 'Of course.' And then he pulled her to him, wrapping his arms around her, and held her. 'I'm very glad you're here, Liberty Snow,' he murmured, and he tightened his hold before releasing her.

Chapter 30

The ship was already on the beach when the sound of voices roused Odrhan from his sleep and he crawled to the entrance of his dwelling and looked out. 'Pádraig, wake up.' It was a larger ship than the one which had brought Ulla and Harald, and it carried six men, one of them a grey-haired giant. Odrhan turned swiftly back to the waking boy.

'Quickly. You must go! Keep low, along the beach. Don't look back but run, as fast as you can, and carry a warning. Go!'

'And you?' The boy's eyes were wide with fear.

'They will not harm me. Now go! God speed.' And he thrust the boy through the door and watched him scramble down the rocks to where the headland would shield him from view.

Quickly he dug a hole in the floor of his cell and buried the chalice there, stamping the surface flat. The rest of Harald's treasure he had long since buried, close to the flat rock where now no one came.

Then he straightened, stood a moment watching them pull the ship higher, and went once more down to the shore.

→ Libby ←

The click of the caravan door woke her.

She glanced at her watch, six fifteen. She dressed rapidly, teeth chattering. By the time she had her boots on and had crawled to the door of her tent, Rodri was striding up the dewed path to-

302

wards the garden. She caught up with him in the dark tunnel where the branches of the rhododendrons made a roof over their heads. 'Wait!' she called, and he turned. 'I'm coming with you.'

'I shan't murder her, you know.'

Maybe not. 'I'll come along anyway,' she said. 'Just in case.'

A smile briefly crossed his face; then he turned and carried on up the path, and she followed him.

Laila had bolted both the front and back doors but he told Libby to wait in the courtyard, and a moment later she heard him on the inside, drawing back the bolts. He smiled briefly at her expression. 'Ways and means, m'dear, ways and means,' and she went after him down the passage to the kitchen.

He crossed to the Aga and bounced the palm of his hand on it to test the heat. 'At least it's still lit,' he said. 'Fill the kettle, will you?' He went over to the fridge and began pulling out food. 'I'm starved, I've not eaten since Oslo.' She realised that he was being deliberately noisy, opening cupboard doors and banging them shut. The sounds must have carried, for it was not long before they heard movement overhead, and moments later Laila appeared at the doorway, a dressing gown tied across her wide midriff. 'You!' she exclaimed, in accents of loathing.

'In the flesh. Tea or coffee?'

She ignored him and glanced at Libby. 'Why is *she* here?'

'She's come for breakfast.'

Laila's eyes flicked from one to the other, and Libby saw that she was looking dreadful, her complexion pasty white without makeup and her usually immaculate hair unkempt. She didn't move from the doorway. 'Where have you been?' she demanded.

'To hell and back.' He took a bite of thick bread and marmalade and chewed, contemplating her. 'To Oslo, Laila, and at the Nordfjord clinic.'

It didn't seem possible that Laila's face could become any

whiter. Rodri continued to chew, his jaws working and his eyes fixed on her. She stared back at him, and the kitchen was silent until the kettle began to boil.

'Give me my passport and my credit cards,' she said at last.

He reached into the chest pocket of his jacket and pulled out a single credit card, which he flicked onto the table. 'The others are cancelled,' he said.

She moved then, coming into the room to confront him. 'You have no *right*—'

'No. But Hector has. That one's in your name alone, there's sufficient on it for your immediate needs. All other accounts are frozen. Standard procedure in these circumstances.'

Libby saw Laila swallow hard, then recover, and hold out her hand. 'Passport.'

Rodri got up and lifted the kettle from the Aga, filling two mugs. He shook his head. 'Not yet. Not until I have Hector safely under this roof. Then you get your passport.'

Libby looked at him. He'd said nothing about Hector comin –

Laila too was stunned. 'Hector? No – he is too ill to travel.'

'Arrangements have been made. He'll arrive under medical escort today or tomorrow, and then a private ambulance will collect him from the airport.' Unwashed and unshaven, Rodri looked dangerous, and Libby suspected that he was only just in command of himself. But when he spoke again, it was with quiet authority. 'Hector will die here, Laila, in his own home with his family around him. And he'll spend the last weeks of his life getting to know his son, and making his peace with the lad's mother, and grandfather. Then he'll die with his conscience clear and his mind at rest, and we'll bury him here, where he belongs.' His eyes were shining, perhaps with anger, but she sensed that some other, more painful passion threatened to overwhelm him.

Laila went on staring at him. 'And me, Rodri? What about me?' Perhaps she sensed a weakness, a crack into which she might slide. 'I too will be here with him.'

She had misjudged her man, and he turned away from her. 'You think Hector wants that?'

'Hector *loves* me, Rodri,' she cried, then added in soft tones, 'and once you loved me too.'

Rodri turned back and gave her a long look, saying nothing. Then: 'Once, Laila, I thought you were the loveliest girl in the world,' he said at last. 'But right now – ' He glanced at Libby. 'Libby came along this morning, I think, to stop me doing something stupid.'

Laila put a hand out to him. 'Rodri, you've no idea how hard it was . . .'

He brushed it aside. 'It was the worst day's work I ever did, bringing you here, and I'll never forgive myself. Maddy's the sweetest girl on earth and her love might have saved Hector, and he'd have had David, his son . . .'

Laila latched on to the last point. 'We tried and we tried, Rodri, but nothing worked,' and she turned to Libby as if in appeal, and Libby felt a sort of compassion for her. 'After his injury, Hector could not—'

Rodri's voice came back like a whip. 'God, Laila! You think I don't know? I've *spoken* to Hector.' She stopped, and the mask of entreaty slipped to reveal a very different look. Rodri saw it too. 'Quite,' he remarked, and Libby sensed a quickening danger.

There was something else.

They remained locked in some private communication for a moment; then Laila snatched the credit card from the table, turned without a word, and left. Libby heard her go upstairs and cross the gallery, and a door slammed shut.

Rodri stared at the place where she had been, then turned

back to Libby and gestured to her mug. 'That'll be going cold, you know.'

———

Then Alice arrived.

'You're back,' she said, looking from Rodri to Libby.

Rodri filled her in with the pertinent facts, and she listened, lips parted. 'So she's not pregnant,' he concluded, 'and she's not going anywhere, as I've still got her passport. We're stuck with her for now, but once I have Hector's say-so, she's on her way.'

Alice closed her mouth. 'Right,' she said.

'Someone in the clinic is going to ring me when they know which flight he's on, and we'll go from there. Today or tomorrow, they said. There's a private ambulance on standby in Glasgow, and I'll go and meet the plane, and escort them back here.' He paused, and gave Alice a concerned look. 'I'll talk to Maddy and explain matters, and see how she wants to handle things with David. It'll be hard for everyone, but for Hector's sake – ' Emotion cracked his voice at last and the mask crumbled. 'Oh God, Alice, you should see him! He's a dead man walking.' And Alice went to him.

Libby got to her feet, sensing that the crisis here was passing, and needing to get back to camp. Alice had her feet on the ground, and was skilled at healing wounds. 'I'll go,' she said. Rodri straightened as Alice released him, looked across at her, and nodded.

———

There was, in fact, no time to dwell on these events, for as soon as she emerged from the garden gate she heard a whistle and saw Callum, out on the headland, signalling to her. Most of the students seemed to have gathered there. She crossed the dunes and walked out towards them.

Declan had arrived and was crouched down beside the opening to Odrhan's cell. She'd forgotten Declan again. 'Come and take a look,' Callum called. And she hadn't told Rodri that he was here.

The students had cleared the fallen stones from the centre of the structure, piling them to one side, revealing it to have been roughly rectangular in outline with rounded corners. An ancient, tiny hermitage, a retreat from the perils of the world. And Declan was there in their midst, examining what might once have been a beaten-earth floor. The students parted as she arrived, and she saw a shallow irregular depression about a metre and a half long which had been cut into the floor; and there, in the centre of the hollow, they had exposed the top of a wooden box. Declan looked up briefly.

'It looks old, but not that old,' Callum said, and she nodded. It was a simple construction, no fancy joints, just planks screwed in place at right angles, and then a lid.

'Screws,' she said, looking down.

'Screws,' agreed Declan. So not ancient, and her mind went back to the drawings she had seen in Rodri's dining room, and to the neat hand which had annotated the drawings. O.D. There had to be a connection.

The rest of the students were crowding round. 'Ooh, buried treasure!'

'Can we just divvy it up and keep quiet?'

Libby cut through the banter. 'Has it been photographed in situ?' she asked.

'About to do that,' said Declan, straightening. 'Then we'll plan it and lift it.'

'Is it strong enough, do you think?' she said.

He shrugged. 'If it begins to break up, we'll stop.'

'We ought to ask Rodri Sturrock before we open it.'

'I was about to go up to the house to ask *Lady* Sturrock. She's up and doing, I presume, and finished breakfast? Kedgeree and silver teapots, was it?' One of the girls giggled.

'Actually, this might not be a great time . . .'

He ignored her. 'Callum, sort out the planning and photography, will you. I'm heading up to the big house to crave an audience. Don't lift it until I get back.'

He set off through the campsite, and Libby went after him. 'Declan, listen –'

He strode on to where he had parked his car beside hers, ignoring her, and they were just in time to see the Land Rover start up from beside the manse and turn in a wide circle. It came to a halt beside them, and Rodri lowered the window. 'Morning, Professor,' he said.

Declan was caught off-guard. 'I thought you were away,' he said.

Rodri raised an eyebrow. 'Did you? And I didn't know you'd arrived, so this is a pleasant surprise for us both. But I'm afraid I'm just off again. I'll be back this evening, though, so I'll look forward to hearing how everything is going.'

'Splendid. And I was just going to introduce myself to Lady Sturrock, so I'll report to her instead.' Declan gave him a wide smile.

'I wouldn't . . .'

'Then she can brief her husband directly,' Declan continued, 'cut through the red tape, so to speak.'

Rodri smiled back in a way that ought to have warned Declan. 'I need, it appears, to remind you—'

Libby interrupted hastily. 'We found a box, buried out on the headland, in the floor of Odrhan's cell.'

'What sort of box?'

'Old but not ancient. Should we wait until you're back before opening it?'

Declan said something under his breath, and Rodri glanced at him. 'No harm in opening it, I don't suppose. What's your view, Professor?'

'I was about to ask Lady Sturrock's permission to do so.'

'Right. Well, have mine instead. And just to be clear on this, it's my agreement that counts here, not hers. I'm off just now to collect my brother from the airport, and from then on it's his. Still not hers. Got that? He's not a well man, though, so he won't want to be troubled right now. I'm sure you understand.'

He nodded briefly at Libby, let out the clutch, and the Land Rover skidded away and up the track. Declan watched it go, then turned on his heel and went back towards the headland.

He was already giving instructions to lift the box by the time Libby got there.

'Callum, how strong do you think—' she began.

'Leave it to us, thanks, Libby,' Declan interrupted, but Callum remained loyal.

'I thought we could slide it onto a sheet of plastic first. One or two planks have warped and sprung, so it might collapse.'

This was achieved readily enough, and between them Declan and Callum lifted the box and laid it on the turf. 'There's something in it,' said Callum as they lowered it, 'but it's not really heavy –'

'So! Let's open it,' Declan said.

Callum glanced at Libby. 'The hinges are rusty. They might break.'

'Just do it,' said Declan.

Callum straightened. 'Over to you, Prof.'

Declan held his look for a moment, then crouched and slid

his trowel under the lid and lifted it. The hinges resisted a moment and then one snapped, and the other went as he lifted it higher. A groan of disappointment went round the students.

No treasure but charnel, human charnel.

'More old bones!' said one of them.

Libby and Callum crouched down to examine them. Long bones, ribs, pelvic bones.

And a skull.

Chapter 31

→ *Libby* ←

Declan did not go up to the house after all, but made his excuses and left soon after, tight-lipped and silent. Libby watched him go, conscious that any successes reported back would be his, and any failures hers, and nothing would change that. And as his car disappeared up the track, she put him out of her mind and began mentally ticking off the remaining tasks. The mound was done, planned, drawn and photographed; there was little more to do at the headland, and the students were now replacing the stones they had moved. The survey of the bay was almost complete, just a few more data checks to be done, leaving only the building recording to be finished off. And then they would go.

But her connection with Ullaness was not yet done, that much she knew. There were things which needed time to play out, but she felt bound here in a different way. And this bond was part of the present, not the past.

The rest of the afternoon passed without incident. The sound of an engine signalled school pickup time and she glimpsed Alice's car turning onto the track. That time already! And she called for tea break. Life here had its familiar rhythms and she'd got used to them.

When tea break came to an end, she followed the students as they trooped back to work, forcing herself to focus on the tasks in hand. Then she heard her name being called, and saw Alice flying down the path towards her.

Libby went to meet her. 'She's taken my car!' Alice said, arriving breathless and gasping.

'I saw it go! I thought it was you.'

Alice shook her head, gulping air. 'She waited until I had the hoover on, then took my keys and wallet, and drove off. Cool as you like!'

Retaliation. 'But where's she going? Rodri has her passport. Unless she found it –'

Alice shook her head again. 'He's got it on him. He told me. And I've got to pick up the kids. Angus and Maddy were going to take Jennet out for the day and I can't reach them. No signal. I hate to ask, but will you drive me to school to get them, then run us home?'

'Of course.'

Alice continued to fume as they jolted up the track a moment later in Libby's car. 'The woman's mad! I'd tell the police except it'll just make matters worse for Rodri.' She drummed her fingers on the door. 'She'll not get far, though. There's only a fiver in my wallet.'

'Did you stop the cards?'

'No, but I will, soon as I get home. We'll be late at school as it is.'

'Where on earth is she headed?'

'Glasgow maybe, to catch them at the airport.'

'Well, that'll go well!'

The playground was empty when they arrived. 'They'll have taken them back in to do homework. I'm sometimes late.' Alice went quickly into the school building while Libby stayed put and lowered the window. A moment later she saw the door flung open again and Alice rushed out, accompanied by a woman.

No boys.

With a sense of foreboding, Libby went to meet them. 'Laila's taken them,' said Alice, her face ashen. 'Morag said she came early, before school finished.'

Libby stared back at her.

The woman was looking bewildered. 'There was a special family event, she told me. Sir Hector's homecoming – and she was in your car. I didn't think anything – '

Libby remembered the expression on Rodri's face last night, and felt a stab of fear. 'Call the police,' she said, 'you must.'

'The *police*?' The teacher looked to Alice.

Alice nodded. 'Aye, she's right.' She rummaged in her handbag. 'Tell them she's in my car and that she might mean them harm.'

'Surely not – '

'Really, Morag, do it! You've no idea . . . Come on, Libby, we need to find Angus.' She scribbled something on a piece of paper, thrusting it at the teacher. 'That's my reg. Pale blue Polo. Rusting. Go!' She pushed the woman in the direction of the school and got back in the car.

Libby started the engine. 'I thought you said Angus and Maddy were out,' she said, as they drove off.

'Aye, but they might be back. If not, we'll catch them at Jennet's.' She held the phone to her ear, and waited. 'Gone to voicemail. I'll send a text and they'll get it when they drive into signal.'

'And Rodri?'

Alice hesitated. 'If I tell him, he'll be torn between them and Hector. And he switches off when he drives.' She turned in her seat. 'Oh God, Libby, where's she taken them?'

Libby looked ahead, driving as fast as she dared along the twists and turns. 'There's three of them, and they're sharp lads. They'll be alright.' But they were children, and Laila had her back to the wall.

'You'd better be right,' Alice replied, chewing her lip, and Libby saw her brush an impatient hand across her eyes. 'It'd destroy Maddy if anything happened to David. Same with Rodri. His lads are his world.'

And there was nothing else they could do. 'Once Morag's alerted the police, they'll soon spot the car,' Libby said, hoping she was right. By this time they had turned off the main road and were following a network of smaller roads, Alice giving directions, and Libby began to recognise the route Rodri had brought her on back in March – a lifetime ago. The yellow gorse was dying back now, the nettles high. And as they rounded the last corner, they saw the narrow inlet of the sea spread out before them. Then Alice gave a shriek and pointed. 'They're here! Look!'

The blue Polo was parked off the road, just above the shoreline, and Libby pulled up beside it. Both women jumped out and looked inside. Discarded schoolbags on the back seat served only to heighten their fear, and they scanned the empty shoreline. Alice yelled: 'David! Where are you? Donald! Charlie!' Oystercatchers rose and flew across the bay, and their piping protest was the only reply. The tide had turned and was ebbing, draining the shallow bay, leaving moored boats tipped on their sides.

It was then that Libby spotted a series of drag marks higher up the beach and gripped Alice's arm. 'The kayaks! Weren't the kayaks there?' And she pointed to lines in the pebbly sand which led down to the water. They ran to the spot and saw a jumble of footprints, small ones, superimposed on each other, and one set that was larger. Oh God.

Alice was looking bewildered. 'She's taken them kayaking? I told you she was mad.'

Mad? Perhaps so. But dangerous. 'Get back in the car,' she

said, pulling at Alice's arm, a pulse leaping in her throat. 'Can we drive to the end of this headland?'

Alice ran after her. 'No. The road stops just after the cottages. Why?'

'We need to see how far out they are.'

Alice seemed to pick up on her fear. 'You don't think –'

An accident, the wind strengthening, a treat gone so terribly wrong, a dreadful tragedy. Laila distraught. So *sorry*! Was it David she had in her sights, Hector's son, but not hers? Or Rodri's boys, by way of revenge?

They drove as far as they could past the cottages and got out of the car again, but found no good vantage point. The slice of ocean that they could see was empty, but it was clear that the wind was picking up, conspiring with tide and current to further Laila's purpose.

Libby looked back down the inlet to the beach and the jetty. There was still water there, but was it enough? 'Is there a boat we can take?'

'Angus's fishing boat is the white one at the jetty, but he'll have left it locked.'

'Let's go and see.' She wrenched open the car door and got back in.

'Can you handle a boat?' Alice asked as they reversed.

'I could once.' They stopped beside the jetty, and Libby ran along it and leapt down into the boat. All the things that her father had taught her years ago at Gosse Harbour would serve her now. But Alice was right, and the door to the tiny wheelhouse was padlocked.

Desperately she scanned the other boats. But who would leave a boat unlocked, and with fuel on board? They might have paddles or oars, but speed was what was needed, and soon the water would be gone from the bay . . . Then she heard Alice cry out, saw her start running towards an approaching vehicle. It was Angus's car, with Maddy sitting beside him, and Libby sank back against the tiny wheelhouse.

And then Angus was on the jetty, lowering himself onto the deck. For a big man, he moved fast. 'You can handle a boat, then?' he said, glancing from under bushy eyebrows as he stuck a key in the padlock.

'Yes.'

'Right. Cast off and we'll be away.' The engine burst into life, barely giving her time to release the bow and stern, and they were off in a choking cloud of diesel.

Angus said nothing as he wove his way through rocks which were now fringed halfway up with exposed bladderwrack. Occasionally she felt a bump or there was a gut-wrenching scrape of metal on rock, and she knew that even had she got the boat going she would never have made it out. But Angus knew these waters and followed the deep channel as effortlessly as an eel until they reached the point where the bay widened to meet the ocean. 'Take her now,' he said, and he left the tiny wheelhouse, a pair of binoculars in his hand. No further instruction, no backward glance. Instinctively she kept the bow at right angles to the waves, letting the prow rise and fall, gritting her chattering teeth.

The weather might have been alright when the boys set off, she thought, but it was worsening fast. Would they have sense enough to recognise the danger, and the strength of character to resist Laila and turn back? David might, and the younger boys would follow his lead. And yet there was no sign of them. Then Angus barrelled back into the wheelhouse and grabbed the wheel from her, pulling it hard to port as he opened the throttle. She held on to whatever she could as the boat corkscrewed over the waves. 'Have you seen them?' she shouted above the roar.

'Kayaks,' he replied, pointing briefly, 'empty.'

She clung on, feeling sick now and unable to stop herself shaking. He tore the binoculars from his neck and passed them to her. 'Off to the port, keep an eye on them. Look for heads in the water.' She went to the door of the wheelhouse, bracing her legs against it to steady herself against the jagged motion, fighting the nausea, and the horizon leapt as she struggled to hold the binoculars steady. Then she glimpsed a red kayak, hull up, at the mercy of the waves. No heads.

The fishing boat rose on another wave, and for a moment she could see further and cried out. Two other kayaks were ahead with figures aboard, still paddling, riding the waves. She shouted at Angus, gesturing to him to change course. He nodded wordlessly, his face like granite, and again she braced herself against the door jamb and watched the writhing horizon. Then she saw another kayak, blue this time, right way up but empty, surfing an incoming wave. Two down, two upright. She slammed her mind closed on the thought.

The waves were flatter now as they left the shore behind them and she was getting a longer view, but she had lost sight of the two upright kayaks. Then she glimpsed something far distant on the horizon, a speck moving fast, throwing up spray on either side.

Angus saw it too and grunted. 'Lifeboat.'

Lifeboat! Maddy must have called them . . . Then the waves flattened again and she saw the two kayaks, paddles flailing madly, not far off their starboard bow, and pulled at Angus's arm. He grabbed the binoculars from her, stared through them a moment, then swore. He thrust the binoculars back at her, swung the boat sharply to starboard, and let out a mighty blast on the foghorn, his face a mask of grim fury.

She took up the binoculars again and, with horror, understood why. The paddles were certainly flailing, but not in the business of propulsion. They were being used as weapons, one attacking, one defending, the latter occasionally back-paddling as opportunities between waves allowed. But even from here she could see that the defending kayak was manoeuvring awkwardly, sluggishly, and then with a great leap of joy she saw why.

Hanging on to its stern she could see two shapes in the water, buoyed up, *thank God*, by life jackets. And now they had seen the boat and one lifted an arm. David, for it was he wielding the defending paddle, didn't turn, but he must have been aware of the boat racing towards them. Laila paused in her attack and Libby saw her turn her head towards them. David took advantage of the moment to back-paddle away as Angus closed the gap between them.

'Take the wheel,' he said, pulling back on the throttle as they approached. 'Easy now, just come alongside.'

For a moment she wondered why he'd handed over now, at this most critical stage, until she saw him reach a boathook from the wheelhouse roof and go to the gunwale in readiness, shouting instructions to her over his shoulder. It was difficult to see where the boys were and she was terrified of driving over them; all she could do was what he told her, and pray. She watched him poised there, and then he leaned right over, boathook outstretched, and a moment later reached down and deposited Charlie in a sodden mass on the deck. It was all Libby could do not to go to him, but Angus's shout steadied her: 'Starboard! Easy – ' She dropped the throttle back while they twisted and danced to the rhythm of the waves. Charlie vomited, and then next moment Angus leaned forward again, and Donald, slippery as a seal pup, was dumped beside his brother on the deck. She heard Angus shouting something down to his grandson and the tone of his voice was fiercely jubilant, and she dashed an arm across her face, blinded momentarily as Angus dropped the boathook on deck and leaned forward with both arms outstretched. A moment later David sprang aboard, landing on his feet, to disappear into his grandfather's embrace.

Libby throttled forward slightly and turned the boat to ease the unsteady motion, and only then did she think to look for Laila.

The red kayak was already some distance away, and Laila was paddling away from them, out to sea, with the calm efficiency of one born to water. The lifeboat must have seen the rescue of the boys, as it now altered course and went in pursuit of her. Angus looked over David's head, his eyes narrowed as he followed Libby's gaze; then he dropped a kiss on the boy's wet hair and released him, taking the wheel from her.

'We'll leave her to the lifeboat crew, I think. Let's get these lads home.'

———————

Later, much later, when Libby thought back over that afternoon, it felt unreal, or like something she'd been told about, that had happened to someone else. At the time the boys' danger had kept her focussed, blocking out the fear, and the release of tension once they were on board was almost more profound than the fear had been. With the boys safe but shuddering on the deck, Angus had told her where there was a tarpaulin, and she had coaxed them to move together into the centre of the boat, away from Charlie's vomit. She'd covered them as best she could, saying meaningless words of reassurance; at least it would keep the wind off them, and it was all that there was. Charlie had curled into a ball like a wounded creature and somehow fallen asleep, his face pressed into his brother's shoulder, while Donald lay there, glassy-eyed and shivering, one arm flung across Charlie. Libby tucked the folds around them. 'It's alright now, we'll soon have you home, and warm,' she kept repeating, wishing she could do more. David sat slightly apart, his back resting on the curve of the hull, his forearms on his bent knees, and stared down between his feet. He moved a little to allow Libby to pass the tarpaulin over his knees, and looked up at her. That familiar single-line frown.

His eyes, as dark and unfathomable as his uncle's, gave her a long, considering look. 'She tried to kill us,' he said. His tone was carefully neutral, slightly puzzled but calm.

'Yes – ' Only the truth would do.

She glanced at Donald, immobile beside him. His glazed stare had not altered, but he must have heard.

'She said my father was coming home today? We were going to paddle round the headland and surprise him. Rodri had said that we could.' Then: '*Is* my father coming home?' David's tone was strained but still controlled.

'Yes. He is.'

'That's good.' He went back to his contemplation of the space between his feet. Then Angus called to her, and she was spared any further reply. But she knew that whatever else happened in these boys' lives, they would carry this day with them forever.

Looking ahead through the glass of the little wheelhouse, she had seen the headland of Ullaness. The roofs and chimneys of Sturrock House were clearly visible beyond, and she could see the church, the manse, and the bright colours of the tents. And out on the end of the headland she could see figures. Angus passed her the binoculars. 'Who's there?' he asked.

She could see Maddy and Alice, as well as Callum and one or two of the students. And there was Rodri, looking back at her through binoculars of his own.

Angus grunted when she told him. 'Right. Then get some-where where they can see you and signal to them. Thumbs-up – anything. And I'll toot on the foghorn. I canna stop here, no water, but I'll pass as close as I can. They need to be knowing, so up you go now.'

Libby obeyed and left the wheelhouse. A fish crate lay in a corner of the deck well, and she pulled it to the side of the boat and stood on it, bracing her knees against the hull, and waved her arms wildly. But how to convey success? She did the thumbs-up, three times with both hands, hoping Rodri had binoculars fixed on her. Angus gave three short blasts on the foghorn, waited a moment, and then repeated, and Libby clasped her hands above her head like a triumphant football fan and then repeated the thumbs-up. The binoculars were still around her neck and she looked through them to see that Rodri was waving back, great sweeps of his arm conveying that he understood. Then David was beside her on the fish crate and he waved as well, and she saw Maddy wave back, then turn to collapse into Alice's arms. David pointed down into the deck well to where his cousins were stretched out, and she saw Rodri's sweeping wave again, before her vision blurred and she tasted salt on her lips.

'They've understood,' she shouted to Angus.

'Right. Then get back inside and hold tight.'

As the engine roared, the boat leapt forward, and Libby looked through an arc of spray towards the headland. The group of onlookers had fallen back, leaving just Rodri there on the rocky headland. She raised the binoculars to her eyes and saw that he was no longer looking towards them but was gazing fixedly towards the horizon, a lone dark figure staring out to where the lifeboat was now a distant speck.

Chapter 32

Angus's boat arrived at the fish-gutting jetty soon after. Rodri would know where they would come in, Angus had told her, and he'd been right. And there all was a confusion of reaching hands, cries and tears, embraces and blankets. Rodri crouched down between his sons, holding them both close, and Charlie, woken from his sleep, sobbed silently into his shoulder, shaking in his grip. Rodri's other arm was wrapped around Donald and he was speaking to him in a low voice. Alice tried to get a blanket around David's shoulders but he shrugged it off, protesting that he was fine, and Maddy was holding on to her father.

Callum, she realised, had come with them, and was now surveying the scene in slightly embarrassed bewilderment. 'You alright?' he asked.

'I'm fine.'

'So everyone's alright?' he asked. 'Except – where's Lady Sturrock?'

'The lifeboat went after her. They'll have picked her up by now.'

'Great. So shall we go? You look frozen.'

'Callum!' Rodri lifted his head, and his eyes met Libby's. 'Take Libby up to the house, will you. We'll all follow.'

In the end it was only Rodri and his boys who went back to Sturrock House, together with Alice. 'Angus said Maddy should take

David home,' Rodri told Libby, as he ushered his sons into the kitchen. 'He's right, of course. Too much for one day.' His drawn face spoke volumes. Too much for everyone. 'Bless you for coming, Alice.'

'We'll soon be sorted, won't we, lads?' Alice was already chivvying them out of the kitchen, forcing a tone of cheerful normality. 'Hot baths first. Dad'll come up and I'll bring you some food. Tea in bed tonight, eh?'

'Dad –' Charlie hung back.

Rodri pulled the boy to him, held him close, his own eyes squeezed shut. 'Aye. I'm here. Get yourself in the tub and I'll be up right away.' He released him and turned to Callum. 'Will you make Libby something to eat? Libby, I need to go to my boys –'

'Of course. Go,' said Libby.

Callum, resourceful as ever, explored Rodri's kitchen with a self-confidence which would stand him in good stead through life. 'What possessed the woman to take the kids out kayaking on a day like this? Is she crazy?'

'Probably.' How much had Callum been told? she wondered. 'Everything alright on site?'

'Yep. Fine. I left Mel starting to lay out those bones, see what we've got.'

A moment later he put a plate of scrambled eggs down in front of her, and she ate, ravenous suddenly. 'You sure you're alright?' he asked. 'It looked pretty wild out there. And those poor kids . . .'

Alice appeared with an armful of wet clothes which she took through to the utility room, and the hum of the washing machine combined with the homely taste of scrambled eggs brought comfort, and Libby felt herself calming. 'I'm fine now, but thanks.'

'Rodri said to offer you a bed for the night,' Alice said as she returned and poured baked beans into a pan. 'I've put in a hot water bottle, same room.'

'There's no need to –'

'Sounds like a good idea to me,' said Callum. 'We'll be fine down on site, and if you're alright now, I'll be getting back.'

'If you're sure. And thank you, Callum.'

He raised a dismissive hand. 'No worries. See you tomorrow.'

'Sorted then,' said Alice, as he left. 'I'll take this up to the boys, and then I'll be off.' If Alice's ponytail was a barometer of mood, then hers was on the upturn.

A moment later, she was back. 'I'm away then. Get Rodri to eat something, will you? I've lit a fire in the library. Hector's got a special bed squeezed into the dining room. I checked on him and he's asleep.' Hector. Libby had forgotten all about Hector. He was here now, of course, but what had he been told?

Alice came over and gave her a hug. 'You look done in, Libby. Go to bed soon.'

'I will.'

Another hug, a smile, and Alice was gone.

And so the kitchen fell silent, empty now of drama, and Libby sat nursing her mug, savouring the stillness and the quiet, and tried to block out the horror. Somewhere in this divided house a man lay ill, his days numbered, while upstairs his brother sat with his sons waiting for the oblivion of sleep to overtake them, and for the healing to begin. That closed look in Donald's eyes as the fishing boat raced for the shore would, she feared, take some time to penetrate.

And somewhere there was Laila, her mad bid for vengeance

foiled by so slight a margin. The image of her in the kayak, paddle raised, was impossible to blot out. Where would the coastguard take her, Libby wondered, and how would she explain what had happened? She must know that she had been seen from the boat, and her intentions understood. And the boys, instead of drowning, could now bear witness. Perhaps the lifeboat men had called the police.

Rodri appeared in the doorway and he stood there looking across at her, his face haggard. He had aged a decade this night.

Libby rose. 'What can I get for you?' she said.

'Nothing, Libby. Only this.' He opened his arms, half appeal, half invitation, and she went to him. He held her for a long time and she felt the tension in him. Then he drew back. 'Angus said you were brilliant. Couldn't have managed without you.'

'He would have.'

'But you were there. And you brought them back. I told Hector.'

'How is he?'

'Asleep.' He released her.

'Alice says you should eat something.'

'Did she? I've another idea.' He led her into the library and pulled cushions from the chairs, piling them on the hearth rug beside the fire, gesturing to Libby to sit, and she did, watched the flames making patterns on the old oak panels. He settled down beside her, a bottle and two glasses in his hand. 'But he's glad to be here.'

He filled the glasses.

'Does he know?'

He shook his head. 'Only that there was an accident and that all's well now.' He handed her a glass. 'The rest'll keep.'

She took it from him, and the fiery spirit drove the last of the cold from her. 'When did you learn what was happening?'

'I picked up Alice's messages when I got back here with Hector in the ambulance, and went with the others out onto the headland. It was all I could do.' He took a long breath, and was silent for a while, his face grim as if reliving the agony of waiting. She knew enough of him to imagine what being unable to act had cost him. Then: 'I'll have to tell him in the morning, though.' The coals moved in the hearth and a blue flame leapt at the coat of arms on the fireback, then died.

'David was asking about him, said he was glad his father was coming.'

Rodri turned his head sharply to look at her, his expression lightening. 'He said that? That's good, very good – ' Then the phone rang and he got to his feet, the glass still in his hand.

He spoke into the receiver, listened, and then grew still. 'I see,' he said, and listened again. 'No, I understand . . . Aye, there's more. Much more. No, no, of course. . . . In the morning. Aye, tell Fergus. . . . Aye, aye, everyone's fine. . . . And thanks, Jimmie. You too.' He put the phone down.

'So perhaps there's a God after all!' he said, in a very different tone, and went for the whisky bottle, raising his glass to the flames: 'To Laila. May she burn in hell,' and she saw that dagger glint in his eye as he tossed back the drink before slopping more into his glass as if all the fury in him were suddenly unleashed. 'One minute she was there, they said, paddling hard away from them, and next she was gone. Empty kayak. They scoured the seas for two hours and then gave up.' He took another swig, and the flicker of the flames shadowed his face. 'Do you know what David told Maddy? He said Laila went for him first, eliminating the strongest, good tactic. Quite out of the blue she smacked him on the head with her paddle, but not hard enough. David's a smart lad and rolled, and when he came up again, he saw her flipping Charlie over, and his brain switched right on to what was happening. He went to help him, but by then she'd tipped Donald up. David reached Charlie in the water, got him to hang on, and then managed to get between Donald and Laila, fending her off until Donald could swim round to him.'

Ice re-entered her soul and she felt herself begin shaking again, remembering what she had seen. 'They were both in the water when we came up to them, hanging on to the back of David's kayak, and he was holding her off with his paddle.'

He swore. 'And for how much longer, I wonder! She'd tried to persuade them life jackets were for wimps, David said, but I'd put the fear of God in them about wearing them, so they did. Otherwise they'd all be dead now.' He drained his glass, and reached down for the bottle again.

'Don't,' Libby said, getting her hand on it first and holding on.

He closed his fingers over hers and gave her a dark look. 'But I intend to get very drunk tonight.'

'And if the boys wake, and need you?' That seemed to steady him. 'It's over, Rodri.'

He seemed to sway where he stood, staring back at her. 'It is, isn't it?' he said, in an odd disbelieving tone. 'All of it. Over –' Then he took the bottle from her, poured himself half a glass, and cocked an eye at her. 'Alright?'

She nodded, and they sat in silence, shoulders touching, and stared into the fire, and the silence lengthened. 'She'd already got rid of one child of mine, you know,' he said in a queer twisted voice, and she turned to him. 'Hector told me. I never knew.

'She must have been pregnant when I first brought her here, though I'd no idea. I think she saw me as a safe bet, and maybe it was a way of hanging on to me. Once here, though, she saw that Hector offered a much better deal, and was still available. Wounded, bed-bound, drugged up – and at her mercy. I'd gone out to the North Sea rigs to get some money so we could get married, leaving her here, where she proceeded to wreak havoc.' He gave a short, dry laugh. 'When I came back, Maddy had vanished, Angus was off looking for her, and Laila had got Hector on the hook. She disappeared briefly, apparently unable to face me, but I expect that was when she got the business seen to. By then it was rather late in the day and there were complications. It only came out later, much later, when they were having fertility investigations and the doctors suspected that she'd been pregnant, and damaged by a termination. She tried to tell Hector it happened years ago, before she met me, but she let something slip, and finally admitted it.' He stopped and stared again into the fire. 'All these years he'd assumed it was he who was infertile, after his injury. They had a massive row, but somehow patched things up, and kept going.'

He stopped again but didn't seem to expect a response, so she stayed silent. Then: 'The lifeboat men couldn't understand how she'd disappeared under the waves so fast. She'd not worn a life jacket, and I reckon her "baby" got waterlogged and pulled her down. Talk about irony.'

'They think it was suicide?'

'She was paddling hard *away* from them, they said. And they asked just now if there was something more they should know.' He reached for his drink again. 'And there's plenty. Anyway, they've told the police, so they'll all be piling round here in the morning. And before then, I shall have to tell Hector.'

———

They stayed there until the fire died down, just sitting, not talking, and Libby sensed him working it all through, a heady mix of relief and exhausted emotion. And the horrors of what might have been. It would take a while, but maybe the coils would begin

to unwind and his load would lighten, and life would look different. And, given time, there would be a different Rodri to get to
know. . . .

Abruptly he rose and pulled her to her feet, taking both her
hands. 'Will you sleep with me tonight, Liberty Snow?'

The question came from nowhere.

'No. Go to bed.'

'You won't?' he said, smiling, and pulled her to him.

'No.'

'Why not?' His face was close to hers.

A hundred reasons. She grabbed on to one. 'What if the boys
wake and come in to you?'

'What if they do?' He looked back at her with an odd twisted
smile. And there, at the back of his eyes, somewhere deep, she
saw the same bruised look she had seen in his son's eyes, the same
need. 'I'd like you close tonight, Libby,' he said. 'The rest is for
another time. But for tonight, it'd be a kindness.'

She reached up and touched his face. 'For kindness, then,' she
replied.

———•———

In the morning she woke to find him gone, and she lay there a
moment and watched the sun slanting through the window to
make watery patterns on the bedroom wall, and smiled. Thank
God there was sunshine, for this day would need it . . . Last night
Rodri had fallen asleep almost at once, having first curled her
body into the contours of his own and then wrapped his arms
around her, consuming the warmth of her – an animal craving
comfort – and she had lain there, feeling the pulse of his heart,
the rise and fall of his chest, the warmth of his skin against hers.
'Thank God you're here,' he said as he buried his face in her hair.
'You smell good, Liberty Snow.'

And she had laughed, glad too that she was.

She had waited until his breathing became regular, then gently extracted herself from his hold. He had stirred, grunted sleepily, then rolled over and gone straight back to sleep, and she too, with her back against his, had slept.

For kindness, she had said, and for the rest, time would tell. But better now that she left him space to cope. Downstairs she found the kitchen empty, but the kettle was steaming gently on the corner of the Aga and so she made tea. Was Rodri with Hector? She drank it quickly, keen now to slip away and get back to the camp. She had no place here where death and deadly intentions stalked the rooms and passages.

So she slipped out of the back door, down the dark rhododendron tunnel, out through the garden gate, and to the campsite. It was still early and no one was up yet, so she slowed her pace and breathed in the astringent air of early morning, and looked beyond the headland to the deep swells of the sea. And there Rodri had stood, his arm tracing a curve in the sky as he signalled back to her. How far offshore had they been? A mile, less probably – the distance over water, just like the distance over time, was deceptive.

She heard voices and waking sounds behind her and turned back to the camp to see tent flaps being turned back and the students emerging. They greeted her with a certain reserve, wide-eyed and uncertain, and she heard whispering amongst them.

'You feeling better?' Callum asked.

'Much better.' But they would have to be told, and it was best done straightaway. She summoned them to gather around and listen: 'In all the upset yesterday with the boys and the kayaks, I'm sorry to say that Lady Sturrock was lost, presumed to have drowned.' That brought gasps and then a shocked silence, followed by a wave of urgent whispering. 'So there'll be police coming and going, and I'll need to go back up there and give a statement. Sir Hector Sturrock also arrived yesterday. He's very ill, and this accident will have been a further blow. So we need to keep as low a profile as we can and then start packing stuff away ready to leave tomorrow.'

'That's *terrible!*' she heard one of them say as they split off into small groups. 'Such a lovely lady.'

'Her poor husband!'

She turned away, but Callum followed. 'God. That's awful. I thought the lifeboat went after her.'

'They did, but she'd gone under. No life jacket.'

'You're kidding!'

She switched subjects, hoping he would leave it there. 'How did Mel get on with the bones?'

'I'll show you.' He led her to the caravan, which he unlocked and entered, sliding along one side to make space, and Libby saw where the bones from the box had been laid out.

'Most of the skeleton is there, just a few phalanges missing, and I think it's a male, mature adult, teeth good. But there are multiple blade injuries, perimortem by the look of them. And there's this.' He turned the skull so that Libby could see the cranium. A great cut mark cleaved the back of the skull, not splitting it entirely but enough for the victim's brains to have spilled out with the blow.

———•———

Pádraig stole back along the edge of the trees, keeping low, until he reached a point where he could watch. And he saw Odrhan walk towards the men who had come from the ship.

He crept closer but could not hear what was being said. Slowly he edged into the dunes and lay there, flattened into the sand, and looked through the grasses, and listened.

'Do you know who I am?' The large grizzled-haired man seemed to be their leader.

'You have the look of your brother,' Odrhan replied.

The man grunted, and one of the men gestured towards a low mound where Odrhan had told Pádraig that Harald was buried. *'And where is Ulla?'*

'She is dead.'

The man nodded, apparently unmoved. *'And the child?'*

Pádraig dropped his head in sudden fear, but he heard Odrhan's response. *'The child died also.'*

The grey-beard threw back his head. *'That is not what I have been told! I hear of a red-haired child who lives on a headland with a man who was once a holy man but who is revered no longer.'*

'You have been misinformed. I live alone.'

'That child is my son!' the man roared, and Pádraig froze.

'The child died, I tell you.'

'You lie!'

'He is in God's hands.'

'Search the dwelling,' the man commanded, and two of his followers ran along the beach to the headland. Pádraig wriggled deeper into the sand so that only his head remained clear.

All day the men tried to make Odrhan tell them where to find him, and Pádraig watched, shaking in horror and grief, sobbing silently. Times many he thought to rise and reveal himself to make them stop, but instinct told him that it would not save Odrhan. In a fury, the grey-beard hacked into the burial mound and then pulled out a round object which he thrust into Odrhan's face, screaming abuse at him. And Pádraig saw that it was a man's head. Then he dropped it and smashed it with a stone. Above them the gulls screamed in outrage.

Odrhan was on his knees now, held upright by a man on either side, and the bearded giant turned back to him, his sword gripped in two hands above his head.

'Tell me!' he roared.

And Pádraig saw Odrhan drop his head, and he knew that he was praying, and he was praying still when the sword descended.

───────

And as Libby ran her finger along the gash, the legend suddenly had immediacy, the murder of Odrhan was laid bare before her, not in romance but in all the horror of reality.

'. . . a blade injury like that,' Callum was saying, 'was either from an axe or sword wielded by a tall man or because the victim was kneeling.'

The caravan door opened and Rodri stepped inside. 'They said you were in here,' he began, and then his eye fell on the skull in her hands. 'Oh God. Another one.'

'It's from the box on the headland,' Libby replied, and turned it so that he could see the back of it. He took it from her and, like her, drew his finger slowly along the edge of the wound, and reached the same conclusion.

'Odrhan?' he said, surveying their faces.

'I think so,' said Libby.

He stared into the empty eyes a moment, then he handed it to Callum. 'Poor bugger. Will he get no peace?' Then: 'I've got to drag Libby away again, I'm afraid, the police are up at the house. Have you told them here what happened?' Libby nodded, and Rodri cut short Callum's expressions of sympathy. 'Thanks. Good of you.' Then: 'If you're ready.'

'Where's Declan?' he asked as they crossed the campsite.

'Gone home.'

Rodri looked at her. 'Good. Then I don't have to drive him off as well.'

'As well as who?'

He gave her an echo of his old unruly smile. 'I fired way over their heads, you know, just as a deterrent. Seemed to do the trick as they didn't come back. But I'd still like to know how your man knew about it.' Then, while she was absorbing that, he stopped and put out his hand to a passing student. 'It was you, wasn't it? You asked about a bonfire on the beach.'

'Well, yes –'

'Right. Then I've a job for you. When you've done your work, you and your mates gather every bit of driftwood you can find and then go into the storeroom next to the dairy and grab a couple of the pallets from there, bring them down and break them up, and build the biggest bloody bonfire you can on the beach directly in front of the house. Don't light it, not until I tell you. Got that? I want it big enough that my brother can see it from the window, big enough so that they'll see the flames in Newfoundland. OK?'

'Okaaay . . .' The lad looked astonished, as well he might, and hurried away.

So much for a low profile. 'That's going to seem very odd,' said Libby, as they set off up the path.

'Is it? They can think of it as a wake. A local custom. And about last night –'

'It's alright –'

'I thought so too. Or at least, it will be, next time. You were very kind, Libby, lovely in fact. That's all I wanted to say. More later.' He opened the garden gate and swept her through. Then he halted under an arch of spent rhododendron flowers. 'You looked just right there, I thought, in my bed. I wanted to wake you to tell you so.'

She laughed in answer to his smile. 'Perhaps you should have.'

'I considered it, but one thing would have led to another, don't you think?' The wind stirred the branches and she saw that the bruised look in his eyes had faded.

'Almost certainly.'

He nodded. 'Then best kept for later. Come on.'

She followed him down the rest of the shrubbery and they emerged into the courtyard. 'What will the police want to know?' she asked him.

'Everything, Libby. Tell them everything.'

Chapter 33

It took some time for Libby to give her statement, and the police went over the details many times. They were in the library, sitting opposite each other at Rodri's desk. Fergus was there, which helped, but this was not the easygoing Fergus who had accepted a nip from the bottle in his tea, this was a different man, deeply shocked by what he had heard. The police had spoken first to Angus and David, and briefly to Rodri's boys, and she saw from their expressions that all the stories were hanging together.

The officer with Fergus was not a local man, and he made her repeat her testimony, coming at it from all angles. 'Could she not simply have been holding the paddle up above the waves?' he asked for the third time.

'It didn't look like that, and David was warding her off, I'm certain.'

Eventually they gathered up their paperwork and prepared to leave. They went back into the kitchen, but she stayed where she was to allow Rodri space to speak to them. A few moments later, he came through to her. 'Alright?' he asked, and she nodded. 'Then come and meet Hector.'

'How did he take it?' she asked, as they crossed the hall.

'He was quiet for a while, then said: "Well, that simplifies things." And that was all, just that.'

A bed had been squeezed into one end of the dining room beside a clutter of medical-looking equipment, but Hector was not in it. He was sat, an emaciated figure in a silk dressing gown, in a winged chair in front of the window, facing the garden. He was calmly smoking and turned his head as she came into the room, and Rodri introduced them.

'I owe you my son, Rodri tells me, and my nephews.'

'It was Angus who—'

He swept her words aside. 'Nothing can repay that. I've been an absent father, a very *bad* father, but enough of one to know what their loss would have meant, to us both.' He looked across at his brother. 'No words can express . . .' His eyes filled, and he turned his head, pulling on his cigarette, his hand shaking. She searched for something to say, but he turned back, in control again. 'And you've been finding various Sturrock skeletons, I hear,' he said, considering her, 'and rattling them.'

Rodri pulled forward two more chairs and she sat. 'I'd no idea there were so many.'

He laughed. Hector Sturrock looked ill and tired, and distressingly like his brother. He'd once had a larger, broader frame than Rodri, but it was now wasted, and although he was a sickly colour he still managed to convey an air of decadence. It was the silk dressing gown with its Liberty print, perhaps, or the lazy way he contemplated her from under drooping eyelids as he drew on his cigarette. 'Best that they're all out in the open, don't you think?' An answer didn't seem to be expected, so she said nothing. And then Rodri told him about the skull they'd just examined, and the cut mark to the skull, and Hector lifted an eyebrow. 'Another one! And so they're true then, the old stories.'

'Perhaps.'

He coughed and spat discreetly into a tissue. 'And Rodri tells me there's some connection between you and us, through some black sheep who rogered the kitchen maid and ran off with her.'

Perhaps he wasn't so very like Rodri. 'Yes,' she said.

'So he was in Newfoundland after all.'

Libby stared at him. Had he known all along? 'What do you mean?'

He gestured vaguely to the papers still on the dining table. 'Somewhere amongst all that stuff there was something, a letter . . .'

But she was no longer listening. Her eye had fallen on an object which had been placed beside a medicine bottle on the small table next to the chair, and she stared at it in disbelief. Hector stopped talking and his gaze followed hers. 'Ah yes – ' he said. 'There is that.'

She lifted her eyes and looked from one brother to the other in silence. Both were smiling slightly, the same quizzical smile. 'The chalice – '

'The same,' said Hector.

So had he had it in Oslo, after all, secreted away? But how had it got here?

Hector seemed to pick up on the thought and shook his head at her. 'Don't look at me, m'dear,' he said, and made a languid gesture towards Rodri. 'There's your thief. 'Fessed up this morning, while you were talking to the police. It was in the manse for a while, I gather, up the chimney, and latterly in the potting shed.'

She looked at Rodri in disbelief.

'True, I'm afraid,' he said.

Hector was enjoying her reaction. 'So another cupboard door opens, and out rolls the Ullaness chalice. Poof! As if by magic. Maybe Rodri should give it to you to bury, and you could find it and be amazed. Gets you out of a fix, eh, Roddy me boy? And you'd do that for him, wouldn't you. It's a small price to pay for coming here, disturbing things better forgotten, don't you think?'

'You broke into your own house, and stole it!' she said, staring at Rodri.

He met her look evenly. 'Strictly speaking, I broke into Hector's house, but yes, and it took some doing I can tell you. Drove through the night to get here from the wedding and then back again in time for breakfast. I rather enjoyed the challenge, in fact, and it opens up new career prospects if Hector throws me out.'

'There's no *if* about it,' said his brother, and reached for a packet of cigarettes and lit another one, flicking a smile at him.

'They'd have sold it, you see, once they knew its value.'

Hector blew smoke up towards the ceiling. 'He's not wrong.'

Libby was at a loss for words. First he'd admitted to shooting at the nighthawks, and now this! 'Have you told him about the cross?' she asked, angry suddenly. Once and for all she wanted the matter settled, out in the open and sorted.

'No.'

'Where is it now?'

He got up and went to the sideboard, retrieved the package she'd given him, and handed it to her. 'It's yours, Libby, not Hector's,' he said. 'Don't let him have it.' But she ripped it across the top, tipped out the cross, and handed it to Hector.

'That looks familiar – and so you're a thief as well,' he remarked, examining it. 'How very well suited the two of you are.'

'Tell him how you got it, Libby.' And so she did, as succinctly as she could, and Hector listened to her with that same focussed look she associated with his brother and the ash grew long on the end of his cigarette.

When she'd finished, he tapped it into an ashtray, then ground out the stub. 'And you found a copy of it on the dead man! How extraordinary. But if the Sturrock man did end up in Newfoundland, who do you reckon is in the mound?' he said.

'I've no idea.'

He grew thoughtful. 'And yet somewhere in those papers there was something. Something about a minister who left his position very suddenly, I seem to remember, it caused a vacancy which was never filled. There's some correspondence about it, I think. He'd aroused some ill-feeling in the community, ran up against the family and so forth. I forget his name, but it's in there, amongst those papers. But even *this* family would hardly shoot the poor bugger and stick him in a sand dune.'

'Well, someone ended up there,' said Rodri. 'Who was bart around then?'

Hector calculated. 'The fourth. Donald Sturrock, and then Mungo came in at number five. He was something of a bastard, I gather, drove the place under with massive debts, then died at a ripe, impotent old age without issue.' He glanced briefly towards Rodri. 'Like me, I suppose, except for the ripe old age, and the impotence.'

'And the issue,' said Rodri.

Hector reached for another cigarette, taking his time to light it, then drew on it and exhaled slowly. 'And I've rather snookered young David's chances, haven't I? He'll curse me to the end of his days, I expect, as will his mother. But they'll get everything I can possibly leave to them. It's not much –' A bleakness had entered his tone. 'And maybe they'll thank me for not saddling them with this place.' He turned to Libby. 'Do you like cold, wet places, where the wind never ceases and the sun rarely shines? And where the past won't let you go . . . ?' Libby felt it unnecessary to reply, repelled a little by this man who was so like, and yet so unlike, his brother.

Rodri deflected him. 'I'd put my money on the minister, then,' he said, 'since he's unaccounted for. And he was holding that little cross.'

Hector yawned, the talking seemed to be taking its toll. 'Maybe so. The family done him in, shot him though rather than cleaving his skull like his monkish predecessor. We're quite capable of that, you know,' he said, addressing Libby again. 'Nasty bunch, the Sturrocks. And there's a bit of a pattern emerging down the centuries, don't you think? Fathering misbegotten lads, murdering churchmen, thievery' – he nodded towards Rodri – 'and more recently, on the distaff side, drowning helpless children.' At that he put a hand over his eyes, and stopped on a sob. Libby glanced across at Rodri where he sat, contemplating his brother with a look of profound sadness.

Better that she left them now, she thought, and she rose to go, but Hector took his hand from his eyes. 'Don't go,' he said. 'I like you. Rodri likes you, Alice likes you, and I'd like to know you better, you're our deliverer, even if you're also a harbinger of uncomfortable truths. Must be the name,' he continued, 'Liberty Snow, Rodri tells me. I was thinking about it this morning. A mix of strong-minded independence and virtue, I decided. God help you, little brother.'

Rodri's expression didn't change. 'Ignore the man. Obnoxious when drunk, insufferable when sober.'

Hector simply smiled back at him. 'I jest, brother. But Laila liked being Lady Sturrock, you know, it was the one thing that really satisfied her. I didn't. I know that much. And I wonder what she had planned for me? There always was something of the Medici about the lovely Laila . . .' His voice trailed off, and again Libby prepared to leave, but Hector waved her back.

'I should get back to the camp,' she said, looking across at Rodri, but Hector reached out and gripped her hand with surprising strength.

'And now I've offended you.'

'You haven't. But I need to get back.'

342

Sarah Maine

She tried to pull her hand away, but he held on. 'Wouldn't do that for the world. And not only because of the boys. Want to know why?'

'Innate courtesy?' she asked, and he laughed, that same dry laugh which made him cough again.

'I've rarely been accused of that, m'dear. No, but for the first time in years I've seen cracks in the shell my thieving brother has built around himself, and I think that might be down to you.' His tone was no longer bantering and she glimpsed charm in his smile, a younger Hector, before life had made a cynic of him. 'I behaved very badly, but it turned out that I took a wrong'un off his hands. He found another for himself, the fool, but it seems to me the gods are giving him a third chance. And then maybe, just maybe, I too will be redeemed – have this, Miss Snow-White, with my blessing.' And he handed her the cross and the envelope that it had been in, and as he did the sketchbook slipped out and fell open against his shoe.

Chapter 34

Something was changing. She felt it stirring deep inside her, overriding the grief and the shame, filling her with a strange new warmth, a sense of expectation – and she was bewildered by it.

She felt light-headed, dizzy sometimes, and hardly dared to trust her feelings as they swung without warning from dark despair to an odd sort of euphoria. The minister was unfailingly kind, and would be kinder still if she allowed him, but she held him at arm's length, wrapped up in this new, strange, turbulent wonder where only one thing mattered.

Alick.

He came more often now, and she knew that he looked at her differently. At first she had been unable to meet his eyes, seeing in his face too close a resemblance to the one which had looked down at her, red and panting as he heaved. But that image was beginning to fade.

And Alick's face was leaner, smoother, and kinder – and so beloved.

It seemed now that he sought her out, joining her on the headland where they would sit, saying little but in a companionable silence as they watched the gannets diving far out at sea, the dark shags flying low and fast. There had been no more talk of spirits; he had told her she must not dwell on such matters, saying that he had been wrong to confuse her. He had been humble, contrite, and had taken her hand. 'You dwell too much on the

343

past,' he said. 'But it's the future that matters, Ellen, and what you make of it.'

'I can't imagine the future,' she said, and he had smiled.

'Then be content with the present moment, Ellen, and let the future unfold.' And the look in his eyes had made her spirit soar, swept along, caught up in a story that was unfinished, a story which had emerged from the shadows of the past and now, if Alick was true, would shape her future.

⇢ *Oliver* ⇠

He had, he realised, been the author of his own misfortune. Warning Alick that Ellen, in her state of grief and upset, was casting him as Harald seemed to have sparked a change in his friend, igniting a latent realisation of his true feelings. He was forever at the manse and Oliver saw that his eyes followed Ellen, and he would hold her in conversation whenever she was in the room. And he sensed there was a warmth now of a different kind, a mutual warmth. Once he spotted Alick leaning against the peat stack, smoking a cigarette, watching her graceful form as she bent to fill the creels, before moving her gently aside to fill them himself. Later he saw him carrying them to the house, deep in conversation, and once he heard laughter. He had spied them out on the headland too.

He became consumed by a jealous, impotent anger. Alick Sturrock was every bit as dangerous as his brother, playing with Ellen's affections, raising hopes that he could have no intention of fulfilling! And he observed despairingly that Ellen stepped more lightly after these encounters, her countenance brightened, her beauty beginning to shine through her grief.

While for himself things grew blacker. The furore over the

digging had died down, but Oliver knew that he had lost ground both amongst his congregation and at the big house. Invitations for dinner became less frequent, and although this did not trouble him, he sensed that his patrons believed he was supporting Alick's rebellion against them.

Matters between the young man and his father seemed to be coming to a head, and this was confirmed one day when Alick arrived with unexpected news.

'*Canada?*' Oliver said, in response to his announcement.

'Newfoundland, to be precise. St John's. Some cousin of my mother has business and banking interests there and is prepared to take me on. Imports and exports, I understand, salt cod out, machinery in. Not exactly what I had in mind as a career, but I've been told very firmly I have to make a living for myself, and so I might as well go somewhere interesting to do it. And frankly, I've had enough of my father's tongue. If it hadn't been for you being here, Oliver, I should have gone mad.'

'I shall miss you.' It was true, but even as he said it Oliver felt a lifting of his spirits, a great joyous leap. As grief diminished and with Alick far away, perhaps, just perhaps, Ellen might come to see . . . And the church was not the right place for him, he knew that now. Despite his protestations, his conversations with Alick had set his mind to questioning again those aspects of belief that he had always found difficult to accept. Like Alick, he would start afresh, become his own man, and tread a different path.

'And I shall miss you too, my dear fellow!' Alick replied.

They discussed what they both knew, or imagined they knew, about Newfoundland, and there was a buoyancy to their conversation, a new optimism. 'And we must decide what to do with the chalice before you go,' Oliver said. It had remained since that day in Oliver's desk drawer, where it troubled his conscience. 'I imagine it's valuable as well as being an important piece. I'm really not happy keeping it here. The difficulty, of course, is how to explain where it came from without re-igniting the whole wretched controversy.'

'Yes. We'll decide. But first there's something else I want to discuss with you, Oliver, something much more important, and I'm going to need your support – but first let me show you these.' He dug his hand into his trouser pocket and pulled out a small package, which he unwrapped. 'What do you think?' In his palm lay two small gold crosses. 'Which is which?'

Oliver bent over them and then looked up. 'Why, they're identical! Though I imagine that one is the copy.'

'Quite right. Well done. But it is an excellent piece of workmanship, don't you think?'

'It is indeed, but why—?'

He broke off as Mrs Nichol tapped on the door and entered bearing a tray. Alick rose to clear a space for her. 'No Ellen today?' he asked, as she set it down.

Mrs Nichol gave him a tight smile. 'She is pegging out the washing, sir. Having a bit of fresh air.'

Alick put the crosses on the desk and moved over to look out of the window, from which it was possible to glimpse the little rise beside the manse where the washing could catch the breeze. Oliver watched him jealously and saw him move the curtain aside to look out. Then he leaned forward. 'Good heavens! Is she . . . is she quite well?' he said.

Oliver went to join him and saw Ellen, sunk down on one of the boulders, bent double and retching horribly. Mrs Nichol came to stand behind them, her mouth working.

Alick swung round to her. 'I asked if she was unwell, Mrs Nichol!'

'She's not been good, sir, these last few mornings – ' Alick stared at her in a way that Oliver found incomprehensible, and he saw that the housekeeper was unable to meet his eyes. Surely the influenza had passed. Why had he not seen for himself that poor Ellen was unwell!

To his astonishment, Alick swung on his heel and was out of the door. Oliver watched through the window and saw him appear a moment later and bend to Ellen, a hand on her shoulder. 'It's mostly just in the mornings, sir,' Mrs Nichol said.

Something in her tone made him turn to look at her, and then the implication of her words hit him. 'In the *mornings*, Mrs Nichol?' he said, and the housekeeper nodded, her face a picture of dismay. He gaped at her and her eyes fell; fleetingly he wondered if she imagined him to be the author of Ellen's misfortune, and in the next instant realised that same question would be in everyone's mind. His next thought was Alick. 'You've told no one, I trust?' he said, and she shook her head. 'Then I must ask you to remain silent. Do you understand? If Ellen is . . . if Ellen's illness is something other than . . . than an illness, then we must take steps –' But what steps could possibly be taken?

The door opened and Alick strode into the room, his face a mask. 'That will be all, Mrs Nichol,' he said. 'I've suggested to Ellen that she goes and lies down.'

Mrs Nichol gave a bob and left without a word, head down.

'Mungo!' Alick spat.

'No!' Oliver stared back at him. 'Did she say so?'

'No, but nor would she deny it. And as it was neither you nor I, my friend, who else could it have been?'

Oliver sank into one of the two armchairs and put his head in his hands. Dear Lord, how completely had he failed her! And she had borne the assault alone, without support, said nothing, and now must bear its consequences. But when had it happened? He tried calculating back.

'And where was your loving God, Oliver, when he forced

himself on her?' Alick's bitterness echoed his own, and he had no answer.

It must have been just before Mungo left. And then he remembered the scurrilous note he had left, and understood what it had told them. Good God, the very day her mother died! But even as he absorbed the blow, a solution began to form in his mind, one that made his breathing become more rapid, and his heart beat strong.

Alick's next words shattered it.

'It was Ellen I wanted to talk to you about. I'm planning to take her with me. There is no place for either of us here – my parents would never agree, of course, so it must be done without their knowledge.' He shook his head, staring down at his feet. 'And now this! But it makes no difference. Mungo's child will be my child, our child, and will be the better for it.'

Oliver's mouth became dry with the taste of ashes. 'You'll take Ellen . . . ?'

'I love her, and how could I leave her now?' The words were simply said, but when he swung round, Oliver saw that his eyes were ablaze. 'It was when you said what you did the other day that I realised that she was a part of me, and has been all my life. I've held back from any declaration because of her grief, not knowing what Mungo— But I will take her with me and make her safe.'

Oliver's dreams crumbled around him.

'But your family – ' he said, through the mist of despair.

'I shan't tell them, and you mustn't do so either. The devil of it is that Mungo is due home any day, and so you *must* keep Ellen away from him. She trembled when I mentioned his name, and if my parents learn what he has done, God knows what would happen to her. They'd stop at nothing to cover it up, you know. Pa's ruthless. No. I'll bring forward my plans, and we will go.'

'But has she said that she will go with you?'

And so to the final nail.

'She did, just now.'

———————

When Alick had gone, Oliver stood staring out of the window, and wondered why it was that here, on the west coast, summer did not fulfil the promise of spring. The bright, clear, sun-filled days which had heralded his arrival had not been followed with warmth and sunshine but had become burdened with overcast skies, heavy with cloud, as if a muslin shroud had been cast over the land. The gorse was brown now, the joy of the yellow iris gone, and the wild roses were shedding their petals, their perfume soured. So soon faded . . . There was rain on the wind.

A storm was brewing, and what a storm it would be –

And he, of course, would be held responsible.

Later, when he spoke to Ellen, he sensed a change in her, a new strangeness. She seemed calmer, and yet even more distant, unreachable but now in a different way, as if she had slipped into another world, a vague world of her own creating. When gently questioned about her encounter with Mungo, she described it as if it was a story, something which had happened to another person; and although she began to shake and clasped her arms across her breast, she told him in detail how she had sought the cool glade, described seeing her reflection in the pool, and how she had bathed her feet and legs there. And then Mungo had thrown pebbles into the pool: 'Three of them, one after another. I thought how odd it was that there would be fish there, and the ripples spread so wide, right across the pool.' And in the same odd story-telling voice she had explained how she could not find her shoes and how Mungo had stepped across the stream in one stride, and taken her. 'He always was a violent man, you know,' she said, in a vague way, and he wondered a little at her words.

He asked her too about Alick, and she had turned to give him an almost ethereal smile of such blissful happiness that he had had to drop his eyes. 'He says that he'll take me away from here, far away, and that we'll raise this child as if it was our own. And this time all will be well.' He asked her what she meant, and she had looked confused and been unable to answer. 'I've loved him always, Mr Drummond,' she said, and repeated, 'and this time it will be alright.'

And so over the next days Oliver found that the manse became a trysting place. What Mrs Nichol made of it all he could only imagine, but he felt powerless to act, accepting that his days here were numbered, and that as soon as Alick left with Ellen then he too would go. It would not trouble him overmuch, he decided, for with Alick gone and Ellen gone, there was no longer any point in staying. He would begin again – alone. Like Odrhan.

Until then, however, he sustained himself by going through the motions, visiting the sick and the needy, conducting services he no longer believed in, and answering whatever summonses came from the big house.

On one such occasion, the details of Alick's imminent departure were discussed with satisfaction by his mother. 'He needs an occupation,' Lady Sturrock had said. 'And this will give him one. He is something of a dreamer, I fear, and this will make him approach life in a more practical manner. He spends a great deal of time at the manse, he values your company, I know, but I sometimes wonder what else draws him there –' She had let the remark hang there, but there could be no mistaking her meaning. 'Alick needs to get out into the world and make his mark, as befits his position. Mungo does too, of course, but Sir Donald has decided that once he returns, he must begin to learn how to run the estate.'

To run, or run to ruin? Oliver wondered.

It was two days after this conversation, and just as the evening shadows were lengthening, that Alick burst into the manse in a high passion. 'Where's Ellen?'

Oliver looked up from his desk. 'She's in the house somewhere. Why?'

'She's not in the kitchen.'

Oliver put down his pen, feeling very old. 'What is it, Alick?'

'Mungo's back, so she must stay indoors! He arrived just before dinner. It was all I could do to sit down at table with him, and then he started goading me, you know the way he does, all insinuation and sly remarks to which you can't respond! Or not in front of Mama, anyway. He's the very devil – ' He flung himself into a chair. 'I had to come away, out of sight of him, or I could not be answerable for myself.'

'Alick – '

'So you must marry us at once – tonight. Everything is arranged. The passage is booked; we'll leave here tomorrow and sail on Thursday.'

Oliver stared at him in horror. 'But I can't marry you, just like that!'

'Why not?'

'Surely you must see – '

Alick's face was rigid. 'No, Oliver, I don't.'

'But, I can't – '

'You damn well can! I know that much of the law. Irregular it might be, but it will be a marriage nonetheless. Mrs Nichol can bear witness.'

'Mrs Nichol has gone to her daughter's.' And Oliver doubted whether she would return; he had sensed a growing disapproval from her. If she decided to speak to Lady Sturrock, then all was lost.

'You must marry us anyway, in the church, in the sight of

God. In the sight of *God*, Oliver! Why should the rest matter to you? And then Ellen will feel safe, she will at least *feel* married, and we can pay for the sheriff's warrant in Glasgow before we sail and make all right and tight. I'll not leave with her unwed!'

And how could he, a minister of the cloth, refuse? If any other of his parishioners had come before him with such a request, especially with a child on the way, he would have had no qualms, for anything was to be preferred to a sinful association. But Sir Donald was unlikely to appreciate that argument; the sin of mis-alliance would outweigh all others.

He became aware of Alick scowling at him. 'You hesitate, my friend,' he said.

'No, Alick,' he replied, his heart leaden. 'I do not. We will find Ellen, and I will wed you tonight.'

Alick leapt to his feet, his face transformed with joy. 'That was why I had the copy made of the cross, you see. It is for her! A wedding present. The two crosses will serve to bind us, and I'll buy her a ring when we get to Glasgow. Where are they?'

'You left them here, so I put them with the chalice.' He re-trieved them from his desk.

'Good. Put them in your pocket while I go and find Ellen.'

And so, that evening, by the light of candles lit on the altar of St Oran's Church, Oliver swallowed his despair and married Alick Sturrock and Ellen Mackay. They exchanged their vows quietly and were bound by the exchange of the two crosses, one of which, if the legend told true, Odrhan had given to Ulla as a token of her conversion, and then buried it with her when she died.

Or maybe it too had been given as a love token, Oliver thought, as he left the lovers alone in the manse and set out to the headland. A crescent moon cast a silvery sheen on the ocean, and from somewhere came the piping cry of a seabird. Had Odrhan loved Ulla only as a godly man, or, as Ellen herself had suggested, had he been her lover? If so, then the monk had fared better than himself.

He went and sat with his back to the ruin, now returned to its former state, and thought of the bones they had reburied under the floor just feet away, and of the skull with its clean-edged cut, a testament to Erik's wrath. At least Mungo would have no reason to come after Alick as Erik had done, hell-bent on retribution and to claim his child. Perhaps he would never know it was his.

Alick had explained his plans to Oliver earlier. 'We'll leave tomorrow evening, after dinner. Everyone will imagine that I'm here with you and won't look for me until morning, and so we'll get a good start. I'll bring the trap down to the manse and be all ready to go; we'll travel to Balemore, leave instructions for the trap to be returned here in a day or two, and travel on from there to Glasgow.'

Oliver rested the back of his head on the stones and let the breath of the soft night soothe him. When Alick was safely away, he would tell Lady Sturrock that he was leaving, and go. Cowardly, perhaps, but it would avoid the inevitable outcry once news of Alick's arrival in Newfoundland, with Ellen, was received.

He looked back towards the church, the scene of his failure, and wondered if his successor would make a better job of it; it pained him to think of it standing empty. As for himself, he would go back to Cumnock perhaps, to the soft lowlands away from this wild western coast.

And so, according to the plan, after dinner next day, Oliver heard the rumble of the trap, and a moment later Alick strode into the study, his eyes alight. He had long since given up the formality of knocking, and with Mrs Nichol still away there was no need for subterfuge. Oliver rose as he entered and found his hand engulfed in both of Alick's. 'All set. I cannot thank you enough, my friend.' Oliver returned him a tight smile. 'Where is she? Is she ready?'

'Upstairs, I imagine, assembling herself.' Earlier Ellen had come down to talk to him, to say her farewells, and from her too there had been a radiance.

'I'll run up and fetch her. I want to be away at once.' Oliver heard him go upstairs, calling her name; then a moment later he heard him descend, and he must have gone into the kitchen for it was a couple of minutes before he appeared again at the study door. 'She's not here! Her bag is there, strapped down and ready, but she's not in the house.'

'But I saw her, not an hour since.'

Alick frowned, and then his brow cleared. 'She'll have gone out to the headland! She was saying yesterday how she will miss the place. Oliver, will you go and fetch her while I put her bag in the trap and turn it, ready to go? I'm anxious to be off.'

And so Oliver picked up his coat and set off once more for the headland.

⇥⇒ *Ellen* ⇐⇤

She had had to come one last time. She needed to say her own quiet farewell to the spirits who she knew, despite what Alick said, were there, just beyond the veil. In the ether. She could hear them rustling through the grasses, their voices echoing in the call of the gulls, their breath soft on her cheek. She had to tell them that this time all would be well . . . A fulmar swooped low, and just for a moment its shadow startled her in the half-light of evening, and her hand closed over the little gold cross that hung from a chain around her neck. Alick could have thought of no better token to symbolise their vows, and it was warm in her hand. She would carry Ulla with her always now.

The sun was low over the horizon and soon it would set, and when it rose again she would be far away from here, fulfilling Ulla's dream to be with her lover, and soon—

'Ellen?' She turned at his voice.

'I'm here. And I'm ready to go now.'

'Go where, my nymph?' A figure appeared from behind the ruin, his shadow darkening the headland.

Ellen froze. Erik . . . ! Somehow her thoughts, and her intentions, had summoned *his* spirit.

'And with whom, I wonder?' He came close and put his hands on her shoulders, pulling her to him. 'I have been watching for you, sweet Ellen. I thought you might come here.'

Reality hit her hard, and she braced herself against him. 'Let me go!'

'I fear I disappoint – did you expect my brother?' She struggled, but he easily controlled her. 'Or was it Drummond?' He held her away from him, examining her face, his eyes dark with mockery. 'And where are you going?'

'I'm leaving, Mungo, with my husband,' she said, and the words gave her the courage to lift her head.

Mungo's face registered surprise, followed swiftly by a frown. 'Your *husband*?'

'So stand aside and let me pass!'

'Not so fast, little nymph, first tell me –'

Then there was the sound of someone else scrambling over the rocks, and he turned.

Oliver heard voices blown back on the rising wind and quickened his steps. As he clambered up the rocks, he heard Ellen, and then

the deeper tones that could be only one man. 'Ellen!' he called
out, and came around the side of the ruin, breathless and his
heart pounding. Mungo turned to greet him, a strange smile on
his face.

'Oho! Well met, minister.'

Oliver ignored him. 'Come away, Ellen.' He put out a hand to
her and she took it, gripping his fingers tight.

Mungo let her go, then threw back his head and laughed.
'My compliments, Drummond, I didn't know you had it in you!
And congratulations, though God knows it must have been an
irregular sort of affair. Did you conduct the ceremony yourself,
give your own responses? A rather thin cloak of respectability,
don't you think, but then she's been under your roof for weeks
now.' Something in his tone warned Oliver that Mungo must be
encouraged to continue in his error. But what had Ellen told him?
'Think of the scandal, my friend, a man of God running off with
his housemaid!'

'Come, Ellen,' he said, and put his hand under her elbow, guiding her past Mungo.

But Mungo took hold of her other arm. 'I'm really not sure
I can condone this, you know, Drummond. I have to consider—'

A movement behind them made all three of them turn. 'Let
her go, Mungo.' Alick spoke quietly, but Oliver's pulse leapt.

Darkness was falling fast now, but there was still light enough
to show the expression of unholy amusement which sprang onto
the face of Mungo Sturrock. 'Alick too! Dear Lord, a veritable
ménage!' He released Ellen, who went over and stood beside him,
and Alick put a protective arm around her.

Oliver saw Mungo's eyes narrow and the amusement vanish.
He spoke quickly. 'Go now, Alick, and take Ellen. I will explain
matters to your brother –'

'No! No one leaves.' And to Oliver's astonishment he saw that a gun had appeared in Mungo's hand. 'So *you're* the lucky man, are you, brother? But this cannot be permitted.'

'Put that away, man,' said Oliver, seriously alarmed now. 'Alick. Go!'

Mungo moved to block the way. 'No, Drummond, *you* go. And take the drab back to the manse. You and I, Alick, are going to bear these happy tidings to Pa.'

'And will you also tell him of the rape?' Oliver asked, putting out a hand to stay Alick, who had moved forward.

Mungo scoffed. 'What rape?' he replied. 'Bring forth your witnesses, minister! Besides, he'd understand that better than this misalliance, believe you me! And he'll send the baggage packing, along with you, Drummond! And you'll be glad to go, if I know his temper.'

'Alick and Ellen are man and wife, Mungo, married in church in the sight of God. Nothing can come between them now, so let them go on their way –'

'And bring disgrace to my family?'

'Disgrace!' said Alick. 'You talk of disgrace! How many brats have you already fathered? Well, this time it will be different.'

That, Oliver thought, was a mistake. He saw Mungo's expression change, and his eyes flicked towards Ellen's midriff. 'Do you tell me that . . . ?'

Alick pushed aside Oliver's restraining arm and stood before Mungo. 'Aye. But we will go, and not trouble you further.'

'What *has* she told you? My dear Alick, the girl was willing! Enthusiastic even –'

He got no further. Alick leapt at him and knocked the gun from his hand. The impact of his assault threw Mungo to the ground and Alick went down on top of him amongst the rocks, kicking and punching and swearing as they struggled.

Ellen cried out to Oliver, 'Stop them! Oh, for pity's sake!' but

Oliver could not get beyond flailing legs and elbows. Then suddenly Mungo was astride Alick, his hair falling forward, his fingers at his brother's throat, swearing viciously.

'Stop them!' Ellen begged, and moved behind him.

Later, Oliver would see that moment played out slowly, theatrically, as if every movement of the nightmare scene had been planned, rehearsed, and perfected, but it was over in an instant. Alick's eyes were bulging, his face suffused, while Oliver could only tug desperately at Mungo's broad shoulders. 'You'll kill him, man. Let him go!' But Mungo removed just one hand to lash out at Oliver, sending him flying back against the ruin. And in that instance of release Alick gave a mighty heave, twisting his torso so that Mungo fell off him and Alick rolled onto his side. And in rolling he presented an exposed back which received the bullet fired from his brother's gun.

The scene froze.

'Christ—'

'Oh God – ' Oliver knelt beside Alick, pressing a handkerchief to the wound, his hands soon covered with blood. He bent his ear to Alick's lips and then sought a pulse.

Slowly, unbelieving, he lifted his head and looked across at Mungo.

Then both men turned to look at Ellen, who was standing stock-still, wide-eyed, the gun still loose in her hand. With a cry as wild as a curlew's call she flung it down and ran to Alick's side.

Mungo struck out. 'Senseless *bitch*!' he cried, and the swipe knocked her off her feet and she fell hard against the stones of Odrhan's cell. Oliver went to her, but the blow had left her senseless. Perhaps better so, he fleetingly thought, and he rose to his feet to confront Mungo.

Darkness had fallen, but in the grey light Oliver could see the horror written on Mungo's face as he stared down at his brother. 'Sweet Christ – ' he said.

And even as the same horror threatened to overwhelm him, resolve formed in Oliver's mind, and it steadied him. 'You call on Him? But He was watching and knows that this was your doing.'

'The hell it was! That bitch – '

'No. Your brother died by your hand.' Mungo looked up at him, thunderstruck, and Oliver knew that every word he said now would count. 'And I will swear to it, on my honour and my soul, in court, and to the end of my days.'

Mungo's eyes widened and he swore. 'You would perjure yourself? For that!' He gestured to where Ellen lay.

'I saw you threaten your brother with a gun, I saw you fight, and then I heard a shot. Who else but you would fire?' Mungo stepped forward, but Oliver stooped quickly to retrieve the gun and pointed it at Mungo's midriff. 'Believe me, I'll fire, for there's nothing left to lose.' Would he have done so? he later wondered, perhaps not, but it was enough that Mungo had believed him. 'As you said yourself, bring forth your witnesses.'

Mungo scoffed but his eyes were wild. 'Your word against mine? Ha!'

'Your gun. Your quarrel. Ellen has spoken to others of the rape.' A lie, but Mungo could not know that. 'You have a reputation. And your recklessness is well known.'

Mungo scowled, and Oliver remained silent, watching him think. 'Against me, and Pa, you haven't a chance!' he said at last, but he sounded less certain, and Oliver pursued his advantage.

'Who else would kill him? Not Ellen, his wife. And not I! I married them just yesterday, as witnessed and recorded.' Another lie, but truth had fled along with Alick's departing spirit, and only justice, at any price, would now serve. A plan was beginning to take shape in Oliver's head and he was thinking furiously. 'I was aiding their departure and you, through jealousy or pride, were trying to prevent them. That much is true, and what other story could possibly be told? By accident or design, your gun discharged. Ellen never touched it.' Mungo glanced again towards the girl's unconscious form and swore. 'Be very sure, Mungo Sturrock, she'll not hang for this.'

'Nor, *damn you*, will I —'

'No, you won't.' Mungo narrowed his eyes, and Oliver met them steadily. 'So listen —'

———

And so, in the darkness which gave them cover, Oliver and Mungo carried Alick down into the dunes. Oliver had taken Ellen back to the manse, given her a sleeping draught, and returned with a spade. They dug a hollow into the side of a low mound and laid him there and, as they rolled him into it, the little gold cross which had sealed his marriage fell from Alick's pocket; Oliver bent to retrieve it, closed the dead man's hand around it, and prayed for his forgiveness.

And they stood a moment agreeing to the story that would be told; then, as the moon came out from behind a cloud, they parted.

Chapter 35

Libby picked up the sketchbook and stared at it, then handed it to Rodri. He took it, puzzled by her expression, and studied the open page. Then he raised his head and looked back at her.

When Libby had first received the package, she had thumbed through the sketchbook, remembering it from childhood days, seeing again the sketches, her own jottings, and the fragment of the legend written in the back. The drawings were of the headland, she now realised, and the figures confronting each other, badly drawn and incomplete, were versions of the painted windows in the library, the same scenes depicted over and over. But then the cross had fallen out of it and driven the book from her mind. She had simply put both back in the package in which they had arrived and brought them up to give to Rodri.

As a child, when she had read the fragment of the legend written on the back page, she'd thought nothing of it, but it was at that place that the book had fallen open:

And so, Ulla stayed with Odrhan, and together they raised the child, in the sight of God, putting aside the evils of the past.

The words had inspired her own childish imagination when she had sat dangling her legs over the wooden landing outside her grandmother's house, considering other endings for the legend.

And they lived out their lives in peace and a sort of content-
ment, lamenting the death of Harald and praying for the
salvation of Erik. And Odrhan loved Ulla, as a godly man,
for the rest of his days. Gosse Harbour 1930.

The handwriting was unmistakable.

'O.D.,' said Rodri, his eyes holding hers. Then he turned to Hector. 'That minister who disappeared? What was his name?'

'No idea. It's mentioned somewhere in all that stuff.' Hector waved a hand towards the papers.

Rodri went over to the table, and while he looked Libby explained to Hector what had brought her here, the stories she had been told, what they had discovered, and what she now surmised; he listened, all trace of cynicism gone from his features, and when she had finished he was silent.

'What a tale,' he said at last. Then his eyes searched her face. 'So it was that which brought you here, all that way. Something unresolved, you say.' He paused, still considering her. 'And do you think you will change our fortunes, Libby Snow?' The smile he gave her was a sweet one, and for the first time she saw David in him. 'We can only hope.'

'Got it!' Rodri said from the desk, and came back to them with a letter. 'I'd skimmed over it before, the first bit's all about needing a new minister, but listen to this: *'Our enquiries confirm that Drummond abandoned his ministry suddenly and without no-tice. It has been asserted that he had alienated his congregation by wanton acts of desecration and indulged in carnal activities with a local woman living as a servant under his roof. She too has disap-peared, presumably in Drummond's company. Furthermore a search of the manse by the Honourable Mungo Sturrock, following Drum-mond's departure, discovered a valuable item, believed to be the lawful property of the estate, secreted away in a desk.'* Libby's eyes went to the chalice. *'No charges are being brought, but as these offences render Oliver Drummond unfit in every way* . . . and so on. O.D. Oliver Drummond.'

Libby looked again at the sketchbook. 'But Jennet said it was a Sturrock man who ran off with a woman.'

'She was wrong, it seems. Because if it isn't Drummond in that mound, then it must be Alexander Sturrock.'

'DNA.' Hector yawned. 'That'll confirm it.'

'So did Drummond change his name to Macdonald? It's a good one to pick. But who shot Alexander?'

'The randy cleric,' Hector said with dry certainty. 'A love triangle. *Un crime passionnel.*'

But Libby was staring out of the window at the desolate garden, and the pieces of the puzzle began to come together. 'Ellen said that *she* had killed a man. Everyone said that she was mad, and once he'd got her away Oliver Drummond probably encouraged them to think so.'

'Why would he?'

'To protect her.'

There was silence as each considered this.

'But why would Ellen shoot Alexander? And where, for God's sake, did she acquire a handy little Webley?'

Libby looked back at Rodri. 'We'll never know, but I think she spent the rest of her life mourning him, and it unhinged her mind.' She looked again at Oliver Drummond's note at the end of Ellen's sketch book. 'He says he loved her all his life "as a godly man." I wonder what he meant.'

'Isn't it obvious?' Hector asked.

There was more silence; then Rodri said, 'And who was her child's father, I wonder?'

Hector gave a dry laugh. 'A recurring point at issue in these parts.'

'There was only ever the one child,' said Libby. 'And he went to the bad.'

'Must have sprung from Sturrock loins, then,' said Hector.

'That's all very well,' said Rodri, 'but someone buried Alexander. Ellen couldn't have done that on her own.'

'Probably the devoted man of God. And for whatever reason, someone must have helped them get away, spreading rumours that they'd gone off together.' The breeze from the open window blew cigarette smoke across Hector's face. He gestured to the paper on the table. 'Mungo Sturrock, for one. Maybe he was throwing sand in everyone's eyes.'

'But the story is that Ellen went off with Alexander,' Libby insisted. 'Lady Sturrock believed that, for one.'

'I doubt she knew. And there was probably all sorts of gossip.'

And all sorts of things they would never know. 'And that's the story which has survived,' said Libby, thinking of Angus and Jennet. 'So much for the oral tradition.'

Hector looked at her, drawing again on his cigarette, eyes narrowed. 'So your ancestress murdered mine, it appears, Miss Snow-White. Seems Sturrock men are badly served by their women, one way or another.'

'But are they well-used by Sturrock men?' Libby replied, and both men looked back at her.

Then Hector gave another laugh, warmer this time. 'Time we broke the mould then, don't you think, Roddy boy? Too late for me, of course, but—'

He stopped, and for a moment Libby thought he must have had some sort of seizure for he had stiffened and become very still, his face rigid as he stared straight ahead, the cigarette halfway to his lips. She followed the direction of his gaze and caught movement in the garden, and then followed his line of vision, and saw that Maddy was on the path leading to the front door, her red hair backlit by the dying sun, and walking purposefully in front of her was David.

———

The driftwood and broken pallets made an impressive pyre, and the students were gathered around chattering and waiting for the command from Rodri to light it. Libby had spent the rest of the afternoon packing what she could, leaving only the tent for tomorrow. Things had happened too quickly, too many things, and the end come too soon – and now there was so much to absorb and consider. Rodri was nowhere to be seen, but his two boys had come down with Alice, bearing trays of food and drink, and rather later Angus and Maddy had joined them. There was no sign of David. Trestle tables had appeared from somewhere, and there was now quite a spread upon them and a barbeque had been lit. What the students made of all this in the face of yesterday's tragedy, she had no idea, but it was good to see Donald and Charlie running around, the nightmare put aside for now.

And then Rodri was there beside her. 'Alright?' he asked.

'Yes.'

'Good.' And he called to Callum: 'Send my lads over here, will you – and then let rip with the fire.'

The boys came running, and he put an arm around each of them. Callum bent to the pyre, and there was a crackle and then a glow as the dried grass caught. A cheer went up from the students as the wood caught, and the flames licked high into the evening sky. Rodri turned to look over his shoulder towards the house. 'They should see that, I imagine.'

'Who should?' asked Charlie, his face lifted to his father.

'Uncle Hector and David.'

'Will David be coming down?'

Rodri turned back to the fire. 'Maybe. Later.'

'Alice says there're sausages,' Donald said.

'Aye, there are. So off you go.'

Libby watched them go. She wanted to ask him how it had gone, the meeting between Hector and his son, but felt she couldn't. It was too deep, too painful. But once again, Rodri seemed to read her thoughts. 'I left them to it,' he said, staring towards the flames. 'Maddy stayed just a little while, and then went to find Alice. She said David was handling the whole situation brilliantly.' He looked over to where the two women were laughing together as they handed out sausages to the students, their shoulders touching, and grunted his satisfaction. 'All seems well there, anyway. Tricky waters to navigate, these.' He spoke almost as if to himself, then turned to look at Libby, the light from the fire shadowing his features.

'So did you get what you came for, Libby Snow?' he asked.

She stayed silent, watching the flames corkscrew into little tornados of sparks and smoke, for there was no simple answer. It would take time to unravel the twists and turns of the story and to follow the threads, as complex a pattern as that on the window-seat cushions, as full of moth holes, misshapen and patched, faded and imperfect.

But there were bright new threads to be woven in. 'Rather more, I think,' she said at last.

'Good.' He slipped his arm around her. 'We can agree on that then, and go on from here. And what happened yesterday will be reported and remembered as a tragedy: a boating accident and a lovely woman drowned trying to bring the boys to safety. That's the story your students will take away, and it's the one we'll all promote, because the truth is unbearable.' He looked over to where his sons were throwing wood on the fire, watched over by Angus. 'And for them, even now, the memory's starting to fade, and when they're old enough to understand they'll say nothing, and begin to wonder what really happened.'

'And it proves that legends are unreliable – ' she said; that, at least, they had learned from the summer.

'Didn't we already know that? But does it matter? Whatever happened was for their time, not ours.' He looked at her, a smile in his eyes. 'You can dig up the whole damned bay if you like and see what else you find – though I quail at the thought. Your best bet would be in the church, as I've a strong hunch that the third baronet might not have found all the loot.'

She turned to look at him and encountered that same slow smile. 'What do you mean?'

'I've found bits and bobs there over the years. It's squirrelled away somewhere. Must tell Hector – '

'So was *that* why – '

At that moment Callum came over with two cans of beer. 'You aren't drinking,' he said.

'I have been,' said Rodri, 'rather heavily, in fact. But Libby hasn't.' He took a can and handed it to her.

'I'll go and fetch a chair, shall I?' Callum said. 'Where would be best?'

'I can still stand, dammit!'

'Rodri,' said Libby, her eyes on the path which led to the gate in the garden wall. 'That's not what he meant – '

He swung round at her words, followed her gaze, and grew still. Then he said, in a low voice, 'Right in the centre of things, if you will, Callum.' Together they watched Angus leave the group and go to Hector, who, still in his dressing gown, stick in hand and leaning heavily on the shoulder of his son, was slowly making his way down the path towards the burning pyre on the shore. 'But well away from the smoke and the flames. The wind's coming in from the north.'

Epilogue

Pádraig stepped ashore and gestured his followers to a place across the little stream. 'There you will find a flattened rock, and it is there you will build. Make that rock the threshold.'

Then he left them and went along the curve of the bay to the tumbled ruin on the headland. Twenty years had not changed it, except for the mosses and lichens. And he thought back to that night when he had run to the village, choking and distraught with the horrors he had witnessed, returning next day with men to help him, and they had buried Odrhan in his dwelling. Then he had commanded them to pull the stones down on top of him so that no one should disturb it, and they had obeyed him even then, a ten-year-old child giving orders. He had made decent the grave of Harald, reburying the severed head, and left with the villagers.

No one went near the headland now, he had been told, it was considered an unlucky place. Once revered because of Odrhan, then avoided because of the woman he kept there, then ignored as Odrhan became known simply as a strange man who dwelt there with a child. And then, after Erik's violence, it was feared.

Old Morag had told Pádraig what Ulla had said, that Erik was impotent and that he had beaten her, but added that she had not quite believed her. Some said Ulla was already carrying him when she arrived, and that he must be Harald's son.

But old Morag, smiling at him, had said that for herself, she thought he had the look of Odrhan.

Turn over for an extract from

SARAH MAINE'S

THE HOUSE BETWEEN TIDES

*

A captivating story of a crumbling estate in
the wilds of Scotland, its century-old secret
and an enduring mystery.

Prologue

The woman stood a moment on the old drive and stared up at the boarded windows, a dark silhouette against the grey walls, then she turned her back on the house and went down to the blaze on the foreshore.

Figures moved in the smoky shadows, small awed groups, lingering after the drama of the auction. They drew back as she approached, a gaunt stranger in a black coat, and a whisper rustled amongst them. *Piuthar Blake!* She drew nearer to the flames. *Bho Lunnainn…* Gusts of wind formed small tornadoes of sparks, and the woman's eyes followed them until they faded over the drained stretches of sand. *Blake's sister. From London.* An outsider now. More of the house's contents crashed onto the pyre—a broken display cabinet from the study, an easel riddled with woodworm. The flames were suppressed for a moment, then leapt to consume the offering—and a way of life.

Earlier in the day there had been a macabre episode when the moth-eaten birds and animals had been brought out, their glassy eyes catching the flames, flashing a sharp reproach. A hotel owner had bought the stag's head from the landing and the rarities had been sent to Edinburgh, while anyone who fancied a tatty guillemot as a souvenir had bid a few pennies. The rest, dusty and faded, had gone onto the bonfire, and she had watched them burn. But she had turned away when the once prized black-and-white diver from the dining room was brought out. It had been found in the back of an old boot cupboard, ravaged by mice, together with more paintings, wrapped in old hessian, too late for the auctioneer's hammer. The paintings had shocked her: the tormented scenes and heavy brushstrokes exposed too painfully the anguish of her brother's broken mind, and she had ordered that they too be destroyed. All except one, a watercolour which she remembered well, painted when his talent had been at its outstanding best, and she lingered over it while the others burned, then put it carefully to one side.

A figure approached her. 'That's the last of it, Mrs. Armstrong.' It was Donald. She turned and nodded, smiling slightly, and they stood together, the flames casting flickering shadows across their faces.

'Do you remember the last fire you and I sat beside?' she said, wistful now for other times, and watched his face until the memory found him.

'The day we all went to see the seal pups? Cooked fish on the beach?'

She gave an echo of her puckish smile, grateful that he remembered. 'A perfect day.' And she turned back to the fire. 'I often think of it.' A smile brightened her face and was gone, and a gull circled them, gave a cry, and flew off across the machair. 'And now there's only you and me.' The flaming easel fell noisily into a void beneath it, sending up a spray of sparks. 'I thought that day marked the beginning of everything, but the world tore itself apart instead—' And hell came to earth on Flanders fields.

She looked towards the foreshore, where they had pulled up the boats that day, empty now, then she glanced back at Donald, seeing in the middle-aged man the child who had once run shouting beside her as they splashed barefoot through sparkling pools left by the retreating tide, drenched in sunshine, the divisions of class overruled by the compact of childhood. But there had been other children too. Her brother, and his.

She strained her eyes across the strand, shedding the pain as she had taught herself to do, and looked instead at the vibrant Hebridean sky. Midsummer half-light. But when the last colour had drained from the west, she knew there would be a pale light in the east, and she clung to that thought, keeping her back turned resolutely on the house.

All day the men had worked to fix boarding across the windows, entombing the house, blinding it. The thud of their hammers still pounded in her head, but at least the job was done, and in the morning she would leave. 'What will become of it, Donald?' The man beside her stayed silent. 'At least the land is in good hands, and the farmhouse is now your own.' She brushed aside his renewed thanks. 'A few papers to sign and then the matter is completed.'

The fire was almost sated now; it had burned quickly, fanned by gusts which blew unhindered across the two miles of open land. 'I don't suppose I'll ever come here again.' Her voice was barely above a whisper, and her cheeks shone wet in the firelight. Donald moved quickly to hold her, turning her face into his shoulder as he might a child, not a woman who was almost old—and she smelt woodsmoke in the tweed and was comforted. A sharp crack, and a spark shot from the fire, igniting the dry grass, burning brightly for a while, then it died, leaving a charred and blackened patch. 'I've been visiting ghosts, Donald.' He tightened the arm which held her, saying nothing. 'And thank God it was *you* who found poor Theo, and brought him home.'

The spectators were dropping away, back across the strand or over the machair to their homes. 'Leave the ghosts where they belong, Emily.' He released her and took her arm instead. 'Come home with us now.'

They left the embers shimmering low on the foreshore, a beacon in the encroaching darkness, and made their way down the well-worn track which linked the two houses. The woman paused just once and looked over her shoulder to where Muirlan House stood immense, dark, and sombre against the streaked lead and crimson of the western sky. He gave her a moment and then urged her forward, towards the glow which beamed a welcome from the windows of the factor's farmhouse.

Chapter 1

~ *2010* ~

The first bone he had dismissed as dead sheep. There'd been others— ribs decaying amidst rabbit droppings and debris from the collapsing ceilings, or bleached vertebrae. But the next one was a long bone, and he held it, considering a moment, then rocked back on his heels.

This was no sheep.

He leant forward, interest sharpening, and scraped at the sandy soil, revealing more stained bones and recognising a tangle of threads from decaying textile. A rotting plank half-covered the remains. He tried to move it aside, but it stuck fast, then he straightened, aghast, as certainty came. The plank was an old floorboard, nailed down, and the bones were underneath it.

He stared down at the remains, thrown off balance, then bent again, his mouth dry, and explored further until he came to the pale orb of the skull. Then he stopped.

The body had been placed on its side with the head hard up against a boulder in the foundations, the chin dropped to the chest, exposing the side of the skull. Exposing not a smooth roundness but a fissured depression, choked with sand. His mind roared as he reached forward to clear crumbs of mortar from the half-buried jaw, flicking an indifferent wood louse from the bared teeth, his hand trembling as he uncovered more of the crushed temple and the dark orbit of an eye. Then he straightened again and stood looking down, the trowel hanging loose in his hand. It was the snapping of fast wing beats that broke the spell, and he ducked instinctively as a rock dove bolted from its roost in an alcove—*bloody bird!*—and he glanced at his watch, twisting it on his wrist. Out of time. The tide had turned, and the wind was strong. Storm coming. He quickly bent to cover the bones again, then grabbed his jacket and ran to the Land Rover.

The empty stretch of sand, which, for a few short hours twice a day joined Muirlan Island to the main island, was disappearing fast. Had he cut it too fine? He revved the engine hard as the vehicle descended the track and he reached the point where track met sand. Then the battered vehicle sped across, through the shallow water, spray arching from its wheels as it rounded the rocky outcrop at the midway point, following the vanishing tracks which had marked his route across that afternoon. Swooping terns accompanied the incoming tide as it flooded the sandy stretches between the headlands, closing in behind him. He glanced in his rear-view mirror at the grey bulk of the house silhouetted on the ridge, and gripped the steering wheel. A body, for Christ's sake!

Then, as he tore across the wet sand, he glimpsed a figure in a long dark coat standing on a little headland, staring out towards the house. A woman? He looked more keenly. A stranger— The Land Rover plunged drunkenly into the last deep channel and he revved the engine again to pull up the other side, releasing his breath as he felt firm ground beneath the tyres. Then he swung the vehicle to the right, wiping damp palms on worn jeans, and headed down the single-track road, skirting the edge of the bay, to find Ruairidh.

The House Between Tides
is available to buy now